MAISEY YATES

Down Home
Cowboy

HQN™

HQN™

ISBN-13: 978-0-373-80199-2

Down Home Cowboy

Copyright © 2017 by Maisey Yates

Recycling programs
for this product may
not exist in your area.

Printed in U.S.A.

Down Home Cowboy

CHAPTER ONE

CAIN DONNELLY WAS sick to death of being alone.

Or, more specifically, he was sick and tired of going to bed alone. It had been a long time since he'd touched a woman.

Four years.

Four years since Kathleen had walked out on him and Violet. And in that time, he had been consumed with trying to salvage what he could of his daughter's childhood. With trying to make a new life for them, with trying to build something that belonged to the two of them, and didn't have his ex-wife's ghost lingering in the shadows.

That was why they had come to Copper Ridge, Oregon, from Texas just a month earlier. The transition had been...rocky so far.

He lifted his beer bottle to his lips and scanned the room. He didn't know how he had allowed his younger half brothers to talk him into going out. He had to admit that his daughter made a pretty convenient excuse for his hermitage. Of course, Violet was sixteen now, and she could stay alone for a while.

Though, if his brother Finn and Finn's new girlfriend, Lane, weren't at home, he probably would have used the excuse of them being in a new place to avoid going out. Out in the middle of nowhere like the Laughing

Irish Ranch was, Violet was likely to get scared. Or some other lie.

But Lane and Finn were at home, and Cain had found himself fresh out of excuses. So he was sitting in the local bar, Ace's or something. Which was the name of the guy who owned it, he'd been told.

The place was a strange collision of surf and turf. There were fishing nets, half a boat hung up on the wall and other little pieces of evidence that Copper Ridge was a coastal town before it was anything else. But there were also Western touches that could rival any honky-tonk he had been to in Dallas.

Including a mechanical bull. Which he had to admit was providing a decent amount of entertainment.

"Are you going to watch that thing all night?"

Cain turned to look at his brother Alex, who had been eyeing a pack of blonde chicks in the corner, and now looked at Cain just long enough to give him a baleful stare.

They were too…young. All those girls, standing in the corner and laughing, scanning the room and trying to see if they could catch the eye of some guy who might buy them another drink. He knew his brothers were up for it. Liam and Alex would happily jump right in the middle of them—in the next thirty seconds, most likely.

Cain felt too old for all of this. He was supposed to be done. That was the point of getting married. He had liked that. That routine. That certainty.

He had been so certain about the decision to marry Kathleen. She'd been pregnant, and he'd always known that if that happened, he'd be marrying the woman. In many ways he'd been thrilled. To have something in his life that he'd felt long denied.

Stability. A family.

He'd become a father at twenty-two, and it had been the proudest day of his life. And for a while, everything had been exactly like he wanted it.

Obviously it hadn't been what Kathleen had wanted.

And *this* wasn't what *he* wanted. But he was just so damn sick of being alone. Being celibate. Yeah, it was the celibate thing that bothered him. He didn't want another relationship. There was no point. Violet was sixteen, and bringing somebody else into the middle of things when their life was already hard enough just wasn't going to happen.

He had never felt right about bringing a woman home for sex with his daughter in the house. And he had really never felt right about spending the night out while he left her at home. Not when his wife had left the way that she had.

So, here he was. Contemplating his celibacy in a bar. Looking at a mechanical bull rather than women. It was all depressing and mind-numbing enough to make him *reflect*.

On the slow breakdown of his marriage, the day Kathleen had packed up all her stuff and left without telling him what she was planning and where she was going.

The day she'd surrendered parental rights to their daughter, because she needed a clean break.

He looked away from the bull-riding spectacle and over toward the bar, where he saw something that most definitely caught his attention.

There was a petite redhead leaning up against the counter, her ass perfectly showcased by the tight jeans she was wearing. She shifted, and her hair shimmered beneath the multicolored lights. Then she lifted her arm, brushing all that glossy beauty to one side. Cain was transfixed by the sight of that arm. Pale, freckled, slim. She looked soft.

Just for a moment, he could imagine touching her so vividly that he could feel that creamy soft skin beneath his hand.

More likely, it was a full-on hallucination. He wasn't even sure if he remembered what a woman's skin felt like.

Maybe she wouldn't be quite so pretty from the front. It was always possible. But he hoped that she was. He hoped that when she turned around she provided him with more fuel for the fires of his fantasies. Because hell, fantasy was all he had.

The beautiful redhead did not disappoint. And she was, in fact, beautiful from all angles. She turned, scanning the bar with a smile on her face. Damn, she was probably there with some other man. Not that he was in a position to do anything about it either way.

Still, it was nice to know that he could get excited about somebody.

"If you're going to sit there looking like you'd rather be anywhere else, maybe you should be somewhere else," Liam said, never quite as easygoing as Alex was.

Cain didn't welcome the interruption of his fantasies. "This is my happy face," he returned.

"You're scaring women away," Liam said.

"That would be *your* ugly face," he said.

Alex laughed. "I love bonding time."

Cain rolled his eyes and took another drink of his beer. Here he was, out. On a Saturday night. And it just felt wrong. He preferred the life he'd had.

Bars, picking women up—he'd done all that in his early twenties. He was just so far past it now. He couldn't even remember what he'd found appealing about it.

"It's better than sitting at home," Alex said, clearly looking for some kind of reaction that he just wasn't going to get.

"Okay," Cain relented, "it was nice to go and eat a hamburger."

"And spend time with us," Alex added. "Because we're so charming."

"I work with you dumbasses all day, every damn day. I wasn't exactly hurting for quality time."

"That makes me feel sad, Cain," Alex said. "I really thought we were making progress with our brotherly bond."

Of the four of them, only Alex and Liam had grown up together. They were also the only two full-blood brothers. Cain had been the product of his father's first attempt at commitment, and then Finn had been the second. Both had been short-lived and unsuccessful.

For the most part, Cain had been raised in Texas, while his brothers had spent their childhoods on the West Coast. All of them had spent sporadic summers at the Laughing Irish, their grandfather's ranch on the outskirts of Copper Ridge—good times, sure. But added up, the brothers had only spent a handful of weeks together during their lives.

Last month, they'd all inherited an equal share in the place and, since then, it had been a labyrinth of trying to figure out how to navigate the new family dynamic. Mostly, he liked them. Mostly, he didn't want to punch them all in the face every day. *Mostly.*

"For me," Cain said, "this is progress. Drinking in public instead of drinking alone."

"Well," Liam said, "you might look like you enjoy it more."

"Like you?"

Liam lifted a shoulder. "Women like this."

"It's true," Alex chimed in, "they do. I go with 'wounded war hero smiling bravely through my pain,' and Liam...well, hell if I know why, but something about looking angry at the world seems to draw them in. You could work that angle, Cain."

"I don't want an angle to work," he said, taking another drink, looking across the room to try to find the redhead again. She had sat down at a table with a couple of other women, and they were eating, laughing. Definitely having more fun than he was.

She laughed at something that must've been particularly funny, throwing her head back and making all that hair shimmer again.

He had to wonder if what he had just said to his brother was true.

"Planning on being alone forever?" Alex asked.

"I'm not alone. I have a daughter. You two don't know anything about that kind of responsibility. I'm not going to bring women in and out of her life just because I want to get laid. It's not responsible."

"Plenty of people have kids and relationships," Alex pointed out.

"Yeah, well, those people aren't parenting Violet. She's not happy with the move, you know that."

"She seems happier since she got her job," Liam said.

"It's hard to tell with her." His stomach tightened

slightly as he thought about his daughter and all of the things he seemed to get wrong with her.

"We've all got shit to handle," Alex said, taking a drink. "But that doesn't mean we can't have fun too."

"You don't know from having shit to handle," Cain growled. Then felt like a dick because for all that Alex played it down, he was a war hero, and given the fact he never talked about his years of service in a substantial way, Cain had a feeling Alex was pretty deeply affected by them.

It was the Donnelly way. The more it hurt, the more you laughed it off.

He forced his gaze resolutely away from the redhead. Because there was no point in fostering any fantasies. He had too much on his plate.

"So," Alex said, "are you just going to sit here all night?"

"I was planning on it."

"Okay. As long as we're clear that it's your choice, and we're not abandoning you." He stood up, clapping Cain on the back. "We're going to go be social." Alex picked his cowboy hat up from the table and placed it firmly on his head, then he and Liam headed over to that group of women they had pointed out earlier.

Cain shook his head, leaning back in his chair, his arms crossed. He wasn't envious of them. In his opinion, they really didn't understand what was important in life yet. They didn't have anything bigger to live for. Not like him. He had Violet.

And, even when she was challenging, she was the reason he got up every morning. No, he didn't envy his brothers. Or their so-called freedom. It was empty as far as he was concerned.

He took one more look back at the redhead, ignoring the tightening in his gut, in his groin. Yeah, he didn't envy them at all. But while he saw their freedom as empty, his bed was empty too. And right now, he was just damn sick of that.

"HE'S CHECKING YOU OUT."

Alison glanced up from her dinner, keeping her expression purposefully bland as she looked across the table at her friend Cassie Caldwell. "Who?" She knew who. She had felt his gaze on her while she'd been standing at the bar. She'd sneaked a covert glance when he had been talking to the guys he was with, and her heart had done some weird fluttering thing that had made her want to punch her own face.

"The really *hot* guy over there," Cassie supplied helpfully. "Well, the hot guy in the plaid shirt who was sitting next to the two other hot guys."

The guy wasn't just hot. He defied such a paltry descriptor. He was broad-shouldered, with the kind of muscles that came from serious labor. He had dark hair, mostly covered by a black cowboy hat, and a square jawline that was visible even with the beard he was sporting.

He was gesturing broadly with very, very large hands that made her feel jittery sensations in parts of her body she preferred to ignore.

He was new, and in a town this size that was noticeable. But there was something familiar about him too.

He shifted in his seat and looked in her direction. Quickly. But she still caught it.

She averted her gaze.

"I seriously doubt he was checking me out." Except she knew he had been, and she was processing the strange, giddy feeling that had come on as a result.

She hadn't felt that in… Well, it had been long enough that she really couldn't remember. Probably sometime back in high school when boys had felt new and exciting, and sneaking off with them had felt like exhilarating rebellion.

Before she had realized just how bad a turn that sort of rebellion could take.

"Well," Cassie said with obnoxious authority, "he was."

Alison shot her friend Rebecca a look, hoping that the other woman would back her up. Rebecca just shrugged. "Sorry," she said, "but I think he was."

"And?"

"Maybe you should go talk to him," Rebecca said, flicking some dark hair behind her ear, her engagement ring glittering in the low bar light.

This was the problem. All of her friends were in relationships. Not just relationships, but *the* relationship. The real thing, the be-all and end-all, soul mates and all of that. Consequently, they had all turned on her. Even Lane, who had stayed home tonight rather than going out because she was spending the evening in with her best-friend-turned-boyfriend, Finn.

Before the great Sexual Finn Awakening, Lane had been the one who had understood Alison's aversion to romantic relationships. But now that Lane had dealt with her own past trauma and moved on, she most definitely seemed to think that Alison needed to do the same. Though, she was a little more gentle than Rebecca and Cassie.

Barracudas were more gentle than Rebecca and Cassie.

"I'm not going to talk to him," she said, taking a sip of her Diet Coke.

"Why not?" Rebecca asked. "Talking doesn't mean anything else. It might be good practice."

"For what? My future as everyone's favorite spinster? I don't need to talk to him for that, Rebecca," she said drily.

"Suit yourself," Rebecca said. "But he was looking at you. And that's a nice ego boost if nothing else."

Alison nodded begrudgingly and took hold of her straw, nudging a piece of ice up to the top of the glass and crunching it between her teeth. There, he probably wasn't checking her out now. Who wanted to watch somebody noisily crunch ice?

Much to her chagrin, she looked back over to where he was—and, also much to her chagrin, felt a stab of disappointment when he wasn't looking back at her. There was no reason to feel disappointed.

But the feeling only increased when he stood and made his way over to the bar, speaking to Ace for a moment before tipping his hat and heading toward the door.

Then he was gone. And she might never have a chance to talk to him. She didn't know who he was. So he probably wasn't local. Since she owned a bakery, and before that, had worked at Rona's diner, which had been one of the more popular diners in town until Rona had retired and closed the place down, Alison was fairly confident that she could spot the out-of-towners.

He was probably one of the tourists that frequented the retail space Rona's had been divided up into. He had probably been some rambling cowboy, just passing through town for a brief moment before moving on. And now she would never see him again.

Relief warred with a strange clenching feeling in her stomach. Something that felt a lot like temptation. Well, temptation had just removed itself. From her sight. Possibly from town. With any luck, she wouldn't have to contend with it ever again.

"The only ego boost I need," she said, dragging her gaze away from the door, drawing in a breath and forcing herself to calm down, "is for people to enjoy my baked goods."

Rebecca and Cassie looked at each other and the corner of Rebecca's mouth twitched.

Alison frowned. "I did not mean that euphemistically. I own a bakery." She wadded up her paper napkin and threw it in their direction. It missed, rather grandly, and rolled sadly onto the floor.

"Sure," Cassie said, smiling.

"My life is full," she persisted, taking a bite of her side salad.

And if sometimes she felt a little bit wistful when she saw a handsome man, then looked at her life and saw nowhere to put him, well, that was understandable. Someday. Someday she would try to sort all that out. But for now, she was enjoying her aloneness. Enjoying her own company. Something she had absolutely not been able to do before her marriage had ended.

She had never wanted to be alone with her own thoughts, because she had hated that sad, small woman that she was. Almost as much as she had hated her husband in the end.

She had absolutely no regrets about her decisions. About the way she had chosen to move on.

One hot-ass guy in a flannel shirt and Stetson eyeing her up wasn't going to change that.

CHAPTER TWO

"HEY, BO," CAIN CALLED, looking around the kitchen and living room area for his daughter, who was on the verge of being late for her second week on the job. "Are you ready to go?"

He heard footsteps hit the bottom landing, followed by a disgusted noise. "Do you have to call me that?"

"Yes," he said, keeping his tone and expression serious. "Though I could always go back to the full name. Violet Beauregarde the Walking Blueberry." She'd thought that nod to *Charlie and the Chocolate Factory* was great. Back when she was four and all he'd had to do was smile funny to get her to belly laugh.

"Pass."

"I have to call you at least one horrifying nickname a week, all the better if it slips out in public."

"Is there public in Copper Ridge? Because I've yet to see it."

"Hey, you serve the public as part of your job. And, unless you're being a bit overdramatic about how challenging your job is, I assume you see more than two people on a given day."

"The presence of humanity does not mean the presence of culture."

"Chill out, Sylvia Plath. Your commitment to being angry at the world is getting old." He shook his head, looking at his dark-haired, green-eyed daughter who was now edging closer to being a woman than being that round, rosy-cheeked little girl he still saw in his mind's eye.

"Well, you don't have to bear witness to it today. Lane is giving me a ride into town."

Cain frowned. He still hadn't been in to see Violet at work. In part because she clearly didn't want him to. But, he had assumed that once she was established and feeling independent she wouldn't mind if he took her.

Clearly, she did.

"Great," he said, "I have more work to do around here anyway."

"The life of a dairy farmer is never dull. Well, no, it's always dull, it just never stops." Violet walked over to the couch where she had deposited her purse yesterday and picked it up. "Same with baking pies, I guess."

"I have yet to sample any of the pie you make."

"I'll bring some home if there's any leftover," she said, working hard to keep from sounding happy. At least, that's how it seemed to him.

"Are you ready to go, Violet?" Lane came breezing into the room looking slightly disheveled, Cain's younger brother Finn close behind her, also looking suspiciously mussed.

Absolutely no points for guessing what they had just been up to. Though he could see that Violet was oblivious. If she had guessed, she wouldn't be able to hide her reaction. Which warmed his heart in a way. That his daughter was still pretty innocent about some things. That she was still young in some ways.

Hard to retain any sort of innocence when your mother abandoned you. And, since he knew all about parental abandonment and how much it screwed with you, he was even more angry that his daughter was going through the same thing.

Though she was actually a little more well-adjusted than he'd been.

Sometimes he was almost tempted to take the credit for that.

Not that it was very great credit. His own mother had been a drunk gambling addict when his father had left, so the threshold for being better than her was not a high one.

"Ready," Violet responded.

Even though it was a one-word answer, it lacked the edge usually involved in her responses to him. He supposed being jealous of his brother's girlfriend was a little bit ridiculous.

"Have fun," he said, just because he knew it would irritate her.

He had lost the power to make her laugh. To make her smile, with any kind of ease. So, he supposed he would just embrace his ability to irritate.

At least he excelled at that.

He could tell he had excelled yet again when she didn't smile at him as she left the room with Lane.

"Wait," Finn said, walking past him and grabbing Lane around the waist, turning her and kissing her deep.

It was all Cain could do to keep from groaning audibly. Between his horndog younger brothers and his incredibly happy other brother he felt like sex was being thrown in his face constantly. Except not in a fun way that involved him having it.

Just him watching other people get it.

Lane and Violet left, and Finn walked back into the

living room. "I'm going to marry that woman," he said, the self-satisfied grin on his face scraping at Cain's current irritation. He had a feeling he and Finn had the same smile. But it had been so long since he'd actually smiled it was hard to say.

"Have you asked her yet?"

"Not officially. But I'm going to."

"She might not say yes," Cain said. He was feeling like an asshole, so he figured he would go ahead and be one. "Or, worse, she might say yes."

Finn was not deterred by Cain's bad mood. "I want to spend the rest of my life with her."

"That's a long time. Trust me. Married years are different than regular years." He had way too much experience living with somebody who didn't even like him anymore. Way too much experience walking quietly through his own house so that he could avoid the conversation that needed to be had, or avoid the silence that seemed magnified when the two of them were in the same room.

He didn't think Finn would suffer the same fate though. Finn and Lane had known each other for years, and they had been friends before they were a couple. Cain and Kathleen had been stupid and young. He had gotten her pregnant and wanted to do the right thing, instead of doing the kind of thing his father would do.

All in all, it wasn't the best foundation for a marriage.

For a while, they had tried. Both of them. He wasn't really sure when they had stopped. He couldn't blame her for that part. For the silence and the nights when it was easier to pretend he was asleep when she slid between the sheets than it was to try to make love with someone who didn't have two words to say to you.

Ironically, he would be thrilled to make love with someone who didn't have two words to say to him now. But hooking up was different than marriage. At least, he vaguely remembered that it was.

"I hope they are," Finn said, obnoxiously cheerful. "I hope every year with her feels like five. Because my time with her has been the best of my life."

Given the way they had grown up, he really didn't begrudge Finn his happiness. He was glad for him, in a way. When he wasn't busy feeling irritated by his celibate status.

Of course, if he really wanted to do something about it, he could. But for a long time it had suited him to stay unattached in every way possible.

Though, in fairness to him, figuring out how to conduct a physical relationship while he was raising a teenage girl was pretty tricky. He had to set some kind of example. And casual sex wasn't exactly the one he was aiming for.

He figured he had to at least try to be a model of the kind of man he wanted his daughter to be with. In twenty years or so, since he wasn't in a hurry for her to be with anyone.

But that good example thing was simple in theory, and not all that enjoyable in practice.

"Good for you," he said, sounding more annoyed than he had intended.

"How's the barn coming along?"

Cain was grateful for the change in subject. "It's coming."

"Show me."

His brother grabbed his hat off the shelf by the door, and Cain grabbed his own. Strange how this had become somewhat natural. How sharing a space with Finn, Alex and Liam—while annoying on occasion—was just starting to be life.

He took the steps on the front porch two at a time, inhaling the sharp, clear air. It was late summer, and in Texas about now walking outside would be like getting wrapped in a wet blanket. That was also on fire. He could honestly say he didn't miss that part of his adopted home state.

The Oregon coast ran a little cold for his taste, but he had to admit it was still nicer than sweltering. The wind whipped up, filtering through the pine trees and kicking up the smell of wood, hay and horse. If green had a smell, it would be that smell that rode the coastal air across the mountains. Fresh and heavy, all at the same time.

It was fastest to take a truck out to the old barn on the property, the one that had originally stood near the first house that had been built when their great-grandparents had bought the land. The house was long gone, but the barn still remained, and with all of his near-nonexistent free time Cain had been fashioning the place into a house for Violet and himself.

"You know," Finn said, as they pulled the truck up to the old structure, "you could always hire Jonathan Bear to finish this out. If you keep going like this, it's going to take you forever."

"You haven't seen what I've done. Anyway, are you in a hurry to get us out of the house?" In the month since they'd come to live with Finn, he'd never seemed to mind them being in the house.

On the ranch in general, yes. But not in the house. He shrugged. "It doesn't make much difference to me. Even if you and Violet aren't in the house Liam and Alex will be. So Lane and I aren't going to start engaging in public sex anytime soon. At our house. However, there's a reason she held on to her cabin."

Lane owned the property down by the lake, and even though she was essentially living with Finn, she still kept that property, and harvested vegetables out of the garden to sell at her mercantile store and to share with them. Cain had no complaints.

"Well, thank God for that," Cain said, his tone dry. "I was seriously concerned."

He and his brother walked through the still overgrown pathway that led up to the old barn. He had started with structural things. A new roof, replacing siding where it had dilapidated. Recently, he had moved on to the interior. He slid the brand-new door to the side, revealing the gutted, mostly hollow belly of the beast.

"Wow," Finn said, stepping deeper into the room. "You've done a lot."

"New wiring," Cain said, gesturing broadly. "Insulation, drywall. I need to texture, and then I'm going to work on interior walls. But, yeah, it's coming along. It will be fine for the two of us for the next couple of years. And when Violet leaves…"

Unbidden, an image of the beautiful redhead he had seen at the bar last night filtered into his mind's eye. Yeah, in a couple of years he would have a place to bring a woman like that.

Not that he couldn't go back to her place, or get a hotel room, but he didn't want to have to explain his absence to a teenage girl who barely thought of him as human, much less realized he was actually just a guy with a sex drive and everything. Both of them would probably die from the humiliation of that.

"It'll be a pretty nice place," Finn said, and Cain was grateful his younger brother couldn't read his mind.

"Not bad. And yes, I know that I could pay somebody to finish it. But right now I'm kind of enjoying the therapy. I spent a long time managing things. Managing a big ranch, not actually working it. Managing my marriage instead of actually working at it. I'm ready to be hands-on again. This is the life that I'm choosing to build for myself. So I guess I better build it."

He knew that at thirty-eight his feelings of midlife angst were totally unearned, but having his wife leave had forced him into kind of a strange crisis point. One where he had started asking himself if that was it. If everything good that he was going to do was behind him.

So, he had left the ranch in Texas—the one he had spent so many years building up—walked away with a decent chunk of change, and packed his entire life up, packed his kid up, and gone to the West Coast to find… Something else to do. Something else to be. To find a way to reconnect with Violet.

So far, he'd found ranch work and little else. Violet still barely tolerated him in spite of everything he was doing to try to fix their lives, and he didn't feel any closer to moving forward than he had back in Texas.

He was just moved.

Finn's phone buzzed and he pulled it out of his pocket. "Hey," he said, "can you pick up Violet tonight from work?"

"I thought Lane was doing it."

"It's her girls' night thing. She forgot."

Well, he had just been thinking that he needed to actually see where Violet worked. "Sure. Sounds good."

"What are you going to do until then?"

"I figured I would do some work in here."

Finn pushed his sleeves up, smiling. "Mind if I help?"

"Sure," Cain did his best to disguise the fact that he was shocked by his brother's offer. He wasn't used to this. He'd been navigating life alone for so long he'd forgotten what it was like to have support. "Grab a hammer."

ALISON STARED AT the sunken cake sitting on the kitchen countertop and frowned. Then quickly erased the frown so that Violet wouldn't see it.

"I don't know what happened," Violet said, looking both perturbed and confused.

"You probably took it out too early. Though, it's nothing a little extra icing can't fix. And it's my girls' night tonight, so I think it can be of use in that environment rather than being put up for sale."

Violet screwed up her face. "It's ugly."

"An ugly cake is still cake. As long as it doesn't have raisins it's fine."

"Well, I didn't put any raisins in it."

"Excellent. Of course, I try to provide raisined items to people with taste bud defects, because we here at Pie in the Sky like to be inclusive. But not in cake. It's just not happening in cake."

Alison was slightly amused that her newest employee seemed to know about her raisin aversion, even if she didn't quite have cooking times down. Violet was a good employee, but she had absolutely no experience baking. For the most part Alison had put her on at the register, which she had picked up much faster than kitchen duties. But she tried to set aside a certain amount of time every shift to give Violet a chance to get some experience with the actual baking part of the bakery.

Maybe it wasn't as necessary to do with a teenager who had her first job as it was to do with some of the other women who came through the shop, desperately in need of work experience after years out of the workforce, but Alison was applying the same principles to Violet as she did to everyone else.

Diverse experience was important on job applications, so that was what Alison tried to provide. Experience with food service, with register work, customer service, food preparation. All of her employees left with expertise in each and every one of those things, plus a food handlers' card for the state. It was a small thing, but it made her feel like she was doing something.

It also gave her a high turnover rate at the shop, but that was okay with her. It meant a lot of work, a lot of training, but when everything went smoothly it also meant that she could put the employees who had been there the longest on training, which gave them yet another set of skills to add to their resume.

Right now she was short on staff, and even shorter on people who had the skill level she required with the baked goods to do any training. So while she could farm out Violet's register training, the cakes, pies and other pastries had to be done by her.

"I'll do better next time," Violet said, sounding determined. Which encouraged Alison, because Violet hadn't sounded anything like determined when she had first come in looking for work. Violet was a sullen teenager of the first order. And even though she most definitely made an attempt to put on a good show for Alison, she was clearly in a full internal battle with her feelings on authority figures.

Having been a horrific teenager herself, Alison felt some level of sympathy for her. But also very little patience. But Violet seemed to react well to her brand of no-nonsense response to attitude. Alison wasn't going to let a chip on the shoulder make her angry, she wasn't going to get into a fight with a child, after all. But she didn't cater to it either.

"You will do better next time," Alison said, "because I can eat one mistake cake, but if I have to continue eating mistake cakes my jeans aren't going to fit and then I'm going to have to buy new jeans, and that's going to have to come out of your paycheck."

She patted Violet on the shoulder, then walked through the double doors that led from the kitchen to behind the counter. The shop was in its late-afternoon lull. A little too close to dinner for most people to be stopping in for pieces of pie. During the summer, they often got people stopping in after dinner, whereas during the school year she got a mini rush just after elementary school let out and parents brought their kids for after-school snacks.

She decided to take the opportunity to check the freshness of her baked goods. She opened the glass-backed display case, grabbed a piece of wax paper and pressed gently on the first row of muffins, then moved on to a loaf of cinnamon chip bread.

A rush of air blew into the shop and Alison looked up just in time to see a tall, muscular man walk in through the blue door. A pang of recognition hit her in the chest before she even got a good look at him. She didn't need a good look at him. Because just like the first time she'd seen him, in Ace's bar, the feeling he created inside of her wasn't logical, wasn't cerebral. It was physical. It lived in her, and it superseded control.

For somebody who prized control it was an affront on multiple levels.

He lifted his head and confirmed what her jittering nerves already knew. That beneath that dark cowboy hat was the face of the man who had most definitely been looking at her at the bar the night before.

He hadn't left town. He hadn't been a hallucinogenic expression of a fevered imagination. And he had found her.

The twist of attraction turned into something else, just for a moment. A strange kind of panic that she hadn't confronted for a long time. That somehow this man had found out who she was, had tracked her down.

No. That's not it. Even if he did, that doesn't make him crazy. It doesn't.

And more than likely he was just here for a piece of pie. She took a deep breath, steeling herself to look directly at him. Which was… Wow. He was hotter than she remembered. And that was saying something. She had first spotted him in the dim light of the bar, with a healthy amount of space between them.

Now, well, now the daylight was bright, and he was very close. And he was magnificent. The way that black T-shirt hugged all those muscles bordered on obscene, his dark green eyes like the deep of the forest beckoning her to draw close. Except, unlike the forest, his eyes didn't promise solitude and inner peace. No, it was something much more carnal. Or maybe that was just her aforementioned overheated imagination.

His jaw was covered by a neatly trimmed dark beard, and she would normally have said she wasn't a huge fan, but something about the beard on him was like flaunting an excess of testosterone. And she was in a very testosterone-starved state. So it was like stumbling onto water in a desert.

Of course, all that hyperbole was simply that. His eyes weren't actually promising her anything; in fact, his expression was blank. And she realized that while he might look sexier to her today than he had that night, she might look unrecognizable to him.

Last night she had been wearing an outfit that at least hinted at the fact that she had a female figure. And she'd had makeup on, plus she'd gone to the effort to straighten her mass of auburn hair. Today, it was its glorious frizzy self, piled on top of her head, half captured in a rubber band, half pinned down with a pen. And as for makeup... Well, on days when she had to be at the bakery early that was just not a happening thing.

Her apron disguised her figure, and beneath it, the button-up striped shirt that she had tucked into her jeans wasn't exactly vixen wear.

"Can I... Can I help you?" She tucked a stray strand of hair behind her ear and found herself tilting her head to the side, her body apparently calling on all of the flirtation skills it hadn't used since she was eighteen years old.

Very immature, underdeveloped skills.

Suddenly, her lips felt dry, so she had to lick them. And when she did, heat flared in those forest green eyes that made her think maybe he did recognize her. Or, if he didn't, maybe his body did. Just like hers recognized his. Oh, Lord.

"Yes," he said, his voice much more… Taciturn than she had imagined it might be. She hadn't realized until that moment that she had built something of a narrative around him. Brooding, certainly, because he had most definitely been brooding a little bit in the bar, but she had imagined he might flirt with a lazy drawl. Of course, it was difficult to tell with one word, but his voice had been clipped. Definitely clipped.

"I have a lot of different pie. I mean, a lot of different kinds. So, if you need suggestions. Or a list. I can help."

"I'm not here for pie. I'm here to pick up my daughter."

CHAPTER THREE

WELL, THIS WAS an interesting situation. By which he meant an insane crock of fuckery.

It was the woman from the bar. Right there in the bakery where his daughter worked. Looking even more like someone he wanted to lick all over than she had at Ace's last night.

Her hair was piled on top of her head, and he wanted to let it down. She was wearing an apron, which was sexy for some strange reason he didn't even want to parse. And she had flour on her nose. He wanted to kick everybody in the bakery out. Wanted to lock the doors and back her up against one of the rough brick walls and take her right there, hard and fast.

And that was thoroughly incongruous with his usual mind-set. And with the fact that even if he did usher everybody out of the dining area, and lock the door, his daughter would probably still be in the back somewhere. Which was something he really needed to remember.

"Your daughter?" The woman blinked, biting her lower lip, which he felt all the way down in his own body.

"Violet. Violet Donnelly."

A realization seemed to hit her on an indrawn breath. The reason he'd looked familiar when she'd seen him in the bar. He was a Donnelly. "Right. Of course." She shook her head. "Of course. She is off about now. I'll go get her."

"Is your boss back there?" He didn't know why he had stopped her, mostly because he wanted to delay her leaving just a second. For what, he didn't know. Torturing himself? Maybe he was into that now. He wouldn't know. It had been so long since he had explored exactly what he was into, he had forgotten.

"My boss?"

"Yes. The owner of the bakery? Alison something? I haven't had a chance to meet her yet, and I thought maybe I would."

"I'm Alison something," she said, her tone dry, her expression strangely resigned. "Alison Davis, actually."

Heat and irritation coiled in his stomach, creating a molten ball that he thought might explode. "You own the bakery."

She didn't look a day over twenty-five to him, much less old enough to own what appeared to be a successfully established business.

"Yes," she said, "I do. Is that surprising?"

"Yes."

"Why?"

Again, he wasn't sure why he was submitting to the banter. He should just tell her to go get Violet. Of course, she was responsible for his daughter's paycheck and, more than that, the only activity she had in town. Which was the only thing keeping Violet from going completely feral.

"Because. You look too young to own a bakery. Not exactly what I pictured. Except for the flour on your nose."

She wrinkled said facial feature, reaching up and

brushing at it with her fingertips. "It's powdered sugar," she responded.

It took everything in him to keep from commenting on the fact that that sounded even more appealing. Because it would be even sweeter if he tasted her skin.

Holy hell. He was in the middle of some kind of severe sexual psychosis. He had been married for years. Which meant that the time of seeing random women on the street as sexual possibilities was long past. His default was not to see women as potential partners.

It still was, he supposed. This...aberration was something to do with her. And she was his daughter's boss. Which was about the most inappropriate thing he could think of.

"Well," he said, "that's important to know."

"In the interest of being strictly correct, yes."

"I'm nothing if not pedantic when it comes to the details of baked goods."

"Maybe I should have hired *you* then."

That at least penetrated his thick skull and made him think about something other than sex. "Why? Is Violet having a hard time?"

"Not any more than usual," Alison said. She seemed much more comfortable with the topic of Violet introduced. "I just meant because she clearly doesn't have any experience baking. So, all things considered, she's doing really well. Just a couple of sunken cakes. But nothing I can't eat."

"Is there anything I can help her...work on at home?" He didn't know why he was asking. He knew next to nothing about baking. As far as he was concerned cake came from the store.

"I can think of a few things, if you wouldn't mind."

"I actually have no idea how to help her. It just seemed like the thing to say."

Alison laughed, and the sound was unexpectedly erotic. It fired through his veins, made him want to earn some more laughter. Possibly because he was mainly accustomed to having women glare at him, yell at him. It had been a long time since he'd made one laugh. Since one had looked even remotely delighted with him in any way.

"Sorry," he said, finding himself smiling. "I'm really not that helpful. But I can taste-test."

"Well," she said, "Violet does have a cake in the back. You're welcome to come back and…have a taste."

"Sure." Cake was not what he wanted a taste of. He wanted to taste that little hollow at the base of her throat. Wanted to see if her skin was as soft as he thought it might be. Wanted to see if she tasted like sugar, or if she tasted like flowers. He wasn't really particular as long as the flavor of woman was layered beneath.

"Come on back," she said, scurrying to the other side of the counter and opening a small, swinging gate, gesturing toward the double doors that he presumed led to the kitchen.

He saw no reason not to comply. So he did. It was tidy behind the counter, plates stacked out of view of the patrons, and napkins and dish towels neatly folded and stacked beside them. She ushered him into the kitchen, and he saw that it was no less organized. There were large mixers, a double oven lining a back wall and Saran-wrapped trays stacked in large holders, full of various baked goods.

And in the back of the room was his daughter, laboriously piping icing onto what looked like several dozen cookies.

"She's practicing," Alison said. "She learned a really basic technique the other day, so she gets to try it out on an order that we got for a client's office party."

Violet's expression was full of concentration, and he was momentarily distracted from the strangeness between himself and Alison by it. By the intensity with which she was focused on her task. By the fact that, for a moment, his daughter look like a stranger to him. Not like a child, and not like the angry teenager he was used to seeing.

She looked content, even though she was deep in concentration and actually applying effort to it rather than just rolling her eyes and tossing out a careless *whatever*.

It struck him then that he didn't know this version of his daughter at all.

"Wow," he said, not sure what else to say.

Violet obviously recognized his voice, because she stopped and looked up. Her expression went flat for a moment, and then came a smile that he could tell was forced. "Oh, hi, Dad. I didn't realize you were going to come by."

"Lane was busy. So I figured I would come and get you."

Violet frowned. "Is it time already?"

"Yeah, but if you want to finish, that's fine. I can wait."

"Yeah," Violet said, "I'm going to finish." She turned her focus back to the cookies. And Cain turned his focus back to Alison.

"Nice place you have."

There were other women—it was all women—bustling around the kitchen, barely acknowledging him as they took cakes out of the oven and moved mixing bowls around, and colored bowls of frosting.

"Thank you. We're working toward doing more than just selling things here at the bakery. We make desserts for special events. And supply cakes for parties, weddings. And we're working on packaging some of our baked goods and getting them in stores. And in various showrooms. So what you see up front is only a small sampling of what happens here."

He gestured back toward the dining area, because he wanted a chance to speak to her without Violet in earshot. She caught his meaning, and led the way back out of the kitchen. He showed himself back into the main room, grateful to get the counter between them. "You seem really busy. I really appreciate you taking the time to train Violet. It doesn't seem like you would have a lot to spare."

"I don't. But, even though there were a few people back there, I'm actually short-staffed right now. And anyway, I'm kind of in the business of training women for the workforce."

"Really?"

She nodded definitively. "Yeah," she said, "that's what I do. I mean, in addition to baking kick-ass pies."

"I'll take two," he said.

"Two?"

"Pies. Kick-ass pies."

"Which kind?"

He lifted a shoulder. "The kind that kicks the most ass?"

"That seems subjective."

He really was out of practice with the flirting thing.

Of course, he didn't want to flirt with her. No, what he wanted to do was throw her down on the nearest flat surface and deal with all of the pent-up sexual energy that was roaring through his body. And he shouldn't want to do any of that.

"Well, in your opinion."

"Okay," she said, making her way over to the pastry case and frowning. The concentration she was putting into selecting the right pie was a little too fascinating for him. He liked the way her eyebrows pleated together, that little crease it made in her forehead. The way her full lips pulled down at the corners.

She had been wearing makeup last night. A bright tint over the natural skin tone on her mouth. But he liked it better now. A soft wash of pale pink. He wanted to taste it. Wanted to bite it.

"I'm ready to go."

He looked up, in the middle of thinking about how he wanted to bite Alison's lip, to see his daughter coming out of the kitchen. Well, that was a great underscore to the first specific sexual fantasy he'd had in about a million years.

"Okay," he said, "I'm just getting pie."

"That's all I've eaten for three days," Violet said.

"If you're whining about pie now, then you really can't be helped."

Violet treated him to a shrug that he had a feeling looked like the gesture he'd just made. "Maybe I don't want to be."

"Fine. Eat a salad and be sad. I'm going to eat pie."

Alison walked over to the register and punched in the code. "Employee discount," she said.

Violet frowned. "You don't have to do that. Especially since I ruined that last cake."

"I'm the one paying for this," Cain said, "maybe consider that before you reject my discount."

"I already told you, Violet," Alison said, "the cake isn't a big deal. It's part of learning."

Surprisingly, Violet smiled. An expression that looked both genuine and not sullen. "Thanks," his daughter said, modulating her tone into something much softer than he'd heard in at least a year.

"Lemon meringue and blackberry," Alison said, looking at him.

"Lemon meringue is my favorite."

Her cheeks turned pink, and he had to admit he enjoyed that. Enjoyed the idea that she wasn't any more immune to him than he was to her. Even if it was futile, it was a nice feeling. "Good. That's… Good."

"Nice to meet you," he said. "Ready?" He directed that question at Violet.

Violet already had her phone out and was texting someone. She looked up just for a moment, just long enough to give him a dry look. "I said I was."

"Okay, then." He took the plastic bag that contained two pie boxes and waved at Alison, then headed out the door with Violet. "You could be a little bit friendlier," he commented when they were back out on the street.

"I was friendly."

"You were standing there texting."

"I already said what I needed to say."

He let out a long, slow breath. These kinds of conversations with Violet were futile. She had decided that he was being ridiculous, and she was going to hold on to that no matter what he said. Just like he always did, he wrestled with how to handle it. He could ground her, but then, the only thing he could ground her from was her phone.

Which was reasonable enough, except summer in a new town meant that it was her only source of social life. There was no school to go to, she had no friends around here. Anyway, she was mad enough. He didn't want to make it worse. He didn't want to cut her off from everyone.

That phone represented her entire life right now. And if she was a different kid in a different situation he might handle it differently. But Violet hadn't been the same since her mother had left.

It had taken a couple of years for Violet to stop looking at him like she thought he might disappear. Like she was surprised that he'd come home. For all of that time she'd been almost supernaturally well-behaved. Quiet. And now, it was like she was making up for lost time. Like she had spent the first two years terrified that he might leave her too, and the second two realizing that he wouldn't. Or maybe now she was testing his staying power; he didn't really know.

All he knew was that being a parent was hard. And doing it by yourself when you knew jack shit about kids—about teenagers—was even harder.

Sometimes he looked at his daughter, at this girl who was closer to being a woman than a kid, and wondered where all the years had gone. Wondered how the hell he was standing on a street in a small Oregon town with a sixteen-year-old. Sometimes he didn't know at all how he'd gotten here. He would have thought that sixteen years into parenthood he would feel like he knew something. Would feel like he understood the gig.

No, if anything, he seemed to be worse at it now. When she was three it hadn't taken any work at all to get her to smile at him. Now it took an act of God.

"Do you want to go out to eat tonight?"

"No," she said. "I'm ready to go home."

It was somewhat encouraging to hear her refer to the ranch as home. Usually, she said something about going back to Uncle Finn's house. This new terminology made him wonder if maybe they were making progress.

"Sure. I bet there's a bunch of food in the freezer that Lane made."

Violet shrugged. "I'm not hungry."

"You will be later."

"You don't know that."

He gritted his teeth. This actually did remind him of when she was a toddler. All kinds of screaming about not being hungry anytime food was placed in front of her. And of course, she would whine about not having anything to eat the minute it was taken away.

"You're right," he said, not doing a great job of keeping his tone even. "I don't know that. I don't know a damn thing." He jerked the driver's side door of the truck open and got in. Violet climbed into the passenger side, slamming the door hard enough that he was afraid she might have broken something in the old rig.

She didn't say anything in response to that. Rather, she just gave him a standard eye roll and long-suffering sigh. He was tempted to tell her she didn't know anything about long-suffering. He was pretty sure he had the monopoly on that at this point.

They drove the rest of the way back to the homestead in silence, and he was grateful. He didn't know how to talk to her. At least, not in ways that didn't do more damage.

When he parked, Violet got out of the car wordlessly and headed toward the house, her eyes fixed on her phone. He looked at the front door, which she slammed behind her, not waiting for him. He decided he was going to avoid the house for a while. He looked back up toward the barn that he was preparing for the two of them, a place where—he hoped—they might find a little more peace between them. Where she might see what the point of all of this was.

That he was doing it for her. For them. So that they could finally move on from everything that had happened in Texas.

He was building a life, dammit. Literally. Building them a place to live, a place to call home. One that wasn't completely overrun with the memory of Kathleen and her abandonment.

She would see. When the barn house was finished, when she settled in here, got going at school, made some friends… Everything would be fine. He would make it fine. The lone alternative was failing the only other person on Earth who had ever depended on him. And as far as he was concerned, that just wasn't an option.

CHAPTER FOUR

ALISON WAS HAVING a hard time concentrating on the chatter at their official monthly girls' night—different from their occasional random get-togethers for dinner simply because it was on the calendar. Which was really crappy of her since Lane had arrived with a shiny new ring on her finger, bursting to tell them about Finn proposing, and she was still thinking about her encounter with Cain Donnelly earlier.

The proposal had been beautiful, romantic and utterly spontaneous. At the lake by Lane's house, and they'd been naked apparently. Alison wasn't surprised. Well, the nudity was kind of surprising—she had follow-up questions about where Finn had been keeping the ring—but the proposal had been inevitable as far as she was concerned.

She'd never seen two people who loved each other more. And that had been true long before they'd gone from Just Friends to more. They were meant to be. Even a curmudgeon like Alison could see that.

And the fact it had been such a certainty in her mind was the excuse she was using for zoning out now. And feeling...well, not left out. But something.

Lane and Rebecca were excitedly talking wedding plans, the diamond rings on their fingers casting showers of sparks across the room as they waved their hands in increasingly broad gestures. Cassie was smiling, sitting there with a dreamy expression on her face, clearly caught up in the romance of it all and no doubt remembering her own wedding.

Bah humbug.

Alison wasn't caught up in any romance. And, she didn't want to be. And somehow, she was the last remaining single girl in her group of friends when just a year ago Rebecca and Lane had been staunchly anti-love right alongside her.

It was a conspiracy.

Her mind wandered back to earlier that day, when she had met Violet's father. She hadn't caught his first name. She knew that Lane would know, but expressing any kind of interest would probably seem suspicious. Then again, maybe not. Seeing as Violet was her employee. And Finn was Lane's fiancé.

It might, in fact, be germane to the conversation. It could be. It was always possible.

"What are Finn's brothers' names again?" she asked, realizing as the words tumbled out of her mouth that it had been a bit of a rough transition.

"Cain, Liam and Alex. Why?" Lane frowned. She tented her fingers, and that diamond ring sparkled all the brighter.

Finn and Lane had been together for only a little over a month. But they had been best friends for more than a decade, and when the two of them had tumbled headfirst into a physical relationship, true love had followed quickly. Though, actually, Alison believed that they'd probably always loved each other, they'd just been hesitant to get involved in romantic relationships for some very compelling reasons.

Alison was glad the two of them had worked it out. She really was.

And she wasn't jealous. Not of the love.

But they all glowed. All of her friends. Every last one of them. And Alison believed firmly, that it was not with love, but with recently had orgasms. And that, she was a bit jealous of.

"Oh, I met Violet's father today," she said, keeping her voice perfectly neutral. "But I forgot to catch his name."

"Yeah," Lane said, "that's Cain."

"And he's divorced, right?" she asked, doing her best to sound not the least bit personally interested. Academic. She was aiming to sound academic.

Lane nodded. "Kind of horrifically, if I've interpreted the comments he's made correctly. And I think I have. But as far as I know his wife just kind of disappeared and left both him and Violet."

Well, that explained a lot about Violet's attitude. Alison had known that she was coming from something of a difficult home situation, but she hadn't exactly known the details.

"That's good to know. I mean, good to know so that I can make sure to relate to Violet in the appropriate way. I've helped a lot of women start their lives over, a teenager should be similar. And it sounds to me like she'll have some of the same issues. Confidence, self-esteem." Typically, Alison worked with women like herself. Women who had lost themselves somewhere inside an abusive relationship and were working on resurfacing.

But, abandonment, feeling lonely, being afraid that you always would be... That was part of it. Alison was intimately acquainted with some of those fears. And she had come out the other side of them. She had gotten to a place where she actually enjoyed her own company, which she considered something of a triumph. She felt very strongly about wanting to help other people reach that same place. Where they knew that the people who hurt them were the ones who were at fault. Where they knew that it wasn't something broken in them.

"I think you're the perfect mentor," Rebecca said, "because you're sensitive, but also pretty firm when you have to be."

"My firmness was hard-won," Alison responded.

"I know," Rebecca said, smiling. But not in that way people did when they looked at her and thought only of how broken she was.

That was just one of the many things she appreciated about her friends. They didn't baby her. They didn't treat her like a sad little fledgling that needed special care.

"Though I have to say, being a good mentor is kind of a depressing thought since it clearly means I don't misbehave enough."

"Are you suggesting we go toilet paper some houses?" Rebecca asked. "Because if so, I'm in."

"No time for that," Lane said, "I have to figure out what color bridesmaids dresses to put all of you in."

Cassie groaned. "I'm pregnant."

"What?" The question was asked in chorus.

"Yes, pregnant. I was waiting for a chance to bring it up. I didn't want to run over the wedding stuff. But baby number three is officially on the way and that means I'm going to be wearing taffeta for two at your wedding, Lane."

"Absolutely not. There will be no taffeta at my wedding. I am a classy lady," Lane said, reaching into the bowl that contained chip remnants and gathering as much as she could into her hand.

"Good Lord," Rebecca snorted, "can't Jake keep it in his pants?"

"I can't keep it in Jake's pants," Cassie said. "My husband is a wicked hot bastard, and I was led into temptation and convinced that it would be okay to do it just once without protection."

Lane and Rebecca looked somewhat wistful and abashed by that. As if they could relate to wanting to take the risk, or perhaps had. Alison could scarcely remember feeling passion like that. Most certainly not for the man she'd been married to for eight long years. Again, she struggled with a bit of envy. Not so much over the babies. Although, sometimes she wished there were babies. But she was thirty-two, and had absolutely no relationship prospects on the horizon. Maybe she would adopt someday. But she certainly wasn't going to be having the traditional husband and white picket fence scenario. At least, not in the next five years.

"I'm going to make sure that Gage keeps it wrapped," Rebecca commented.

Rebecca was the youngest of their group, and was of course not quite as biologically predisposed to having full-blown ovarian explosions when people announced pregnancy as Alison and Lane were.

"I'm on the pill," Lane said, "to avoid just that sort of thing. Because Lord knows lapses in judgment happen. Especially with Finn."

"Stop it," Alison said. "You are talking to an extremely celibate woman. And it just feels mean."

"What about that hot guy that was checking you out

at the bar the other night?" Rebecca asked. "Do it with him."

"What hot guy?" Lane asked, looking between Alison and Rebecca. "There was a hot guy?"

"Some sexy cowboy checking her out when we went out the other night."

Suddenly, everyone was looking at her. "I said it then, and I'll say it again. I'm not going to get involved with anyone."

"Clearly, you have needs that have to be met," Lane said.

"Well, they're not going to be met with him."

"Why not?" Rebecca asked.

"There's no reason for it to be him. Nothing happened. He… He was looking at me. That's it. For all we know he could've been staring because my makeup looked funky and I had lipstick on my teeth." She really didn't want to get into the fact that it was Cain Donnelly who had been looking at her. There was too much small-town weirdness happening without her letting her friends in on it.

And Lane would enjoy it too much. And try to matchmake or something. No thank you.

"He wanted to get into your pants. Literally the only reason men stare at women."

"Thank you for that, Lane," Alison said.

"You're welcome. And, now that I've pointed out the very helpful piece of information, maybe you can admit that you actually had a guy who wanted to get with you and you passed it up for no good reason."

Alison sputtered. "I have good reason."

"Tell me your reasons. I want a list of them," Lane said, crossing her arms and staring her down.

Alison held up a finger. "I don't want a relationship."

"Who said anything about a relationship? I was talking about hooking up."

"Well, I'm not in a place in my life where I feel comfortable doing that."

"Uh-huh. I don't believe that." This was when she wished her friends would treat her a little more like a fragile fledgling.

Alison threw up her hands, exasperated, then leaned in and took a piece of pie off the tray that was sitting on the table between them. "It doesn't matter what you believe. What matters is the truth. And the truth is that I… I don't feel… Like I should sleep with a guy just to sleep with him."

"You don't have to *sleep* with him," Rebecca said, her tone sly. "Just have sex with him and leave."

Alison looked at her younger friend. "Rebecca. I'm shocked. This coming from you, who has literally only ever been intimate with the man you're in love with."

Rebecca made a dismissive sound. "I was not in love with him the first time I was *intimate with him*." She put air quotes around that phrase. "In fact, I was decidedly *not* in love with him the first time."

"Settle down, you horrendous bitches," Cassie said. "If Alison wants to stay celibate, Alison can stay celibate."

"Thank you," Alison said, her tone arch.

"And," Cassie continued, "if she wants to become a nun, she can become a nun."

"Okay," Alison said, shooting her friend a deadly glare. "I'm not even Catholic."

"If you're not devoting your life to the church, Alison, I feel like you might devote some of it to having a little bit of fun, but that's just me," Cassie said.

"Wow, your support waned quickly."

Cassie grabbed a second piece of pie for herself. "I'm supportive. I'm very supportive. But in this instance my support includes giving the opinion that if a hot guy—correction, a hot cowboy—is checking you out…"

"It was Cain Donnelly," Alison exploded, forgetting why she hadn't wanted to share the information in the first place. "Okay? Are you satisfied? I discovered today that the man who checked me out at the bar was Cain Donnelly."

Cassie and Rebecca just blinked in silence.

But Lane exploded with laughter. "Oh, my goodness. That is *funny*."

"Why is that funny? I finally found a man who made me consider the benefits of a little bit of medicinal penis and he happens to be the father of one of my employees."

"And a man less likely to show a woman a good time I cannot think of," Lane said, wiping a tear from beneath her eye as she continued to hoot like a deranged burrowing owl.

Alison thought back to that strong, muscular frame, those large, very capable-looking hands, that angular jaw…

"He looks perfectly able to show a woman a good time to me," she said.

"Oh, sure, physically. He's hot. They all are," Lane said. "All the Donnelly men, I mean. Did you not notice that there's a family resemblance?"

"No," she said. "I mean, later when I realized, yes. But I don't think of Finn that way and it just…didn't occur to me."

She'd been caught up in more than just looks. It had been about the connection. The electricity.

"Every Donnelly is hot," Lane said. "But Cain has extenuating circumstances, and he's not the most charming individual at the best of times. Though for him I'm not really sure what constitutes the best of times."

For some reason, Alison felt instantly defensive of him. Which was crazy, because tall, dark and not-getting-in-her-pants did not need her defense. "He was really nice when I talked to him."

"Well, this sucks." Cassie looked deflated. "She finally meets a decent guy and he's complicated."

"All men are complicated," Lane said. "Some are just worth it."

"Why does it have to suck?" Rebecca asked. "You could still hook up with him."

"No," Alison said definitively. "That's too many connections. When I thought he was just a guy passing through town I was almost kind of open to the idea. Of course, then he left the bar and I figured I would never see him again. But when he walked into the shop today... I thought maybe. I thought maybe it was fate. But then it turned out he was Violet's father. And no. First of all, I have so much of my own baggage that I am required to pay oversize luggage fees. So I don't want a guy who's carrying that much of his own. Second of all, Violet needs... Something. Stability. Someone she can talk to. And I feel like she's really getting somewhere at the bakery. I want to help her. Like I've helped other people. I can't do that if I have my hand in her father's pants."

"I don't know," Lane said, her expression taking on a dipped-in-honey sweetness that spoke of nothing but trouble. "You do like to help the needy. Cain is awfully needy."

That brought to mind some very choice images. Hot, sweaty ones. Of how she might help Cain's needs. Wrap her fingers right around that need. Test its strength. Lean in and...

"Dammit," Alison said, sliding her fingers through her hair and cradling her forehead on her palms. "Don't tell me things like that."

"I can tell you a few things about the Donnellys," Lane continued. "I mean, assuming certain anatomical traits are hereditary..."

"Stop it." She let out a heavy sigh. "Lane, you of all people should understand why I don't want an entanglement. And, until recently, you didn't want one either. Don't betray me just because Finn liked it and put a ring on it."

"I would never betray you," Lane said. "But I don't really consider endorsing a sexy man a betrayal."

"You just said he wouldn't be any fun," Alison said.

"Right. You've seen him, so you know that actually isn't true. I mean, physically, he would be a lot of fun."

"You're a bunch of perverts," Alison said. "Anyway, my life is full. I'm fulfilled. My business is going well, I'm making a difference. I don't need to be distracted."

"I make a difference in a man's life every night," Lane said, looking very smug indeed.

"Go away, you're disgusting," Alison said. "Good thing my pie is delicious."

"Does it take the horrible taste out of your mouth of how disgusting I am?" Lane asked.

"Can we talk about anything else, please? It seems to me that many people in this specific circle are either getting married or having babies and I think that both of those things should get more airtime than the hookup that I'm *not* going to have."

Her friends begrudgingly complied with her request, but for Alison, the evening was pretty much tainted. By the memory of Cain Donnelly and how gorgeous he was. How much she wanted to trace that square jaw with her fingertip, feel his beard and how rough it might be. See those green eyes sharpen with interest. And by how much she wished... She just wished things were different. Or maybe she didn't. Maybe she felt relieved.

Or maybe she was caught somewhere between the two things. Which was a strange experience indeed. Regret and relief warring for pride of place inside of her.

Whatever, it was a get-out-of-jail-free card. She knew who he was, and who he was made him off-limits.

So, she wasn't going to have sex. Which meant she could just eat more pie, because nobody was going to see her naked anyway.

And so that was what she did.

CHAPTER FIVE

THE MORNING WAS cold and clear, the sun rising up over the mountains just as Cain finished with milking the cows. He walked across the paddock and leaned over the edge of the fence, watching as the rose gold burned away and shimmered into a true, bright yellow gold that washed over the tops of the mountains, over the trees, gilding the edges and setting the fields below on fire. Little yellow-and-purple flowers all ablaze in the day's early light.

There was something about this part of the day that Cain had come to love. It had taken some getting used to. Getting up at five in the morning and dragging his ass out into the cold with a thermos of coffee and a can-do attitude. But over the past couple of months it had become his favorite moment.

Nothing had gone wrong yet. There was still a world of possibility ahead. And sometimes, it felt like it was just him and the mountains.

"Good morning, jackass," came a voice from behind him.

And Alex. Him and the mountains, and his annoying little brother Alex.

"It was a good morning," Cain said, turning and facing the other man, who was currently grinning from ear to ear like an idiot. Which basically summed Alex up.

"I'm not feeling the love."

"You shouldn't be."

"What were you pondering?" Alex asked, making his way over to the fence to stand next to him.

"The joy of silence. And of being an only child."

"Well, you pretty much were growing up."

That was true. Their dad had liked to spread it around, and he had liked to procreate. But he hadn't liked to raise the children he created. So, even though there had been variations in their childhoods, they'd had that in common.

"I was," Cain said. "And you know what? I was happy."

"I have yet to see evidence that you've ever been happy a day in your life," Alex said, ripping him cheerfully. Alex did everything just a little bit too cheerfully. Sometimes, Cain thought he glimpsed something else beneath that good-natured cheer. Something darker, something that Alex clearly didn't want anyone else to see.

Alex had served in the army for more than a decade, and during those years had spent a lot of time overseas. Cain knew that his younger brother hadn't come out of that service without some scarring, mentally, if not physically. But he did a damn good job of hiding it.

Which made Cain suspicious that what was under all that was pretty dark. But he wasn't going to go poking at it with a stick. If he did that, his brother might return the favor.

"If I remember correctly, I have been happy once or twice," he said. The day of his wedding and the day of his daughter's birth came to mind. Nothing else jumped out in his memory.

"I would be happier if I had a refill of coffee. How about you?"

"It's about that time," he acknowledged, brushing his knuckles against the brim of his hat and tipping it back on his head. "Actually, it feels past time."

Suddenly, he felt tired. The kind of tired that had nothing to do with sleep. The kind that weighed a man down.

He hadn't slept for shit last night. Every time he closed his eyes he'd imagined sifting his fingers through red hair, touching soft, pale skin. He'd been so hard it had been physically painful. But he had refused to do anything about it. Had refused to give himself any relief.

Because his damn body deserved to be punished for wanting to get it on with the single most complicated woman he could have found in a small town. And, given that it was such a small town, most women were going to be complicated in some way or another. So, that was saying something.

Really, the only woman that could possibly be more complicated would be a married one. And even then, maybe not so much. Because, as long as it was a secret…

Not that he would ever go there. His own marriage might have been an unmitigated disaster but he respected the institution too much to go sticking his dick where it didn't belong.

Just as they were approaching the house, the front door jerked open and out came a very stormy-looking Violet, wearing black leggings, a plain gray T-shirt, and a hoodie with only the bottom zipped, the hood up over her hair. She stomped down the stairs and stopped in front of Cain, seeming surprised momentarily as she very nearly ran into him. "Where were you?" she asked, expression furious.

"I was out doing my job," he said, trying to keep his tone measured, even though he could sense that this was about to become a fight.

"Well, I'm late to *my* job," she said, nearly shouting. "Why didn't you wake me up?"

"I didn't know you were opening this morning, Violet," he said, much more patiently than the situation warranted, he felt. "And it's your responsibility to set your own alarm."

"I did," she said. "But it didn't go off."

"Technology failure," he returned, "that's not my fault. But if you head over to the truck I'll get ready to drive you over."

"You should have been around, instead of out playing cowboy, or whatever the hell you're doing."

He couldn't do much of anything but stare at the little viper whose diapers he had once changed. "Playing cowboy? This is my job. This is our legacy."

"No. We had a ranch in Texas. And I know you sold it for a crap ton of money. You don't have to work here, you're just choosing to work here. Because I guess you really like being too busy to do anything for me."

"That's it. Get into the truck before we both say something we're going to regret," he said, grinding his teeth together.

"No. I mean, I'm going to get into the truck," she said. "Because I'm late for work. But not because you told me to."

"Violet. At this point, I don't give a damn why you get in the truck, but you need to do it. And you need to shut your mouth for about thirty seconds and then think very carefully about the next thing you let come out of it. I'm going inside to get coffee. Wait for me."

Alex didn't say anything as the two of them headed into the house. And he continued to say nothing as Cain went over and poured himself a travel mug full of coffee.

"No comment?" Cain asked finally, because surely his younger brother, who had a smart remark for everything, had a smart remark for this.

"No comment at all. Except that teenagers are hell. I should remember, seeing as I was one of the worst."

"She overslept, and somehow I'm the bad guy."

Alex laughed. "I have a feeling at this point you could buy her a pony and be the bad guy."

"Too fucking true," he grumbled, feeling seriously aggrieved as he strode out of the kitchen and made his way out to the truck, where Violet was waiting, her arms crossed, her expression the physical embodiment of the storm cloud.

He jerked the driver's side door open and got in, starting the engine with a little more violence than was strictly necessary.

They began the drive toward town in silence, and Cain told himself to keep it that way. To keep his temper in check. Because Violet was a teenager, and she was testing boundaries. Because she was angry, because ever since they had left Texas she had felt disenfranchised and stuff because she'd had to leave her friends behind. So it wasn't about him. It really wasn't. It was about the change. And he needed to remember that.

That lasted all of ten minutes.

"You think I did this for me?" he asked. "You think that I sold everything I spent your entire life building because I thought it would be hilarious to start over somewhere? Just for fun?"

"I think you'd rather work yourself to death than sit in the same room with me for more than five seconds."

"I sat in a truck with you from Texas to Oregon, I don't think that's the real issue here. That was a long-ass drive, Violet. I didn't avoid that, did I?"

"Whatever," she said, propping her chin up on her hand and staring out the window.

He was so mad at her, and he wanted to leave her on the side of the road. But suddenly he was overwhelmed by the urge to laugh. Because the drama was just a little too much, and a whole lot familiar. He could remember doing the exact same thing at Violet's age. Of course, when he'd been angry at his mother it was because she had stayed out all night at the casino and gone home with a strange man.

Violet had no freaking idea how good she had it.

"We were dying there," he said, his tone rough. "Waiting for her to come back. And I wasn't going to wait anymore."

"You didn't ask me."

He tightened his grip on the steering wheel. "No. I didn't. This isn't a democracy, this is a dictatorship. I wasn't taking votes."

She made that horrible, cat-hacking-up-a-hair-ball sound that teenagers made when they *just couldn't even* with you.

And after that, he let it rest. Because he did have to take her to work, not leave her on the side of the road.

"I'm going to get in trouble," Violet said when they pulled up in front of Pie in the Sky. And in that moment, she sounded so young, so small, and so defeated he just couldn't be mad anymore.

"No, you aren't. Alison seems nice. She'll understand that your alarm didn't go off. It was a mistake. It happens."

She looked up at him then, her eyes suspiciously bright, the expression in them pleading. But she wasn't going to ask for his help, of course not. She was just going to sit there looking miserable until he offered it. And of course he was going to offer it. Because dammit, it felt good to have her need him.

Usually, he had no idea what in the hell he could do for her. But this, he could do.

"Come on. I'll walk you inside."

The fact that she didn't argue with him confirmed his suspicions about the fact that she did want his help. As soon as they entered the bakery Violet scampered behind the counter, grabbing an apron as she went, disappearing into the kitchen. A few seconds later, Alison appeared.

She was wearing much the same thing she'd worn yesterday, all that red hair piled on top of her head again. She looked up, pausing, her expression like someone who had been hit by a truck. "Oh. I didn't realize you were here," she said, reaching up and patting her hair, then dropping her hand quickly and smoothing her apron in what looked like a nervous, fluttery motion.

He affected her. He made her nervous. Well. Hell.

"I figured I would walk Violet in. I know she's late."

Alison frowned. "Right. I put her to work on cupcake duty. I really needed the help this morning."

"Her alarm didn't go off. You know how phones are." Or, he figured it was something to do with the phone.

He didn't really know how phones were. He had no clue what he was saying.

"She needs to get a backup," Alison said, her tone not unkind, but definitely firm. "But I have no trouble talking to her about that. She's sixteen, I think she can take the responsibility for it."

That rankled a little bit. Because he had decided to come in and take the responsibility for it. Because he wanted to be the hero here. Violet might be too little for him to pick up and put on his shoulders, but he could do this. "Yes," he said. "But she is still learning. She's never had a job before. And she's used to me getting her up in the morning for school. But with the way things are working here at the ranch I'm out early. I wasn't back in time to be her backup today. And she's not used to that. She'll learn, but you can't expect her to get it right the first time."

Alison blinked. "Are you scolding me?"

"Maybe."

"I'm not sure how I feel about that," she said, resting her elbow on the counter and leaning in ever so slightly.

"You don't seem too offended," he said, resting his own elbow on the counter and moving in toward her.

"I'm in my place of business," she countered. "So I'm being measured in my responses."

"I would hate to see your temper in full force."

"Is that a redhead joke?"

"I don't think so." He leaned in just a little bit more, and when her breath caught, an answering catch hit him low in the stomach. "You seem a little defensive about that though. It makes me think people have commented on your temper before."

"Not for a while," she said, a soft smile playing with the edges of her mouth.

He wanted to taste that smile. And again, like she'd done the first time they'd talked here in the bakery, she licked her lips, as if she could read his mind about all the tasting he wanted to do.

"Alison, the rest of the cupcakes are too hot to frost."

Both he and Alison looked up quickly, Alison's head whipping back toward the kitchen, when Violet came out wringing her hands and looking lost.

Violet. Yes. He had brought Violet to work. And he had been... Well. Damn. He had been flirting with her boss. And he had decided he wasn't going to do that.

"That's fine," Alison said. "You can watch Sabine do doughnuts. It's pretty easy. I think you'll be able to pick it up pretty fast."

"Bye, Dad," Violet said, turning and heading back into the kitchen. Clearly, he was dismissed.

"I'd better get back," he said. And he really needed to get his damn head on straight.

"Right. Well. Get your daughter an alarm clock."

He touched the tip of his hat with his fingertips and drew it down. "Yes, ma'am," he said, thickening his drawl on purpose.

He wasn't sure what he expected, but he liked the result. The color rose in her cheeks, pretty and bright, and for a moment he just enjoyed the sight. He wasn't going to do anything about her response to him, but, apparently he hadn't forgotten how to do this entirely. That was good to know.

"I'll be back later," he said. And he didn't wait for her response before he walked out of the shop and back onto the street.

ALISON WAS STILL flustered a couple of hours after Cain left. She had been ready to stand firm when it had come to Violet and her lateness. But then… Then… Stuff had happened. And she still wasn't entirely sure what it had been. Well, okay, it had been flirting. She was reasonably sure. But why? Why did she have to respond to him like this? And what was even the point of him making it blatantly obvious that he was…that there was electricity between them?

She heard a loud groan from across the kitchen, and turned just in time to see her problem child pulling another sunken cake out of the oven.

She could fire Violet. She could blame it on the cake. No one would ever have to know it was because she thought Violet's dad was hot.

No. She wasn't going to do that. The entire cornerstone of her business was helping women. If she compromised that mission because of a man… Well. Hypocrisy, that's what it was.

"You're still having trouble, Violet?" she asked, once she had her rogue thoughts under control.

"I don't know what I'm doing wrong." She looked so distressed that all of Alison's petty thoughts faded away.

"I'll tell you what. I'm going to help you. I'm going to spend extra time on this with you."

Violet shifted uncomfortable, tucking a strand of dark hair that had escaped her ponytail behind her ear. "I don't know if I can get down here for that. Or stay late or anything. My dad has to get up super early to work and I don't have my license yet."

"Okay," Alison said, feeling determined now. She had been passive, once upon a time. That was not her way now. Now, when she got the bug to do something, she dug her heels right in. "Is there space to cook at your place?"

"I guess so. We're staying in my uncle Finn's house, and his kitchen is gigantic."

"Do you think anyone would mind if I came over after shift and helped you with a few things?"

Violet blinked, obviously surprised by the offer. "No. Probably none of them will be around. Finn will be with Lane, my dad will be… Well, anywhere but in the house. My other two uncles… Mostly I don't want to know what they're up to."

She wasn't quite sure what to make of the comment about her dad, but it suited Alison to think he wouldn't be around. "Perfect. Actually, if you want to text your dad and let him know that I can drive you home…"

Violet frowned. "You don't have to do that. It seems like you're doing an awful lot for me." And that clearly made the teenager uncomfortable. But Alison was willing to make her uncomfortable for the sake of proving she was valued.

She'd needed that. And no one in her life had given it.

"Yes," Alison said. "I am. But you should never feel like don't deserve that, Violet." Alison felt passionate about this part of her job, about this part of the bakery, and her calling. Because she had spent so many years living in a dark hole. Thinking that she didn't even deserve to see the sun, not after what she had submitted herself to for so many years. It was difficult to ask for help when you'd half convinced yourself that it was your own fault you needed it.

Now that she was in a position to offer help to other people, now that she wasn't in quite such a desperate situation, she wanted them to feel the freedom in accepting help. In feeling that they deserved it.

Especially somebody as young as Violet. She wanted her to always know that she could ask for extra help if she needed it. That she wasn't a burden. That she could offer help herself when she saw the need, and she was able.

"I don't understand why you're being so nice," Violet responded.

"This is something that I can do. I'm good at baking. And I'm good at helping other people learn how to do it. Or if not baking specifically, then job skills in general. Why wouldn't I want to pass that on?"

"I don't know."

"You don't have to know. But I do want to help. So after work we're going to tackle more cake. If you think you're up to it."

"Definitely," Violet said, looking a little more certain now.

"Great."

Alison attacked the rest of the day with a solid sense of determination. She felt…a renewed sense of something. And she was rolling with it. By the time they closed up shop, she was feeling even more amped up.

Last night's sense of…whatever that had been had faded. She didn't need attraction. She didn't need flirting. She had this. She was making a difference.

"Are you ready?" she asked Violet, grabbing a few of the ingredients she would need to do some more specialized baking tonight and piling her arms high with them.

"Yes," Violet said. "Do you need help?"

"Yes. If you could get those icing bags and a couple

of different extracts—whatever you're in the mood for—
that would be great."

Violet complied, pausing briefly in front of the various flavored extracts. "What should I choose?"

"If we were making your birthday cake, what would
you pick?"

"Lemon. And vanilla. Lemon for the cake, vanilla
for the frosting."

"Then choose those. We are going to make a badass
lemon vanilla cake."

Violet looked absolutely delighted by that. And Alison wasn't sure she had ever seen the teenager delighted
before.

Violet was almost chatty on the drive out of town,
up to the ranch that she and her father were living on.
Alison had never been to Finn's house, though given
the fact that Lane was almost living there now, she
had a feeling that she would have been invited up soon
enough.

The house itself was set back from the main road,
at the end of a long, winding driveway. A stunning log
creation that almost seemed to flow with the nature
around it. "This is... Well, it's beautiful," Alison said
as she pulled up to the expansive dwelling.

"I guess so," Violet said, her enthusiasm noticeably
dampened.

"You don't like it here?" Alison asked, turning her
car engine off and unbuckling.

"I don't know. It's not that I don't like it, I guess."
Except she clearly didn't.

"An issue with ranch life or small-town life?" Alison asked.

"I don't know. It's just different. It's cold and there's

nothing to do in town. We lived on a ranch in Texas but we were closer to a city."

"I've never lived anywhere but Copper Ridge," Alison said. "Though I've fantasized about running away a few times."

"Really?"

"Yes. I just don't know where I would run to."

"Adults can't really run away. They just move." Violet let out a heavy sigh. "They have all the control."

"That isn't true," Alison said. "Adults can most definitely run away. Mostly when they feel like they aren't in control. Anyway. Let's get all of the baking stuff." She got out of the car, inhaling a deep breath of the sweet, pine-scented air. She loved her little apartment on Main Street, right above the bakery. Right in the heart of town. But sometimes, she craved an escape. A sanctuary.

She certainly wouldn't say no to a luxury cabin in the middle of the woods.

She and Violet collected the ingredients, and the two of them walked up to the porch together. Violet pushed the door open, and Alison followed her inside.

Then she followed the girl into the most beautiful kitchen she had ever seen. The rest of the cabin was nice, but there was nothing like a custom kitchen with a view to get Alison's heart pumping. For some strange reason, the sight threw her mind back to the tiny house she'd lived in on the outskirts of town only four years ago.

Four years. It felt like a lifetime. Like it had been another person. Pale, beaten down.

For some reason, when she took a step forward she could almost feel that tacky yellow linoleum beneath her shoe. She shook her head. She was walking across a gorgeous stone floor, in a beautiful home that bore absolutely no resemblance to the house she had once shared with her ex-husband, Jared. There was no reason to think of him now. And yet, she found herself thinking of him sometimes at the strangest moments. Moments that shouldn't remind her of him, but somehow did.

Resolutely, she set the ingredients down on the granite-topped island in the middle of the room, the sudden motion and the noise that it made forcing her back into the present. "Okay," she said, "let's get baking."

CHAPTER SIX

WHEN CAIN CAME back in from his evening chores, the house smelled amazing, and the sound of clattering dishes was filtering out of the kitchen. He wondered if Lane was here cooking something for dinner. That was his favorite part of his brother having a girlfriend. The fact that she fed all of them, and happily. In fact, she saw to it like it was a mission.

Lane owned the Mercantile in town, and specialty foods were her passion. That meant that she simply wouldn't let any of them go unfed on her watch, or fed on cruddy, frozen meals.

It suited him just fine. Though Finn's disgusting happiness and constant look of satisfaction got a little bit old. But there was food.

He made his way into the kitchen, and stopped, feeling like he had been slugged in the stomach.

Because there she was, red hair piled on top of her head, bent over in front of the oven, showing off an ass that was even more perfect than he had imagined it might be. He knew it was Alison. There was no one else it could be. Nobody else affected him like this. Wasn't that a joke?

"What's going on?"

Both Violet and Alison jumped. "Baking practice," Violet responded, lifting a red spatula.

"Okay," he said, but it wasn't okay at all. Because temptation had walked right into his house, and he was doing his very best to stay away from temptation.

"I thought… I thought you knew," Alison said.

"No," he returned.

"Sorry," Violet said, looking more angry than sorry. "I said that Alison was bringing me home. I didn't think you needed details. I figured I wouldn't see you at all."

What struck him was the way that his daughter's body language had changed since realizing he was there. When he had walked in she had looked happy, at least the small blips he had gotten of her before his gaze had fixated on Alison's butt. And now she was back to looking angry. Angry and tense.

So, it was just him, then.

"The cake is almost done," Alison said. "Do you want to do the honors, Violet?"

Violet gave him a wary look. "I guess."

"It's okay that I'm here, right?" Alison asked him.

That woman. She had no problem coming at him from the front. Of course, not exactly the way that he fantasized about her coming at him from the front. He'd like to come at her from behind. He tried to ignore the kick of heat that pooled in his gut at that thought.

"Of course," he said. "Have you had dinner?"

He didn't know why he was testing this line. Or maybe he did. Because she was here. She was here in his house. Baiting him with her perfect ass. And if she was going to do that, then he was going to push right back.

"No," she said. "But that's fine."

"What's fine?"

"You don't need to feed me."

He crossed his arms and leaned against the door frame. "I didn't offer to."

"Dad," Violet said, jerking him out of the interaction, and out of the haze that had descended upon him. "What's your problem?"

"Nothing. But I do think that Alison should stay for dinner. And then we can enjoy the cake afterward. I was just giving her a hard time."

"Whatever. You're weird. Can I…" She shot a sideways glance at Alison. "I just want to talk to my friends until dinner."

"You're not on the clock," Alison pointed out. "But thanks for asking."

"Well, I didn't want to deprive you of my company," Violet added.

"Go talk to your friends," Cain said. "We'd hate for them to experience Violet deprivation."

Violet walked out of the kitchen, pulling her phone out of her pocket as she moved away from them to head up the stairs.

His stomach tightened, a strange sense of anticipation stealing over him. Oh, yes, he remembered this. Very vaguely. That crackle of possibility that sizzled over your skin when you were near somebody that you wanted. When you wondered if you were going to have them.

It had been a long time. But he still remembered that.

And he wondered where all his common sense was. That common sense that told him he needed to steer clear of a woman who was so involved in his daughter's life.

But then, flirting wasn't sex.

It had just been so long since a woman had looked at

him like that. With color in her cheeks. Since he had felt this kind of excitement. Since he had wanted.

"I hope she's better for you than she is for me," he said, not really meaning to lead with mention of his daughter. But then, he supposed that was a pretty fitting metaphor for his life. Violet came first. No matter what. Even when he would rather just be a man, just talk to a beautiful woman, he couldn't really. Because he was a father. First and foremost.

His ex-wife might have forgotten that. But he hadn't. He never would.

"She's fine, honestly. I don't know what's going on between the two of you, but with me she's fine."

"Normal teenage stuff, I guess." he said, making his way over to the fridge and opening the freezer. There were several meals that had been premade by Lane there, ready for them to heat up when necessary. "Did you like your parents when you were a teenager?"

"No," she said. "Not even a little bit. But I don't like them very much now either."

"That...isn't encouraging."

"Do you have a better relationship than that with your parents?"

He laughed. "Hell no."

"Right. Well, then."

"Do you have a food preference?" he asked. "It looks like there's pasta, pot roast and...meat loaf? All made by Lane Jensen."

"Then all of it will be good," Alison said. "Lane is one of my best friends, so I've eaten most of her food."

"Right," he said, "I know that she's a good friend of yours. She talks about you a lot. And she kind of helped Violet get the job at your bakery, right?"

"Oh," Alison said, leaning against the island in the kitchen, tucking a stray curl behind her year. "Right. What else has she... She talks about me?"

She looked concerned by that. Which seemed strange to him. "She hasn't told me anything."

"Okay. Good to know."

"I'm voting for pasta," he said lightly, taking a metal pan out of the freezer. "I had a long workday."

"Have you always been a rancher?" she asked. "I mean, Lane did tell me a little bit about you. Or, I mean about Violet. But I applied some of it to you."

"Right. Well, then you know we just moved here from Texas. And yes, I have always been a rancher. I sold the spread back in Dallas. That was beef, this is different. But I like different. Violet not so much."

"Well, you know what they say. You can please some of the people some of the time... But you can't please teenagers ever."

He laughed, making his way over to the oven and sticking the pan of pasta inside. "True. Very true."

"Really though, she's not bad as far as teens go. She's a good kid."

He felt a momentary flash of... Something. Jealousy almost? That this woman, this stranger, got something from his own child that he didn't. And then, he was just pissed. Pissed that he was standing here with a beautiful woman, the first woman he wanted to touch since his divorce, and he couldn't.

Because of his daughter who hated him anyway.

"Do you want to come sit in the living room while that warms up?"

That was better than inviting her up to his room, which was what he actually wanted to do.

"Sure," she said.

They both walked into the living room, and he took a seat on the couch. She took the chair across from him. Probably for the best.

"She's a good kid," Alison repeated, keeping her eyes focused on the window, on the view outside. Which was pretty spectacular. His grandfather had had the custom home built a few years ago, if Cain understood the timeline correctly. It was nestled in the center of the mountain, taking advantage of the scenery of the valley and the fields below.

"You said that," he responded.

"Yes," she said, "I did. And I mean it. She's a good kid. But I think she needs to take a little more of her own responsibility. She could be driving herself to work. And she can definitely get herself up in the morning."

Irritation streaked through him, heat that rivaled the heat of attraction that had been firing in his gut just a moment before. "Excuse me?"

"She can take more responsibility than she is. I understand that you're feeling protective because you just moved here…"

"Look, I know you think that you know the situation because Lane told you some things, but you don't. I do feel protective of her. Very protective. She's been through enough."

"Yes. But I have a feeling that part of the reason she's sometimes surly with you is that you're hovering a little too much."

"No. That isn't it. Just ask her. She feels like she doesn't see me. She's mad at me because I have a job, and because I don't talk to her, which she doesn't actually want. Because she hates me." He was not going to let this woman, no matter how sexy, tell him anything about his relationship with his daughter.

Because you're such an expert about your relationship with your daughter?

He ignored that obnoxious inner voice.

"Hovering over her and driving her to work, and coming in to talk to her boss when she's late isn't the same as spending time with her," Alison said calmly.

"How many children do you have, Alison?" he asked, crossing his arms.

She frowned. "None."

"That's what I thought. So, you'll understand if I don't take your advice on mine."

"I don't have any children, but since my bakery essentially functions as job training I see a lot of different kinds of women. And I've learned to work with a lot of different personality types. I've learned the most effective ways to build different kinds of people up, to give them confidence. I want Violet to understand that she can accept help, and that it's a good thing to get help. But I also want to see her standing on her own two feet."

"You think I don't want that? You think that because you spend a few hours a day with her you know her better than I do? I've been raising her for sixteen years. Four of them by myself. You don't have any right to make commentary."

She stood up, making her way over to the window, twisting her hands in front of her. "All right. Maybe I don't. And fine, I don't know anything about kids. But I do know about women. And she's almost a woman."

He didn't want to hear that, even though he'd been having similar thoughts earlier. He stood too, agitation pouring through him. "She's still a kid. And she needs certain things done for her. She's had it rough. Her mother abandoned her and she needs...she needs more from me because of it, okay? She needs to feel taken care of."

Alison turned to face him, her cheeks pink, this time from anger, and not from any kind of attraction. "If you're going to purposely misunderstand me, then I don't see the point of having this discussion."

She started to walk back toward the kitchen and he reached out and caught her arm. She looked down at where his hand was curled around her, and she jerked away, her expression wary. "Don't."

"Sorry," he said. "Did I hurt you?"

She blinked, her expression schooled into a perfect, blank slate. "No."

He knew she was attracted to him. And he'd bet money that was why she'd reacted the way she had when he'd touched her.

He expected her to walk past him. To walk away then. But she didn't. Instead, she just stood there, looking at him. And he forgot what they were talking about. He forgot that they'd been arguing. And the tension—tension that had been associated with anger only a second ago—shifted, changed.

He forgot everything. Except that she looked like heaven. And a little bit angry, but that just made him want to reach out and smooth the crease between her eyebrows, then trace the shape of her face, down to her chin, slide his thumb across her lower lip and see if it was as soft as a rose petal, like he suspected it might be.

He took a step toward her. Again, he expected her to move away. Again, she didn't. No, instead, she held her ground, and she licked her lips again.

Before he knew what he was doing, he reached out,
hooking his arm around her waist and drawing her up
against him. She looked startled for a moment, her hands
held up like he had her at gunpoint. But that only lasted
a moment. Then she softened, her spine curving as she
melted against him, pressing her palms to his chest.

"This is a bad idea," he said.

She nodded slowly. "Yes."

But she didn't push at him. Didn't try to pull away. So
he began to lower his head, slowly, those rose-petal lips
so close to his own he was already anticipating the taste.

"No," she said suddenly. "Oh, no." And then she did
push against him, extricating herself from his hold. "I
can't do this. I don't do things like this. I'm sorry. I really need to go."

And then, as it seemed to be the pattern in his life,
Alison stormed from the room, leaving him standing
there to wonder what the hell he had done wrong now.

CHAPTER SEVEN

ALISON WAS ALL the way back at her apartment by the time she caught her breath. She hadn't said goodbye to Violet. Hadn't stayed to help her frost the cake. She was a terrible mentor. And she felt guilty. Very, very guilty.

But she'd had to get away from Cain.

What had she been doing? She had nearly… She had nearly kissed him.

She went over to the cupboard by her stove and opened it up. She took out a bottle of wine and poured herself a generous portion.

She took a sip, trying to get a handle on her shaking hands. But she couldn't. She had to… She had to process all of this. She hadn't been that close to a man in four years.

When he had reached out and grabbed her arm, it had scared her. It had felt like a flashback to something else. Back to someone else. But then he let go of her, easily and quickly. He'd been worried that he'd hurt her.

And then, well, then he had looked at her like she was something amazing. Something he'd never seen before, and all she had wanted to do was lean in to that.

She knocked back her glass of wine, taking a long, strong sip, her other hand braced on the counter. Was this a relapse? All it took was one burning look from a gorgeous man and she was ready to lie on the ground and write *welcome* across her chest?

No. It wasn't the same thing. Not even remotely the same as the reasons she had hooked up with guys when she was in high school, why she had married Jared. That hadn't ever been about physical desire, unfortunately.

That had been about her pathetic need to feel loved by someone. Anyone. In whatever shape that love would take.

This was different. She didn't want Cain to love her. She had wanted him to press her down on that couch and kiss her until neither of them could breathe.

She took another gulp of wine.

It was difficult to figure out, right then, why kissing him would have been a bad idea. Why letting him lay her down on the couch and drive them both crazy would be such a terrible thing.

He was gorgeous. Like, honestly the hottest guy she had ever seen. She had never before wanted a guy just because she wanted him. Because she wanted to feel his hands on her skin. Because she wanted sex, not some kind of connection. Not some kind of solution to that howling, empty thing inside of her.

She wasn't empty now. She had her bakery. She had all of the women that she had helped so far, and the women she was helping now. She had a good group of friends. She had her own apartment that she kept in exactly the manner she wanted.

She bought the kind of wine she liked and the kind of food she enjoyed. She no longer had to cook dinner promptly at five o'clock or face the possible ramification of having a dinner plate thrown at her head if it was too cold, or if she had done something wrong.

She could eat at eight if she wanted to. And she could cook whatever she wanted. Or she could go to a restaurant.

Yes, her life was in an entirely different place now than it had been a few years ago. She was a different person. Or, more accurately, she was the person that she should have been all along.

Too bad that person was starting to want sex.

She closed her eyes and thought back to that moment Cain had looked at her. The way he had touched her. The problem was, she wanted sex, and not an entanglement. It seemed to her that Cain's life was a giant entanglement right now. Particularly with her own.

He was definitely the wrong person to experiment with. What she needed was an actual stranger. A man who would be in town only for a night. Someone she couldn't possibly have any obligation to. Somebody whose life she couldn't get drawn into.

She didn't trust men, that much was true. But even more, she didn't trust herself.

She wasn't going to involve herself quite so personally in Violet's affairs. Not anymore. She would not be taking any more trips up to the ranch. She needed to get some distance between herself and Cain Donnelly, that much was certain. Otherwise she was going to make a very bad decision that she would regret later.

Sure, it might be much later. After the heat and fire in her skin had abated to a slow burn. But, regret it she would.

She had too much regret in her life already. She wasn't in the market for more.

Cain reached the top of the stairs and wished he had brought a bottle of whiskey up with him. And his brothers—damn them—were never around when he wanted them to be. They'd all gone out, and there had been no buffer between himself and Violet.

The night had been a disaster. Violet had ended up angry with him because Alison had left, and she had blamed him. Not incorrectly, but he wasn't going to explain to his teenage daughter exactly what had happened.

Better to let her think he'd been unfriendly than... too friendly.

But all of this had resulted in an extremely sullen meal, followed by her storming off to her room a couple of hours ago.

He had done what he always did. He ignored it. He stayed downstairs until he was ready to collapse, and now he was headed to bed. He sighed heavily.

What he really wanted to do, more than anything, was call up Alison. Say screw responsibility and pass out after having an orgasm, instead of passing out after drinking too much. Alone.

But he couldn't do that. First of all, because Alison had been the one to pull away from him—almost like she was afraid of him—before she had run out the door like she was most definitely afraid of him.

Also, because running away from home to go get laid while his daughter was pissed off at him was probably not the most adult or responsible thing to do. Of course, he'd just about had it with responsibility.

Still, there were no vacations from it when you had a child. Even if that child was close to being an adult, as Alison had so irritatingly pointed out to him earlier.

That pissed *him* off.

That she was right, mostly. That it didn't erase the fact that he felt like he'd done the right thing earlier going in and trying to smooth things over for Violet, because she had obviously needed him to.

Alison was coming at it from the point of view of a boss, as somebody who helped people with training and independence and stuff. He just wanted his daughter to look at him like he wasn't horrible.

He looked down the hall, toward Violet's room. Maybe he had to talk to her. Maybe this whole giving her her space thing wasn't the answer. He was so hesitant to make more waves, but it didn't seem to be working.

Maybe he needed to make some waves. Maybe, in that way, Alison was right. Maybe he needed to push Violet harder, expect more from her.

He began to walk toward his room, then redirected. Tonight. They were going to talk tonight. He wasn't going to tolerate any more of this silent treatment. He wasn't going to accept any more of this being frozen out. No. It ended now.

He stopped in front of her door, hesitated for a moment and then knocked. There was no answer. "Violet?" He knocked again. Nothing.

Immediately, the image of her having some kind of medical episode flashed into his brain. Even if he had no idea what kind of medical episode it might be. He could see her, in his mind's eye, crumpled on the floor, unable to answer him or move for some reason.

He pushed the door open, fully unreasonable panic rioting through him.

And the bedroom was empty.

Her window was open. Up on the second floor.

"Shit. Shit. Shit." He made his way over to the window, looked out, looked down. And he didn't see anything. Didn't see anyone. He had no idea where she could be, who she would have gone with. He didn't even know why she would sneak out.

Suddenly, he felt like an idiot. Of course, he had imagined that she was hurt, or sick, or something. It had never occurred to him that she might sneak out. He didn't think she knew anyone here in Copper Ridge, but he didn't know that for certain. Of course he didn't. He had never asked. He assumed that she was always texting friends back home, but for all he knew she was texting other kids here.

He didn't know how many other times she had done this. He didn't know what she was doing.

He tore back downstairs. "Finn!" He realized that his brother might already be upstairs, and he should have rattled some doors up there.

Alex came out of the living room, Liam following close behind. And Finn came down the stairs behind him. Finn was only half-dressed, and was likely coming from bed where Cain was reasonably certain his brother had left Lane.

"What's up?" Finn asked.

"Violet's gone."

"What?" Finn asked, immediately looking concerned.

"What do you mean gone?" Alex asked.

"I mean I opened her bedroom door to check on her,

and it looks like she climbed out the window. I don't know where the hell she could be. I didn't even know she knew anyone here."

"Damn," Liam said. "I guess things haven't changed very much since I was in high school."

Cain felt absolutely grim. "That's not exactly comforting."

"Okay, the first thing we should do is look around the property. The barn, and that kind of thing," Finn said.

"I don't know," Cain said. "If she's on the property then she's safe enough. But what if she's out somewhere else? And who's driving? Who's she with? What's she doing?" None of the potential answers to those questions were any good, as far as he was concerned.

"I'll tell you what," Finn said. "Lane and I can canvas the ranch, you can go down into town."

"We'll go too," Alex said.

"Yeah," Liam added. "Actually, if there's one thing I remember about spending summers here it's where we used to party."

"That's actually helpful," Cain told Liam. "Come on. Let's go."

"As soon as we're done looking, we can join you in town," Finn said.

"Great," Cain said. "Text me."

His brother nodded, then went upstairs, Cain assumed, to collect a shirt and his fiancée.

Outside, Cain waited impatiently for his brothers to climb in the truck, then started the engine and tore off down the driveway without any real sense of direction.

"There was a barn that we used to party at," Liam said. "On somebody's property. But they didn't use it anymore. We can always look there."

"She doesn't know anybody," Cain said. "Nobody except for her boss."

Alison. He had to call Alison.

He didn't have her number. Great. He just had the bakery number. He didn't know enough about his daughter. That was the refrain that played over and over in his mind while he drove down to town.

He dialed the bakery, let it ring. All he got was the machine.

"Text Finn and ask for Alison Davis's cell number." He barked the order at Liam.

Liam complied and about thirty seconds later, Cain dialed the mobile number and got a voice mail. Which wasn't that surprising, considering she probably had to get up about as early in the morning as he did.

He bit back a curse and left a brief message all while driving down the main street scanning every building— for what, he didn't know.

"Just keep driving," Liam said. "Trust me. I'm pretty sure we can figure out where everybody congregates these days."

"You really think nothing has changed since you were here getting drunk and banging local girls?" As soon as he said that, he cringed. Because his daughter could very well be getting drunk. And at this point, she was a local girl.

"I think kids are kids, and unless that old barn has been knocked down, it probably serves just as well as a party place as it did back in the day."

He dialed Alison again. "Alison, this is Cain. I'm looking for Violet. She sneaked out tonight. I don't know who any of her friends are, I don't know who she talks to. So if you've seen anybody coming in and talking with her, I would appreciate information. Thanks."

He left his phone number and threw the phone down onto the seat, cursing as he continued to drive. He followed Liam's instructions, but wasn't exactly aware of doing so. When they turned onto a dirt road, and he saw the old barn up ahead, light visible through the cracks in the boards, he knew that his brother had been right.

"How do you know these things I don't?" he muttered as he pulled up to the barn.

"I just know what the troubled kids get up to."

Great. That meant his daughter was a troubled kid. Just perfect.

He cut off the truck engine, pausing when his brothers climbed out after him. "I should probably go in alone, don't you think?" Cain asked.

"Hell no," Alex returned. "This is what family is for."

Liam smiled at that, and the three of them walked up the dirt driveway to the barn. There was music thumping out from the old wooden structure, and he could hear laughter and high-pitched squeals.

He hoped that Violet was in there. He really did. Even though he was going to be angry, he really wanted her to be here. Because he didn't know where else to look. Didn't know where else to even begin. He didn't want her to be here, but he so very desperately needed her to be.

"This is kind of exciting," Liam said, smiling broadly. "I've never been on this side of a party being broken up before."

"Well, I'm glad you're enjoying this," Cain responded.

"One of us has to." And then Liam broke away from

the group, striding to the barn and shoving the door open like he was *Hawaii Fuckin'-Five-0.* "All right. Break it up." He turned back around and smiled at Cain. "Fun," he said.

Cain moved deeper into the barn, along with Alex. There were kids everywhere, drinking, making out, doing God knew what else. He was trying not to look too closely.

"Are you the police, man?" Some kid with bloodshot eyes pointed that question at Liam.

"You wish I were the police," Liam said. "As it is, I'm just a guy looking for his niece. And I'm probably meaner than any cop you've ever met. Her name is Violet. Dark hair, about this tall." Liam held his hand up just beneath his chin.

"Look, man," the guy said, "if you aren't the police…"

And Cain was officially done with this bullshit.

He grabbed hold of the kid, turning and slamming him up against the barn wall. "Violet Donnelly. Do you know who she is? Do you know where she is?"

"I don't know. I don't know a girl named Violet." The kid looked scared now, and Cain felt satisfied by that. Because he should be. Every little bastard in here should.

"There she is," Alex said, pointing toward the back of the barn.

Some of the other kids had picked up on the fact that they were busted and were starting to flee the building like rats off a sinking ship. But not Violet. Because she was half reclining on a beanbag in the back, with some jackass plastered to her face.

Cain saw red.

"Violet Donnelly," he shouted from across the barn, taking long strides over to where she was and grabbing the back of the kid's T-shirt, hauling him off his daughter. "You get your ass out to the truck," he said, ignoring the protests of the young man whose shirt he was still holding on to.

She blinked. "Dad?"

And that was when he realized that she was drunk. His daughter was drunk. And this guy had been kissing her.

"She's been drinking," he said, pushing the little dickhead pawing his daughter back. The kid swayed, and Cain figured he was drunk too. But that wasn't going to stop Cain from teaching him a lesson he'd remember. "Let me tell you something, you little earthworm, if a woman's not fully in her right mind, then you better back off. And if you have to get a woman drunk to get her into you? There's something wrong with you in that case. And if you enjoy taking advantage of women, then you're beyond help. Is that what you like?"

"No," the kid said, "no." He was visibly shaken and Cain was more than okay with that.

"Also, the issue here is, she is a girl. Not a woman. She's sixteen, so I sure as hell hope you're drinking underage in here."

"I just… She likes me."

"Well, that's too bad for both of you, because you're never going to see her again." Maybe he was being unreasonable. At this point, he couldn't tell. But he didn't care either. All he wanted to do was light the place on fire, burn it to the ground. He wanted to leave nothing but ash and ruin in his wake.

Reasonable was for another day. Reasonable was for another moment. Reasonable was for another man.

"Dad," Violet said, "you're embarrassing me." She wrapped her arms around her midsection and looked down, her dark hair falling into her face.

She was wearing some ridiculously tight minidress and chunky boots, and showing way too much skin for his liking.

He didn't even know where to begin lecturing her.

"Oh, I have just started to embarrass you." He turned around and faced the group of teenagers that remained. "All of you go home. All of you. Before I call the police and have you arrested for underage drinking. And, just in case you didn't know, I'm Violet Donnelly's father. That's right. I'm her dad," he said, pointing to her. "So, if you intend to hang out with her, you have to contend with me. I'm sure most of you won't, but I feel like she won't have lost any good friends."

"Dad." Violet pulled away from him, crossing her arms and walking out of the barn with her head down. She was scowling. He couldn't see her face, but he sensed it. And he was glad. He was glad she was angry, he was even a little bit glad that none of these delinquents would probably ever speak to her again.

He was angry, and he wasn't thinking straight. She had scared the ever-loving hell out of him, and now that he had seen for himself she was safe, he was just mad.

"We'll ride in the back," Liam said, hopping into the bed of the truck. Alex followed suit.

He didn't really know if they were doing it for his benefit or their own, but he was happy to go with it either way. Although, happy might be overstating it at this point. "Suit yourselves," he said, opening the passenger side door and gesturing for Violet to get inside.

She stumbled on her way in, crawling into the seat and groaning. And something in his heart twisted, something in his stomach tumbling right along with it. His daughter was drunk.

He slammed the door shut and leaned against it for a second, pressing his hands to his forehead and counting to ten. Like he had done when she was a toddler and she was frustrating him. But she wasn't a toddler. She was sixteen, and she was drunk. She had been making out with some guy. She had sneaked out. She had friends here, and he didn't know who any of them were, but he had just yelled at all of them.

"Damn you, Kathleen," he said. "Damn you to hell." He cursed his ex-wife as he rounded the front of the truck and made his way to the driver's side. She had left him here to do this by himself. Had left both him and Violet in over their heads.

He was angry. So angry. And he wasn't sure he had fully realized how angry until this moment. He took a deep breath, then got into the truck. He and Violet were both silent until he turned out onto the main road.

"What the hell were you thinking?"

"I don't want to talk to you," she said, the words petulant, and slightly slurred.

"I don't care," he said, raising his voice slightly. "I didn't want to have to come track you down in the middle of the night. I didn't want to open your bedroom door to find you gone, with no idea where you might be. So right now, what you want is low on my list of priorities, Violet."

"I'm sorry, now you care where I am? Why? Just because you noticed I was gone? Do you really think that was the first time I sneaked out?"

Her words cracked over him like a whip. Of course it wasn't the first time she had sneaked out. He was an idiot. He was a damn idiot.

"Why? Why didn't you talk to me?"

"We don't talk," she said. "Ever. So why are you acting like you care about who I hang out with or what I do?"

"Of course I care. That's a stupid thing to say."

"Maybe I'm stupid, then."

"Choose your words carefully, kid," he said. "I'm not in the mood. And you're giving me your phone."

"What the hell? Dad, that's not fair."

"I don't care what's *fair*. It doesn't have to be *fair*. You just have to do what I say."

"Yeah, that sounds about right. That's how you uprooted my entire life and brought me out to this shithole!" She was getting shrill now to go with the slurring.

"Because I am your father and I make the decisions about what happens in our lives. You do as I say, when I say it, because you don't know what the hell to do with yourself. And if that was in question at all before, it isn't now. I didn't know where you were tonight, Violet. I went upstairs and you were gone."

"That was kind of the idea."

He was ready to explode, God help him. "Anything could have happened to you, don't you understand that?"

"Now nothing ever will. I think you scared Reed off forever."

"I hope I scared his punk ass. It will save me the trouble of killing him. He was drunk. You're drunk. What the hell would have happened if I hadn't showed up?"

"I don't know."

"That's the problem," he bit out. "You don't know. I can think of a thousand things, Violet. Would he have tried to drive you home? Would he have stopped somewhere and tried to take things further?"

"What?"

"Sex, Violet. I'm not going to baby you. You're out here doing this stuff, and you have to understand what it all might lead to."

Silence settled between them and heat prickled the back of his neck as he realized that he actually didn't know if she'd had sex or not. He'd assumed not. She'd never had a boyfriend. But clearly there was a lot happening he didn't know about.

They'd kind of had The Talk a few years ago. He'd bought her a book and said if she'd had any questions, she could ask. And she hadn't asked. Which in hindsight...yeah, he wouldn't have asked any questions either in her position.

Had he royally screwed this up? He didn't know how to deal with this on his own. It would probably help her to have a woman to talk to and she didn't have one. She had him. And he sucked.

"I didn't like the way he was touching you," he said, his voice low, gravelly. His emotions were on edge and he didn't know how to get hold of them again.

"I did."

"You're drunk."

"That doesn't matter."

"The hell it doesn't, Violet. It affects your decision-making ability. God knows it's going to affect his. Especially when you're both too young to be drinking. And when you're in a position like that, you're vulnerable. If he had decided to keep going, and you didn't want him to…"

"I can handle myself." She curled up into a little ball and leaned against the passenger door, her cheek against the window.

It reminded him of when she was little, and she'd fallen asleep like that in the truck on the way home from swimming in the river.

Why couldn't it be simple like that anymore?

His chest tightened, every muscle tense.

"No. That's the thing, in a situation like that you couldn't. I understand it feels good to think you could control it, but he's stronger than you. And he's also not my asshole kid, so I can't yell at him, I can only yell at you. I'm scared," he admitted finally. "I'm scared about what's going to happen to you, and what might have happened to you tonight. And the only thing that scares me more is that you aren't. At all. You think it was fine, and you know what? That's why you need someone to tell you what to do. Because you aren't old enough to understand the consequences of your damned actions."

She didn't say anything. And when they pulled into the driveway and up to the house, he realized it was because she'd fallen asleep. The scowl that usually marred her brow was absent now, her cheek still pressed against the glass.

His stomach twisted hard, his past and present colliding like freight trains, with all the mayhem you'd expect a crash like that to cause.

He unbuckled his seat belt, then reached out and unbuckled her belt, sliding her over to his side of the truck before getting out and scooping her up into his arms.

Alex and Liam were already out of the truck, both

of them headed resolutely to the house. Neither of them lingered. Which he had to admit was decent of them. Surprising, considering they were generally a bunch of assholes.

He adjusted his hold on Violet, and she made a sleepy, croaky sound that reminded him so much of when she was little, it made his breath catch.

But she was drunk. And she clearly knew people here. Knew a boy. Enough to make out with him. And Cain himself didn't know a damned thing.

He carried her into the house, up the stairs, and laid her down in her bed. He walked over to the window and closed it, resolutely. But he would never take for granted that she was going to be in her bedroom when he came to check on her again. Would never just believe that she was where she said she would be, that she wasn't hiding something.

It made him miss the days when his daughter hiding something meant her curling her grubby hand around part of a cookie and sneaking it before dinner.

This was bigger. This was something he couldn't control, couldn't protect her from. He took a deep breath and walked out of her bedroom, closing the door behind him.

It was official. He was in over his head. He hated admitting it. But he had done everything he knew to do. He had tried to give her space. He had moved them from Texas, from that house that held too many ghosts, too many memories, and brought them here, and he was no closer to Violet than he'd been before they'd left. She hated him, and he was damn close to hating himself.

He was a man who had made a living out of riding the range on a thousand-pound animal, a man who had spent countless hours working the land, battling the el-

ements. He had waged war with barbed wire, mended
fences out in the blistering heat and the pouring rain.
Had gone out when the floodwaters had risen and made
sure each and every one of his animals was safe.

He had never felt at a loss. He had never felt like
there was anything he couldn't master, bend to his will
as long as he applied enough grit and sweat.

But there didn't seem to be enough grit and sweat
and good intentions in all the world to fix this situation
with Violet. It was something more than physical labor,
something he couldn't hit with a hammer or bend with
enough force.

His entire body was filled with restless energy. Or at
least, that was the sensation he chose to embrace. It was
either that or give in to the dark storm that was brewing
inside of him. He chose the energy. The adrenaline rush.
He stormed down the stairs and through the entryway
of the house, slamming the front door behind him, taking long strides down the road that led to the old barn.

It was cold, but he didn't care. Soon, he would work
off the chill.

He went inside and flicked on the work lights, flooding the empty space with a warm glow. He was never
going to sleep. So he would work all damned night if he
had to. And he would find something. Something that
would help him solve this problem. Or he would die of
exhaustion along the way.

CHAPTER EIGHT

BY THE TIME Alison arrived downstairs in the bakery, she was working on her second cup of coffee. She hadn't slept well last night. Or rather, she had slept hot and sweaty and dreaming of Cain's hands on her body.

She groaned, selfishly glad that Violet wasn't coming into the bakery today. Because it eliminated the chances of her seeing Violet's father. Or at least, it reduced them. And maybe, without Violet around to remind her of Cain, Alison would think of him a little bit less.

She snorted. Because, seeing as she was thinking of him at five thirty in the morning, she was obviously not going to think of him less today.

She lifted her mug to her lips while she opened up the home screen on her phone. And saw she'd gotten a voice mail at some point last night. She hit play and held her phone to ear, her heart hitting her sternum when she heard the familiar drawl.

It was Cain.

He couldn't find Violet.

Terror clutched at her throat, and she hoped that there was a follow-up message. There wasn't. So she had no idea if he had found Violet or not. But she did have his phone number. And she did know that he got up early. Plus, if he hadn't found his daughter, she imagined he wouldn't have slept at all.

She quickly dialed the number that he'd left. As it rang, she asked herself how on earth she had ended up in this position. Where she was dialing the man she wanted most to stop obsessing about before the sun had even risen.

It's about Violet, she told herself. *Totally reasonable. Absolutely and completely reasonable.*

"Hello?"

Oh, no. He sounded like he had been asleep. His voice was all rough and rusty and sexier than it had a right to be. It was an intimate thing, to hear a man sounding like this, to hear the first words he spoke in a day.

She bit her lip. "It's Alison. I'm sorry if I woke you up, but I just got your message. About Violet. Did she make it home okay?"

He cursed violently. "Right. That. Yeah. She's home."

"Oh, thank God."

She heard some rustling, shifting, and she realized that he was still in bed. She wondered what a man like Cain wore to bed. She personally wore flannel pajamas festooned with goats in party hats. She doubted Cain wore pajamas festooned with anything, let alone farm animals.

She wondered if he wore anything at all.

Then she realized he had confirmed Violet was home, but nothing else. "She's okay?" Alison pressed.

He laughed, a strange, humorless sound. Not one she typically associated with laughter. "Well, that all depends on your definition of okay. She's in one piece. Nothing injured except for her pride. And probably her social life."

"Oh, no."

"Yeah. She was out at some barn, on somebody's

property, with a whole group of teenagers. They were drinking. And about the only good thing I can say about it is that she chose a night to get drunk when she didn't have to work in the morning. She gets to sleep her hangover off. Which is actually what *I* was trying to do. Because, interestingly enough, when you find out your teenage daughter has been out getting in that kind of trouble, the first thing you want to do is start drinking too."

Alison frowned. "I bet."

Cain let out a heavy sigh. "Would you mind… Would you mind if I came in this morning and had a talk with you?"

For some reason, Alison felt immediately defensive. Chastened. But then, in her experience those words didn't end well. Her parents had never wanted to talk with her when she was a kid unless she was in trouble. No teacher at school had ever wanted to have a chat if things were going well.

Jared had certainly never wanted to talk with her. He had only ever wanted to scream at her.

But this was Cain, and she had a feeling this wasn't about her. So she was just going to have to shove that baggage to the side, and stop being such a baby. Wallowing wasn't helpful. That was something that she went through with the women that she brought on at the bakery. You were welcome to feel emotion. Alison had no problem with tears, especially when someone was in pain. But choosing to exist in pain was pointless, at least in her opinion.

So she had to take her own advice about that.

"Of course. I have enough people on shift this morning that I should be able to spare a moment for coffee next door."

She hoped that he didn't think she was asking him out. Especially not in his sleep-deprived, hungover state. "I'm not hitting on you," she said, the words tumbling out in a rush.

There was a pause, then a strangled sort of laugh, different than the one from earlier. "I wasn't thinking you were."

"Just so we're clear. I'll meet you out front. And then we can go to The Grind and we can talk about Violet."

"Just so we're clear," he said, parroting the words back to her, his tone grave.

"Right. See you… Well, in about twenty minutes?"

"That's a stretch. Give me a chance to rinse last night off me."

That made her wonder exactly what all he had done last night. And then, it forced her to picture him in the shower. He had said he was hungover. She wondered if that meant he had gone out drinking. Oh, Lord. What if he had hooked up with somebody? That made a strange, sour sensation roil her stomach. She didn't like it. Not at all.

"Great," she said, not quite able to give the word any sort of arc, the syllable falling flat. "See you then."

She was not going to run into the bathroom and check her face. She was not. More to the point, she wasn't going to dig in her purse for makeup and slap some on really quick. No. She wasn't.

That mantra was still repeating itself in her head as she walked into the bathroom, purse clutched tightly in hand. She scowled all the while she put a little bit of blush on her pale cheeks and slicked some gloss over her lips. And continued to scowl while she dug in the bottom of her endless bag for the travel mascara she kept in there.

Once she'd finished primping, she studied her reflection, satisfied that she looked slightly less like a ginger ghost with the help of that dusting of color. Not that it mattered. Cain was just coming to discuss the issue with his daughter, and it didn't matter whether he discussed that issue with an actual woman, or with a ginger ghost.

Snarling at herself, she stuffed the makeup back in her bag, not bothering to reorganize it, then ferociously did the zipper up before walking back out into the bakery. She popped into the kitchen, where a couple of the employees—Meg and Lucinda—were already pulling croissants from the oven. "I'm going to step over to The Grind for a few minutes. Can you hold down the fort while I'm gone?"

"Sure," Lucinda said, waving. "Everything will be fine here, Alison."

Lucinda was one of her longest-lasting employees. The older woman had spent years out of the workforce while she raised her children, and when her husband of thirty-five years had suddenly disappeared with another woman, it had left her without a source of income and a whole host of businesses that were reluctant to hire her because of the gaps in her resume.

Her children did their best to help her out, sending their mother money when she would allow it, but Alison knew that it was good for Lucinda's self-esteem for her to have her own source of income, for her to feel like she was making it—at least in part—on her own.

"Thank you," she said, "you're a goddess, do you know that?"

Lucinda smiled, flour dusted across her cheeks. "Of course I do."

Only two years ago, Alison knew, Lucinda would not have felt that way. And the fact that she did now... It proved what Alison did here was important. This bakery was important. She really did make an impact by making people feel empowered, enabled.

She built herself up with those sorts of thoughts while she waited for the clock to tick down, while she waited for Cain to arrive. About ten minutes earlier than she logistically expected him, she found herself standing in front of Pie in the Sky, her arms crossed, vigorously rubbing her hands over her elbows to try to keep herself from freezing to death in the crisp morning air.

She was acting weird.

No, she countered, she was acting concerned. She was concerned about Violet. And, given all of the bolstering she had just done for herself over the past few minutes, she knew that she was going to be able to use her concern.

She was just eagerly anticipating her conversation with Cain because she wanted to help. Because this fell in line with her passion for making sure that women—and honestly, in this case especially this young woman—were on the right path.

Right now, it sounded like she was on the path that Alison herself had been on at that age. And Lord knew that had ended in a bad place.

She certainly wasn't anticipating it because Cain was hot. No. Not at all. It had nothing to do with the fact that he was tall, broad-shouldered, muscular and...

She looked down the sidewalk, just in time to see said tall, broad-shouldered and muscular man ambling toward her. He was wearing a tight black T-shirt that showed off his physique and fitted jeans that sent her imagination into overdrive.

He had on a cowboy hat that matched the T-shirt, pulled low over his face, and she had to war with her desire to see his face, and to enjoy the little thrill that shot through her because of the anticipation she felt due to the fact that she couldn't see it. That she would soon.

Then he lifted his chin, his expression grim, and no less handsome for it.

Her heart thumped hard against her breastbone, and it became more and more difficult for her to believe her own line about her altruistic motivations.

"You look like you could use coffee," she said, pasting a falsely bright smile on her face.

"What I could use is another drink. But, since I have to be of some use today, you're right. Coffee is probably best."

"I suppose I shouldn't bother to say good morning," she said, clasping her hands in front of her and squeezing them together tightly.

"No."

"Okay, then. This way." She breezed past him, walking just one building down to her friend Cassie's coffee shop. "The Grind has the best coffee in town. And I supply most of her pastries. Though I have to say, she makes a mean scone."

It was kind of nice to eat somebody else's goodies, actually, which was something she enjoyed about going to Cassie's.

"My favorite is the cherry chip," she added, realizing as they walked into the small, quaint little building that Cain probably really didn't care what sort of scone she enjoyed. "But you probably just want a black coffee," she said.

"Actually, a scone sounds good," he said. "Butter is a lot like alcohol when applied directly to a problem."

Alison laughed. "I want to get that put on a T-shirt. Seriously. As a bakery owner, I have to agree."

He smiled at her, and for a moment, she got lost. Forgot why they were here. Forgot where they were standing. And what they were supposed to be doing. This beautiful man was smiling at her, and she just wanted to enjoy it.

She blinked, jerking herself back into the present moment. She had to get a handle on herself. Seriously. This was about Violet. This wasn't about the fact that she was feeling giddy over a handsome man.

It was Cassie—of course—who came to the counter to help them. She looked between the two of them, her expression a study in near-comical neutrality. But possibly only to Alison since she knew the other woman so well.

"Good morning," she said, sounding a little too chipper.

"Hello," Alison said, working at keeping her smile bright. "I would like my usual and a cherry chip scone. I believe Cain is in the market for something stronger."

"Just a black coffee," he said. "And the same scone she's having."

Cassie arched a brow, clearly dying for some sort of detail. Or for an indication as to why the two of them were together early in the morning. Alison made the executive decision not to give her friend any. After all, Alison wasn't used to being the subject of speculation that wasn't just sad.

So this felt pretty good. And Cassie could just continue to wonder.

"Coming right up," Cassie said, her eyes narrowed and fixed on Alison, who was practicing her best saintly expression. Honestly, she could sit for an artist working on a holy scene in a stained-glass church window, she was nearly certain.

She fairly glowed with light and innocence.

At least, she thought she did.

The disapproval Cassie was radiating suggested she disagreed.

"This okay with you?" Cain asked, indicating a table by the door.

"Sure," she said, taking her seat, looking around the room as he sat across from her.

She wondered what everybody else was thinking. If they were wondering what sad Alison was doing sitting with this hot guy. Or maybe, just maybe, sitting with him they didn't think of her as sad Alison. Because who could be sad sitting with a guy this hot?

"I'm going to cut right to the chase," Cain said, his hands pressed against the top of the table. "Violet likes you."

Right. Violet liked her. Not Cain. And that was why she was here. Violet.

She knew that. And it was what she wanted. But still. It made her stomach sink an inch or two. "Cain," she started, but he cut her off.

"She seems to respect you, and we can't speak two words to each other without having a fight. I completely lost my mind at her last night." He looked down at his hands. Consequently, so did she. They were very large. "You know, I had all these ideas that if my kid was ever in a situation where she needed help, I was going to be cool about it. But the problem is it's wrapped up in fear, and this rebellion thing that she's going through, and even though I know she needs help it's hard for me to sit there and tell her that I'm here for her, and be supportive, and laugh and say that I got into trouble at her age too. That I fooled around with people I shouldn't. It all seemed funny when it was me. Because I was young and stupid, and I didn't know any better then either. But I do now. I know everything that can go wrong. I know every possible thing that could happen to her. I have seen too much damn *Dateline*, Alison. I know too many ways to catch a predator."

"You're her father," Alison said carefully, "you aren't her friend. Of course you're not going to buddy up to her and talk about your youthful indiscretions. Why would you?"

She shook her head. Then Cassie called her name from the counter.

"I'll get it," Alison said, getting up from her seat and making her way over to the pickup station. She went to grab the plates with the scones, and the cups of coffee, but Cassie reached out, wrapping her fingers around Alison's wrist.

Alison did a double take, her eyes connecting with her friend's intense gaze. "What is going on?" Cassie hissed, her voice low.

"Perhaps I just got finished having very acrobatic sex with him upstairs," Alison said quietly, her brows raised.

"*Did* you?" Cassie was nearly squeaking, and as much as Alison was enjoying this, she figured she needed to set the record straight, and quickly.

"No. I'm here to talk to him about his daughter."

"That's lame. You should be having acrobatic sex with him."

"Your opinion has been noted. I'll take the scone and the coffee and leave the commentary, thanks." She left Cassie scowling behind the counter and brought all the goodies back to the table.

"Anyway," she said, sitting across from Cain, trying to block out the words *acrobatic sex*, which kept playing over and over in her head.

She knew nothing about *acrobatic sex*. Had no idea what it would even look like. Didn't want to. She gritted her teeth against the prickle of longing that worked its way up her spine, made her face feel hot.

"I don't have a line to her. Not right now," Cain said, unaware of the direction her thoughts had veered. "I pretty much haven't since her mother left. I tried. I sent her to therapists, I did what I thought I needed to do to make sure that I minimized the impact of Kathleen leaving. But whatever, she's still mad at me. And maybe I deserve it. Maybe I'm a bad father. I was a bad husband."

That little prickle of pleasure turned cold, made the back of her neck feel icy. "In what way?"

"I don't really know, since my wife didn't exactly stick around for a postmortem. She just left one day. She left, and she never came back. That's the beginning and end of it. We never talked about it. She never said she was unhappy. I mean, I knew that she was. I knew that we were. She didn't like me. It wasn't just that she didn't love me. She didn't even want to sit across from me at the dinner table. She actively avoided me. But we never talked about it. We never talked about how to fix it. And in the end, she hated me enough that she left Violet too. I never wanted that failure to come back on my kid, but it has. And now… It's the same. It's exactly the same thing. Violet doesn't want to be in the same room as me. She doesn't want to talk to me. She won't smile at me. But she smiles at you. She talks to you."

Unease wound through Alison. "If you're asking for me to give you intel on your daughter, I'm going to have to decline. Because as much as I think you're in the right here, as much as I feel like she can't be sneaking out and getting drunk, I'm not going to abuse her trust. I'm not going to engage in anything that looks remotely like stalker behavior."

That wasn't really a fair comment, and she knew it. Cain was Violet's father. He was well within his rights to know what she was doing, when she was doing it and who she was doing it with. But still, all of this crashed up against the issues she had with her ex, and it was difficult for her to separate the two.

"That's not what I'm asking for. But if… Give me a clue about what I can do better. If you could help me figure that out. If you can get to know her well enough that you could help me with that. And, if you hear about her doing anything that might put her in danger, if you see her with people that I should know about…"

"If I thought that she was in any kind of danger, you know that I wouldn't allow that. I'd blow that whistle, trust me. I would be the narciest narc to ever narc."

"What kills me is that I never really looked into how she was spending her time here. I just assumed that she was texting friends from Texas. I didn't know she'd made any friends in Copper Ridge. And I feel like that's my own stupid-ass mistake. I feel like that's me burying my head in the sand."

Alison thought of her own parents. The ways in

which she had constantly failed to meet their expectations. All the times that they had gone through her things, tried to force her to stay in and study. And the ways it made her feel further and further from them, like they were strangers. And a lot of that was down to her own stupidity.

What she'd said to Cain was true. He was the parent, and it was up to him to keep tabs on Violet. In that regard, her parents had only been doing their jobs.

But Cain loved Violet. That much was obvious. Her parents... They had been so cold. Frozen. Caught up in lives that they didn't like very much, intent on trying to add value to their existence by forcing their daughter to be what they needed her to be.

Alison had rebelled hard. She had been searching for something. Something that she didn't have. At least she understood that much about rebellion. That it came from anger. From trying to fill a void.

"It seems to me that Violet has a lot more of a reason to be mad at her mother than at you. But you're the one who's here. So you're the one whose life is being made difficult because of it."

"The result is still the same. I don't know what the hell I'm doing."

Alison shifted uncomfortably in her seat. "Neither do I, since I'm not a parent. As you pointed out to me the other night."

"Yeah," he said, "well, I thought what I was dealing with then was a case of a grumpy teenager. I thought I was right, back then, all those days ago. Now... Now, I think maybe I'm a dumbass."

"I doubt you're a dumbass."

"You doubt it. But you aren't sure?" He lifted his coffee to his lips.

"Hey, I don't live with you."

"Despite what I told you, I think the fact that you aren't a parent is actually helpful. Like you said, she's sixteen, and she can take some responsibility. You see the situation differently than I do. I just... I can't be neutral. When she was late to work, I wanted to fix it. I wanted her to appreciate something I did for her. Maybe that wasn't the best thing for her, maybe it was just what I wanted. But you seem to actually want the best thing for her."

Alison laughed, picking a white chocolate chip out of her scone and popping it into her mouth. "I don't know about that. I get a lot out of helping people."

"Well, I would like it if you helped me. And then you can consider that warm glow you get payment."

"Gee. Thanks." She smiled, this time picking her scone up and taking a bite, chewing thoughtfully. "Violet is a good kid. And she trusts me, I think. I'm not going to do anything to violate that. I'm happy to come over again and help with baking stuff. But I'm not playing double agent."

A bolt of lightning she hadn't anticipated seemed to strike the table between them and reverberate through her body. Maybe he was thinking of what had happened the last time she'd been there. They'd had a fight, but more than that, he had touched her. And when he had done that, she had burned.

"Great."

"Actually," she said, feeling relieved, because suddenly she had an idea. And having an idea made her feel exuberant. Made her feel like she was on the right track. And it did a great job of distracting her from the situation at hand with Cain. The situation being that her form was exceedingly warm for his. "I told you that I'm starting to coordinate with one of the local wineries. Making individual desserts for farm-to-table dinners and things. And before that gets kicked off I'm going to be making some prepackaged goods for them to sell in their showroom. If Violet could specifically help me with some of the concepts for those projects, it might… I don't know. Give her something. Something to look forward to, something to feel ownership of. In my experience, that's what people need. It's when they lose that that they start to lose themselves."

"You sound like you're speaking from experience."

If that was a subtle way of asking for information about her life, it wasn't terribly subtle. But he wasn't wrong. She was more than familiar with that scenario she'd described. With what it was like to lose yourself, and to allow more and more terrible things to happen and to accept them as normal, because you didn't know what you wanted anymore. You didn't know what you deserved. And you didn't know what else could possibly be out there for you. Like you had gone too far down a dark tunnel and could never find your way back.

But she didn't want to talk to him about that. She didn't want him to know about her past. It wasn't relevant to the conversation anyway.

"I wasn't exactly an angel during my teenage years," she said, instead of giving away any secrets about her more recent history. Ancient history was much safer. "My relationship with my parents was difficult. And I did what a lot of teenagers do. I acted out. But I didn't have anything constructive to occupy my time with. So I found some destructive things instead."

"That sounds like…things I don't want to know about."

"Probably. But, you know, the usual things. Cheap beer and… Well, frankly sex is cheap, Cain."

She regretted those words the moment they left her mouth, because as soon as she spoke them, she was no longer applying them to teenage her, or to the activities that bored teenagers might get up to. No. Instead, she was thinking about how she might apply them to him. To her and him together. And it was clear from the spark in his eyes that his mind had gone to the exact same place.

He curled his fingers more tightly around his coffee cup, and she found herself mesmerized by them. They were long, blunt and strong-looking. His hands looked rough from all the physical labor he did, and she wondered how they would feel against her skin.

The idea was so compelling that she didn't do anything to stop herself from thinking about it.

No, she didn't do anything to stop herself at all.

"I'm not sure I agree with that," he said, his voice rough. "Sex seems like something that's pretty damn expensive to me."

She couldn't quite figure out what he meant by that, and her brain was too fuzzy for her to try. "Well, when I was sixteen and didn't have a job, it was much more affordable to me than going to the movies."

She had been searching for that kind of passion, the kind of connection that she couldn't find anywhere else in her life. She wasn't good at school. Certainly not good enough for her parents. They were disappointed in her. Always disappointed, and distant. In fact, getting yelled at by them would have been nice. Because at least then it would have seemed like they cared. So she had been looking for heat, for laughter, for something that felt big and bright.

At the end of all that, she had found Jared. Then she had found out just what a sad little person she was. How much passion could cost, and just how much she was willing to take in the name of having somebody tell her they loved her.

That was the saddest part. Realizing that it hadn't mattered to her if somebody showed it, as long as they would say it. She had gone so many years without hearing it. She had been so damned needy.

Another reminder that back then, sex had been about trying to solve a feeling of emptiness inside of her. It didn't feel like that now. That wasn't what she wanted to do with Cain. It had nothing to do with her emotions at all.

That was... Well, it was somewhat encouraging, really.

"I guess it depends," he said. "I had sex and ended up with a kid."

"To be fair you didn't end up with a kid every time. Unless you've only..."

A slow smile spread over his lips, and she felt a corresponding blush rise in her cheeks. "Oh, no, honey. Don't you worry about that. I've had enough experience to know what I'm doing."

Those words sounded like a promise, and they were most certainly a promise she hoped he fulfilled. With her.

No. It's too complicated. He's Violet's father, and you're supposed to be helping her.

But she wanted him. And why did that have to be complicated? He didn't know about her past. And yes, there was that little issue of the fact that he wasn't just passing through town, but making a home here for himself and his daughter. But she was in her thirties. It wasn't like she couldn't have an affair and then forget about it.

She didn't want a relationship, and she had no reason to believe that Cain did either.

She wanted to say that. To make an offer. To reach out and brush her fingertips over his knuckles. But her arm was heavy, her hand felt like lead. Well, she couldn't make a move on him here anyway. Because, if anything happened between them, it was going to have to be a secret. She didn't want an actual relationship, and she didn't need every well-meaning woman in town giving her the third degree about him, and every man who thought she needed sheltering interrogating Cain about his intentions.

And she really didn't want that mess infecting her relationship with Violet.

Cain needed her help. He had asked for her help. And she was giving it. But she needed a little bit of help too. Help getting out of her sexual dry spell.

She cringed internally as she replayed her own thoughts. Because it sounded an awful lot like she was considering making some kind of trade for sex. Though, she supposed it wasn't really any different than the kind of crap she'd gotten up to as a teenager. A guy brought a six-pack of beer out into the woods, and you'd drink it with him, and then give him a blow job. That was just how it worked. Everybody was happy.

She was giving him the equivalent of a six-pack, the least he could do was give her…

She imagined that dark head between her thighs, giving her something that no man ever had, and she went warm all over.

"I suppose I should get back to the bakery," she said, shoving the last of her scone into her mouth, and taking a gulp of her latte. Her mouth was full of scalding milk, and she winced as she worked to swallow it. It burned all the way down.

"I'll walk you back," he said, taking hold of the plates and busing the table for them, then returning for his coffee cup.

"Thank you," she said. "Thank you… For walking me back."

They made their way out onto the street, and she could feel his presence behind her. It was so dynamic, so masculine. Until he had come into her life, she would have associated that with danger. For so long, all things masculine had been negative. And only recently was she starting to sort through those connotations. Only recently did she feel less fearful, did she feel like she missed certain things about men.

Well, physical things, mostly.

Of course, it helped that she lived in a town full of decent men. Men who were constantly around reminding her that the entire species wasn't terrible. Sheriff Eli Garrett was one of the best there was, and he and his wife, Sadie, had given her nothing but support right after she'd left Jared.

Jack Monaghan had been one of her first regular customers, buying more pie than one man could feasibly eat and look like he did.

So many men, so many *people*, in the town had all rallied around her, because they knew what she had been through.

The fact that Cain didn't know what she had been through made him his own kind of attractive. What would it be like… To have a man look at her, but without pity? To have a man treat her like a woman and not a victim.

She knew what it was like to have a man make her a victim, and she knew what it was like to be treated like an object. To be treated like a thing.

On the other end of the spectrum, she knew what it was to be coddled. Most men around town looked at her like they wanted to wrap her in a fuzzy blanket. And then put her down for a nap or something, rather than lie down with her.

But she wasn't fragile. At least, she didn't want to be fragile anymore. Some of that was because of the town and the people in it, their concern for her. Their insistence on treating her with special care. And some of it was just her. Clinging to the past. Using it as protection to keep herself from more pain.

Maybe she could let go of the past, if she held on to Cain. Even just for a little while. Actually, it was the perfect solution. Because there were so many reasons that she wouldn't get caught up in him emotionally. Because of everything he was going through. Because he had a daughter to worry about. Because he was a bitter divorcé, like herself, who probably wanted absolutely nothing to do with the institution of marriage ever again.

Safeguards. Because as much as she liked to think she wouldn't need them, it was good to know she could have them.

And he was… She stopped walking and turned to look at him. She was tempted to call him safe. Except that seemed far too bland a description for a man like Cain.

Then again, Alison wasn't one who took safety for granted. Because she knew what it was like to be with someone who wasn't safe. Still, that term seemed limiting. She didn't have anything to be afraid of, as far as Cain was concerned. But *safe* seemed too simple. Also, *safe* wasn't exactly what he made her feel when he looked at her with those compelling green eyes. No. She did not feel *safe*. She felt like she was on fire. She felt like she couldn't breathe.

Mostly, she wanted. Wanted in a way she hadn't for a long time. Maybe ever.

It struck her then that this was all part of moving forward. That this was part of that process they called healing, which hurt and agitated, and had rarely been comfortable.

For the first two years after leaving Jared her entire being had felt like a limb that was being rejuvenated after having the blood flow cut off. Fuzzy at first, numb. And then it had started to hurt. Every new movement forward, every uncertainty.

For the past couple of years, she had been comfortable. But she supposed that wasn't enough. She supposed that now she needed to be put back to full use. So to speak.

"Would you come inside for a second?"

"Okay," he said.

He was looking at her with a strange expression on his face, and it occurred to her then that she had been staring at him for at least thirty seconds without speaking while she parsed all of this in her head.

"Just for a second," she said, holding up her hand and pushing the door open. He came inside. There were a few people in the bakery already, most of them drawn in by the trays of fresh croissants to bring to work, or the array of doughnuts. But, for the most part, it was empty. Still, she was going to need a little bit more privacy. "Could you just…"

She moved to the side, gesturing to the small, walk-in pantry where she kept the large bags of dry goods, for transfer to the kitchen canisters later. She opened the blue door and ducked inside. To his credit, Cain followed without questioning her much. Then she closed the door behind them.

His dark eyebrows shot up, but otherwise, his expression remained pretty much neutral. And she realized that she had taken a step too far. There wasn't really an easy way to explain this away. And beyond that, she wasn't sure she wanted to. Maybe that was why she had trapped him in a pantry. Because she had known that it wouldn't give her an easy out. Because she had known that it would look like exactly what it was.

"Hi," she said, backing up against the shelf, her shoulder blades butting up against a bag of flour.

"Are you taking me on a behind-the-scenes tour?"

"I'm going to cut to the chase," she said, her breath coming in short, sharp bursts. "I'm helping you out, with Violet. And I'm happy to do it. Because I like her and I want to see her succeed in life. But I… I…"

And for some reason, words failed her then. Maybe because the only words that came to mind were ludicrous. So she decided that she was going to go ahead and dispense with words. Or maybe *decided* was a bit too strong of a word. Either way, before she fully knew what she was doing, she found herself moving toward him, stretching up on her toes.

And then, for the first time in four years, Alison's lips touched another person's.

CHAPTER NINE

CAIN'S MIND WAS a blank. A moment before he had been sipping coffee, and now, he was sipping on Alison's lips. If it was a bad idea, he certainly wasn't thinking of that now. He wasn't thinking of anything at all. Except how damn soft she was. How beautiful. The way her petite curves molded to his body, the way she sighed, like a particularly contented cat, as she melted against him, parting her lips and sliding her tongue against the seam of his mouth.

He felt like there was a fire in his gut, spreading out through his veins, setting each and every inch of him ablaze. He was so hard it was a physical pain. The instant attraction he had felt for Alison had been nothing. A drop of water in the ocean. And now he was submerged in the whole damn sea.

He slid his hands down her back, cupping her ass, and he had a feeling he was taking things too far, too fast, but he couldn't bring himself to care. No, instead he cupped that soft, sweet flesh, grabbing as much of her as he could. Because he was greedy. Greedy for more. For everything.

It had been a long time, and that was a good excuse for why he had absolutely no control. But it wasn't the bottom line. Hell no. It was just her. He remembered enough about sex to know that. To know that no matter how good it was, it wasn't usually like this. Wasn't usually beyond reason. Wasn't usually beyond control, and thought, and every other thing that made him a man and not just a raging beast.

Right about now the only thing that made him a man and not an animal was the fact that he had opposable thumbs. Otherwise? Nothing. He was pure instinct. Pure need. Male. Female. Need. Have.

He was shaking. Shaking like a damned virgin. Like he was a teenager, not the father of one. And he wanted… Well, he wanted nothing more than to shove her jeans down her generous hips and push himself into her body. To satisfy the raw desire that was coursing through him like floodwater, threatening to consume him, threatening to sweep them away.

He moved his hands upward, before pushing his fingertips beneath the waistband of her jeans, groaning as he came into contact with bare skin. He half expected her to back off, to break the kiss. But she didn't. Instead, she arched against him, threading her fingers through his hair as she tasted him even deeper.

He turned her around, pressed her back against the opposite shelf, reaching up and knocking into a couple of canisters, sending them crashing down to the floor. He gripped the edge of the shelf, uncaring about the mess he had just made. He didn't care about anything. Not a damn thing except satisfying both of them.

She was sweet. And being inside of her would be even sweeter. Uncovering all that pale skin. Her breasts. Her…

He gritted his teeth. He was on the verge of embarrassing himself, and a man of his age and experience should not be having that issue. But damn if she didn't have him so close to the edge his head was about to blow off.

It occurred to him then that they were making out in a pantry, in her place of business. But on the heels of that thought came a lightning bolt of pleasure, so intense it about bowled him over when she pushed her hand up beneath his shirt, soft, tentative fingers making contact with his stomach.

He reached down, grabbing hold of her wrist, curling his fingers around her slender arm and drawing it up over her head, pressing it back against the shelf. He rocked forward, letting her feel the evidence of his desire for her.

She gasped, wrenching her lips away from his, her golden eyes wide. He thought for a moment that she was uncomfortable. That she would want to stop. But instead, she screwed her eyes shut again and moved forward, pressing her lips to his again.

She rolled her hips forward, answering that blatant invitation he had made when he had pressed his hardness against her.

Then his phone started to buzz in his pocket. He wanted to ignore it. He wanted to take it out of his pocket and throw it across the small space. No, he wanted to take it out of his pocket and crush it in his hand for daring to interrupt the most action he'd had in years.

But he didn't do any of that. Instead, he broke the kiss, taking his phone out and looking at the screen. It was Violet. Of course it was Violet.

It didn't escape his notice that last night he had interrupted her make-out session and now she was interrupting his. But he was a damned adult, and he was entitled to his.

"I have to take this," he said.

Alison nodded wordlessly, shrinking back from him. "Hello?"

"Dad," came the sound of his daughter's croaky voice. "I'm sick."

He bit back a growl, his lingering irritation nd arousal warring with concern. He knew exactly what kind of sick Violet was. "You're hungover."

"Are you working? Come inside and help me."

No. He wasn't working. He was with a woman. For the first time in so long. And he couldn't tell her that. He also couldn't deny his daughter for the sake of continuing a secret make-out session in a closet.

Because he wasn't a teenager. Even if for a moment he'd felt like one.

"I'll be home soon," he said, hanging up. She would be mad at him for not saying goodbye. But he was still mad at her. Not just for last night, but now for this.

"Do you have to go?"

Alison's eyes were bright, her lips pink and swollen and he wanted so badly to kiss her again. To keep the whole world firmly on the other side of the pantry door. But he couldn't. Dammit. He couldn't.

"Yeah," he said. "Anyway. It's probably for the best."

Alison shook her head, a curl tumbling down from the top of her head, falling into her face. "I don't think it is. What I was trying to say before is… We're both busy. We're both in difficult places in our lives. You asked me to help you out with Violet, and I'd like to do that. But…well, I'm very attracted to you. And I would really like it if you could help me out with that."

He couldn't seem to look away from her. "What are you asking me?"

"I want you. Physically. Your body. Maybe I'm not saying this right. I haven't done this in a long time."

"Propositioned a guy or had sex?" He was not in the mood for any beating around the bush. He needed to know exactly what was being said. And his blood was still mostly drained out of his brain and pooled south of his belt, so he needed her to speak plainly and slowly.

"Well." She hesitated. "Both, really."

He had a hard time believing that. Because she was gorgeous, and she kissed like a wet dream. So he had no idea in all the world why she couldn't have sex whenever she wanted it. Why she should be in any kind of dry spell, he didn't have a damn clue.

"This shouldn't have happened," he heard himself say, and he could have kicked himself the moment he spoke the words. But it was true. He was still holding his phone in his hand, because his daughter had just called. His hungover daughter who needed him to come home and deal with her. Not just to help her because she was sick, but who needed to be disciplined. Who needed to be assured that he loved her. Who needed... Something. Something he didn't know how to give, obviously, or they wouldn't be in this situation.

And just a moment ago he'd been pissed off because she'd interrupted the kiss. Because he let himself get distracted, he let himself be more invested in what was happening here in this pantry than he was in what was happening in his house.

"Why not? I don't want a relationship, if that's what you're worried about. I'm really...busy. I have the bakery, and pie is really very demanding. Well, not as demanding as croissants. Croissants are one of the more demanding pastries."

"I don't even have time for this," he said, wishing he could say anything else. Wishing it wasn't true. "I can't. My life is a shit show. You don't want tickets."

"I mean, that's kind of the thing though. I have tickets. I'm involved. And, since I'm involved, it just seems like…" Suddenly, she trailed off. Then she blinked rapidly, the color leeching from her face. "Oh, my gosh. I almost had sex with you in my pantry. I have customers out there. I have employees out there."

He cleared his throat. "Well, yeah."

"I don't do things like that."

"All the more reason for us not to, I suppose."

She nodded mutely. Then she took a deep breath. "Why don't you leave? I'm just going to…hang out here. Until it doesn't look like the two of us are walking out of the pantry together."

"Well, we went in together."

"Maybe people didn't notice." The color was returning to her cheeks now, flooding her face, brighter than usual. Now, she was getting embarrassed. And she was getting mad. So he had a feeling that he just needed to comply with what she was asking him to do, or he was going to get a canister thrown at his head.

"Violet works tomorrow?" he asked.

She nodded, biting her lip, clearly going out of her way not to say anything.

He nodded in return, held her gaze a beat longer than he needed to. Any longer and he would have pulled her back into his arms. He backed away, then walked out of the pantry. The two people that were sitting in the dining area of the bakery looked up, stared at him for a long moment. He grabbed the edge of his hat and tipped it firmly. "Good morning," he said, striding through the small shop and out the door.

I made the right decision, he told himself as he headed toward his truck. He had to take care of the situation with Violet. And he couldn't afford any distractions. And if his body still throbbed, that was all right. It was a sacrifice he was making for his daughter. Even if she would never know that he had made it.

Whoever had said virtue was its own reward had never kissed a pretty little redhead in a pantry and walked away aching. There was no reward in this virtue. No, this virtue felt a whole lot like a stick in the eye.

Or a crowbar in his pants.

Not for the first time, he felt like a man walking through an alien landscape. What the hell was his life? As he got into his truck and drove down the still somewhat unfamiliar streets, headed home to handle the aftereffects of his daughter's night of drinking, he could only be grateful for his truck. The one he had driven out of Texas.

Right about now, it was the only thing that felt like it hadn't betrayed him. The only thing that hadn't changed beyond recognition. A small consolation, but he would take it.

He had to take what he could get, after all.

He thought of Alison, standing there all flushed, bright-eyed, her pink lips swollen. Yeah, he would take what he could get. And since he couldn't get her, his old truck would have to be his consolation.

Which was about as rewarding as all his fuckin' virtue.

"What's up, Bo?"

Cain didn't bother to modify his tone when he entered his daughter's bedroom. Even though he knew he would be met by a groan of pain. He was not disappointed on that score. He was caught between wanting to baby her and wanting her to feel the full force of her stupid decision—within the safety of her own home, of course.

"I'm sick," she said, sounding completely miserable. She was buried beneath her blankets, only a few pieces of dark hair that looked like bedraggled antennae visible. "And don't talk so loud."

"You're hungover," he said, not lowering his voice one bit. "And, by the way, I would have figured that out even if I hadn't caught you last night. Trust me, I know a hangover when I see one. I am, in fact, intimately acquainted with them."

"Stop it," Violet said, burrowing deeper beneath her blankets and pulling them up over her head.

"Consider this Consequences 101."

She resurfaced, opening one eye just slightly. "You're being mean. If you've had a hangover before I don't understand why you're being so ridiculous about mine."

"Because I wasn't sixteen when I had them," he said, this time raising his voice, because he was just in a mean-ass mood. "And this is how you learn. I learned. You're the one who chose to make it lesson time, Bo."

"You're ridiculous," she said. "Jade's parents are the ones who got us the drinks. I don't see why you care so much."

"Great. Thank you. If you could provide a last name to go with Jade, I will happily report her parents to the local authorities. In the meantime, let me remind you that Jade is not my daughter, you are. Also, if you had asked me if you could have a beer in our kitchen, we might be having an entirely different discussion right now. You didn't. Instead, you sneaked out. You put yourself in a dangerous situation. No plans to get back home, clearly no designated driver. And if something had happened," he said, repeating himself from last night, and not caring at all, "I wouldn't have known how to help you. Where to find you. I would have gotten a call from the police."

"I don't understand why you care so much all of a sudden," she said, sitting up and wincing. "You never care what I'm doing. You never ask."

"Fine. I'm asking now." He was trying to remember some of the things that Alison had said to him. About Violet being older. About her needing more responsibility. And it was work—it cost him—to try to think of Alison without just thinking of kissing her again.

Remembering what it had been like to have her soft body pressed against his.

"I don't want to talk now."

"You don't get to play this game, Violet. You can't be angry at me for not asking, then say you don't want to tell. Was that your boyfriend last night? Do you have a boyfriend, and I don't know about it?"

"He's not my boyfriend. And he is most definitely not my boyfriend after last night, since no boy wants to date a girl who has a psychopath for a dad."

"Fine with me. Since no psychopath dad wants his daughter to date a little punk in skinny jeans who thinks an incapacitated girl makes for a great make-out buddy."

"I wasn't incapacitated," she mumbled, grabbing her pillow and hugging it to her chest. "And this is why I don't talk to you."

"I thought *I* didn't talk to *you*." He remembered again

what Alison had said about rebellion. And he did his best to use that to talk himself off his rage ledge.

Violet was sixteen. And frankly, getting into a shouting match with a sixteen-year-old was the height of idiocy. But he wanted to. Because she was angry, and that anger wasn't rational. She was firing at him with verbal shotgun shells hoping that at least some of the shots would connect with the target—which at the moment was him. He knew that. Logically, he knew it. It didn't make him less mad. Didn't make him want to fight back any less.

Still, he took a deep breath, and he did his best to keep his cool.

"You don't."

Okay, she was completely committed to just being angry. Fine.

"Well, I'm talking now. Don't talk back if you don't want to. Really, I wouldn't mind. You're mad at me. I get that. I don't get why, but I get that you are. You think I should have talked to you about this move, but this family isn't a democracy, Violet. I made the best decision that I could for us. You weren't happy in Texas either. Tell yourself whatever you want, but you were mad there too."

"It was my home," she said, scowling angrily. "We had a nice house there. Our own house."

"Okay, so this is about sharing a house with your uncles? Because it's only temporary. I'm building us our own place. You know that."

"No, it's not about them. They're fine. It's just… I don't want to be here."

"You didn't want to be in Dallas," he said, making his tone even more firm. Because if he knew anything, he knew that. "You hated it. You hated me, you hated everybody. This attitude isn't new. You're just blaming the move now. Blaming me. If you're mad at your mother, I understand that. And I get that she's not here to yell at, to abuse. And I am. But I didn't leave you."

She threw the covers back, still dressed in last night's clothes, then cursed, pressing her hand against her forehead. "No," she said, "I guess you didn't. But she left you. She probably wouldn't have left me if it wasn't for you."

He felt like she'd slapped him. Because it was every thought he'd already had thrown right at him, and there was no way he could dispute it. No way at all. He wanted to throw all the blame on to Kathleen, but every time he did that he remembered the way she had been with Violet when Violet had been a baby. When she had been a little girl. How much his wife had loved their child.

He had never been able to reconcile that woman with the one who had waiked out the door one day four years ago, never to return. If her love for Violet had waned, he hadn't seen it. But her love for him certainly had.

It was his darkest thought about the divorce. About Kathleen's abandonment. He had never blamed Violet. Not even once. He had been afraid that she blamed herself. That had kept him awake at night. It had been the reason he had sent her to therapy.

But knowing she blamed him...

Some selfish part of him sort of wished she had blamed herself. So that he could comfort her. So they could be angry together. So that they could condemn Kathleen together. But that wasn't it. She blamed him. And he didn't know where to go from there. He couldn't dispel it. Couldn't defend himself. Not when he wasn't sure if she would believe any of it.

He let out a hard breath, then pushed his hair back off his head. He had to go do something before he said more things he was going to regret later. "I'm going to make you some eggs."

Violet wrinkled her nose. "What?"

"Eggs and onions and a bunch of spicy shit to help with your hangover. I know how to do that. That's about the only thing I know how to do. Just wait here."

He walked out of the room, making his way downstairs and into the kitchen. Hangover cures he had a lock on. It had been a long time, but he had spent his college years in something of a haze. So, since he was at a loss for words, since he was at a loss for just about everything, he figured he would scramble some eggs.

He opened up the fridge, not bothering to be gentle with the ingredients, not even the eggs.

He was so in over his head with this. With her. And about the only time in the past twenty-four hours he had felt like he knew what he was doing, what he wanted, was when Alison's lips had connected with his. At least he understood that. At least he knew where that was going.

Here, in his own house, he felt like a raging asshole. Like an idiot. Like he didn't know which end was up.

With Alison, he had felt like a man. And he hadn't realized just how disconnected from that feeling he had been. Purposely, he had to admit. Because his brothers were right. If he'd wanted to go out and hook up, he could have.

Apparently, half the time he had been at home, using

Violet as an excuse to stay in while the rest of them went out, she hadn't been here anyway.

Kathleen had left, and it had been the most convenient excuse in the world that he had a daughter at home and that he couldn't get back out there. Hell, he didn't want a relationship anyway. And still, the idea of engaging in random hookups bothered him. Not so much because of him. There had been a time in his life when he had done it, after all. But because of setting an example for his daughter, and things like that.

The idea of hooking up when he was drunk and sad with women who were drunk and sad seemed… Sad. But that wasn't what Alison was proposing. She wanted him, she had been straight up about that. And she didn't want a relationship.

He cracked three eggs into the pan and started to scramble them furiously. It was just the kind of arrangement he had been telling Finn he wished he could have.

Except that damned complication of her being his daughter's boss.

"Well," Alex said, walking into the kitchen. "Good morning."

"It's not and you know it," Cain returned, knowing he was growling while scrambling.

"How's the kid?"

"Lucky I didn't lock her in the root cellar."

"We don't have a root cellar."

"How about a dungeon? Because that sounds perfect right about now."

"I'll tell you what, you make a man glad he's childless," Alex said. "You make a man glad he never got married either."

"Always glad to be your cautionary tale."

"You make a great one. Though honestly, if any of us was going to be a cautionary tale, I would have laid money on Liam. Maybe me. Because God knows I could have come home from Afghanistan in a coffin. Fortunately, I'm fine."

Cain eyed him neutrally. "I have my doubts about that."

"What are you talking about?" Alex lifted his hand, curled his fingers. "Everything intact."

Cain had a feeling there were injuries he couldn't see. But, considering he couldn't sort out the problems that were already on his plate, he wasn't going to take Alex's on as well. Not unless his younger brother offered. And he had a feeling that was about as likely as Violet coming downstairs with a smile on her face to let him know she thought he was Father of the Year.

"Well, great. Somehow, I've managed to be the biggest mess of the four of us."

"Don't think that gets you out of ranch duty," Alex said, pouring himself some coffee. "Are you ever going to come out and do work? The cows were taken care of already. Hours ago. But Finn said something about needing help moving some of them from one pasture to another."

"Are you going to head out?"

"I'm done for the day. I have some other things to take care of. Stuff I've been avoiding for the past month. But I can't let it go anymore."

"What kind of stuff?"

Alex's face went rigid. "Just stuff." He shook his head. "Do you remember Jason Campbell?"

Cain frowned. "No. From where?"

"Here. He and I hung out sometimes in the summer

when we were growing up. Enlisted together. Met up at basic. We ended up being deployed at the same time."

"I didn't know about that," Cain said.

"Yeah. Well, anyway, he's dead."

Alex said it so matter-of-factly. So flatly. And there was no offer of elaboration. So Cain didn't ask for it. Instead, he offered an apology. Which was—he'd learned—one of the safest things someone could offer you when you told them a piece of particularly sucky information. Usually, though, people offer platitudes and advice. Which almost never helped.

"I'm sorry," he said.

"He left me some land. I've been avoiding going and collecting all of the details. But I'm going to have to."

"He left you land?"

"I told you all when I got here that I didn't need this ranch. I meant I didn't need it because I needed more land. Or more money, or anything like that. I have a fine income. Plus, apparently I have a small farm or what-ever somewhere on the outskirts of town."

"Then, and don't take this the wrong way, why the hell are you here?"

Alex laughed shortly. "Damned if I know. Something to do with family. Brotherhood, and things like that. But I need to get started handling this. I need to figure out what exactly Jason wanted from me. I have a meeting with his lawyer. Not even the same one Grandpa used. Who knew Copper Ridge had more than one lawyer, right?"

Cain snorted. "I suppose people get divorced and sue each other here just like they do everywhere else."

"Yeah. I guess so."

Alex let out a long, slow breath. "I guess if I go take

my dead friend's land he's really dead. Unless, of course, he decides to haunt me out in the cornfields."

"Entirely possible."

"You seem too pragmatic to believe in ghosts," Alex said.

"I wish. But then, some of the worst ghosts I've had to deal with have been the ghosts of the living." He thought of Kathleen again. Of the damage that had been done to both Violet and himself because of her. And how now that she was gone, there wasn't any less friction between them; now that she was out of his life she wasn't any less his problem. Except now, he was utterly powerless to do anything to fix it. She wasn't even here to yell at.

"Are you scrambling eggs for me?"

"I am making a hangover cure for my sixteen-year-old."

"Wow. Put that one in the baby book."

That actually made Cain laugh. "I'm tempted to. And then, when she has kids and they become horrible teenagers, I'm going to show it to them. So that they know what she did, and then they might cause her even a fraction of the trouble that she's causing me."

Alex smirked. "I hate to break it to you, but one drunken make-out session is not even scratching the surface of the kind of trouble Liam and I used to get into."

"I believe it. But don't you give her any ideas."

"Hell no. But it's the circle of life. When you're a teenager, it seems like a great idea, and when you're an adult thinking about yourself, it's a great story. But when you are the adult dealing with a teenager... You just think it's all dangerous and a bad idea."

"What's that about?"

"Maturity. I think. I wouldn't know." He raised his hand and mock saluted. "Anyway. I have to go see a man about a horse. Or, several horses, as the case may be."

Alex turned and walked out of the kitchen. Cain turned his focus back to the food he was making. But now, his mind was fixed firmly on ghosts. The ghosts that lingered in every corner. Ghosts that he and Violet had apparently brought with them from Texas, even though he had been so bound and determined to leave them behind.

When he went back upstairs to give Violet her breakfast, she was sitting up, hunched over a pillow like a cave creature. She took the plate wordlessly, not meeting his eyes. Then Cain went back downstairs, heading outside and seeking out any hard labor he could find. He had a lot of anger and a lot of sexual frustration to work off, and he wasn't sure there was enough acreage on the Laughing Irish Ranch to even put a dent in either.

All the while he was working he kept flashing back to that kiss in the pantry at Pie in the Sky. And after a while, he quit pushing it aside. After a while, he embraced the memory. He let it fill his brain, fill his body. And then it wasn't anger he was trying to burn through, oh no.

His blood was running hot and fast as he went over to the pile of logs that had yet to be split into kindling. He picked one up, propping it up and setting it on its end. Then he picked up an ax. He brought it down hard on the wood, but the motion did nothing to ease the tension inside of him.

He picked up another full log and repeated the motion. Establishing a steady rhythm of ax hitting wood. There was something about it that reminded him of sex.

Or maybe it was just that everything reminded him of sex now. That hard, steady pounding...

He gritted his teeth, and he imagined grabbing hold of pale, shapely hips as he pounded into her. He was certain of precious few things these days. Almost nothing. But he knew he wanted Alison. He knew it was a bad idea. Knew that the fact she was tangled up in his shitty personal life was an issue.

But despite the complications, there was one thought shining bright and clear, brighter than the last rays of the sun as they disappeared behind the mountain, signaling the end of a truly long and horrendous day.

He was sick of going to bed alone. He was sick of wanting and not having. He was sick of what he had become. Abandoned husband. Failing father. Rancher who worked his knuckles bloody every day, then woke up at the ass crack of dawn to do it again.

For just a while, he wanted to be somewhere different. With someone who smiled at him. Who looked at him like she didn't want him gone every time he walked into the room.

He wanted some oblivion for a few hours. And didn't he deserve it? Or maybe he didn't. Maybe he just wanted it, and that was okay.

But he was at the end. Of his rope. Of whatever the hell. And he needed. He just needed. He hadn't realized how much until Alison had stretched up on her toes and touched her lips to his. He had known that celibacy was getting old, but he had been able to endure it. She had opened the door. She had blown the lid off that semblance of control he had been living with for so long.

And now, it wasn't just a vague desire. Now, it was actual need.

He swung the ax down, embedding it in the top of the next piece of wood. He was breathing hard, his blood pouring through him like fire.

He had responsibilities. He should probably see to those.

But he was already halfway to his truck. And he was deliberately forgetting about everything here on the ranch. Everything in the house. Everything in his life that he didn't want to think about. The only thing he cared about right now was that thing that was blazing hot and bright inside of him. That desire, that need, that excitement, that had been absent for so long.

He had spent a hell of a long time concerning himself with what other people wanted, what they needed. Well, now it was his turn. He was going to go get what he wanted. And what he wanted was Alison Davis.

CHAPTER TEN

ALISON TURNED THE closed sign and closed the blinds on the storefront windows, then let out a long, slow sigh. It had been an extremely long day. Not because of anything that had happened at the bakery. Mostly because of the somewhat disastrous make-out session that had happened in her pantry.

Reflexively, she touched her lips, grateful for the fact that she was currently alone.

Really, the make-out session itself had not been disastrous at all. It had been… Well, it had been spectacular. If she had ever had a kiss that good, she couldn't remember it. He was so… So hot, and hard and strong.

All those brilliant, masculine things she had come to miss. And the way he had wrapped his fingers around her wrist, held on to her so tightly, not like she would break, but like he might if he had to let go.

And he didn't want more. He didn't want any more than that one kiss.

She frowned, lowering her hand down to her side, curling her fingers into a fist. She took a deep breath, walking across the bakery and flicking the main lights off. Only the little antique-style pendant lights were still on, glowing their particular golden shade, casting little pools onto the floor.

She closed her eyes, massaging her temples. Well, she

was fine. That was the bottom line. She had put herself out there. She had tried. And he had said no. She had gone to the verge of begging, and she had felt ridiculous in the end, had felt like hiding in the back and weeping for the rest of the day.

But she was tougher than that. And she would not let a man make her cry that easily. No way. Absolutely not. Hurt feelings, a little bit of embarrassment… That wasn't worth her tears. Any man would be lucky to have her proposition him, and just because Cain Donnelly couldn't appreciate the good fortune of being offered her body, didn't mean another man wouldn't appreciate it. When she got around to wanting to go proposition the male populace in general, that was. Right now, she was still mostly Cain-oriented, and not so much sex-oriented. But that too would pass. If there was one thing she had learned in recent years it was that things passed, and life went on. She was about to walk to the little doorway that led to the stairs to her apartment when she heard a knock behind her on the door. She jumped, turning to see a large, dark silhouette in the doorway.

She might have been nervous if it wasn't Copper Ridge. Or maybe she still would have been nervous if she hadn't seen the cowboy hat. But because she could make out the shape of it clearly, she knew with absolute certainty who it was.

Maybe it wasn't even the cowboy hat. Maybe it was just the intense, visceral reaction that happened deep inside of her. Because nothing else felt like this. Nothing else felt like Cain.

Heart hammering in her chest, she moved quickly across the dining area, turning the locks on the door and jerking it open. He didn't say anything; he didn't have to. His green eyes were full of intensity and fire. And the kind of intent that couldn't be mistaken for anything else.

"Come in," she said, stepping out of the way and allowing him enough space to come inside.

He did, and she locked the door behind him, drawing the blinds down over the window. Again, not waiting for him to say anything. Because she knew. There was only one reason he was here, looking like that, at this hour. Anticipation fired through her. Anticipation, but no nerves at all. Which was not how she would have expected this to go.

But she was certain. So certain. This feeling, this need that had gripped her from the moment she had met him owned her. Body and soul. She had realized earlier there was no point in fighting it, and she wasn't going to.

Then he reached out, wrapping his arm around her waist and pulling her up against his hard, muscular chest. Just like he had done at his house that night. He had been angry with her then too. He was angry with her now, it was clear. But he wanted her, right along with it.

She marveled, just for a moment, that his anger didn't frighten her. Only a couple of years ago it would have. But not now. Not him. Never him.

He changed his hold, planting both hands on her hips, drawing her up against him and letting her feel every hot, hard inch of him growing between them. It had been a long time since she had felt that, and even longer since she had gloried in it. But she was glorying in it now. She was gloating. She was downright smug.

"I was fine," he growled. "I was doing the best I could handling everything in my life. And I didn't need anything outside of that. Until I saw you in that bar. And you took everything and turned it inside out. You made me want. You made me need." He released his hold on her, drawing his hand up and gripping her chin between his thumb and forefinger. "I'm pretty pissed about that."

"The feeling is mutual," she said, the words coming out in a breathless rush. "Except I'm not mad."

"You aren't?"

"No."

He shifted, those green eyes all sharpened intensity, trained on her, piercing her right through. "How do you feel? Tell me."

"Scared," she said, the truth slipping between her lips before she could stop herself. Oh, not scared of him, no. But of the thing between them. She'd wanted a man before. She'd burned before. But that had been a little flame in the hearth next to this. Something comforting to rest by during a long, emotional winter. This wasn't that. This was something else entirely. Bigger, hotter. A forest fire, raging out of control and scorching everything in its path, could never be anything but scary.

"That's not exactly a ringing endorsement." He didn't ease up his hold, but still, she was afraid that he might.

"Excited too," she said quickly. "Definitely excited."

That word seemed wrong. It didn't quite fit. But then, *scared* didn't really fit either. This was something else. Something new. Something that had woven its way around every secret place inside of her, waking up need, desire that she had shut down so long ago. Like power being restored to a long-forgotten city.

For the past four years she'd had goals. And she had met them. Fulfilled them. She had been proud of them. Of all her accomplishments. She had felt happiness in that time, of course she had. She had felt pride, and a sense of determination and purpose. All things that had been absent from her life for the entirety of her marriage.

But this... She hadn't had this. Maybe she never had.

"You know what's about to happen, don't you?"

She laughed, a full, throaty sound that seemed like it had come from a stranger. Some sensuous, confident woman that she was certain she was not. Except, maybe right now she was. Maybe with him, she could be.

He didn't know otherwise. She was the woman that had made him drive all the way down from his ranch, the woman that had made him want, when before he hadn't. He had said so. That was all she was to him. Not a victim. Not the sad, grasping, insecure creature she sometimes saw herself as in those dark hours between midnight and sunrise when memories scuttled in like spiders from dark corners.

"I know," she said, feeling bold and reckless. More things she could hardly remember ever being. She lifted her hand, pressing it against his cheek, a shaky breath escaping her lips as she felt the heat of his skin and the roughness of his whiskers against her palm. "This isn't going to end with a kiss." A smile grabbed the corner of her mouth and tugged it upward. "Or maybe it will. But a lot is going to happen in between. Between this moment, and that last kiss."

"Hell yeah," he said in a voice like gravel as he closed the distance between them, his mouth meeting hers.

This time, there was no one around. This time, there was no one right outside the door to wonder what was taking so long, or what was happening. Though, she imagined that if anyone was standing out on the main street now, and they looked inside, squinted real hard, they might be able to make out her and Cain's silhou-ettes in the dim light. She found she didn't care about that either. Not about anything. Not anything but this kiss and what would happen next.

His kiss was like oxygen. As if she had been drown-ing for years and this was her first sip of salvation.

It woke her up.

An insistent pulse beat at the apex of her thighs and she arched her hips, glorying in the feel of his arousal pressed against her. And while she didn't want to get into any comparisons, this was definitely different than anything she'd experienced before. When she had been a teenager sex had always been wrapped in insecurity. In being afraid of rejection, afraid of doing the wrong thing. In her marriage, it had been a bargaining chip, a peace offering, a flag of surrender.

But she didn't care. Not now. Not with him.

Cain wasn't going to reject her. He wanted her. She could feel how much he wanted her. And truly, she didn't give a damn about doing the wrong thing or the right thing as far as he was concerned. Because she wanted. And this was all about what she wanted. How long had it been since she had focused solely on that?

For so long it had been a matter of survival. Of climb-ing out of the wreckage, putting one foot in front of the other as she walked away from that burning pile of re-fuse that had been her life. Just putting distance between the woman she had been and the woman she was now. But this was more than forward motion. It was better.

And now that she had discovered it, she wanted it. Wanted it all, wanted it now.

She pressed her hands against his chest, dragging them down slowly, glorying in the feel of his muscles, that hard chest and stomach. He was incredible, and so much more of a man than anyone else she had been with. So much more of a man than she had imagined she would want. But she did want him. And that realization nearly made her cry.

Which was stupid. *So* stupid. But it was such a relief to know that even though Jared had left a lot of things broken inside of her, maybe less was permanently destroyed than she had originally thought.

She wanted this man. This strong, uncompromising man. She didn't fear him. She *wanted* him. That was good in a million indescribable ways.

Ways that she would never tell him, but that she held close to that bright, burning ember inside of her as she allowed it to stoke the flames even higher.

And if it wasn't that great realization making her burn even hotter, it was his hands. Large and warm and roaming over her curves, down her back, over her butt.

"Do you know what my life has been?" he asked. "For four damn years, I've woken up in an empty bed, gotten up and started work. Then made sure that my daughter was taken care of before going right back to work. Sunup to sundown. That's who I've been. That's all I've been. But that's not what I want tonight. Tonight... I'm going to be a selfish bastard. Tonight I want to just be a man. Not someone's father. Not someone's ex-husband." He slid his thumb along the edge of her lips. "I want to bury myself so deep inside of you that I might get lost."

She felt like that should scare her, bother her. His stated intent of selfishness when *she* was the one who wanted to be selfish. Instead, she found it reassuring.

They were both out for themselves. And they were both being honest about it.

In a way, it took all the pressure right off her. He would grab hold of his pleasure, while she took care of her own. While they used each other for their own ends. So, she wouldn't have to worry about what he was enjoying, what he wasn't. That was his problem. And she had every confidence that he would see to it.

"I'd like to get lost with you," she whispered.

By tacit agreement, they didn't speak after that. And she was glad. Because she didn't want to talk anymore. She didn't want to know him any better. Didn't want to be so unbearably conscious of the fact that this was the same Cain Donnelly she'd had coffee this morning with, to discuss the difficulties he was having with his daughter. The same Cain Donnelly whose daughter she would see early tomorrow when she came in for shift.

No. She wanted the same thing he did. Wanted him to just be a man. Her lover. The fantasy she hadn't even known was her fantasy until she'd seen him in Ace's bar.

And whatever he wanted her to be, she would be for him.

That gave her a feeling of power too. They didn't know each other. And they wouldn't. But they would see each other naked. They would touch each other. They would taste each other.

Yeah, that was exactly what she wanted. Exactly what she needed.

"Shirt," she commanded. "Off."

A smile hitched his lips up and he reached down, gripping the hem of that tight black T-shirt that had been playing havoc with her hormones since she'd seen him this morning, and tugged it slowly over his head. For a moment, she fought the urge to whimper and bite her lip, and then she just gave in. Because if this was for her, she wasn't going to fight any urge she had. She was going to indulge. And she was going to enjoy. And she wasn't going to do anything to hold that enjoyment back.

He was gorgeous with the shirt on. But off? Those gloriously defined muscles were a thing of beauty, the dusting of dark, masculine hair over the top of them making her fingertips itch with the urge to touch him. To feel the differences between them. That striking contrast between the hard and the masculine and the soft and feminine. Something that she was so ready to revel in after years of drought.

And so she did. She stepped forward, placing her hand on his chest, drawing it down to his stomach, then tracing a slow line across the top of his jeans. His chest pitched up, a harsh breath on his lips that ended on a raw groan.

She leaned in, pressing her lips tentatively to his chest, right where she imagined his heart was. Then she gave in to the wild, completely uncivilized, completely un-Alison urge to lick him. She was rewarded with a feral, masculine sound, with his frame tensing beneath her touch.

She drew her tongue slowly down that hard wall of muscle, down to his nipple, where she laved in a leisurely circle.

His hand shot up, grabbing her hair, tugging her head back. "You're testing my control here."

The way he was holding her...with the same sort of possessive grasp she remembered from the pantry earlier... It left her vulnerable. Perhaps that should bother her too. But she wasn't bothered. Instead, it sent a lick of arousal between her thighs that felt like a long stroke against her slick folds. Amped up her desire to even greater heights. Her *need*. Oh, how she needed this.

She let her mind go blank of thoughts on what she should feel. On what she would be expected to feel in a situation like this given what she had been through. Because she didn't care about any of that. She cared only about this moment. This man. As if he was the only one.

"Well," she said, glorying in that husky, stranger's voice that came from her lips, "we don't want that. If you leave me unsatisfied I'm going to be very cranky."

He curled his fingers around her wrist, drew her hand away from his chest and claimed her lips with his own again. Then she found herself being hauled up into his arms, big hands gripping her thighs and lifting her, urging her to wrap her legs around his waist.

One hand splayed against her back, he took two steps deeper into the dining area, setting her down on one of the little bistro tables in the corner. It rocked slightly and she braced herself on the edge by curling her fingers around it.

"Oh, my," she said. "Well, I don't think this table has ever been used in quite this way before."

"Don't people eat dessert here?"

"Well, yes."

"Good," he said, "because I'm about to have my dessert."

He took a fistful of her T-shirt, wrenched it up over her head and flung it down onto the floor. And before she had a moment to process the fact that he had just done that, he unhooked the catch on her bra and sent it in the same direction as her shirt.

She had a momentary flash of concern that the loss

of bra would prove a disappointment to him, since she wore a pretty padded one in an attempt to balance out her top half with her hips.

If he noticed that her breasts were smaller than advertised, though, he certainly didn't seem to mind.

He didn't stop there. He made quick work of her jeans and her underwear, tugging them down her thighs in one smooth motion. And there was no chance for her to get caught up in displays of modesty. No. Because, before she could fully process the fact that she was completely naked, spread out on a table in her bakery, he had lowered his head, fastening his lips to one tightened nipple before drawing it deep into his mouth.

The sensation was such a shock, the heat of his lips and the slow glide of his tongue a sensory overload after so many years of *nothing*. It was such an incredible rush of pleasure that she didn't even bother to fight it. She just let her head fall back as a tormented cry escaped her lips.

Sex had never been like this before. And, if it had been, she would have probably sought it out a whole lot sooner.

But all thoughts of comparisons left her mind as he moved his hand to cover her stomach, the warm weight resting there both steadying and arousing. Of course, any feelings of steadiness fled when his hand began to slide down between her legs, his mouth still lavishing attention on her breasts. His touch was confident, and he moved his palm down to that place where she was wet and needy for him, cupping her in a possessive hold before rocking the heel of his palm slowly against that sensitized bundle of nerves.

She gasped, arching her hips upward, encouraging

him to do more. But it was clear to her that Cain wasn't going to be rushed. That he was not a man who was going to take cues from her. She supposed that was the flip side to all that talk of them pleasing themselves. He was bigger. He was stronger. And what he decided pleased him would take precedent.

It was a strange feeling, submitting to being at his mercy, submitting to being at the mercy of any man, when she had been so adamantly against ever experiencing that powerlessness again. But, as he spread his fingers slowly, parting her slick folds before sliding his thumb over her clit, then bringing the tip of his finger down against the entrance to her body, she realized it wasn't all bad.

Then, she really did have to fight against the urge to close her legs, to make it go a little slower. To make it stop altogether.

Not because it didn't feel good. But because it felt *so* good. Because it felt so big. Because it was threatening to take over everything, every thought, every other feeling. Her sense of time, and place, of who she was.

The fact that she might be anything at all but a creature designed purely for his pleasure.

He began to press his finger inside of her while he sucked harder on her nipple, the intense sensation making it difficult for her to breathe. She couldn't do much of anything but arch her back into him, press her hips upward, a silent entreaty for him to go deeper, harder. Again, his movements remained maddeningly controlled, the press of his finger intractably slow.

He lifted his head, kissed her neck, the edge of her jaw, up to the corner of her lips. And when he captured her mouth again he pressed his finger deeper, and she gloried in the penetration. In the invasion. The feeling of being possessed, even though she yearned for so much more.

"You want me," he said, the words ground out against her mouth as he pushed his finger all the way inside of her, the delicious friction making her ache for more.

She could only nod her head, all words, all thoughts deserting her completely.

Of course she wanted him. She was made of that want. She was liquid with her need for him, ready for all of him. Ready for the foreplay to end, ready for him to be buried inside of her, just like he promised.

"I want you too," he said, letting his lips drift across her cheek, to the shell of her ear, back down her neck. He shifted his hand, adding a second finger to the first, the feeling of fullness—foreign after so long—sending electric sensations skittering along her veins. "And I'm going to have you," he said, "all of you. I want you all over my fingers. My tongue. My cock."

The dirty, illicit words twisted around inside of her brain, sank down into her soul, only making her want him more. She was still reveling in them, in the great, yawning cavern of need they had created inside of her when he knelt down in front of her, mouth pressed against the tender skin of her stomach, then lower still, a hot kiss on her inner thigh. His fingers were still buried deep inside her when he lapped at her, right at the source of her desire for him.

She froze, slapping her hand against the back of his head, sifting her fingers through his hair. "Cain…"

"I told you," he muttered, pressing his face deeper against her, "I want you on my tongue."

This was just what she had fantasized about the other

day. Something that no man had ever done for her, because in the past, when her partners had made sex all about them, it most certainly hadn't included something that they didn't get anything out of.

"I thought you were going to be selfish," she said, gasping as his hot tongue slid in rhythm with the fingers he was working in and out of her body.

"I am," he said, the vibration of that low voice against her tender skin skimming down her spine, hitting her like an electric shock. "I'm having dessert."

And that was when he started to devour her. And any thoughts, any protest she might have made, was lost completely.

She arched against that wicked mouth, into his talented hands as he continued to torment her.

The orgasm was barreling down on her like a storm she couldn't outrun, didn't want to. She had never experienced anything like this before. In the past, climax had always been something that she had to make a concerted effort to experience. But not now. She couldn't have held back if she tried.

He pressed his lips to her firmly, sucking her deep into his mouth as he pressed his fingers deeper, and release broke over her like full, angry clouds hovering over the sea. Like a downpour. And she just let it wash over her completely.

She was breathing hard when he withdrew from her, rose up over her, kissed her deeply, with the evidence of her desire lingering on his tongue.

"You have no idea how much I needed that," he said.

"How much *you* needed it?" she asked, the words coming out weak. "I don't think I'll ever recover."

"Good."

He straightened, stood back, his hands going to his belt buckle, working his jeans down his narrow hips. Her eyes were glued to the stark, large outline of his arousal at the front of them, and when he exposed himself completely, her heart leaped into the center of her throat. She had known that he was more of a man than any other she'd been with before, but she hadn't realized just how far that would extend.

Really, she couldn't have asked for more. She couldn't have asked for better. If you were going to indulge yourself, you hardly wanted fat-free frozen yogurt. No. Since this was an indulgence, she wanted it all. And Cain Donnelly was the human equivalent of full cream gelato. Thick, heavy, probably bad for her, but destined to feel oh so good at the time.

"I need you," she said, not caring if she was on the verge of begging. She didn't have any restraint left. She just wanted.

He bent down to retrieve his jeans, reaching into the pocket and taking out his wallet, where he fished out a condom.

She could only be grateful for that, because she was too far gone to think of it. Possibly too far gone to care. He tore the package open, rolling the protection over his thick length quickly before tugging her to the edge of the table and positioning himself at her entrance.

She was so wet, so ready from her last climax that the first couple of inches slipped in easily. She let her head fall back, her eyes closed, reveling in that slow, sweet pleasure of being filled as he rocked his hips forward, taking her slowly.

He leaned forward, bracing his hands on either side of her, his green eyes intense, that strong, square jaw held tightly, a muscle there jumping. The tendons in his neck were standing out, a testament to the willpower he was exerting by going so slowly.

She wasn't sure she liked that his willpower was intact. Not when hers was crumpled up and discarded on the floor along with her clothes. She lifted her hand, brushing her fingertips along his jaw. He closed his eyes, his expression pained, and she felt his cock jerk inside of her.

She slid her hand slowly down around the back of his neck, drew his head down as she lifted herself up, tracing his mouth with the tip of her tongue. Then she wrapped her legs around his lean hips, urging him deeper, grinding her pelvis against him, a streak of white-hot pleasure cracking through her like lightning.

She honestly hadn't thought it was possible for her to have another orgasm so close to the last one. Not considering how strong it was. She had been more than willing to have him inside of her without coming again, just for the sheer pleasure of the penetration. But she was already on the verge of another climax, and if it was on offer, she wasn't going to say no.

He withdrew slowly, then thrust back in strong, and still, he was a bit too controlled for her taste. She abandoned his mouth, angled her head to the side. "You like being inside of me," she whispered, in that same throaty, stranger's voice. "Do you feel how wet I am for you?"

A fractured groan escaped his lips, and he bucked forward hard, bringing him into even greater contact with her clit, that streak of pleasure turning into a deep pang of need.

"Yes," she said, rocking against him. "Yes, Cain. Like that."

"I'm not going to last," he said, growling through gritted teeth.

"I don't need you to last. I just need you. Hard. Now." She had never said anything like that to a lover in her life. Had never thought she would. She had never been this vocal, this demanding. But when she saw the flare of heat in his eyes, when he moved his hands to grip her hips, blunt fingertips digging into her skin, she knew that she had made the right choice.

Because any control that he'd had before was gone. He was holding her like a man should hold a woman. Strong, certain. His thrusts were hard, almost brutal, but that was what she wanted. This was hers. Her moment. Her pleasure. And she wanted all of it. She wanted to claim this moment. This little stolen space of time with this man who wanted her as much as she wanted him.

This man who saw her as a woman. Not as an object of pity. Not as a project. He had a need as deep as hers, he needed to be a man again, and he had chosen her to fulfill that basic, elemental desire.

The power, the pleasure that realization brought on was all-encompassing.

She rocked her hips against his, chasing that fire, chasing that need. She wasn't afraid of the wildfire, not anymore. She was running right at it with open arms. And if it incinerated her completely… Well, that was a risk she was willing to take.

She turned her head to the side, her eyes catching sight of those strong, masculine forearms holding on to her so tightly, his strength so evident. She pressed her face against him there, inhaling that sharp, masculine scent. He smelled like sweat and dirt. Hay and sunshine. Because he had been outside working all day, and she didn't think he had gone in for a shower. But she didn't care.

She was too caught up in this. In him. In that raw, real essence of him. Of this. She wanted to capture it all. She didn't want any of it blunted, didn't want any of it sanitized.

It had been a long time since she'd been present during sex. Much longer than four years. She'd never told Jared no. But, in the end she hadn't wanted him either. Hadn't wanted those hands that had hurt her to give her even a spark of pleasure.

It had become another way she had allowed him to use her body. She'd been his brick wall. To scream at when he was enraged. His punching bag to vent that anger. And his source of release when he needed it.

By then, she hadn't been a woman. She had been a thing. The thing that had belonged to Jared. His Swiss Army wife. A tool for his every need. But she'd lost any sense of her own needs. Her own dreams. Her own desires.

This was different. It was sharp and clear and unbearably real. Cain's hands were warm, his body hard above hers, his mouth insistent as he tasted her, long and deep.

But one thing became abundantly clear as he gripped her hips harder than ever, as he chased his release and she chased hers.

This wasn't taking. It was giving. She wasn't a thing to him. She was a woman. And the first thing he had done, as part of his own satisfaction, had been to get on his knees and see to hers.

His pleasure was entwined in hers. He wanted her to feel good.

That was a revelation. A concept so foreign she had

difficulty wrapping her mind around it. But she didn't need to. Because her legs were wrapped around him, and he was thrusting home, hard and deep, kissing her in a rhythm to match, and there was no thinking. Not now.

It didn't matter what had come before. Because this was now. Beautiful and endless, like that first day of summer always felt back when she'd been in high school.

As if this moment was just the first of many. As if the sunshine and warmth, the freedom, would never end.

But then all too soon the tension in her stomach began to wind tighter and tighter, like the last few grains of sand in an hourglass slipping through. That first orgasm she had welcomed, but this one, she wished she could delay. Wished she could turn the timer over and start again. So that it wouldn't end.

She so wasn't ready for it to end.

His back was slick with sweat, his muscles tense, his movements becoming more and more erratic, that frayed effort testing her control, winding tight the spring inside of her until she could hardly breathe through the need for release.

He lowered himself down, his mouth crashing into hers. She closed her eyes, gritting her teeth as streaks of light flashed behind her lids, her release grabbing hold of her, her internal muscles pulsing around his hardness as he lost control completely, thrusting into her once, twice more before freezing over her, his own climax making him shudder and shake.

It was perfect. That moment of ecstasy. That moment of nothing. Where there was nothing beyond that shared instant of breathless passion.

But then the world started to creep in around them, and the reality of what had happened settled on her. She was completely naked now, lying on a table in her bakery with a man buried deep inside of her.

And as that reality took hold, she realized that she was still happy with the decision. It hadn't been a decision, not really. It had been need. Pure and simple. There had been no real decision-making at all.

It had been desire that was bigger than she was, and she could never regret that she had experienced it. That she, Alison Davis, had been swept away on a tide of passion that only a few years ago she would have said she didn't possess the ability to feel.

A limp, colorless woman who was cracked, bruised and beaten down would never have done something like this. This wasn't her healing, no. It was the evidence that she had already healed. It was beautiful, blindingly brilliant.

But it was over, and that really sucked.

He leaned forward, his muscles shaking as he did, and he brushed his lips against hers. And there it was, that kiss that they had both acknowledged it would end with.

"Cain," she said, pressing her fingertips against his biceps, feeling all that weakened strength beneath her touch. "I don't want that to be our last kiss."

CAIN COULD BARELY BREATHE, let alone think. Let alone try to untangle the words that Alison had just whispered. He was still inside of her, and he knew he needed to move, since he was probably crushing her into the hard surface of the table. But everything in his body had gone lethargic, making him far too satisfied to contemplate shifting position.

He didn't really want to untangle Alison's words. Because that meant dealing with things like time, reality and the English language, and he wasn't feeling in the right headspace to do any of that.

No, what he wanted to do was give it about ten minutes, get a new condom and start all over again. Four years of celibacy was a hell of a lot, and one round of incredible sex was hardly going to burn it off. No, all it had done was remind him why sex was something wars were started over.

It was that damn good.

Better than whiskey, it burned things clean, made things feel clear. At least in the moment. Made that moment, that bright, white-hot moment of release seem like the perfect one. And he had had so many years of imperfect that it was exactly what he had needed.

Delicate fingertips fluttered against his chest, and he looked down at the face of the woman he was still on top of.

"What?"

She giggled, honest-to-goodness giggled, making her internal muscles pulse around him as she did. His breath hissed through his teeth and he moved away from her then, because safe sex demanded that he did.

"Something funny?" he asked.

"Kind of. I mean, I'm sort of amused by the idea that I screwed your brains out. So you didn't hear what I just said."

"You would be correct." He looked around. "Bathroom?"

"That way," she said, gesturing to a blue door with a little sign in the back. All the doors in this place were blue. Kind of an antique, washed color that complemented the exposed brick nicely. And he really didn't care about any of those details, because he'd just had sex.

"Be right back."

He strode into the bathroom and took care of the condom as quickly as possible, walking back out and realizing that it was a little bit strange standing in the middle of what was a public place during daylight hours wearing nothing but his skin. He had gotten up to a fair amount of mischief back before his marriage. And he had definitely had sex in places other than a bed, but the closest he'd ever come to public sex was parked somewhere up in the woods in the back seat of a car.

Not exactly the quaint, small-town bakery he now found himself in.

He'd hoped Alison might start putting herself back together while he was in the bathroom so he could gain some control of himself.

But she was still naked, standing in the center of a bakery, looking like the best treat on the menu.

"So, what did you say?" he asked.

She cleared her throat. "Earlier, we talked about this ending with a kiss. Well, I don't want that kiss you just gave me to be the end of it. It was too good."

Her words echoed exactly what he had been thinking earlier. Though, he had been thinking of an immediate round two. He had the box of condoms right out in his truck, and he had no problem bringing them in and suggesting it. He had a feeling, however, that she was talking about something else.

"I'm definitely listening."

"I know you have a lot on your plate. And I... I have a lot on mine. So, I'm suggesting that while we're both dealing with all those things on our plate, we help each other with a little bit of stress relief."

"Stress relief. As in…"

"As in all the orgasms we have time to give each other."

Cain rubbed his chin. "I mean, I like the idea behind that."

"I'm going to be honest with you," she said, taking a deep breath. The slow intake of air caused her breasts to rise and fall gently, the slight bounce in them captivating his attention entirely. It had been four years since he had seen a pair of naked breasts. In person. Pictures really didn't do them justice. Well, pictures were pretty good, but he really did prefer them live.

"Sorry, if you're making detailed plans right now you're only going to have to repeat them later. Because all I can do is look at you."

She rolled her eyes, an expression of mock irritation written across her face. But her cheeks turned pink, and he could tell that she was secretly pleased with the attention she was getting.

"I've been really busy setting up the bakery for the past few years," she said, bending down to collect her T-shirt, which she pulled over her head, without the bra. That was not a whole lot less distracting as far as he was concerned. Then she picked up her jeans and put those on too. She grabbed her underwear and her bra, holding them in her hand. "And I haven't exactly made room in my life for men, by which I mean sex. I still don't have room in my life for a man, by which I mean an emotional commitment. But I really have missed the sex."

"Yeah, well, I've been in a little bit of a post-divorce

dry spell, myself. By which I mean, the entire post-divorce period."

"Really?" She lifted a brow. "That surprises me."

"You've seen what I've been dealing with. It shouldn't be that surprising. Plus, I don't really want Violet to go out and randomly hook up, so it didn't seem like something I could do."

"How old are you, Cain?"

"Thirty-eight."

"Well," Alison said, "she's sixteen. So, for her hooking up really isn't the best idea. But you're certainly entitled."

"I should have consulted with you a long time ago, since you seem to think I'm entitled to sex."

She smiled. "Maybe I missed my calling. Maybe all this time I was supposed to be some sort of therapist."

"Butter, remember. Butter is better than therapy."

"How about sex?"

"Better than butter."

"Not really tempted to get into that as my line of work, but if you and I can come to some sort of agreement…"

"I have to sort out all of this stuff with Violet. And as much as I want to blow it all off and… Well, blow being an interesting choice of words…"

"I'm not asking you to take any time away from your family. But you were able to come over here tonight."

He nodded slowly. "True. And we do live with my brothers, so they'd be able to keep an eye on her, and on everything else while I'm away." They had made the offer before, and he had always turned it down. Right now, he really couldn't remember why. Right now, he felt like past Cain was a bit of a dickbag.

"Good. Because I have to say, after breaking my sex fast in such a spectacular way, I'm not looking forward to jumping right back into a drought."

"Same goes."

"You are just…" She smiled again, a smile that could only be called dreamy. He really couldn't say how long it had been since a woman had looked at him like that. Maybe never. "You're just very good."

"You make a man want to be good, honey. You're so beautiful, it makes it easy to be thorough."

That only made her smile harder, and the jolt that gave him was almost as powerful as the jolt he'd gotten from his recent orgasm. Almost.

"You're not so hard on the eyes yourself."

"I'll take it." He lifted a shoulder. "I've certainly been called worse."

He bent down, picked up his jeans and started to tug them on. She groaned. "Why do you have to take my show?"

"Because I really should go home," he said, grabbing his T-shirt next and pulling it on. "I didn't tell anybody where I was going. Usually, I can get things covered. But I probably shouldn't disappear without notice."

"Do you… Do you have to tell your brothers about us?"

He glanced up, raised a brow. "I mean, I should probably let them know that I met someone. But I don't see why they have to know it's you."

She looked relieved about that. "Good. And please don't be offended by that. It's just that this is a small town, and things get complicated quickly. There's a lot of gossip. And we really don't want that kind of thing getting around. I don't want Violet knowing—" She cringed. "I really don't want Violet knowing."

He shook his head. "I don't either. If there's one thing I'm not explaining to my sixteen-year-old, it's my sex life. And if she knew that my sex life was tangled up in her work life, I might end up in the position where I have to. And that just isn't happening."

"Okay. So we agree on secrecy."

"Fine with me."

"I guess...call me. Call me when you...want sex?"

He would be calling her in ten minutes. But he still had a life to take care of, and he would have to remember that. It wasn't just seeing to Violet. It was taking care of the ranch, continuing work on the home that he was renovating for Violet and himself. Important things that he couldn't let fall by the wayside just because he was finally getting some.

"Sure." He took his hat from the table where he had left it and put it back on his head. Reflexively, he tipped it forward, and was gratified by the color that rose up in her cheeks.

Hell, if she had grumpy cowboy fantasies, he was her man. And he was going to go ahead and enjoy being the fulfillment of something rather than being a wrecking ball.

"See you later," he said, turning and undoing the locks on the bakery door before stepping outside into the crystal clear night and closing it firmly behind him. He took a few steps down the street, then stopped, planting his hands on his hips and drawing in a long, deep breath.

The air was damp and mingled with the scent of salt from the sea. The waves crashing against the shore just beyond the buildings sounded almost like the impending roar of a storm.

Strange, for the first time in a while, to feel everything still and at peace inside of him while the raging went on outside.

This was good. This was better than good. It made him feel like he had his boots firmly planted back on the ground. He had stepped out onto this very street a couple of times in the past week, feeling disoriented. Feeling like he wasn't sure how he had gotten here. But he damn sure knew how he had gotten here tonight. He had gotten in his truck and he had driven. He had chosen to come down here. Chosen to be with Alison.

And he would have a chance to be with her again. And again, and again. No emotional entanglements, just a chance to work some of that darkness out of his soul. For a moment, that thought made him feel just a tiny bit guilty. Because if Alison was anything, it was softness and sweet sugar. And he was… Well, all rough hands and dirt.

But she didn't seem to mind. And he had to figure that if he needed a little bit of what she had, maybe she needed a bit of what he had.

Yeah. That made sense to him.

And he had to admit, even if only to himself out here on this dark, empty street, that being needed felt pretty damn good.

CHAPTER ELEVEN

"THANKS FOR HELPING with all of this, Lane," Alison said, surveying the trays of miniature pies, cookies and cupcakes that were about to be taken out to Grassroots Winery for a wedding.

Grassroots Winery was nestled deep in the trees, between Copper Ridge and the neighboring town of Gold Valley, so it was a little bit of a drive, and it was nice to have company.

She didn't particularly want to be alone with her thoughts this morning. Not when they were still full of Cain and his body and his...everything.

"No problem. I needed to make a delivery out that way anyway. And needed to pick up some more wine for the Mercantile." Lane owned a specialty food store in town, and the two of them had a lot of fun trading ingredients that Alison turned into baked goods.

Both of them had begun working with Lindy Parker recently when the other woman expanded her efforts at the winery. Lindy had recently gotten divorced, which put her in control of the winery, and she was making the most of it.

"Still, I hate to take advantage of my friend with a truck at every opportunity."

Lane grinned. "You hate to, but you do it often enough."

"Guilty."

She was guilty of a few other things too. Such as trying to get her rear out of the bakery to avoid both Violet and flashbacks to last night, when Cain had taken her so expertly in that quaint little dining room where people were currently sitting and eating their morning pastries.

She had sanitized that table extra. Because while no one in there would ever know what had happened, she knew.

She had hoped she would be able to get over it, but when Pastor John Thompson had taken a seat in that very spot with his Bible and croissant, embarrassment had spread over her skin like fire. She had been tempted to do a few Hail Marys, and she wasn't Catholic. Neither was Pastor John.

Until she got a handle on all the memories, it was best that she get some fresh air and escape the scene of her most recent indiscretion.

Except she didn't really feel like it was an indiscretion. It was a decision, in many ways. Sure, one that had been made by the incredible attraction between them, but when it came to sex, if you weren't doing it for love, you had better be doing it for desire like this.

Love, she didn't care much for. What had happened last night on the other hand, well, she cared for that a whole lot.

She got into Lane's truck, and Lane started to drive out of town, heading away from the coast, inland to the mountains that cut a jagged line across the sky. The highway that led to the winery was long and straight, lined by tall, dense trees. Evergreens that stood sentry year round, a thick carpet of ferns covering the ground beneath them.

Everything seemed clearer this morning. Beautiful, more than usual somehow. Like she was looking at it with fresh eyes, rather than the same tired eyes that had taken in this scenery for most of her life.

She could have left town four years ago. Could have left all this behind. But, in that instant, she was more glad than ever that she had chosen to stay. That she had chosen to dig in and call these roots her own, rather than ceding them to the man who had already taken so much from her.

Because if she had left, then she wouldn't have had this moment. This moment of absolute clarity. This moment where she had the opportunity to look at something old and see it as new because something inside of her had changed. It was abundantly clear that that was what had occurred. That what had happened last night with Cain had altered something, shifted something, added something that was missing.

"You're quiet this morning," Lane commented.

"Sorry," Alison said, jerking her focus away from the scene below. "Just tired."

"You don't seem tired. You seem…contemplative."

"Interesting. I don't feel more contemplative than normal." That was a lie. She was exceedingly contemplative. Deep in contemplation, as a matter of fact. But nothing she was ready to share. Although, with her, sharing always felt like a complicated thing. Usually, the deep ruminations were tied up in her past, and it was always difficult for her to decide if she wanted to talk about those things, or if she wanted to pretend they had never happened.

It changed on any given day.

"I guess things are really tough between Cain and

Violet right now," Lane said, her tone conversational and light. Too conversational and light. Because Lane was far more intentional than she was pretending to be right at this moment.

"I had a talk with him," Alison said, attempting to keep her voice neutral. "The other morning. About that. He's hoping that I can figure out how he can communicate with her better, or something. Or at the very least let him know if I see her hanging out with people she shouldn't be."

Lane sighed. "He's a good guy. A great guy. But he's very… He's not the kind of guy who radiates sensitivity. And right now, I think Violet might need a little more sensitivity in her life."

"Spoken by one formerly rebellious teenager to another," Alison said, "I'm not sure there's much that can be done. You decide to make mistakes, and you go make your own mistakes."

Lane grimaced. "I guess. I mean, I don't think anything would have stopped me from sleeping with my boyfriend back when I was in high school. I'm not sure there's anything my parents could have done on that score, but…the way they reacted when they found out I was pregnant, that I wish I could change. If I had known that I was loved and supported it all would have been very different. I mean, I still might have given the baby up for adoption, but I wouldn't have left home."

"Well, to be perfectly honest, if I had known my parents cared about me at all, I probably wouldn't have been out in the woods getting drunk back when I was sixteen. If my father had shown me even a tiny bit of affection when my mother died. If, when she knew she was dying, my mother had at least had a deathbed confession of love, maybe I wouldn't have found Jared quite so appealing. But Violet must know how much Cain loves her."

"I can see why you would think that," Lane said. "But the thing is, he's not very verbal about it. He does a lot for her, and *I* can see what that means. I can see that it means that he loves her, and so can you. But I'm not sure that a sixteen-year-old girl who was abandoned by her mother is going to interpret it in the same way."

"I guess not," Alison said, feeling strangely defensive of Cain. Though she supposed at this point it wasn't that strange if she felt defensive of the man who had made her body feel better than it had in years. Maybe better than it had ever felt.

Grassroots Winery was right next to a river, the sound of the rushing water audible through the thick grove of trees that separated it from the sleek, manicured lawns and paths around the buildings.

Alison knew there was a dining area down by the water, but it didn't get a lot of use outside of summer since it was a good ten degrees cooler there thanks to the rushing rapids and dense tree cover.

Pale light filtered in through the pines, casting a golden glow over the grass, dappling the parking lot. It smelled different here, miles from the ocean. Like wood, moss and pine. Heavy and rich like the forest itself.

The tasting room was fashioned from a beautifully reconstructed old barn, the beams glowing a deep amber color in the sunlight, the grounds around well manicured and lushly green.

The vineyard stretched gloriously behind the tasting room, tables and a gazebo situated in perfect placement for catching the vast mountain view behind the winery in wedding pictures.

It wasn't Lindy who greeted them though, but a petite blonde who looked to be in her early twenties. She had a pale, drawn look to her, in spite of the fact that she affected a broad smile when Alison and Lane approached.

"Hi," she said, "welcome to Grassroots. Lindy told me that you would be here, and that I was supposed to direct you to the tasting room. I'm Clara."

Alison thought the other girl seemed vaguely familiar, like someone she might have known back when she was a child.

"Have we met before?" Alison asked.

"Probably," Clara said, forcing another smile. Alison couldn't help but notice that her smiles disappeared completely between them, her mouth edging into a firm, grim line. There was something about the solemn expression that gave her déjà vu.

"I doubt you and I went to school together, but do you have older siblings?"

This time Clara didn't attempt a smile. "A brother."

"Okay. What's his name?"

"His name was Jason," she said, her voice flat. "He's dead."

Alison felt immediate regret. If there was one thing she knew all about, it was the insensitive questions of strangers, or, sometimes even more oppressive, the silence of them. "I'm sorry," she said simply.

"Me too. Lindy hired me to fill a temporary vacancy here at the tasting room, and that worked for me. Staying busy is best for me right at the moment. Anyway, you aren't here to hear about my tragedies. If you want to bring the baked goods inside, I can have some of the other staff members take care of putting it all away."

"I'll be doing the wedding cake tomorrow," Alison said. "I'll deliver it just before everything starts, and I'll be here to help serve."

"Perfect," Clara said. "Do you want my help carrying in trays?"

"You probably shouldn't leave your post. We've got it."

Alison and Lane headed back to the truck to collect the trays of pies and cookies, and when they had a decent amount of distance between themselves and Clara, she groaned. "Nothing like asking the wrong question."

"You didn't know," Lane said. "It's not like you did it on purpose. Not like when that old bitch in the diner asked you how Jared was when she knew full well that you had left him because he was an abusive ass. And that Sheriff Garrett had basically run him out of town on a rail after he made a scene at the Fourth of July barbecue."

"Oh, yeah." Alison stepped up onto the bumper of the truck, then leaned down and picked up a tray filled with pies. "I had almost forgotten about that."

Except of course she hadn't. It had been the thing that had finally made her go. Not more beating in private. That full, public humiliation. Not just in the parking lot of the diner after work, but at a place where she had been trying to…she'd been trying.

Sadie Garrett had invited her to bring pies for the first annual barbecue on Garrett Ranch, and for the first time in years she'd felt a spark of something.

And her husband had come in swinging his fists, and

he'd ruined it. Like he'd ruined everything in her life during the course of their marriage.

Sadie had helped her find just enough with that offer of baking pies, that she'd been able to see a different future.

And she'd taken it.

Unlike when she'd been nineteen, she hadn't let a painful event propel her right into another one. Into another person who would just use her without giving anything back.

She had decided to stand on her own two feet. And she'd been doing it ever since.

Lane grimaced. "Sorry to bring it up."

"No. It really is okay. I guess that's the thing. Sometimes, it's not the worst to remember bad things. Sometimes it's actually good. I'm in a really good place right now, Lane. And a few years ago I didn't think that was possible. A few years ago I didn't see anything stretching ahead of me but..." Her throat tightened unexpectedly, emotion gripping her. "Well, anyway. I'm in a good place now. And everything that happened in the past... It can't hurt me now. He can't hurt me now."

She was feeling particularly renewed after reclaiming that long-forgotten part of herself last night. Quite happily renewed, even.

"That's good. Very good that he's not holding you back anymore." Lane let silence lapse between them for about half a second, then her whole tone changed. "So does that mean that you can call Cain now and tell him that you want his body?"

Alison nearly stumbled, quickly reclaiming her grip on the pie tray. "What?"

"You *want* him. You have wanted him since you first

saw him. I wasn't there, and I could still tell when you recounted it. So what's holding you back?"

"The little matter of the fact that his daughter is my employee," she said, lying like a lying liar, "and that everything in his life is so complicated." She cleared her throat. "Plus, who even knows if he wants me?"

"He's a man. He is a man who has been alone for a very long time."

"Wow. That's friendship for you. None of this, of course he wants you, Alison, because you're so beautiful, and witty, and charming, and of course he won't mind the fact that you're barely a B cup out of your Wonderbra, Alison. Because you're a special glitter princess who has no equal."

"Is that really a Wonderbra?" Lane asked, directing her gaze to Alison's breasts.

"*I don't know.* It's an off-brand. But it is padded. My point is, I'm not looking for an entanglement." She took one hand off the tray and gestured broadly. "And… *and…*"

"And you slept with him already, didn't you?" Lane asked, her eyes suddenly far too keen and intelligent for Alison's taste.

Alison turned her focus determinedly to the landscape. "I can honestly tell you I have not slept in that man's presence."

"Right. But have you seen his penis?"

Warmth and color flooded Alison's face. *"Maybe."*

"Ha! I knew it! Were you ever going to tell me?" Lane's tone was borderline shrill.

"Yes," Alison said. "I was going to tell you."

"Even if I hadn't guessed?" she pressed.

"Yes. I'm pretty sure."

"*Pretty* sure?"

"It just happened last night. It's not like I've been keeping it some big massive secret for weeks."

"How did I miss that?" Lane looked at her, her expression filled with scrutiny. "You're glowing. You have sex glow."

"I do not have sex glow," she grumped. "That isn't a real thing."

"Yes," Lane said, "it is. Trust me. I know. Because I was feeling really upset about the fact that Rebecca and Cassie were radiating it a few months ago when I felt bleak and lifeless and definitely without a glow."

"Well, now we're all glowing." She lifted her hand in a gesture of triumph, then the tray wobbled slightly and she grabbed it again quickly. "I glow, you glow."

Lane's expression brightened and she quickened her pace down the path toward the tasting room. "Wow. Finn's *brother*. You're sleeping with Finn's brother."

"Don't say that like it's significant. It isn't. I like Cain a lot, but this thing that's happening between us… It's only physical."

"Why? Why would you limit yourself like that?"

"I don't consider it a limitation. From my point of view." She paused for a moment while they walked into the tasting room. There were tall tables made from barrels situated throughout the room, with roughhewn stools positioned around them. Twinkling lights hung on crossbeams overhead—a special decoration for the wedding, she had a feeling—and there was a large rustic chandelier that also seemed to be made from parts of old barrels.

Alison made absolutely sure the room was empty before she continued to talk. "From my point of view relationships have never been about freedom. My life, the way that it is now? It's the best it's ever been. And now I have the very best part of a man on top of it. His body. And all the freedom and autonomy that I want. My life can continue to be all about me while I have great sex. That, my friend, is what they call having your cake and coming too."

"I don't think that that's... I don't actually think that's the saying," Lane said, setting her tray down on the far counter. Alison did the same.

"Whatever," Alison said, "it's what I say."

They walked back out of the tasting room and toward the truck, a strong breeze from the ocean sending her curls straight into her face. She smoothed them back while Lane continued to lecture.

"I would just hate for you to discount relationships because of something bad that happened to you. And I'm aware that this is a different conversation than the one the two of us had a few months ago. Where we were both kind of supporting each other's desire to stay single. But..."

"I know," Alison said. "You've crossed over. You've reached the other side. You pierced the veil. And now you see the light, and you have love, and you're living your happily-ever-after. I'm not trying to minimize what you went through, Lane. I understand that having the baby and being abandoned by your boyfriend and shunned by your family was really difficult. And I completely get why it took you a long time to decide that you wanted to move forward with your life. But this is different for me. I actually thought I found my happy ending once. I thought I had my Prince Charming. I didn't marry Jared knowing he was going to use me for a punching bag. I just wanted love. I wanted what everybody else wants. And I thought I *had* it."

She folded her arms over her midsection, trying to keep the unexpected twinge of pain that had popped up from spreading. As if she could keep it localized by gripping her own ribs. "But that's not even the worst part. It's what I became over the course of that marriage. It's all the pieces of myself that I lost, that I gave to him, that I've only just now started to get back. I don't want to lose those. Not again. It isn't just that I didn't like the man I was with. I didn't like the woman I became. I like who I am now. I'm not going to risk that."

Lane frowned, her dark eyebrows locked together. "Right. I guess I can't argue with that."

"No," Alison said, "you can't." They walked on in silence for a moment, no sound but the gravel crunching beneath their feet.

"He's good in bed though, right?" Lane asked finally.

Alison huffed a reluctant laugh. "I mean, in theory. I had him on a bistro table."

"You *what*?"

A smug smile tugged at the corner of Alison's lips. She was never the one with a story. She was never the femme fatale. The fact that she was right now both amusing and wholly satisfying.

"In the bakery," she continued, suddenly feeling downright chipper.

"You're going to have to tell me which table. So that I can avoid it. Or don't, I guess. But then every table is a potential sex table. It's Schrödinger's sex table."

"The one in the far corner, in the very back. There. Now you know. You don't have to wonder. You won't be plagued with speculating."

"Thank you."

She hesitated for a second. She'd told Cain to keep all of this to himself, and not to go telling his brothers. But Lane was…linked to the Donnelly family and there was no getting around it. "I don't suppose the odds are great that you aren't going to tell Finn?"

"I tell Finn everything. I always have. I mean, even before we were together, he was my best friend. I don't really do the secret thing from him. I mean, except for the giant secret that I kept from him for years about my past. But that's not how I do things anymore. I share now."

"Cain doesn't want his daughter to know. And I don't either. It would make things really weird. Can you even imagine knowing that your dad is having sex with someone, let alone somebody that you have to interact with? Also, he has a whole thing about it seeming like a bad example."

"He doesn't want to have to get into the whole *do as I say and not as I do on a bistro table* conversation?"

"Not especially."

"You can trust Finn. I mean, you can trust him not to spread it around, I don't know if you can trust him not to say something to Cain and in general be an ass, because he kind of excels at that."

"That's fine. I mean, Cain was going to tell them that he was sleeping with somebody, because he figured he would need his ass covered sometimes."

"Wow. You guys have this all planned out, don't you?" Lane sounded a bit too amused by that. Especially when there was nothing funny about it. "Yeah. We do," Alison said.

"So did Finn and I," Lane said, her tone now dripping with smugness. "Good luck with that."

"Don't say that. You don't know me. I think I can handle this."

"Honey. I *do* know you. And, for as long as I've been your friend, you haven't had a relationship at all. So, I'm just saying, things might not go as smoothly as you think they will."

"I don't see why not. We're very compatible in every way. Both of us really liked what happened between us, and neither of us wants a relationship. Plus, it isn't like you and Finn. Cain's not my friend. He never has been. I saw him, and I wanted him. And now I'm having him. I've had a shortage of that kind of thing in my life. I'm taking it by the horns, so to speak."

A sly smile curved Lane's lips. "Grabbing hold of it with both hands."

"Stop it," Alison scolded.

"What? I'm just saying."

"Well, *just say* your way into the tasting room. We've got stuff to do. I can't sit around and trade double entendres with you." She cleared her throat, shooting her friend a very prim expression. "But it definitely takes both hands if you want to grab onto it."

Lane let out a crack of laughter. "Okay. I can let it go now. Because that satisfied me so very deeply."

"Good. I'm glad that you're satisfied."

And for the moment, Alison felt like she might be too—a rare and wonderful occurrence. She was just going to enjoy it. Because up until now she had had spare few moments of enjoyment, and she felt like she deserved this.

Heck, from where she was standing, feeling like she

deserved much of anything was a pretty big achievement in itself.

She paused in front of the tasting room, looking at the scenery around her, then down at the tray of goodies in her hands. All of these steps she was taking. All the richness, the layers and textures she was adding to this existence that she had carved out for herself in such a desperate, bloody-knuckled way in the beginning. It was all starting to look beautiful.

And she was happy.

CHAPTER TWELVE

"Alison is coming over tonight."

Cain looked up from his dinner and stared at his daughter, who had just come flouncing into the kitchen before hoisting herself up onto the island next to where he was eating. "Okay."

He was impressed that he had managed to keep his tone neutral, considering every male hormone inside him had stood up at full attention at the mention of Alison's name. He wondered why she hadn't texted him to let him know. But then, he had to wonder if it was because she was trying to keep her interaction with Violet separate from her interaction with him. Or at least trying to keep their personal connection separate. She was supposed to use her connection to Violet to give him some insight.

"What are you working on tonight?" he asked, trying his best to seem unaffected by the mention of Alison, and interested in what was happening.

"I suck at making cakes. Like, I'm the actual worst at it. So, she's probably going to give me more remedial cake instruction, so that she doesn't have to fire me." Violet made a comically dramatic gesture that he had a feeling was completely genuine.

"Okay," he said slowly. "Do you really think it's that bad?"

"Yes! I keep torpedoing cakes."

He was stuck trying to figure out the best thing to say, trying to figure out exactly what she needed to hear. He really had never been very good at the whole verbal communication thing. Not in marriage, not in fatherhood. And, when Violet had been little, he hadn't had to. He had tossed her up in the air, blown a raspberry on her stomach and made her entire day.

But now…she needed more. She needed something else. And he didn't know how to offer it. Maybe it was time he admitted that.

Which meant starting with talking.

"Are you feeling okay after the hangover, Bo?" he asked, trying to sound much more okay with everything than he was.

Violet shot him a wary look. "Yeah. I feel fine."

"The breakfast that I made you helped?"

"Yeah." She looked down at her hands, peeling at some paint on one of her fingernails. "I don't understand why you're talking about it without breathing fire now."

"Because I breathed all the fire I had. It's used up. Now, I just want to figure out how we're going to move forward. I can't have you going out and not know where you are. I understand that you're mad at me, and I understand it isn't just about last night. Bo, I don't know what I'm doing wrong. I can't tell you that your mother didn't leave because of me. Mostly because she did." He shook his head. "It sure as hell wasn't because of you, honey. It wasn't. It was a combination of me and her. Everything that went wrong. And I… I'm mad. I'm mad at her because she left. I'm mad at me because if I had noticed sooner, maybe I could have fixed it. Maybe

I could have said the right thing, done the right thing. But I didn't. I completely fucked it up."

His daughter looked a little bit…bemused at hearing him say those things. At hearing him swear like that. But, it was honesty hour. He was trying to fix something, trying desperately to make sure he didn't leave anything broken. "I really want to make sure I don't do the same thing with you. I want to make sure that we fix this. That you don't walk out of here one day and never come back."

Violet blinked, and he could see that she was holding back tears. And that she was angry about it.

"I'm not going to do that." She sucked in a sharp breath. "I came with you this far. If I was going to run away, I would have done it back in Texas."

"Before we got to this hellhole, as you've labeled it?"

"It's not a hellhole. It's more of a hellmouth. Not quite at the center of the devil's unholy kingdom, but still pretty bad."

"Well, that's giving of you."

Violet heaved herself down off the island and started to pace. "I don't want to be mad at you. I don't want to feel awful all the time. I don't know what I want. I don't really know who I am."

She stopped pacing then, her hands down at her sides, her expression one of absolute defeat. Her green eyes— eyes that were the same color as his own—full of that same sadness he felt sometimes.

That broke him. Broke him straight down to his core. Anger was actually easier to deal with than this. Than her apparent desolation. Than her sadness. All that pain that she carried down deep.

But honestly, he wasn't surprised. Kathleen's leaving had affected him, and he was a grown-ass man who had more than enough anger, and had had more than enough reason to want some distance from her. Kathleen was Violet's mother. And there was going to be a whole lot more hurt and a whole lot less relief involved for her than there was for him.

"You're mad at me," he said. Mostly because he just wanted everything to be said.

"Sometimes. Sometimes not."

"That sounds about right. Sometimes I get mad at you too," he said. "But mostly, I get angry at me."

"Why?"

"I already told you. Sometimes I think it's my fault. What you said to me earlier. I believe it too."

"I don't think I do really." Violet tucked her hair behind her ear. "I don't. I was mad at you because I was embarrassed. Embarrassed that you saw that. Embarrassed that my friends saw you get mad. It would have been better to not get caught. Then, you wouldn't know that I did that, and they wouldn't know that you are a jackass."

He laughed, in spite of himself. "Well, I am kind of a jackass."

"And one of my friends said you were hot," Violet said, her entire face turning red. "And I pretty much don't think I'm ever going to recover from that."

He laughed again, because he really couldn't help himself now. "Wow. I went in there to embarrass you and it worked on so many more levels than I could have possibly anticipated."

"Dad. I thought we were trying to have a moment."

"I'm sorry. I'm having a moment now. A moment of

pure triumph. That is…gold. It is actual gold. How horrifying is that for you?"

"Seriously. You're the worst." Except she didn't sound even half as angry with him now as she had earlier.

"The worst. But kind of hot."

"No. That's disgusting. You're my dad. You are not hot. You are old."

Right on that note, in walked Alison, carrying an armful of baking accoutrements, followed by his brothers, Liam and Finn. "Where do you want these?" Finn asked.

"Over there is fine," Alison said, gesturing to the island at the center of the room.

Finn complied, carrying everything over there and dumping it on the high gloss surface. Liam followed shortly behind him.

"Thank you," Alison said brightly, turning her smile on to both of them.

Cain's stomach tightened, and he recognized vaguely that he was feeling jealous. Jealous of his engaged brother, and his younger brother, who he could probably still beat up.

Though Liam had some kind of brooding appeal that women kind of lost their shit over. Also, tattoos.

Plus, Liam was much closer to Alison's age. At least, Cain assumed so. He didn't know exactly how old Alison was. Late twenties, maybe. And—as his daughter had just kindly pointed out—he was old.

"I didn't realize you were coming by tonight," he said, in what he hoped wasn't a terribly transparent bid to turn her attention on to him.

"Sorry," she said, biting that lip he had sucked on last night. "I should have called."

"It's okay. You're always welcome to come."

He hadn't really meant to infuse that statement with a double entendre, but he was more than happy to let it stand. More than happy to let her mull that over.

"Well," she said, sounding a little bit flustered now. Damn, that was satisfying. "We should probably get started. It takes a while to bake a cake. And it's already late."

Cain frowned. "You open the bakery awfully early. Are you sure this isn't too much?"

She waved a hand. "No, it's fine. I have a wedding cake to do tomorrow, so I'm going to be at home most of the day until I go serve. That means I get to sleep in until at least six."

Violet pulled a face. "That's not sleeping in."

"Yes it is." He, Finn and Liam spoke that in unison.

Her face grew even more horrified. "So being an adult is basically just never getting to sleep in past sunrise?"

"Well, and being in charge of your own grocery purchases, which means you can buy whatever you want," Finn pointed out.

"And eat cereal for dinner," Alison said.

"Yeah," Cain agreed. "That."

"I think I'll take sleeping in over cereal for dinner, but you're really selling the adulthood thing."

"There are other attractions to being an adult, Violet," Liam said. "You're just too young to hear them."

Violet stuck her tongue out. "You're gross, Uncle Liam."

"And you're a brat. Anyway. I have to go. Headed out to the bar tonight."

"Spare us all the details of the debauchery. I'm way

too young to hear about how many chicken wings you ate before you feel asleep in front of *60 Minutes*," Violet said, her parting shot as Liam grinned and left the room, Finn right behind him.

That left Cain, Alison, Violet and a whole lot of weird energy.

"I can leave you guys to your baking," he said.

"You don't have to go," Alison said. "You want to learn how to make a cake?"

He looked at her, at her petite frame, at her curves— which he now knew were slightly exaggerated by the bra she wore, but he didn't give a damn—at the way her thin T-shirt molded to said curves. Yeah, there was pretty much nothing else around here that he would rather look at than her. And he didn't see the point in pretending otherwise.

"Sure. I can always use a new skill." He patted his stomach, which was flat and hard, and he knew it. "But I have to be careful not to eat too many sweets."

Alison laughed, a high unnatural sound. "Right. Because you have to watch your figure?"

"Hey, if I don't no one else will."

"Fair enough." Alison set about preparing the ingredients, and then began to instruct Violet on how to assemble everything.

"I killed that last cake too, so you know. The one that we started here," Violet said. "Why did you leave?"

Alison looked stricken. "Oh. I guess… I guess I forgot to talk to you about that. Because of all the…" He could see her looking for a reason, probably because she didn't want Violet to know that she knew about her little drinking escapade. And she definitely didn't want Violet to know about *their* little escapade. "I've been busy. Because of the wedding cake. Anyway, I got a text from a friend, and I had to go. And I meant to tell you."

Alison was actually a pretty damn bad liar, but Violet didn't seem to notice. Probably because it didn't occur to her that an authority figure would lie to her. That adults were just as fallible as teenagers. A strange thing, considering she had been abandoned by her mother. But a testament to her age. Things were generally black-and-white to her. Kathleen was bad because she had left. And she didn't know what to make of Cain at this point because he had stayed, but she also blamed him a little bit. Which made a lot of sense when he really thought about it. That dealing with their relationship was hard because it contained both good and bad feelings. It was hard enough for him, and he was a grown-ass man. It was probably a lot harder for a sixteen-year-old. Not for the first time he wondered if he waffled between being too easy on Violet, and too hard on her.

Honesty was just going to have to be the new policy.

Except when it came to his sex life.

"Well, I need you to supervise me before this cake comes out of the oven, or I'm going to flatten it again. And I'm getting really tired of looking at sunken cake."

"It's just something you have to learn, Violet," Alison said, her voice assuring. "It's not a failure, it's just part of learning. You don't get things right the first time. There's no guarantee you'll get them right the second time. Or the third time. But you'll never get it right if you stop."

Her words were applicable to a host of things, and hit a little too close to home.

"You could be a motivational speaker," Violet said,

and he had to fight the urge to scold her for her tone. Alison could certainly handle herself. And the interaction.

"I thought of that. But I prefer life with a little bit more butter." She looked over at Cain and treated him to a secret smile. One his daughter completely missed because she was fully absorbed in her own situation.

He wanted…well, he wanted to be alone with Alison. He wanted to move up behind her and grip her hips. Draw her back into his body so she could feel just what she was doing to him without even trying.

But since they were currently in the kitchen watching his daughter bake a cake he figured that was probably an inappropriate thought to have.

Still, that didn't stop him from taking a long, appreciative look at her as she bent over the counter, talking to Violet about baking times and rising cakes and… luckily he was thirty-eight and not eighteen, or the cake wouldn't be the only thing rising.

"So, Violet," Alison said, her tone light and conversational. At least she was forcing it to try and sound light and conversational. "If you aren't busy tomorrow, I have that wedding I'm bringing dessert to, and I would love help with the service."

Violet looked up. "Oh. Like with serving guests?"

"Yes. I always go to the reception to cut and serve cake because there's a particular trick to it. If you want to help me, I'd pay you your regular hourly rate and you'd get a little more experience to add to your resume." Alison shot Cain a quick look. "I can take you from the bakery and bring you home after."

"Dad?" Violet asked.

"Fine with me," he said, and managed to not add anything about how it was funny she seemed perfectly capable of asking his permission to do things like go to a supervised work shift, but not if she could go under-age drinking in a barn.

They were being civil. So he was going to be civil.

"Okay, then," Violet said, "that would be great."

Violet actually looked happy for the rest of the cake-baking session. And Cain could only marvel at it. He ended up staying in the kitchen the entire time. And about halfway through he realized it wasn't just inter-esting because of Alison's body.

No, it was good to watch Violet do something she enjoyed. To watch her succeed. He even liked seeing Alison excel, liked watching her operate in her natural environment.

Of course, at some point, the whole thing started to feel a little overly domestic to him. And that only gave him a renewed sense that he and Alison really needed to keep what was happening between them, well, be-tween them.

One thing he wasn't in the market for was this kind of happy-family situation. Mostly because he knew that ultimately that didn't exist. Happy families. It was all a weird smoke screen. Something that lasted for a cou-ple of years at best before it started to erode like rocks being pounded by waves.

Or, in the case of his first marriage, waves on sand.

Drunken lust and a baby were a pretty crappy foun-dation. Both he and Kathleen had tried for a long time to build off it. But ultimately, it wasn't strong enough to bear the weight of the life that had piled up on top of it.

He hadn't really seen evidence of anything else being a whole lot better. His brother Finn and his fiancée, Lane, were a notable exception. But then, the two of them had been friends for years before they had ever taken their relationship to the next level. And he figured if anybody had a chance of making it work it was people like that. People who knew everything there was to know. Who had no surprises left.

He couldn't imagine that being remotely as hot as what he and Alison had. As that kind of dark, forbidden attraction that had a shot of the unfamiliar in it, making the whole thing a pretty potent cocktail.

He supposed, though, that for the purposes of what Finn seemed to want—home and family and all of that—familiarity was better than heat. Cain just wanted the heat. And nothing else.

He was already up to his eyeballs in domesticity. He didn't need any more.

This time, when the cake came out of the oven it was perfect. Violet's exuberance at the victory was enough to make Cain momentarily forget everything. Everything except for seeing Violet enjoy something. Seeing her feel proud of herself. It wasn't until he saw that smile—a smile that went all the way to her eyes and made them sparkle—that he realized that all the little spots of happiness in between her moods weren't the kind of happy she used to be.

But this was.

"I'm going to have to leave that with you," Alison said, patting Violet on the back. "But it's perfect. And I know that you have frosting down since you've been helping with that for a couple of weeks now. Just let me know what kind you want."

"Just buttercream is fine," Violet said, surveying her work. "I can't believe it. I actually did it."

"It's not that hard," Alison said. "You just needed a

little bit of confidence. Maybe we move on to piecrust next?"

"But aren't there like nine thousand ways to mess that up?"

Alison laughed. "Oh, at least ten thousand. But you mastered this after it got in your head. So I wouldn't worry too much about anything else. If you don't get it right the first time, or the second time, or the third time... Maybe on the tenth time. And that's okay."

Alison began collecting her things.

"I'll walk you out," Cain said. "I think I might go work on the barn house for a while anyway."

"Barn house?" Alison asked.

"I'm remodeling an old barn for Violet and me to move into eventually."

Violet rolled her eyes. "Yes. I'm super excited to go move to a barn while we could be living here."

"But I'm cleaning a stall out just for you," he said. "How about giving me some credit?"

"Fine." Violet turned to Alison. "My dad is making us a really great place to live. Because he's awesome and he builds awesome things. And he isn't going to make me sleep in a stall."

"Good," Alison said, "because I was genuinely concerned that he might."

"Yeah. Well. Good night, Violet," Cain said, as he moved toward the door. "I'm just...going to check on some things in the barn."

Violet lifted an eyebrow. "Okay. Good night."

They stepped outside onto the porch and paused for a second. "Thank you," he said. "For helping her with the cake. Which was my official statement to you as a father. And now I'm about to make an official statement to you as a man. Let's go park."

Alison laughed, then pressed her hand up against her lips. "You want to park?"

"I bought myself a little bit of time by saying I was going to go outside and work. And Violet expects that you're leaving. So, I figure I can get in the car with you, and we can drive partway down the driveway and pull off the road."

"Get in my car, then."

He looked back over his shoulder, just to make sure nobody was watching out the window or anything. And then he headed toward Alison's car with her. He got into the passenger seat and didn't bother to buckle. She climbed in and started the engine.

"This is ridiculous," she said, looking at him, her smile saying that even if she thought so, she was enjoying the ridiculousness.

"Yeah," he said. "It kind of is."

His life had been heavy on unenjoyable ridiculousness for a little bit too long, and he couldn't remember the last time he'd had fun. Couldn't remember the last time he had sneaked around with somebody. More than seventeen years ago, that was for sure.

"I'm not complaining," she said, putting her car in Reverse. "Down the driveway?"

"I'm definitely not complaining. And yes."

She headed down the long, winding dirt driveway, and when they came to a small turnout he directed her to pull off.

"You might want to kill the lights," he said, looking over at her.

She complied, plunging them into darkness. There

were lights left on the dashboard, little orange glows accentuating the darkness, giving him just the barest hint of an outline for Alison's face. He leaned across the space between them, cupping her cheek and kissing her, deep and long. He didn't see the point in going slow. The entire evening had been a study in torture. In going a hell of a lot slower than he wanted to.

She tasted sweet, like she had been sampling some of the sugar she had been baking with earlier. He wanted to lick it all off her. Mostly, he wanted to lick her.

"Back seat," he growled against her mouth.

"You mean you don't just want to kiss?" she asked, her tone far too innocent to be genuine.

"You should know better than to go parking with men like me."

"You seemed so nice back there when I was baking the cake."

"That's how we get you."

She unbuckled, and he opened his door, getting out and then getting into the back seat. She got in at the same time he did. He growled, wrapping his arm around her waist and pressing her down into the seat as he kissed her with every ounce of pent-up hunger that had been building inside him since she had walked into his house tonight.

The car wasn't big enough for him to stretch out all the way, but he settled between her thighs anyway, wrapping her legs around his hips as he continued to kiss her.

"That was torture," he said, sliding to her neck, licking a trail down to her collarbone. "Looking at you and having to keep my hands to myself."

She pressed her palms against his chest, dragging

them down to his stomach. "You think it was easy for me? When all I wanted to do was touch you, everywhere."

"Where do you want to touch me? Show me."

She slid one hand down to cup his hardening cock. Then she squeezed him tightly, running her fingertips along the length of him through his jeans. He loved this. Loved that she wasn't shy about what she wanted.

He pushed his hand underneath her shirt, unhooked her bra and then pulled her T-shirt up before flinging the undergarment into the front seat. "Finally," he said, lowering his head and drawing one nipple into his mouth. She really did have the most amazing breasts, and he didn't think it was only because it had been so long since he'd touched a woman.

"They're smaller than they look. Because of the bra."

"Like I care," he said, nuzzling her other breast before lapping it with the flat of his tongue. "Doesn't matter how big they are. All that matters to me is how much you like it when I do this." He sucked her into his mouth again.

She gasped, arching her back up into him, encouraging him to go harder. And he obliged.

"I do like that," she said, her tone breathless, her fingers laced through his hair, tugging slightly.

"Good." He moved his hand down her stomach, reveling in the soft feel of her skin beneath his hands. His own skin was calloused, but she didn't seem to mind. He undid the button on her jeans, then slowly lowered the zipper before pushing his hand down beneath the waistband of her panties and stroking the glorious, wet flesh he found there.

She flexed her hips upward, arching into his hand,

her excitement and anticipation sending a shock of arousal straight down to his cock.

She gripped his shoulders, rolling her pelvis in time with his movements, chasing that release of hers that he could tell she was right on the verge of. Already. And he had barely touched her.

He pressed a finger inside of her, sliding his thumb over her clit, relishing that harsh gasp of breath on her lips and the intense pulse of her internal muscles as she climaxed. She grabbed hold of his wrist, holding his hand still, but pressing his palm down hard against that sensitive bundle of nerves as she rode out the orgasm.

She shuddered, her entire body shaking as the harder pulses calmed down to steady waves. He eased himself away from her, so hard now he was sure he was going to pop his zipper open.

She let out a long, slow breath. Then pushed herself up so that she was sitting. He couldn't see her expression, and for a moment, he was afraid that she was going to get out of the car and say that she needed to head home. That she was good now that she had gotten hers.

Instead, she placed her fingertips against his shoulder and shoved him back. Not hard enough to actually move him. He doubted she could do much of anything to move him, but he didn't see any point in fighting against her. In fact, he wanted to see what she would do next.

He wasn't disappointed. She reached out, undoing his belt, then the closure on his pants, drawing them down as much as she could in the cramped back seat. She curled her fingers around his thick length, squeezing him. He groaned, relishing the soft feel of her delicate fingertips against him.

The only thing that would make it better would be

if he could see her. If he could watch her touching him like that. Those slender fingers on the most masculine part of him.

But then he couldn't think. Then she leaned forward, her hot, slick tongue darting out and sliding over the head of his cock. He could barely make out the shape of her in the darkness, the pale, elegant curve of her spine arching as she took more of him into her mouth.

And he was lost. Lost in the dark, heady pleasure and the hedonistic rhythm that she established using her lips and tongue and hands. His damn head was about to explode.

His sweet little baker knew how to handle a man, that was for sure. And he was grateful.

He placed his hand between her shoulder blades, slid it down along her back, beneath the waistband of her pants so that he could get a handful of her ass. He squeezed her tight, then moved his hand over that smooth skin.

She made a low, throaty sound as she opened wider to take him in deeper, her hands sliding down between his thighs as she continued to tease him.

She did something particularly good with her tongue and he bucked his hips lightly, grabbing hold of her hair to try and steady them both so he didn't lose it completely.

"Careful, darlin'," he said. "I don't have a handle on all my control right now."

She didn't say anything; instead, she squeezed the base of his dick, then tilted her head, licking his length like a lollipop.

He reached down, gripped her chin and stopped her

movements, tilting her face upward. "Baby," he said, "I want to be inside of you when I come."

She touched the tip of her tongue to his thumb, and he rested it down against her bottom lip. She bit him, then sucked his thumb into her mouth. If he didn't feel the slight tremble in her lips he would have been tempted to believe that she was in total control here. But she was just as turned on as he was. Just as close to the edge.

He lifted his hips, reaching into his back pocket and taking out his wallet. Then he took out the condom packet he had placed in there earlier. Because he actually had a reason to carry around a condom again. Another thing that was part of a bygone era. Or had been. Until Alison.

"You do it," he said, handing the packet to her.

She sat up, tearing open the condom before discarding the wrapper, rolling the latex onto him, her grip firm. His breath hissed through his teeth as she rolled it down over him slowly, taking her time as she smoothed it over each inch.

She pushed her hands beneath his T-shirt, pulling it up over his head, then planted her hands on his bare chest, urging him to lean back against the car door. Then, she shifted, climbing onto his lap. He reached out, pushing her jeans farther down her legs, and she did her best to kick them off, taking her underwear with them. Then she straddled him, positioning herself on the head of his cock.

She gripped his shoulders, lowering herself slowly onto him. He planted one hand on her hip, the other on her ass as he guided her down completely, until she had all of him inside of her.

She froze for a moment, then leaned in, pressing her

forehead against his. She breathed out, a jagged, shaking sound that touched him down deep, not just physically, but somewhere else.

He lifted his hand, grabbing hold of her hair, pushing his fingers deep inside of it as he drew her head closer, kissing her fiercely before thrusting upward. She gasped then, and came alive.

She began to move over him, her fingernails digging into his shoulders as she rode him. As she drove them both closer to the point of ecstasy. Drove them both crazy. He tightened his hold on her rear, blunt fingertips digging into that pliant flesh, but if it hurt, she didn't seem to care. If it hurt, she seemed to like it.

That worked for him, since he couldn't tell if he was in agony or ecstasy as all that slick heat fisted around his body, driving him to the brink. Tormenting him as much as pleasuring him.

There was no sound except for their harsh breathing, the sound of skin on skin as her movements intensified, as they both started to shake, started to lose control. He needed her to go over. Now. Because he didn't have any ability left to resist. Because he needed to come more than he needed air. He reached between them, pressing his thumb right against her clit, then drawing it back to where their bodies met, then forward again.

She curled her fingers into his shoulders, her nails digging deep into his skin as she buried her face in the side of his neck, the moan of pleasure on her lips sounding as though it had been dragged out from deep inside of her. Then, he felt her break, internal muscles squeezing him as her climax hit hard. And he followed, not bothering to hold on any longer.

This was what he wanted. For the two of them to lose it together.

He gripped her hips, holding on to her tightly as he thrust into her hard, once, then twice, freezing as the wave overtook him too. He gritted his teeth, white lights flashing behind his eyes, the orgasm so intense he couldn't even breathe through it.

He wrapped his arms around her, desperate to feel every inch of bare skin he could against his. To feel those small, perfect breasts pressed tightly against his chest. She was breathing hard, her face still pressed against his neck, her entire body gone pliant in the aftermath of her release.

He wanted to stay like this the entire night. But, as sanity returned, he became aware that he was pressed up against the window, the door handle and armrest digging into his lower back, and that if he stayed like this much longer he was going to feel it for the next three days.

"I suppose I'd better let you go," he said, his arms still wrapped around her. He tilted her face up and lowered his head, kissing her, slowly, leisurely. Taking his time tasting every inch of her mouth.

She shivered. "Well, now I don't really want to go."

"I'm going to have to get back. And you have a big cake to bake tomorrow. And then you have to wrangle my teenager."

She laughed unsteadily, pushing away from him and digging for her clothes. "True."

He opened the car door and stepped outside, pulling his pants into place and taking the condom off as he did. He looked around, not really sure what he was going to do with the protection.

Then Alison's hand was sticking out of the car door,

a paper coffee cup in it. "This is empty, put it in here. I'll throw it away on my way in."

He took the cup from her, sticking the offending item inside and then putting the lid back on. "This is why adults don't do this," he said. "Unless they have to, I guess."

"It's kind of fun. I haven't done anything like this for a long time."

His stomach tightened, the moonlight catching her face, casting all that beauty in an otherworldly glow. "I'm not sure I've ever really done anything like this," he said, before he could modify the words.

"Well," she said, also getting out of the car, then trying to step into her jeans. "I can honestly say I've never done anything like this and had it feel this good." She braced herself, planting her hand on his chest as she wiggled into her pants. "Believe me when I tell you you were much, much better than the pimple-faced sixteen-year-old boys I used to take out to the woods back when I was in high school."

He laughed. "I take that as high praise."

"You should. You're the best I've ever had by a mile. In car, or in bed."

"You don't have to say that, I feel good enough that I don't need the extra ego boost."

"It's true. If my—if the last person I was with was better, I probably wouldn't have waited so long to jump back into the game."

He was curious, he couldn't help it. Even though he shouldn't be curious. And he absolutely shouldn't wonder about her past. Because that wasn't the point of this. They were all about the present. At least, they were supposed to be.

"Who was he?"

She was battling to get through her T-shirt in the dark. "Who?" she asked, her voice muffled.

"The last guy."

She pushed her head through the neckhole of the shirt, smoothing it down over her body. "Not really important."

"You say that. Which makes me think it is."

"Just… My ex."

"Ex-boyfriend?"

"Ex-husband."

The admission hung in the air between them, as thick as the mist that was starting to descend, lower and lower as the hour grew later. "I didn't know."

"Yeah. I know. It's fine." She took a deep breath. "It's better. This way. The divorce."

Divorce sucked, and it was complicated, and he knew better than anybody that being happy about it in some ways didn't mean you weren't hurt by it in others. "Divorce is hell," he said. "Kind of no matter what. At least the road that you had to be on to get there."

"I'm over it," she said. "It's been four years."

"For me too. I'm not sure I'm over it, though. I mean, I'm over her. But not necessarily everything I went through. Not necessarily all of the fallout that was left."

"It's different for you. Because of Violet. Because you'll always be connected to her through Violet. We didn't have any kids. I'm glad. Because when I cut ties with him, it was clean. No reason to ever go back. No connection remaining. Honestly, for me, divorce was only good."

"You weren't happy?"

She shook her head. "I couldn't even remember being

happy anymore. But. It's done. I don't think about it anymore, and I don't want you to think about it." Except she was lying, and he could tell. She absolutely did think about it, whatever she wanted him to believe.

Still, there was no point in pushing it. He never should have asked the question in the first place. Personal details were immaterial when it came to the two of them. Because all they were doing was having sex. That was it. Beginning and end of story.

"Suit yourself."

He turned and started to walk away. "Where are you going?" she asked.

"I'm going to walk back up to the house. You can't drive me. Then they'll hear the car engine and get suspicious. I'm just going to make it seem like I'm walking back down from working on the barn."

"Okay," she said, closing the passenger side door and walking around the back of the car to the other side. "I'll see you. Maybe after I drop Violet off tomorrow night."

"Sure."

He wanted to grab her and kiss her one more time. But, because he wanted to, he didn't. He needed to start fighting some of his urges around her, or things were going to get tangled up quickly. He was already giving in to his curiosity where she was concerned, and that had to stop.

He took a deep breath, inhaling the clean scent of the night air as he started to wander up the driveway again. But then he stopped. Waited until she got her car started. Until she got it into gear and began driving down the road again.

He had to make sure she was all right. That was just gentlemanly.

He watched until her taillights disappeared, another thing he told himself was just being a gentleman. And he certainly wasn't regretting that he wasn't with her. That he couldn't go back home with her. Get into bed with her and hold her all night. He'd had sex with her twice, but he'd never had the luxury of having her in bed. With all that soft space and hours between sunset and morning for them to explore each other.

Someday. Someday they would do that.

He shook his head and turned back toward the house, nothing but the sound of his boots crunching on the gravel to keep him company.

He didn't want to get too cocky, because historically that hadn't worked out well for him. But right at the moment, it seemed like things were going okay.

He looked up at the night sky, at the little patches of velvet blue and bright white stars that were fighting their way through the clouds.

The mountains and trees cast inky shapes against the gray. It certainly wasn't the wide-open space of Texas, but it was beginning to feel a little more like home.

Beginning to feel a little more like what he had hoped it might when he'd first decided to uproot Violet and himself and drive across the country.

Like their life. Like his life. One that wasn't so tied up in the past.

He shook his head. Whatever happened next, whatever happened in the future, right now was pretty good.

And it had been a long time since he had been able to say that.

CHAPTER THIRTEEN

IT WAS A beautiful day for a wedding. And if Alison wasn't such a marriage Scrooge she would very likely be thinking that this venue would be perfect for her own wedding.

But it wasn't her wedding. She was never going to have another wedding. Anyway, her first wedding hadn't been anywhere near this extravagant.

Really, it hadn't been much of anything at all. She and Jared had made it legal at the courthouse, and that was basically the beginning and end of it.

Well, unfortunately the end hadn't come until eight terrible years had passed. She frowned, putting the truck in Park and looking over at Violet. She had borrowed Lane's rig again to get the massive cake all the way to Grassroots without incident. She had feared that if she stuffed it into her tiny back seat it wouldn't hold up.

That brought her back to much better memories than her previous marriage. Like to what she had managed to accomplish in the back seat of her Camry just last night. She had managed to fold up a cowboy and fit him back there, and ride him like she was saving a horse.

Suddenly, the awkwardness inherent in the fact that she was fantasizing about the father of the girl sitting next to her made her throat tighten, and she cleared it, trying to get a handle on her brain. They had to get through this wedding without her having errant fantasies.

But she was thirty-two years old; it should be easy enough for her to control herself.

"It's pretty here," she said, "isn't it?" Because she was desperate to get her mind on something other than the night before.

She and Violet both got out of the truck and surveyed the scenery for a moment.

"Yeah," Violet said. "Weird though."

"How?" Alison asked.

"Oh, it's just…our ranch in Texas was in the middle of nowhere and all the trees and everything were totally different. The air smelled different."

"Do you miss it?" Alison asked. She'd never left a place before, so she didn't know what it was like to feel homesick like that.

"Sometimes," Violet said. "But sometimes…sometimes I'm glad because there's fewer bad memories."

"Violet…"

"We should do the cake," Violet said, rapidly switching the subject.

Alison decided to honor that.

She surveyed the scenery. Then, she paused when she saw a man walking past. "Excuse me?" She looked back at Violet. "We need help to move this behemoth. He'll do."

The guy, dressed in a dirty white T-shirt, white cowboy hat and battered jeans, turned toward them and started to walk in their direction.

"Can I help you, ma'am?"

Okay, he was pretty cute, and definitely charming, but being called ma'am didn't do a whole lot for her self-esteem. And whatever. He was probably in his early thirties so he had no call to *ma'am* her. "Maybe," she said. "We need help moving this giant cake into the tasting room."

"Normally I would volunteer myself, but I'm not real steady on my feet these days. I can get you a cart though."

"That will do."

"I'm Dane Parker," he said, extending his hand. "I work here, temporarily. Just helping my sister get back on her feet. She just went through a divorce."

"I was sorry to hear about that," Alison said.

Dane's smile turned sharp. "I wasn't."

"I can appreciate that. Nice to meet you," she said, reaching out and taking hold of his hand. It was rough and calloused, a lot like Cain's. A working man's hand.

"And you are?" he asked, turning his attention to Violet.

"Violet," she said, her cheeks turning noticeably pink.

Dane Parker smiled, a little too friendly for Alison's liking. "Very nice to meet you."

"Violet is working with me to get some job experience. Her first job. A summer job. Until she goes back to high school in the fall."

His smile barely slipped, but she saw the momentary shock, and noticed him take a step back. "That's very nice. I'm going to go get that cart for you. I could carry it, but I doubt you want to chance it."

"Yeah, lope away, cowboy," she muttered as she went to the back of the truck and opened the tailgate.

"He was cute," Violet commented, her tone muted.

"He's the kind of guy that's a little *too* cute," Alison returned.

"What's that supposed to mean?"

"The kind of guy that gets you in trouble." Alison cleared her throat. "Actually, you would get him in trouble at this point. He's way too old for you."

"I didn't mean I wanted to date him," Violet said, looking mildly horrified by the idea. "I meant that I appreciated looking at him."

Alison shook her head. "Sorry. I may be projecting. I made some pretty bad decisions when I was your age."

Violet frowned. "Really? You don't seem like the kind of person who makes bad decisions."

Alison tilted her head to the side. "How did you come to that conclusion?"

"I don't know. You own the bakery. And you're doing all this stuff. You just seem…responsible."

So responsible that she had done it with a guy in the back seat of her car last night. But she kept that to herself. "Well. I learned the hard way that being responsible for your own self is important. You can't hand that to anybody else, Violet. Because nobody is as invested in your future as you should be."

"Well…"

"Will this work?"

She turned to see Dane Parker standing there with exactly the kind of cart she needed. "Yes," she said. "It will more than work. Actually, I think we can take it from here. Thank you for the help."

This time, when he grinned, the full force of that smile—the one she had a feeling had brought stronger women than her to their knees—was directed at her.

"If you need anything else just let me know. It was nice to meet you."

"You too," she said.

"Well," Violet said when he was out of earshot, "he likes you."

"I'm up to my eyeballs in cake," she returned, sounding prim even to her own ears. "Sexy cowboys have to get in line."

Actually, that sexy cowboy would have to get in line behind the one she was currently sleeping with. Wow. For a moment there she had to stop and wonder whose life she was living. Not that she was in a hurry to jump into another man's bed. Quite the contrary. She was content to let the thing with Cain play out as long as it might.

No other man had elicited the kind of response in her that he had, not even other good-looking men. There was just something about him. Something that went beyond the physical.

Well, there was certainly plenty of physical. But if that was all she'd been after, any man would have done. Any good-looking man, that was.

But really, as cute as Dane Parker was, she had absolutely no inclination to grab him and drag him into the back seat of any vehicle at all.

"Is that a choice that you have to make? Cake or men?" Violet asked, helping Alison maneuver the cake out of the back of the truck and onto the cart.

It was a beautiful, simple design with four layers of lightly frosted white cake heavily laden with berries. She would add cream when she served it, and a few extra berries for good measure.

In spite of the fact that she was pretty cynical about

romance where she was concerned, she did like to watch other people find happiness. And she liked contributing to that happiness in any way she could. In this case, via a very lovely cake.

"No. I don't think you have to choose."

"I wondered," Violet said. "Because you know..." She trailed off. She cleared her throat, then started again. "Well, my mom didn't seem to be able to have a husband, or a kid and anything else. Like, she had to burn it all down to go do something else. So I wondered if that was an accepted truth that nobody tells you when you're in high school because it's depressing as fuck."

Alison's heart clenched tight. "No. That's not the case at all, Violet. I have a specific set of circumstances. I mean... I kind of got lost in a bad relationship and it's taken me some time to dig out of that. It's a good thing to be alone sometimes. But not after you already have a husband and a child. Please, don't think I'm putting my stamp of approval on what your mother did."

"Have you ever been married?"

Ugh. "Yes. But we had serious problems that... He... He wasn't a good man, Violet. And those are the kinds of decisions you make when you're really desperate for somebody to give you the kind of love that you think you're missing. In my case, it had to do with attention. And what I thought of as passion. My parents withheld their approval for me pretty much at all costs. So, I was looking for a man who was different than that. Who made me feel... I don't know. Something exciting."

"It's nice to have somebody pay attention to you when you feel like you're mostly ignored," Violet muttered.

"Right. But when you're reacting to feeling like

you've been wronged, whether you actually have been or not… You can make really, really bad choices."

"Is this a roundabout way of lecturing me because my dad told you about what happened?"

Alison froze, sucking her lower lip between her teeth. "Um. I… Why would he have talked to me?"

"Because he can't help himself? Because he has to get all up in my business all the time? I mean, I knew he would tell you. Because you see me, so he probably has you watching out to see if there's any shady characters hanging around me."

Alison grimaced. "Okay. He might have…said some things to me."

"Right," she said, suddenly going all brittle and distant.

"Don't be mad. I'm not making stuff up. And I told him that I wasn't going to report back to him. So, if you're worried about this being covert ops, it isn't. I promise. But I am going to say something if I think I should. And I'm just saying that sometimes we do things because we're reacting…"

She pushed the cart up into the tasting room, which was empty for now. Everyone was still at the ceremony, and wouldn't be filtering in until the reception.

"What did you do?"

Alison let out a frustrated sigh. "I slept with guys I shouldn't have. Then I married one that I really shouldn't have. And I let him treat me badly for a long time because I felt like I had gone too far to turn back. Because I was too stubborn to admit that I had made a bad choice when I had kind of grandly stormed away from everything, from all good decision-making, from my family. I'm just saying, don't make decisions just to make your parents mad. You can't make your life about getting back at people. It just backfires."

She glanced over at Violet, who was looking a little bit shocked.

"You wanted me to be less vague," Alison said. "So, that's kind of the situation."

"Well, I haven't done anything like that." Her face turned red. "I do like him though. The guy. I'm sure that my dad told you there was a guy."

"He might have mentioned it. But you have your whole life to get involved with guys. That's one reason I took a break to focus on myself. Because I spent so many years wrapped up in someone else, in a relationship, that I kind of forgot to figure out what I wanted to be. I think you can do both. I just... I couldn't. But you are strong, Violet. Definitely stronger than I was at your age. I think you're going to be okay."

"If I were stronger maybe I wouldn't feel so confused all the time. But I thought I knew what I wanted. I thought I knew how my life was going to go. I thought everything was secure. And then my mom left." Violet blinked. "She wasn't bad, Alison. That's what scares me. Because it's not like she neglected me all of my life. It isn't like she was evil. I can't even think of her as being evil now. I miss her. I shouldn't. What she did was wrong. To me and my dad. It's not like he hurt her or anything. He's not bad either. I get frustrated with him sometimes, but he's not bad."

Alison's chest felt so tight she could hardly breathe. "I can't pretend to understand why a mother would leave her daughter, Violet. I can't justify it. I do know that it had nothing to do with you."

"What if it is me?"

"It's not. You could be the worst, most awful little monster on the face of the planet, and unless there's something broken in your parents, they're going to stick with you. Thinking that it's you... There's no benefit to that. Trust me. Again, we'll use my marriage as exhibit A. I thought there was something wrong with me, and I thought it was magical that he paid any attention to me. I thought that having a man love me, no matter how broken that love was, no matter that it didn't look like any kind of love I had ever heard about or imagined, made me incredibly lucky. It made me want to stay, no matter what. Because my parents had convinced me that I was never going to be good enough.

"My mother got sick and I canceled all my plans to go to school to help take care of her. She still didn't think I did anything right. Until she died, she didn't think I did anything right. It hurt so much and I was... lost. My friends had left town, I'd given up on going to school. I was just...here. Profoundly unwanted by the only family member I had left. So, when Jared wanted me—even though his version of wanting could be so angry and jealous. Controlling.—I thought that I had to take that. It took me a long time to realize that it was my parents who were broken, it wasn't me. And it was Jared who saw that I was broken and picked up those pieces so that he could use them for his own ends. It wasn't me. It was never me."

She took a deep breath, perilously close to confessing much more than she wanted to. Not so much because she didn't want to confide in Violet, because she wanted this girl to understand. She didn't want her to make the same mistakes that Alison had. But she didn't want Cain to know the truth. It would ruin things. It would turn that hard, certain grip of his soft and gentle, and she didn't want that. She didn't want him to be careful. She didn't want him to look at her like she was a victim, not when he had been looking at her like she was a woman.

"How do you… How do you convince yourself of that?"

"Sometimes? You have to stop and do it every day. Sometimes, it gets heavy, and you're convinced that it must've been you, even if you went through a long period of time where you knew better. It's a process. And I think if you remember that it isn't just going to be finished, and that sliding back into believing those lies isn't a failure, you can really start to move on. But anytime someone has hurt you, mistreated you, especially someone you're supposed to trust… It's hard. I know it. But your dad loves you. So much. He was down at the bakery the morning after your incident desperate to talk to somebody about it."

The corner of Violet's mouth quirked upward. "My dad was desperate to talk?"

"He was. He's worried about you."

"He says that. But mostly he just gets mad at me, and then he goes to work on the ranch, or to work on the barn thing that he's remodeling."

A little kick of defensiveness rallied in Alison's chest. "He does that for you."

"I think he does it for him, but that was nice of you to say."

Violet had clearly misconstrued the reason behind Alison's statement. "No, I think he really does do it for you. I think he doesn't know what else to do. What else to do beyond going out and physically working at something. Because you're right, he doesn't strike me as a talker." Cain was a man of action, she had witnessed that firsthand. And she had no issue with that, since it was exactly what she was looking for. But Violet needed something else.

She had a feeling that he was getting there, that she had walked in on the beginning of him trying to connect with her last night. But it was going to take a long time for Violet to internalize any of it.

When it was your own parents, your own mother, who made you feel like you didn't deserve love, approval, and in Violet's case made you feel like you weren't worth sticking around for, it was hard to overcome. Alison knew, because she had waded through that swamp for years. She just hoped that she could help Violet avoid making the same kinds of ridiculous mistakes she had.

"We need to get in our positions," she said.

Violet nodded, rallying, helping Alison push the cart across the room and set the cake on the table. Then they stashed the cart behind the bar and took their positions. Alison gave Violet a quick tutorial on how to do the cream and the berries, so that service would go quickly.

The entire room was laid out beautifully, tables stationed throughout the rest of the interior, clear Christmas lights wrapped around the chandelier and the beams. The little pies and pastries she had brought over yesterday were distributed on one table, and pasta and other foods—provided by Lane—were on another.

Soon, people began to trickle in, filling their plates up first with food. Alison watched from her position, feeling a strange sort of aptness to the whole thing. Most of the town was there, part of the party, celebrating together. And she was just kind of separate. Set apart. It had been like that when she and Jared were married. Because she was the sad woman with the abusive husband that no one could quite bring themselves to make eye contact with.

And then afterward she had been the victim. The object of pity, a project that people had wanted to help. But it had been very difficult to find actual friends. Just another reason she prized Lane, Rebecca and Cassie so very much.

That they had brought her into the fold, and they hadn't treated her like damaged goods. That they were patient with her irritation when she felt like she couldn't talk about her past, and then with her reluctance to actually do it when the topic came up.

She hadn't realized how truly isolated she had become in her marriage until she had started forging connections with people again. Hadn't realized just how special it was, how essential it was, to have that network of people who cared for you. Who were there to help pick you up when you fell, or just sit down on the floor with you for a while if that was what you needed.

She looked over at Violet, and noticed that she had a wistful expression on her face. "Everything okay?" she asked.

"Yeah," Violet returned. "It's just kind of crazy to see everyone all dressed up. I mean, I don't really associate Copper Ridge with fancy events."

"Madison West is something of a town princess," Alison said, keeping her voice low. "The daughter of one of the richest men in town, though he's had a lot of controversy over the past couple of years. And her husband, Sam, is actually a famous artist."

Violet's eyebrows shot up. "An artist?"

"Yes. And blacksmith."

Violet snorted. "Okay. That's a little more what I would expect from Copper Ridge."

"It's a great place," Alison said, meaning it with every part of herself. "I could have left at any time, but I decided I wanted to stay. I've never regretted that."

"Yeah," Violet said. "I'm not sure I'll stay."

"Well, that's up to you. And it will be here waiting if you ever decide to come back."

"I haven't slept with anybody," Violet said, her voice hushed. "Just… Just so you know."

Alison felt something tighten at the base of her spine that reminded her vaguely of panic. "Okay," she said, shuffling a few plates around, trying to keep her hands busy. "That's… Probably good."

"I kind of would like to."

"Well…well, I mean you're sixteen and there's…a lot of time to do that."

"I guess."

She let out a long, slow breath. "Why do you want to? Because you want to know what it's like? Let me tell you that doesn't end very well. That ends after about five minutes and him having way more fun than you."

"I just… I mean, sure. But, it seems like it would be nice to be that close to somebody."

Alison shook her head. "Okay, this I have some experience with. You don't. You don't feel closer to him. You feel good for a minute, and then afterward sometimes you feel more alone than ever, because the thing that you just did was close—so close—to looking like a real connection, but then at the end of it he goes home, and so do you. And that hole inside of you just gets deeper."

Violet blinked and looked down at the cake. "Some-

times I just want to do something. Something big.
Something that will quiet everything down. Because
the inside of my brain is so loud, and sometimes it all
hurts so bad."

"Then make it something that's for you," Alison said.
"Not something that's also serving some random guy. If
you meet someone, and you love him… And frankly, are
more than ready to handle the potential consequences
of failed birth control, then those are good reasons. But
just wanting to fix something isn't. Because sex doesn't
fix anything. Usually, it just breaks it worse."

She tried very hard not to let her own words sink
down too deeply inside of her. It was fine advice for a
sixteen-year-old girl. Violet did not need to be having
sex. And was emotionally unequipped to handle the
fallout from that. Alison was not. She'd had a lot of experience, a lot of mistakes made that she had already
dealt with and sorted through, emotionally speaking.

She was thirty-two years old. She already knew that
sex wasn't going to fill any kind of emotional void. Plus,
Cain was good at sex. So, it wasn't some physical disappointment she was submitting herself to for a little
bit of attention.

She knew exactly what she wanted, and she was getting exactly that. She had no regrets. And she was going
to be fine. She wasn't a hypocrite, because she was a
grown-ass woman and Violet was a kid. A kid with a
wide-open daisy-field expectations when it came to boys
and being physical with them.

Alison had already run that particular gauntlet. She
had met disappointing, unsatisfying, underwhelming,
speedy, tiny, mouth-breather and bully. Basically Alison
and the Seven Douchebags. There was nothing she was

looking for that she hadn't already found. She wasn't looking for anything with Cain. She was just having. Experiencing.

Because she had the maturity level to deal with that. She did.

"You're going to be fine, Violet. It's hard, being sixteen. It's hard even for those perfect, sparkly-looking cheerleader girls with both parents and a house in a cul-de-sac. It's really hard for people like you and me. Who have already experienced the kind of pain adults don't handle well. I mean, you can see how much your mom leaving hurts your dad. Why would it hurt you less? It won't. Of course it's going to hurt you even more. So all of that stuff that you're feeling… You're not being dramatic. You're not making things up. It's real. It's real and it hurts and it was never going to do anything less. But sometimes, you can't make feelings go away. Not really. All you can do is hold them back for a minute. With alcohol, with sex, but those don't fix anything. The only way you can get rid of the feelings is to feel them. Really feel them. And then try to walk forward."

"Does it ever quit hurting?"

Alison thought about that. Really hard. Because she had never been abandoned by her parents. They had just been emotionally distant. And leaving an abusive marriage wasn't really the same thing. She had been the one to walk both times. They had been very painful situations she was walking away from, but she had stayed until she was good and ready to deal with the fallout. That was different than having somebody wrench themselves from your life.

"It changes," she said, trying to be as honest as possible. She didn't want to tell her that it was going to be okay. That it would never hurt. Because what would happen if Violet reached the end of the decade without her mother and it still hurt? And she was afraid it always would? Was afraid that she was broken in some way. "It changes, and eventually it becomes bearable. Eventually, it becomes part of who you are. I think that sounds scary, but it isn't. These hard things, they can make you stronger if you let them. You can use them as a road map to guide you. To the place that you do want to be, by reminding you what kind of person you don't want to be."

That was certainly true for her. If Alison knew anything it was that she didn't want to go back to being the kind of person who could be with a man like Jared. Somehow, she had contorted and twisted and shrunk herself down to fit into that marriage, and when she had emerged she had been reduced. Lifeless and colorless. It had taken a long time to find that color. But she had. And now she was aware that was something she couldn't simply take for granted. Now she was aware that it wasn't a permanent part of her that could withstand any manner of abuse and indignity. She had to take care of herself. She had to prize her own happiness.

She figured there was probably a way to come to that conclusion without living in an abusive situation for nearly a decade, but that wasn't her story. That wasn't her experience. And all she could do was take that horror and try to use it for good.

"Well, I'm not going to abandon anybody." Violet put her hand on her chest. "Because it hurts."

"That's something." She reached out, putting her hand on Violet's shoulder. "It really is."

Then, the room erupted into applause, and both she

and Violet looked toward the entryway of the barn. And there they were, the bride and groom, huge smiles on their faces. Madison West looked absolutely perfect, her blond hair left loose and cascading around her shoulders, her formfitting lace wedding dress making her look like an edgy fairy-tale princess.

Then there was Sam, a surprise in a traditional tuxedo and black cowboy hat, looking rugged and absolutely taken with his bride.

Both she and Violet traded glances and shared a wistful smile. Alison had no idea why she felt wistful. She didn't want this. She didn't want a wedding. Didn't want a husband. Didn't even want a man who looked at her like she was the center of the universe. Because she knew that no matter how it started it could all go badly in the end.

She kept telling herself that, over and over again as her heart clutched tight watching Sam McCormack gaze lovingly at Madison.

She didn't want it. Because no matter how much the man may love her, eventually, she wouldn't be able to love herself. Some people just weren't meant for love or marriage.

She was one of them. She was better off alone.

CHAPTER FOURTEEN

"How did the wedding go?"

Cain had decided to bring Violet to work that morning, and it was only partly because he wanted to see Alison. He leaned over the counter, holding his cup of coffee from The Grind as he tried to make a decision about which pastry he wanted.

"Good," Alison said. "You know, even if she is a little bit difficult right now, Violet is a really good kid, Cain. You should be proud of her."

She reached across the counter, her fingertips brushing lightly against his knuckles, the gesture, casual enough, sending a sharp shock of heat all the way down to his groin. It was weird, trying to affect this casual manner with her in public. When they were talking about Violet, and he was just the father of one of her employees, rather than the man who had screwed her senseless in the back seat of her car the other night.

He hadn't had time to see her yesterday. The wedding had gone late and she had been busy. Then, by the time she had dropped Violet off at the house, he had seen the dark circles under her eyes that were like bruises punched there by someone's thumbs, and he had figured it was best to just let her go home.

She had looked a little relieved when he had said good-night, so he had figured in the end it had been

the right choice. And it shouldn't have been difficult for
him to spend one night without sex. Not after four years
without it. Now that he had been reminded of how good
it was, however, going without was a lot harder—no pun
intended—than it had been previously.

He had spent some time in the shower taking care
of business. He wasn't going to take some damned cold
shower and deny himself the release. No. He had too
many years of punishing himself. And honestly, the
world was punishing him enough. He might as well get
whatever pleasure he could from it.

"I'm glad you think so," he told Alison now. "Actually, it's really encouraging to have your insight into
that. Because half the time all I see is this angry kid
that I don't know how to handle. Mostly because I'm
angry too. How do you defuse somebody's anger when
you feel it for them? When you feel it for you? I haven't
figured that out yet."

This was perilously close to being soul-baring, and
all he and Alison were supposed to be doing was body-
baring. But again, those lines. Those blurry lines that
were starting to intersect. He didn't like it.

"I don't think it's a bad thing to be angry for her. It
probably helps. Though it might help her a little bit more
if she knew that's how you felt."

"She doesn't know?"

Alison hesitated. "What kind of food do you want?"

"What?"

"You're having a turnover. A marionberry turnover.
Go sit down. I'm going to bring it to you in a second."

He scowled but walked over to the tables, then he
paused for a moment. He deliberately selected the one

he'd made love to her on the other night. Mostly because he wanted to remind her.

When she made her way out from behind the counter, she stopped, a plate in hand. Her mouth flattened into a line and tilted slightly to the side, her eyes narrowing. He grinned.

He could practically feel the force of the breath she let out from across the room. So, he just leaned back in that chair, nice and comfortable, widening that smile.

"Are you twelve?" she asked, setting the plate of turnover in front of him and sitting across from him.

"No, ma'am. Which you know. As you are intimately acquainted with certain aspects of me."

She blushed and looked around the room. "Stop that."

"It's the ass crack of dawn and barely anybody is here."

"Your daughter is here. Cooking in the back room. And you're out here being indecent."

He had to laugh at that. "I know. What would she think if she knew? I mean, I remember being a teenager, and I certainly assumed that the days of indecency were long past for my parents. Though, my father was hell-bent on proving that wasn't the case by spreading his seed hither and yon with whatever woman he came across. He was done with that by the time I was sixteen though. Or, if he wasn't, he didn't claim any of those other kids."

Alison frowned. "I don't really know your family situation. I mean, a couple of things from Lane. You didn't grow up with your brothers."

"No. I'm the oldest. I grew up in Texas, spent summers here. Finn grew up in Washington, but not near Liam and Alex, who were mostly in Washington too.

That's where we all converged. At the Laughing Irish Ranch, our grandpa's ranch. He recently passed away."

"I knew that from Lane. I'm sorry to hear it," she said.

"He was a crusty old bastard, but he was a good man. Which is more than I can say for our father, who is mostly a horny old goat. Probably see him less than we see our grandfather. Who is dead, if you recall."

The corner of her mouth tilted upward, like she couldn't quite decide if she was supposed to smile about that.

"You can laugh," he said. "It's actually damned funny."

"Is it?"

"Kind of. I guess the Donnellys are destined to be left at one point or another. Some of us twice."

"I wouldn't say it was destiny. I would say it was bad luck to know more than one asshole."

"Some of us have bad luck, right?"

He watched her face closely. He could see the ghost of something—some deep emotion—flash in those golden eyes. She had been married, and divorced, she had confessed that the other night. So, even though she was reluctant to talk about it, he knew that she had been through something similar to him.

That whole till-death-do-them-part not panning out. The marriage just ending up done because someone decided to quit. And she said it was different for her, because she had done the leaving. Still, he didn't think it was ever easy.

Divorce sucked.

And if the divorce itself didn't suck, then every little thing that led you to that point did. Either way, you came out with a few scars. But they were talking about the two of them. They were supposed to be talking about Violet.

Here he had just been concerned about blurry lines and he had gone and sat at the table he had screwed her on. Clearly he had some issues with boundaries, whatever he told himself.

"I guess so," she replied finally, looking back behind her again, as if she was checking to see if there was anybody in the bakery who might find the two of them sitting together incriminating. He knew that Cassie at The Grind had been more than a little suspicious about the two of them associating with each other. At the time, there had been nothing happening between them. That was not the case now.

"You were telling me what a great kid my child is," he said, picking up the turnover on his plate and taking a bite.

It was perfect. Tart berries, flaky crust, encrusted with sugar on the outside to give it that little bit of sweetness on top of the sour. A hell of a lot like Alison herself.

"She is. But she's hurting, Cain. And I think she feels really alone in that. I don't want to violate her trust and, in fact, I promised her that I wouldn't. She kind of expects that I'm reporting back to you in some regard, because she isn't an idiot. She knows that being over legal drinking age is thicker than water, I guess. She's a kid, so of course if there was anything dangerous that she was involved in I would tell you. Because I want to protect her. But…she has a good head on her shoulders. We talked about a few things… Some kind of deep things, that I think she probably wouldn't be very comfortable saying to you. But if she just knew that you wanted to talk…"

"What did she say to you?"

"I can't… I can't tell you. Not really. Not in detail. If you want to know what's happening with Violet you're going to have to talk to her."

Irritation fired through him. "But she talked to you," he said. "You could just tell me."

"I could. But then she wouldn't trust me anymore. And you wouldn't be any closer to her, you would just be the NSA wiretapping her personal life. That's not the same. It's not the same as knowing somebody cares. And she needs that."

"I love her. More than my own fucking life. Everything that I've done over the course of the past couple of years has been for her. Everything. Right now, I'm working to make us a place to live, on top of working at the ranch. I brought her here so that we could start healing. So that we weren't living in this house full of ghosts. With both of us waiting for her mother to walk back through the door one day and say that she was an idiot, and that she was sorry. I couldn't put either of us through that anymore. I gave up everything that I had worked for for her."

"And I don't think she sees it that way. Have you said that to her?"

He leaned back in his chair, taking the two front legs up off the ground. "No. But I shouldn't have to."

"Why? Because she should recognize what you're doing perfectly with all the great and wizened maturity she has at sixteen? Because she should have to change the way that she feels appreciated, rather than you changing the way that you show it?"

Oh, that was just too damn close to being valid criticism. He didn't like it. It jabbed him right in the side.

"Just because you've spent a few hours with Violet doesn't mean you know her. And just because you've spent a couple of naked hours with me doesn't mean you know me."

"You asked me to do this, Cain. You wanted me to talk to her. Don't get mad now because I'm telling you something you don't want to hear."

"I wanted you to tell me if she was getting into any kind of trouble I needed to know about." He was digging in now, getting defensive. And he could feel himself doing it, even knew that it was maybe a little bit unreasonable. But he couldn't bring himself to care.

He was mad. Because apparently Alison spent two seconds in Violet's company, and Violet unloaded everything onto her. And he had… Well, he had nothing. He had nothing from her at all. That was unacceptable.

"Well, she is having trouble. She's having trouble with you. She doesn't know how to talk to you. She doesn't feel like you care about her. Don't you want to know that?"

He damn well didn't. Not from the woman he was sleeping with. Not from anybody, really. But most especially not from her. It was all that tangled up string. Those different lines they had running that were a serious problem.

"I'm going to go. I'm going to go work. To build something for myself and for my daughter, which is important, even if a sixteen-year-old who feels like she's not getting enough attention—because she's not the center of the world as she can see it twenty-four hours a day—can't see that. She is the center of my world, that's what's infuriating about this. Everything I do is for her."

He stood, shoving the rest of the turnover into his

mouth, and walked out of the bakery. He started to walk down the street, headed toward where his truck was parked, when he heard footsteps angrily stomping behind him on the pavement. He turned to see Alison coming after him, her cheeks red.

"She can't see it," Alison said. "She can't. It doesn't matter what you think she should see, she can't. Maybe my parents did love me, Cain. But I never thought they did. And it led me to a really bad place. I made a complete mess of my life because the people who were supposed to love me couldn't show me that they did. You're better than they are, you are. But Violet has been through more than I had at that point. Even if it doesn't feel intuitive to you, even if it's hard, you need to drop some of this brick wall you've built up in front of yourself. Because it isn't her fault that your father left you, it isn't her fault that you've learned to protect yourself because people have abandoned you in the past. None of this is her fault."

"You don't think I know that?" he growled, advancing on her. "I've never blamed her. Not for one second. I blame myself, if anything. So now I'm trying to fix it."

"Is this how you tried to fix your marriage too?" The question was hushed, but it hit him with the force of a fist to his gut.

"You don't have the right to comment on my marriage," he said through gritted teeth.

"Why not? You just build fences around everything and nobody has the right to remark on it, because it hurts you? Honestly, Cain, I don't think you know how to talk to anybody. I think you keep everybody at a distance, including your daughter. I assume you did the same thing to your ex-wife."

"It figures that you would take her side without even ever having met her."

He turned away from her again, stalking around the corner, and he could sense Alison following behind. "What's that supposed to mean?"

"By your own admission," he said, stopping and turning to face her. "You ended your marriage. You left your husband. Why was that? He didn't make you feel loved while he went and worked his knuckles bloody for you? Is that what it is?"

She drew back like he'd hit her, her eyes full of anger, and pain, and he regretted his words almost immediately. But he was mad. Because here she was passing commentary on the woman who had abandoned him and his child as if he had been in full control of something that could have fixed it. There was no fixing somebody who was awful enough to abandon her own daughter. There just wasn't. There was nothing he could have done. Even if he could have been better, he couldn't have stopped her.

"If she had only left me, Alison, we would be having an entirely different conversation. But she didn't. She left Violet too. She was broken. I could've been the best damn husband in the entire world and I couldn't have stopped her from doing that. If it had just been me… If she had stayed in the area, if she had told us where she was going, if she had showed up to court to work out a custody agreement rather than me ending up with full custody by default… Then maybe I would say that you're right. But she didn't. And so you're not."

Alison wrapped her arms around herself. "The way I see it, it's two separate issues. Your ex-wife was definitely messed up. And what she did was wrong. But that doesn't mean you shouldn't try to identify some of the things that went badly in your relationship and make sure you're not repeating them. It doesn't mean you don't have to change."

"Right. So your husband had to change?"

She took a step toward him, her expression furious. "I had to change. I had to change everything that I was. To get up enough courage to leave him, to start over, I had to change everything about myself. I have spent the past four years painstakingly changing everything that I became when I was married to that monster. You don't know my marriage. You don't know my life. If I were you I would tread really carefully around that subject, Cain."

He wanted her to tell him. He wanted her to tell him so that he could know what they were fighting about. He wanted to be able to have that conversation, but it was futile, and it was fruitless.

Because they weren't supposed to get to know each other. They were supposed to talk about Violet. They were supposed to have sex. Those things didn't need to wind together, they didn't need to have a confessional between the two of them. Talking about past sins and failures. They weren't supposed to change each other. They were just supposed to soothe each other, give each other a little release. That was it. He shouldn't want to know. And yet he did.

He wanted to keep having this fight, and he couldn't for the life of him figure out why. Except that he felt like she was close to scratching at the truth, to knocking down that brick wall she had accused him of building up between himself and the world, and he found he was curious to see what was behind it.

But he wasn't going to. He was going to walk away.

"We just won't talk about that subject, then," he said. "Because that's not what this was supposed to be about. I appreciate you talking to Violet." He wasn't sure he did. "But I think it's something I'm going to have to work out for myself."

"And us?"

He paused. "Maybe not the best idea. Because it's messy. It wasn't supposed to be messy. It was supposed to be good. Neither of us needs complications."

She shook her head. "Good point. I'm way too busy for complications."

"Yeah, well. Me too. I have enough drama and fighting in my life without adding it here."

Her cheeks darkened with rage. "This is hardly drama. I was trying to have a conversation with you. Don't make it about me being hysterical. I've had enough of those accusations to last me a lifetime." He knew that they were talking about her first marriage again. Something in him felt hungry. When she brought it up, when she skirted around the edges of that particular topic, he felt hollow. Starving for a little bit more of her.

That was a new feeling. One he couldn't say he had ever experienced before.

With Kathleen, the only thing he had been hungry for was her body. And it had resulted in a connection that had been a lasting one. Because they'd had Violet. And from there they had tried to make a marriage.

He paused there for a moment, looking at Alison. He had never really wanted to know everything about Kathleen. They had known each other, sure. They had been married for thirteen years. But he didn't think they had ever screamed at each other on the street. Not like this. He had never wanted to get to the bottom of what a fight was really about. Not like this.

Thirteen years and he had never once yelled at her. She had never yelled at him. No, it had been a whole lot of quiet resentment that both of them had let brew because neither of them had wanted to examine it. Least of all him.

That was… It was unsettling to realize he had now experienced something more with a woman he had been involved with for only about a week than he had with the woman he had pledged to stay with forever. The woman he had spent more than a decade with.

What had he done with Kathleen? He had walked on eggshells around her while she had seemed to tiptoe on glass, and then he had gone out to the ranch to work. Work himself until he was exhausted and there was no question about them having a conversation. In the end, no question about them having sex because both of them were too tired.

But they made themselves too tired. They both had.

It was bleak. Just the memory was bleak. And so much harsher in hindsight than it had been in reality. Time and distance away from that kind of existence had made it look exactly like what it was. Something that nobody would willingly endure if they had a choice. Well, he supposed that Kathleen had had a choice. To just walk away completely. To make a clean break.

Not spending the next few years arguing over custody. She had opted to not see him at all.

Standing on the street, yet again, he felt like he was looking down at a stranger, rather than comfortably occupying the body he had inhabited for the past thirty-eight years. A stranger that he could see clearly, and without bias. A man who had been married without really being married. Sure, he had kept his vows, had never even thought about straying, but he had been no manner of husband. Not really. He hadn't been plugged in, hadn't been connected.

It took two people to create that atmosphere, and he knew it. But his part in it had been very real. And that had all been covered up by blame. The blame on Kathleen for leaving, the blame on himself for being so terrible she'd had to leave. But the truth was actually much more insidious than that. It wasn't about the way he was with her. It was about the way he was.

"I have to go," he said.

"Okay."

"I think Lane is picking Violet up from work."

He would make sure that she was.

Alison wrapped her arms around herself. "Okay." She looked miserable, small and devastated, and he hated himself. But he didn't know what else to do. Or maybe he did and he just wasn't ready to do it.

"Great." He tipped his hat and turned back toward his truck, jerking open the door and getting inside, gritting his teeth as he jammed the key into the ignition and started the engine.

But nothing was great. Not about this, not about anything. He felt like he had missed an opportunity back there, but he wasn't sure he wanted to go back and claim it. Wasn't sure it was even possible.

So he just drove away. And when he got to the ranch, he started work like nothing had happened. The only thing that was different was that he recognized the pattern. That he felt himself walking a well-worn track, even though he was in Oregon instead of Texas.

Working instead of talking. Walking away instead of saying all the things that should be said, even if they were mean and unfair. Even if they made waves.

There had been waves in his marriage—they had just been beneath the surface. And part of him had been convinced that as long as they didn't grow into massive swells that everyone could see, they wouldn't do any damage. But that foundation had been cracked beyond repair without shouting in the street.

Now this conversation with Alison might have put a crack in him. And he'd be damned if he had any idea how to fix it.

CHAPTER FIFTEEN

ALISON WAS FURIOUS. She was furious the entire rest of the day, all through baking, all through serving customers, all through doing everything that had given her joy for the last four years. Stupid Cain Donnelly had ruined her joy. Asshole.

Of course, she supposed that wasn't really fair. She was one who had taken off after him down the street like an enraged bat winging her way out of hell. She was the one who had pressed things. And she supposed that she shouldn't really be surprised that in the end he had gotten nasty with her, because she had gotten nasty with him.

She had felt angry and raw over what he had said about her marriage. Because it hit perilously close to the bone. To things that had been said to her in those initial years of mistreatment. When people had asked her what she could be doing to make her home a more peaceful place. What she had done to make her husband angry.

Her own father had asked her that once, what she was doing to make Jared so upset. Because of course, it had to be her fault in some way. She hadn't spoken to him again after that.

From her father's point of view Alison had always been trouble. She had certainly made her parents angry often enough, though they hadn't demonstrated it with fists, but with cold silence.

His assertion that perhaps she had been inflexible, that perhaps she had been the one who had needed to change, while expecting him to make all the changes, had come from him knowing absolutely nothing about the situation. But still, it was so close to being an echo of all those old, terrible things that it was gnawing at her.

More than that, her blood was still humming with the fight. She wanted to go back at him. Wanted to find him again and scream at him. There had been something cathartic about it. Something freeing.

To get angry. To feel angry. And to expend all of it all over this big strong man without any fear of him. Yes, his words had hurt, yes they had struck in tender places, but he hadn't frightened her.

She had been able to speak her mind at him, and God knew that she had about a million *more* things on her mind that she wanted to subject him to.

Seething, she grabbed a rag and began to wipe down the counter where it was already pristine and clean. She hadn't been so mad in a long time. She didn't know what it was about Cain Donnelly that seemed to call up the extremes in her emotions. In her body. Extreme need, extreme rage.

She threw the towel down into the milk crate beneath the counter that housed all of the dirty linen. Then she paced, each turn sharper than the last. She covered the small space back behind the register.

No. She wasn't done with him. She was not done letting Cain Donnelly have a piece of her mind. She was going to give him more. Several pieces. She wasn't going to let all those things he had said stand. Wasn't going to let him deflect all his own crap and make it about her.

She didn't start coming up with justifications for her decision to confront him until she was halfway to her car.

It was for Violet, of course. Because he had a relationship with his child that could still be salvaged, and she was now invested in that. Because Violet had made her a confidante, and she wanted to honor that.

It certainly wasn't just because Cain had made her really mad and now she wanted to go be even madder. No. That would be petulant.

About halfway to the Donnelly ranch, she wondered if it was so bad if she was being petulant. If she didn't deserve a few moments of petulance out of so many years of reason, out of so many years of hiding.

And by the time she was driving up the winding dirt driveway and pulling up in front of the impressive log home, she had fully decided that it didn't actually matter why she was there to yell at Cain, as long as she did. Because he deserved it. Bottom line, he was infuriating, and enraging, and she was going to let him know.

Alex, the youngest of the Donnelly brothers, was walking across the driveway area when she pulled in. She threw her car in Park and got out. "Where's your dumbass brother?" she asked, not bothering to modify her tone. She wasn't going to modify anything.

"I have three of them, you're going to have to be more specific," Alex said, crossing his muscular arms over his broad chest. The only thing she knew about him was that he was younger, and that he had been in the military. His hair was still cropped close to his head, and he certainly had the build of a man who engaged in a lot of physical labor. She should have chosen him to hook up with. He seemed easier. Easier in every way. Cain was tricky. But, sadly, Cain was also the only one she wanted.

"Cain. I need to talk to Cain."

"I should have known you were here to see that particular dumbass."

She didn't bother to ask him why he might have thought that. It was because of Violet, or because he suspected something was going on between the two of them. Her anger was making her reckless, and that in itself was a gift. Because recklessness was something that she hadn't been able to afford for a very long time.

"Yes. That particular dumbass."

"Last I saw him he was headed out to the barn house. The place he's working on for him and Violet. It's just up that dirt trail there. You can walk or drive if you want."

"I'll walk," she said, "thanks." She curled her fingers tightly around her keys, squeezing her hand until the metal dug into her palm. She took long strides up the dirt path, not caring that the dust was starting to cover her black shoes as she walked. Then she saw the old building, simple and unpainted on the outside. Cain's truck was parked in front of it, a bunch of lumber sticking out of its bed.

She walked right up to the truck, cocked her foot back and kicked the tire. "Oh, mother..." She swore profusely, grabbing hold of her toe. Well, now her anger had hurt her, which, had she been in a more reasonable frame of mind, she might have taken as an omen to go ahead and settle down.

She was not going to take it as an omen. No. She wanted her rage, dammit. Sore toe or not.

She stormed into the barn then, only to see Cain there working, shirtless, his drill poised halfway up the wall, every muscle in his body tense and on glorious display. He was angled just slightly to the side, giving her an incredible view of both his well-defined back and his washboard abs.

He was a work of art. An infuriating work of art, but a work of art nonetheless. And, even through the haze of her anger, she could appreciate that.

"I'm not finished with you," she said, kicking an empty bucket off to the side to punctuate the sentence.

He turned, not even having the decency to look startled. "Hello to you too."

"You don't know my life, Cain Donnelly. You have no idea what I've been through, and trying to make commentary on it in order to throw the focus off yourself was a cheap move. It was a coward's move. I thought you were better than that. I thought you were a jackass, but I didn't think you were afraid."

"Oh, is this what we're doing now?" He crossed his arms, still holding on to the drill; for some reason all of that was just really hot. Sweat beaded on his face, on his chest, his stance aggressive and masculine. He was holding a freaking power tool.

"Fighting? Yes."

"Well, have at it. Scream at me. It's everyone's favorite pastime."

"Don't play the martyr. It doesn't suit you. Your shoulders are far too broad for me to believe you're being crushed beneath the weight of all the dissatisfied women in your life." She took a step toward him. "I don't believe you're being crushed. I *do* believe that you have your head up your ass."

"Oh, that's right, you were going to tell me all about how I had my head up my ass out there on the street."

"That's right. I was. Before you ran away."

"There's a big difference between running away and deciding you don't want to have a conversation with someone who doesn't know shit, honey. Trust me."

"Right. That's pretty rich coming from you after you made an active attempt to tell me everything you knew about what kind of wife I was. And all the blame that I put on my poor husband. Because of course, I can't actually be making a valid point about the fact that you don't like to talk about anything. No, it has to be the fact that I'm a bitter divorcée. But that's just lazy. It's lazy, and it's crap, Cain."

He held his arms wide, the drill still in his hand and she was momentarily distracted by all that gorgeous, exposed masculinity. By the way his pants rode low on his lean hips, exposing those beautiful lines that served as an arrow down to the most masculine part of him. Those lines she just wanted to lick, even when he was being a jerk.

Actually, she kind of wanted to lick them more now that he was being a jerk. She didn't know what that was. Probably had something to do with the survival of the male species though. That they became slightly more lickable when they were being asses.

"You're doing the kind of work that you're comfortable with," she said. "You're out here pounding nails and whatever else, ignoring the fact that all you really need to do is sit down and have a conversation with your daughter about what's bothering her."

"Contrary to what you might believe I did try that. She told me that she blamed me for her mother leaving. That she was mad at me. So, I think that sums up her behavior."

"She's scared. She's scared because the rug that held her life in order has been ripped out from under her. And even though your intentions were good in leaving Texas, I think it was just more change for her. And she feels lonely. She feels like you don't understand her."

"What the hell am I supposed to do about that? She's a teenager. Being misunderstood is her natural state."

"You were mad at me that she confided in me, but you refuse to sit down and have a conversation with her. That isn't my fault. You need to figure out what you want. And then you need to figure out if you're willing to do the legwork to have it. But I can't do it for you."

"I don't want you to."

"Yes, you do. You just don't want to admit it."

"You are reaching," he said, taking another step toward her, dropping the drill onto the floor. It made a loud noise, and she jumped, looking down at the offending item. "It's fine," he said. "I haven't put in the new flooring so it didn't damage anything."

She looked back up at him. "I didn't care about your stupid floors."

She didn't. Actually, she hadn't thought about his floors at all. She was too busy being surprised she hadn't been startled by that showing of temper. She really wasn't. It was fine. He was angry. She was angry. And it was this kind of wonderful, glorious controlled burn. They could feel everything, all the things, and it wasn't dangerous. To be around this man who didn't frighten her, and yet could be angry, could get right up in her face.

She knew that most men weren't abusers. She did.

And she wasn't holding Cain to a low standard just because Jared had been an asshole. No, that wasn't it at all. It was her lack of fear that she marveled at. That she gloried in. And the way that they were able to strike sparks off each other in this way that wasn't dangerous. That didn't end with her being a victim, her being shut down. He could yell, and she could yell right back. And they could disagree, and he could be angry, and he might be upset, but he wasn't so threatened that he had to shut her up with a fist to her face.

"You aren't any less upsetting than I am, you know," she said, taking a step toward him. "You ask for help, but you won't take it." She moved closer to him still, inhaling, taking in the scent of him. He smelled like sweat, skin and sex. Even though they weren't having sex, he smelled like sex to her. She had a feeling that as far as she was concerned, she would always associate sex with Cain. That he was now an integral part of her sexuality, woven deep into the fabric of her desire. And she was too exhilarated, too turned on to care. Even now, even angry, she was so damn turned on. "You won't budge. You refuse to see middle ground. That you can be both doing things wrong *and* not be completely at fault. But you pendulum swing wildly between being a martyr and being a stubborn dickhead who can't accept the fact that he might have done something imperfectly."

"That's what being a parent *is*," he said. "I have to have some level of confidence that I'm doing things right. I'm raising a human being. I have to be invulnerable to her, or how is she going to feel safe?"

"She's not five. She's sixteen. Be honest. Her seeing you vulnerable is better than her seeing you as an inflexible ass. What's the worst that could happen if you sit down and have a seriously honest conversation?"

"She keeps the conclusion that she already had. That it's my fault. And then in the end she's going to leave too."

Alison took a step back, her breath momentarily stolen by that. Because she couldn't pretend that that wasn't a serious concern, or a hard admission. Couldn't pretend that those fears wouldn't stop her in her tracks.

"I guess you just have to trust that she loves you enough that even if she is mad she's going to stay."

He shook his head. "She's not going to stay with me forever, that's the thing. But I would like her to come home and visit me. I would like her to be part of my life. She's everything I have in the world, Alison. Everything I've given my life for the past sixteen years. And when she's gone, what will I have left?"

She felt defused, and she didn't like it. "You'll make a new life," she said. "But she isn't going to be gone from your life completely. You'll always have her."

"Right. Who knew that being a parent was so much existential bullshit?"

"I didn't. But, as you pointed out before, I'm not a parent. I can only tell you that you have a great daughter. A great daughter who loves you. And who wants to connect with you. So do it, dammit. Cain, just do it. Don't hold yourself back like you did with your wife."

He frowned. "How do you know I did?"

"Because I've met you. Either your divorce changed you completely or you've always been a wall."

"You think I'm a wall?"

"I *know* you are. A brick one."

He reached out, wrapping his arm around her waist

and tugging her up against his body. "Because I'm hard?"

"We agreed that we weren't going to do this."

"I'm not doing anything." He reached up, pressing his thumb against her upper lip, tracing the outline of her mouth slowly, deliberately, while his green eyes burned into hers. "We're not doing anything."

"Right. Absolutely nothing." Her voice sounded unsteady, weak and whispery to her own ears. And she despised it. She preferred that angry woman that had charged in here, ready to take control of everything.

But she hadn't anticipated getting drawn back into this. Hadn't realized that all it would take was for him to touch her again and she would be lost. She probably should have, but she had considered herself immune to such things. That was before. BC, in fact. Before Cain.

She resisted that. The implication that he had changed her in some way after she had done so much work to take control of her life and herself. But she couldn't dispute it. Couldn't dispute the fact that he had gotten in her head, in her body, changed something fundamental inside of her that she wasn't sure she could ever change back.

You can. A physical affair is hardly going to change you irrevocably when eight years of abuse didn't. You managed to overcome that, you'll overcome this too.

"Then again, I've spent the past four years doing nothing. And this feels a lot different." He leaned in, his breath fanning over her cheekbone. She trembled. All the way down.

How many times had a man made her shake? So many. More times than she cared to count. More times than she cared to remember. But not with need. Cain took this feeling and twisted it. Turned it away from fear so that it was facing the bright, white light of desire. As far away from that sense of cold isolation and terror as she could possibly get.

He made her crave this. Made her enjoy it. This sense of being out of control. Of surrendering. Only a few weeks ago that would have been unfathomable. That she might turn and embrace this sensation that had once been her worst nightmare.

That had been about a man's hands on her body. This was about a man's hands on her body. One had been about strength causing pain. This was about strength giving pleasure. One was about control used to intimidate, this was about control wielded with expertise. The way that he could use that control to limit himself, to extend her pleasure.

One had been about taking. The other about giving.

So when she trembled for Cain it was an entirely different sort of shiver. One of anticipation instead of reluctance. One that made her want to fight to let all of that burning inside her shine outward so that he could see it too. Instead of one that enticed her to retreat deeper inside of herself. To hide. To disappear.

Both of these things were about a man's hands on her body. But the way those hands were used made all the difference in the world.

"Yes," she said, her voice a hushed whisper. Not because she was afraid to speak loudly, but because she didn't want to shatter the spell of intimacy that had woven its way around them. Didn't want to go back to shouting. She didn't want to minimize herself, to whisper to make him retreat. She wanted to make him come closer. "It is different."

He brushed her cheek with the backs of his knuckles, those rough workman's hands gentle, even as his calloused skin abraded hers.

She had a feeling that if she leaned in, if she kissed him, she would be allowing him to hide behind that wall of his. That she would be hiding behind one of her own. But she didn't know what to say. And she didn't even know if they should say more. If they should strip more barriers away for each other's sake. No, that wasn't what it was supposed to be. He didn't need to strip himself bare for her, not in an emotional sense. He needed to do that for the other people in his life.

She only needed him to strip off his clothes for her.

And returning the favor for him actually did strip down some of the walls inside her. Because doing so was a reclaiming. A reshaping. Remaking the way that she saw her own body and what it could be used for. What she could want. What she could have.

Limp. Pale. Hurt. She had been those things for so long. And on her own she had become strong. She had become bright and colorful. But this was her rediscovery of what it meant to feel good. Of what it meant to feel need. Of what it meant to have that need satisfied.

This wasn't the easy way out. Not for her. And as for him? Well, he wasn't supposed to be her problem. Yes, it had become complicated between them. Yes, there were feelings—feelings that had gotten pretty deep pretty quickly—when it came to seeing his relationship with his daughter work out. But in fairness to her that was wrapped up in the fact that she cared about Violet.

That's all it was. It had to be.

So she stretched up on her toes and she kissed him. And when the kiss ignited, when the conflagration between them exploded she welcomed it. She didn't care that his chest was slick with sweat, or that he smelled a little like the work he had been doing all day. No, she liked that. Gloried in his masculinity. It added to the rawness of it all. Highlighted their lack of control. Because this hadn't been planned. Neither of them had gone and gotten dressed up for a date.

There were no breath mints, he hadn't put on his Sunday best. She hadn't straightened her hair or put on fresh makeup or tried to make herself more acceptable for him. Because neither of them had to work to make this attraction flare up between them. No, they would have to work to make it go away. Would have to fight to tamp it down.

The knowledge of that... That he wanted her after a long day in the bakery left flour on her nose and her red hair frizzed out like spun sugar made it all the more potent.

She grabbed hold of either side of his face, poured everything she had into the kiss as he walked them back toward the wall and pressed her against it, the boards rough behind her, his hard body uncompromising and hot in front of her.

He claimed her mouth, kissed her neck, licked a slick trail across her collarbone and down between the valley of her breasts. Then he reached behind her, wrenching her shirt up over her head, leaving her in jeans and a bra. Then he slid his hands down her waist, to her hips, to her thighs, gripping her legs and lifting her up, encouraging her to lock her ankles around her body.

It opened her up to him, allowed him to press the hardened length of his arousal against that place where she was already wet with her desire for him. He rolled his hips forward and she gasped, holding on to his shoulders as tightly as she could, fingernails digging in.

He pressed his face against the side of her neck, growling explicit words against her skin, the vibrations reverberating inside of her. "I need you," he said, punctuating that statement with the scrape of his teeth against tender flesh.

"Yes," she said, because all she had inside her was simple agreement. One word. The rest was all feelings. Feelings, and sounds of pleasure, desire, need. But words? No. She could hardly remember her own name.

He reached down, undoing the button on her jeans, shoving them roughly down her legs. She wiggled, trying to help him out, only managing to get them just below her knees. Then, his arm wrapped low around her waist, he worked at the front of his own pants, managing to free himself from the confines of the denim.

Still holding on to her, he reached back and pulled his wallet out of his pocket, retrieving a condom. Then, in a feat of coordination that Alison herself knew she could have never managed, he managed to tear open the package and protect them both in one deft movement before nudging the fabric of her panties aside, the blunt head of his arousal pressing against her entrance.

She flexed her hips forward, encouraging him to go deep, to take her now. He gripped her chin with one hand, his arm still wrapped tightly around her, her body held up both by his strength and the wall behind her.

Then he kissed her, deep and dirty and exactly like she wanted him inside of her. But he didn't give her what she wanted. Instead, he teased her. Sliding in just a bit before pulling back out, and repeating it again.

She released her hold on his shoulders, sliding them

down his back, to his ass. She gripped him hard, pulling him firmly against her as she pushed her hips forward, allowing herself more of him than he had been willing to give. She gritted her teeth, her head falling back as pleasure erupted inside her, little sparks of light flashing behind her eyelids.

That was when his control snapped. He moved his hands, gripping her rear tightly as he bucked up all the way inside of her. So deep it was difficult to tell where he ended and she began. So deep it could never be called anything but a possession. That should bother her. It should scare her. Because she had been a man's possession. In the basest and most terrible way that could be applied. A thing to be hurt, a thing to be used. But this felt different. And she had no idea how it could.

Something about it took her breath away, the depths, the beauty of it. It made tears prick at the backs of her eyes, and she hated it. Hated it almost as much as she needed it. She couldn't turn away from it. Couldn't stop him, not now. Even as panic tumbled through her like an avalanche. Oh, not because she was afraid of him. Not because she thought he would misuse her. But because it wrenched the lid off an empty well inside of her she hadn't known existed. And now that she knew it was there she wanted it to be filled. With him. Forever.

Now that she knew it was there, she could only ache at the realization of the emptiness. The profound hollowness that extended so deep and wide inside her. And she couldn't escape the sense that he might be the only one that stood a chance at filling it.

She screwed her eyes shut tight. *No. You're supposed to fill it. You know better than this. You do.* She took a deep breath, steeling herself against all that emotion that was rolling around in her chest.

She tried to focus on the feeling. On the physical. The physical that had rocked her from the first moment she had seen him. That had awakened all those places in her body that had been asleep for so long. But she feared now he had awoken something else, and she had no idea how she would ever forget it was there now that she had become so aware of it. But she would try. Yes, she would try.

She focused on the strength of his grip, on the shift and bunch of his muscles beneath her fingertips. The short, sharp growl he made in her ear as he drew closer to his release. The hard, thick heat of him filling her with each and every thrust. And the way it drove her closer to release, the way it ratcheted up all the tension inside of her to near unbearable levels.

And when her release washed over her, it was easy to forget anything but that present moment. But the blinding, intense pleasure that lit every nerve ending inside of her on fire. He had turned her into a creature of need, and only he could satisfy his creation.

Later, that thought would disturb her. But right now, there was nothing but his hot skin beneath her palms, his hard muscles tensing beneath her touch. His big body spasming as he found his own release.

When they finished, there was no sound except the fractured breathing echoing in the half-constructed space. She realized then that anyone could have walked in at any time. Neither of them had even thought of locking up. She didn't even care. If she could go back and change it, she wouldn't. Because if either of them had thought with clarity even for a moment, they might not have ended up making love against a wall.

And she was really glad they had.

"So much for it being over," he said, his voice rough. He reached out, brushing his hand over her cheek, sifting his fingers through her hair. He didn't sound overly regretful. Which was good, because she wasn't either. Resigned. He sounded resigned. Not exactly overjoyed, but she would take it.

"I guess so," she said, letting herself lean against him for a moment. Letting herself take a deep breath, inhaling his masculine scent.

"We're breaking rules all over the place tonight. This was supposed to be done. And it was supposed to be simple. I wasn't supposed to wonder about you," he said, those green eyes looking into hers intently. "But I do. Tell me, Alison." A crease appeared in the center of his eyebrows, his gaze sharpening. "Tell me about your ex-husband."

CHAPTER SIXTEEN

CAIN REALIZED ALMOST immediately that he had made a mistake in issuing that command. But it didn't change the fact that he wanted answers. She had called her ex-husband a monster and he wanted the details. Felt compelled to seek them out. This was the first time he had ever wanted to push somebody for information about their life. It was one of those things that had always seemed like a tit-for-tat situation. He was not a tit-for-tat kind of guy.

But he wanted to understand her, this woman who had crashed into his life and reduced his control to rubble. Wanted to understand more about this woman that made him want things he had never wanted before. Who made him want to know things. She was the one who had created the need in him, after all. So, shouldn't she be the one to satisfy it?

"You don't want to talk about this right now," she said, twisting to the side, moving away from him and pulling her jeans back up into place.

She bent down, seeking out her T-shirt and tugging it on too quickly for his taste. He regretted that he hadn't gotten her completely naked this time. She had apologized for the padded bra last time they were together. But he honestly didn't care. He liked them bare. He liked the illusion beneath her clothes of slightly larger breasts too; really, he just liked them.

"Yeah," he said. "I'm pretty sure that I do want to talk about it, which is why I brought it up." He shifted his stance, pulling his own pants back into place. "I think you might be the one who doesn't want to talk about it, Alison. Which is okay, but don't tell me what I want."

"You just finished having sex with me up against the wall. And you want to talk about my ex-husband? The last man that I slept with?"

"We've spent an awful lot of time talking about my past."

"Because I've been trying to help you deal with the present problem. Jared has nothing to do with any of this."

"Jared." He tested the name out. Decided he didn't like it.

"Yes. And I don't like to talk about him."

"That doesn't mean you shouldn't."

"The entire point of all of this is that we don't know each other," Alison said. "Muddying the waters by... You know, getting to know each other, seems like a bad idea."

"Maybe it's a good thing. Because we aren't looking for permanent connection. Tell me whatever you want about him. You don't have to be fair, you don't have to be measured, and all that other stuff that we try to do when we talk to people about past relationships. You can tell me things that you haven't told anyone else." He shrugged. "Because in the end, it won't matter. It will be like you told your secrets to that wall you accused me of being."

She shook her head, pushing her fingers through her

hair and laughing a little bit. "No. Because it will change the way that you see me. And that's going to ruin what we have." She gestured widely between the space that separated them. "And I need to feel like a woman again, Cain. I need it so badly. You have no idea what being with you, without brakes, without you acting like I need to be coddled, means to me."

"So tell me what it means to you," he said, crossing his arms and leaning back against the wall. He wanted to go to her, wanted to comfort her. But, considering he was pushing the communication thing, he figured he should maybe hold off on the physical contact.

It was all a little bit much. All a little close to relationship stuff.

"Do you know the worst part about living in a small town?" She turned to face him, forcing her lips to turn upward. "I'm going to tell you. Everybody knows who you are and what happened to you without you telling them. Because somebody has. Especially if you have an interesting backstory." She shook her head. "They know their own version anyway. And they have their own opinions on where you were wrong, and where you were right."

"I imagine that gets claustrophobic after a while. But I suppose if it's unbearable you could always leave." She hadn't. That much was obvious. It made him wonder why.

She didn't leave him in suspense. "Yes. But, then… You don't get a chance to change the story."

"And that's what you're doing. You're changing your story."

She crossed her arms, holding her midsection tightly, as if she was afraid she was going to fly apart. "Yes. Because I would rather be Alison Davis, owner of Pie in the Sky, supporter of women, good friend, good neighbor, than Alison Davis, beaten wife." She looked away from him, her throat working, her cheeks pale. "And I never wanted to be that to you." Then, she turned to face him again, her eyes shining bright. "But now I will be. He abused me. My husband abused me."

Those words made Cain feel hollowed-out, like she had reached inside of him and pulled out something essential, but for the life of him he couldn't figure out what it might have been. Not his heart, because it was still beating in his chest, raging in fact.

"What do you... How?" That was probably the worst question to possibly ask. How had he abused her? But he wanted to know. He had to know. Mostly because he felt murderous, and if he was going to kill a man he needed to know exactly what his crimes were.

Alison closed her eyes. "I don't like talking about this." But then her eyes fluttered open and she took a deep breath and continued. "He seemed fine at first. Of course he did. And I was...desperate to have somebody in my life permanently. To have somebody that wanted me. My parents... I was such a disappointment to them. And because I knew I could never measure up I did my damnedest to be an even bigger disappointment, so that I could at least get some attention. But it was all just quiet disapproval. Cutting remarks that seemed small, but it didn't take long for them to start burning all over. Whatever. I guess that's just an excuse now. For why I was able to be fooled. For why I married him so quickly." She frowned. "And why I stayed."

"You don't have to justify a quick marriage to me," he said. "Violet's mother... It wasn't like we had some epic courtship and decided we wanted to be together for the rest of our lives. She got pregnant. So we got married. Because it seemed like the right thing to do. Because it was something my father didn't do. And I was going to be there for my kid. There. Don't feel stupid about marrying him quickly. I've been there and done that."

"That's a much less pathetic reason than just wanting someone to say they love you, even if they don't act much like they do." She took a deep, shuddering breath, and he didn't press again. He didn't say anything else.

She was quiet for a few moments, then she continued. "It was all right for about a year. But things were stressful, and we never had any money. I got a job at the diner, and that helped. Still, he was working long hours at the mill and he was stressed. Stressed about finances, and it started with him saying awful things when he would get angry." He could tell that she was telling him a very well-rehearsed story, that this was something she had told other people before. That she'd found a way to somehow detach herself from this explanation of events so that she could get through it. Her tone had taken on a flat, emotionless quality. He didn't like it.

It was kind of scary. As though the Alison that he knew had exited her body completely, and left behind was a hollow, mechanical version.

"He started drinking more. The first night he hit me, I thought about leaving. If I had only left that night, Cain." Her voice broke slightly, and that was how he could tell she had departed from the narrative, at least just for a moment. "If I'd left that first time I don't think I ever would have come back. But I didn't. Because I loved him, and him hitting me once didn't make it go away. And then... After once turned into twice, after that turned into… Just being beaten. Worse than a dog. After that, it felt like if I left I would have endured all of that for nothing. If I just walked out, if it was that easy, then all of it was for nothing. All those years of my life for nothing. Then after that I just didn't care. You wouldn't know her, that woman."

She curled her fingers into fists, took a step away from him. "I hate her. She was so weak. She didn't even know how to smile anymore. I used to be friends with Sadie Garrett in high school. And when she came back to town almost five years ago she came into the diner and she didn't even recognize me because I looked so different. Not because I changed my hair or anything. Just because… At least back in high school I was rebellious. At least back then I had some spark of something. But by the time Sadie came back it was just gone. At a certain point Sheriff Garrett intervened—he had tried before, but I… I didn't press charges. But my husband came after me in public, at a town barbecue and…it pushed me to do something. I actually followed through. I pressed charges. I left."

"Then she wasn't weak," Cain said, his voice rough. "You shouldn't hate her so much. That woman that you were back then. She left. That's not weak, that's strong."

"I didn't feel strong. I felt terrible. Sometimes I missed him," she said. "You wanted to hear something that I hadn't told anyone else. Well, that's it. I can never admit that. Not to anybody. Because during the eight years I was married to him I forgot what my dreams were, I forgot who I was. I forgot that there could possibly be a future without him. Everything revolved around him. Around his moods, around his desires. It was all about him. And I didn't know how to be me anymore.

So, separating from that… It wasn't fun. I didn't like it. My life was just blank. It was nothing. And slowly, so slowly, it started to change. I quit the diner, I started working on getting the bakery open. I started helping other women like me. Women who are in that dark, terrible place where they're starting over, and they need to, but they don't like it yet."

She sighed heavily. "And now you're looking at me like you think I might break. This is why I didn't want you to know. Because I liked it when you backed me up against the wall in the pantry, because I like it when you touch me and it isn't gentle. I don't want you to start treating me like I'm made of glass because of this. I'm the same person, it's just that you know about what happened to me."

It had changed things though. He was only just beginning to process the implications of it all. Because he had been too shocked, too utterly blinded by rage and a bone-deep sorrow that shook him to his core. To know that this woman, this brilliant, strong woman had ever been made to feel pain, fear…

God help him, if he ever saw that ex-husband of hers he really might kill him.

He was only just now beginning to build a relationship with his brothers, but he wondered if they were the sort that would help him hide a body. Alex would. He was pretty confident in that.

She had also been concerned that it would make him see her differently. And she wasn't wrong. Because it was difficult for him to imagine the strong woman who had had no difficulty going toe-to-toe with him from the moment they'd met ever cowering in fear beneath somebody's fist.

He clenched his teeth, pressing his fist against his forehead, trying to stem the anger that was pouring through him.

"You want to know how I let it happen?" she asked, her voice small. "I can see that you're trying to figure it out."

"No. You didn't let anything happen."

"I stayed. I stayed for eight years."

"Don't blame yourself for that bullshit. Ever. There is never... My wife left me. She left me, she left my child. My daughter is hurting deeply because of that woman, and I would never raise a hand to her. Violet is a walking trauma for me, and I would never raise my hand to her. You know who hits when they're angry? Toddlers. Boys. No kind of man. Your ex-husband was no kind of man. I wouldn't raise my fist to a woman, Alison, but I swear to God if I ever met him he'd sure as hell see who I would raise my fist to. Possibly raise a shotgun too."

She nodded slowly. "I know he was wrong. I do. But I also know that everybody always wonders how I could have stayed for that long. Not what I did to make him hit me, though my father asked that once."

He swore. "Nothing. You didn't do anything."

"I know," she said again. "I really do. It's been four years, and I've come through an awful lot. That doesn't mean... I don't even know why I stayed, Cain. It's hard for me to figure out how it all happened that way. But in the end, I think it was just that slow breakdown that happened over the course of years, where I changed slowly, bit by bit, until I didn't realize how much I had lost. How much of me was gone."

He didn't know what to say, didn't know what the right words were to offer comfort. And that was when he realized comfort wasn't what she was looking for. She wasn't looking for anything from him. Not words, not validation of any kind. She had found that a long time ago, or she never would have been able to walk away like she had.

It didn't stop him from wanting to offer something all the same. But he had a feeling it wouldn't be well received. Anyway, talking to people about things wasn't his strong suit. Punching out the ex-husband, now that he could do. Building her something, fixing something, he could do that. But this stuff, standing here, when he had nothing in his hands, nothing to give, nothing to fix, he didn't have a damn clue what to do in this kind of situation.

He knew it wouldn't help. He knew she might not like it, but even so, he took a step toward her and reached out, pressing his thumb against that little dent in her cheek just beside the corner of her lips. "You look like you're all here to me."

Her forehead crumpled slightly, her eyes looking shiny. Then she tightened her lips and blinked, her expression going smooth again. "Thank you. It's taken a long time to fill in all the holes, but I think I might finally be all here. That's why it's hard for me to explain all of this. Because all those rationalizations that I made back then seem so thin and transparent. I can see through that woman's excuses. The reasons that she gave herself for why she had to stay. But she couldn't." She paused for a moment, and he could see her struggling to get the next words out. "I couldn't. I couldn't see through the excuses back then. I was too lost in it. Too beaten down. Not just physically, emotionally. It's the emotional stuff that ultimately kills you. Because it's the reason you stay. The fear, the loss of yourself, the feeling that it doesn't matter what happens to you… That's the thing that gets you in the end."

"I'm glad you remembered," he said, his chest feeling uncomfortably tight. "I'm glad you remembered that you matter."

"I'm not sure I remembered it. More like I just discovered it for the first time. As far as being my own person, I'm behind a lot of other thirty-two-year-old women. But I'm figuring it out."

He laughed. "Remember when I met you, and I didn't think you were the owner of the bakery because you were too young? You're not behind."

"I'm definitely making up for lost time." She looked him up and down, her expression turning lascivious. It was definitely a conscious effort at transformation. She was done addressing the hard things. That was fine with him, because he wasn't really sure what to do with them. "A side effect of low self-esteem is having a lot of bad sex. You are very good sex, Cain. And that's sort of the last piece of myself I had to put back together."

"I guess that's all part of moving on, right?" Now he was thinking about himself. "Eventually you start wanting the things that you wanted before." He smiled. "Which, in my case is pretty simple stuff. Good food. And a naked woman. I'm not really sure I ever wanted to get married before Kathleen got pregnant. It just happened. But I'm damn sure I don't want to get married again."

"You're singing my song," she returned. "I like my life. I like my freedom. And, trust me, when you've had so much of your freedom taken from you you're not in a hurry to give it up again."

"I don't want to take any of your freedom. I just want a little bit of your time."

She smiled. "I think that's a song lyric."

"Is it? Well, it's true either way. We can have just this for a while. And if you ever think of something else you want to say…about anything. You can tell me. Because I'm sure as hell not going to tell anyone you know."

"Consequence-free sex and a consequence-free confessional?" She looked thoughtful. "That seems almost too good to be true."

In a way, he knew that it was. But he was more than willing to keep up the fiction. Things were already changing inside of him since the revelations she'd made about her past. He didn't want to change the way he felt because she had said she didn't want him to change the way he looked at her. But it was impossible. It was impossible to know that she had endured all of that and not regret some of the things he had done to her. The ways that he had approached her. Impossible not to want to modify the way he was with her moving forward. And abso-damn-lutely impossible not to look at her with a newfound respect.

"You're strong," he said again. "You really are." Maybe she did believe that now, but he didn't see any problem with saying it again.

"I'm a victim," she returned, the word flat. "It's hard to feel any pride about that."

"You were victimized," he said. "But then you took action. You changed your life. You changed your situation. You shouldn't define all of who you are by something that was done to you. Look at all the things you've done for yourself. What you are is strong. What you are is a survivor. You're Alison," he said simply, except it wasn't simple at all. She was so many things, contained in one person. "You make a mean pie, you help other people. You give a fantastic blow job."

That made her laugh. "I hope they put that on my gravestone."

"Hell, it's honest. I'm gonna remember all those things about you a hell of a lot more than I'm going to remember something some prick did to you because he was a weak, sad asshole."

"I like the way you think. Of course, I'm not sure that's the way it is with the rest of the town. But that's why I stayed. Well, there are a few reasons. But that's one of them. I didn't want him to have the final say on how people remembered me. And if I had slunk out of town after the Garretts' Fourth of July barbecue years ago, after he came and got in my face in front of half the town… Then that's what they would remember. I'm trying to rewrite the story. Write a new ending."

"You're doing a damn fine job of it."

"Thank you. And, if I may say, I'm enjoying the chapter that you're adding. Though it's making my life story rated X, it's going to make it a much racier memoir."

Just that statement brought back a rush of memory that made his blood run hotter, faster. "That's a good thing, isn't it?"

"It is. It's a new wonderful experience to want to have sex with a guy just because I want him. And not because of anything else. A physical-only affair is basically the best thing that ever happened to me."

"I haven't been the best thing that happened to anybody in a long time. Maybe ever. I'll take it."

She smiled at him then, and he felt it resonate somewhere deeper inside of him. Maybe because he was so aware now of how hard-won those smiles were. Of how far a journey she had been on to get them back. Maybe just because they somehow felt more valuable. Because he understood them. Because he understood her.

That wasn't supposed to happen, but it had. He couldn't even bring himself to be sorry about it.

"I'm certainly enjoying you. I'll probably see you… Maybe not tomorrow. Violet is off. But maybe I'll see you in a couple of days?"

He wanted to say he'd see her tomorrow. He wanted to make it definitive. Wanted to separate the reasons that they were coming together even more from the situation with Violet, from convenience. Because this wasn't about convenience for him. Not anymore. It was just about Alison. He wanted her. Not some other woman. He couldn't pretend that he wanted her simply because she was the easiest to access either. Not now. Not with everything he knew about her. She was amazing. Incredible. Generous in ways that he knew had to cost her.

He wanted her. No one else.

But he wasn't going to say that.

"Yeah. Feel free to text me or call me. I'll just be here. Working."

"Well, I'll be at the bakery. Baking."

"Sounds good."

She nodded. "See you around, Cain."

Then she straightened, and turned and walked out of the barn. And Cain was left standing there, feeling once again like his life had changed completely, and not quite able to figure out how.

CHAPTER SEVENTEEN

IT WAS DIFFICULT to walk into girls' night with her head held high, considering that she felt she had last night's activities written all over her face.

But everything was all set up in Rebecca's store, the Trading Post. Wine, scones, some sort of phyllo dough-wrapped appetizer compliments of Lane, and Alison had brought the pie. There was no avoiding the place, there was no avoiding her friends.

And, really, she might as well broadcast it. Lane already knew, and if she hadn't gone and spilled the beans, Alison would be surprised. In Lane's position she might have, she had to admit. Because good, sex-centered gossip was very hard to pass up.

And in the end, she was going to tell them about it anyway. It was just that... She would kinda prefer to wait until everything had died down. Until the affair was over. Until she had done her moping over the loss of Cain—because no matter that she was doing her best to keep her feelings from becoming involved, she would mope in the end, because the loss of sex this good could only ever be tragic. Yeah, she would rather wait until then.

That, however, required a little bit more finesse, and a little bit more smoothness than she possessed. So instead, as soon as she walked through the door by way of greeting she said, "Yes, I had sex. Please issue questions one at a time."

Surprisingly, there were no questions asked. Instead, her three friends stared at her with their mouths wideopen.

"Really? You three are all up in my business when I don't want your input, and now that I've come in making proclamations you have nothing?"

"In fairness," Lane said, "it's a little bit of a surprising announcement."

"You knew already," she said. "And I don't believe for one second that you didn't tell."

Lane gasped—a little bit overdramatic in Alison's opinion. "I did not. I was going to allow you to tell everyone on your own. Which I suppose you just did."

"Stop acting wounded. If I hadn't announced it tonight, you would have done it in the next few hours."

Lane lifted a shoulder. "True."

"I've eliminated all the meaningful glances and winking and nodding before the grand confession. I have confessed. I am having a purely sexual relationship with Cain Donnelly. It is amazing."

Rebecca blinked. "Wow."

Cassie smiled. "Well-done."

"Yes. I thought so. And, the best part is I'm able to help him figure out some of the issues with his relationship with his daughter, and I get what I want too."

"That really does sound like a no-strings relationship," Lane said, her tone comically serious. "I think you're well on track to everything going completely smoothly and not developing feelings for him."

"I didn't say I don't have feelings for him," she returned. "He's a really nice guy. Also, you can't exactly feel…neutral about the guy that is putting you in a multi-orgasmic space. Warm and fuzzy feelings are certain to follow. That isn't the same as relationship feelings though."

"If you say so," Lane responded.

"I do."

"Would it be so bad to be in a relationship, Alison?" Rebecca asked gently. "I don't want to push you. I'm the last person who wants to push you. I know what it's like to feel…like it isn't going to happen to you. Like it can't. But Gage is the best thing that's ever happened to me. Kind of hilarious, since I spent a lot of years thinking that Gage was the worst thing that had ever happened to me. It's amazing what can happen when you let yourself heal."

Alison bristled at the lecture. "I'm healed," she insisted. "I'm really glad that for you healing took the form of forgiveness, and love eternal and all of that stuff. Really. But for me healing has meant learning to be comfortable with myself. Learning to be by myself. I'm happy to introduce sex into my life now, because celibacy was definitely getting old. But I'm not interested in sharing my independence. In giving anything of myself to somebody. And having to consult someone before I go out for the night, or figure out how to juggle someone else's schedule and mine. I just don't want to." She ignored the little tug of longing inside of her that was set off by those words. Mentally, she thought it all sounded inconvenient, but something inside of her responded emotionally, and she didn't know why that was. She didn't like it. So she wasn't going to acknowledge it. "Right now, love for me has to be all about loving myself."

There was an inauthenticity to that statement that had never been there before. She had said those words, those exact words to her friends in other conversations, and back then, she had believed them. Now, she wasn't so sure what that meant. If it was even true.

"Loving yourself can be awfully lonely," Cassie said, "though I support it in theory. I'm just not sure the loving yourself means having to be alone."

Alison forced a smile. "I have you guys. I'm not alone. You have no idea how much this friendship means to me." She swallowed hard. "I've been thinking a lot about the past lately. Mostly because of all of this stuff with Cain. Because you can't make a major change without…reflection and things. One of the reasons I think it was so easy for me to get lost in my marriage was that I didn't have anyone around me to talk to. I didn't have friends to remind me of what I was worth, when I had forgotten. I'm not alone. I have the three of you. And that has changed my life in ways that I don't even have words for." Suddenly, she felt emotional and precarious. Like she was standing on the edge of a cliff about to fall off. About to tumble into the sea and drown. "I'm just so thankful that you became my friends."

Lane reached out and wrapped her arm around Alison's shoulders. "And I'm glad that we've been able to do that for you. But don't forget that you've done a lot for us too. You really helped me deal with everything when I was processing the changes in my relationship with Finn."

"And threatened Gage with bodily harm when he first showed up in my life. At the time, that was very helpful," Rebecca said, nodding.

"I would most definitely mete out bodily harm on

anyone who tried to hurt one of you," she said, her tone fierce.

"We would do the same for you," Cassie said, "you know that. And none of us would ever encourage you to do something that we think wouldn't be good for you."

"I know that," Alison said. "But, seriously. Just be happy that I'm getting laid. I am. And stop matchmaking. The idea of a relationship is... It makes me feel claustrophobic. I didn't like that person that I used to be. The person that I am when I'm...in love or whatever."

Rebecca shook her head. "That wasn't love. I'm sorry, but it wasn't. I just... I know what it's like to feel kind of sour about it because somebody who was supposed to love you didn't do it right. But I think it's important to know that just because you call something love, doesn't mean it is. My mother left us, Alison. And I spent a long time feeling like I wasn't worthy of love because of the way my mother was able to leave me. But she was the broken one, not me."

Alison took a deep breath. "I understand what you're saying. And I appreciate it. It's just different for me. We're allowed to have different dreams, right? There isn't only one way to be happy. And I have the bakery. I have you guys. I have all of these women that come through that I get to help. Best of all, I have tons of distance from that time in my life that was so dark. I've changed. I'm a different person. I'm happy with that."

Again, she ignored the little stab of emotion in her chest.

Rebecca looked down. "I'm happy for you." Her friend looked back up, meeting her eyes. "So, it's good?"

Alison laughed. "That's the beauty of a physical-only relationship. If it wasn't good, I would be out."

"Good point," Lane said, her tone overly cheerful.

Alison could tell that her friends still wanted to argue the point about love. She appreciated it, she appreciated them. She also didn't expect them to understand. They'd certainly all had traumas in their lives. Cassie had been married once before Jake, so she specifically knew what it was like to try to move on after the dissolution of something that was supposed to be permanent. But while her marriage had ended badly... It hadn't been the same as what Alison had been through.

Her friends were wonderful. And she knew that they loved her, just like she loved them. But that didn't mean they were right about this. It didn't mean that they could identify with her specific situation. They were sympathetic, and as empathetic as they could be, but they didn't know what it was like to feel so cold, brittle and fragile.

To gather up the pieces of yourself that were left and walk away. To painstakingly rebuild everything you were piece by piece.

Only she did. And she would never, ever take the chance that she might have to go back and do it again. It wasn't Cain she didn't trust, or men in general. It was herself.

She didn't expect her friends to understand that either.

"I feel like we need to have some celebratory pie."

"Because you're having sex?" Rebecca asked.

Alison forced a smile. "No. I don't want to celebrate that tonight. I'll celebrate it later. With him. Right now, I want to celebrate us. Right now, I'm celebrating our friendship."

"Well," Lane said, "I'll eat pie to that."

HE WASN'T GOING to break down and call Alison. He was going to give her space, because she seemed to want space. And if she didn't want space, then she could close that gap herself. It didn't have to be up to him. Anyway, he was having quality time with his brothers. Since Lane was out with her friends, even Finn had joined them.

It had taken a lot of convincing to get Cain to go out with Violet still at home. But the fact of the matter was he couldn't hover over her all the time. He also couldn't lock her in her room, unfortunately. Since child services frowned on things like that.

He had asked her to stay at home. He had to hope that she did.

He took a sip of beer and looked around the room. The bar was filling up, people getting in line to ride the mechanical bull, more people milling around the dart-board and mixing alcohol with sharp, pointy things, which felt like it was maybe a bad idea. He figured, however, that a lot of people went out on Friday night for the express purpose of engaging in bad ideas.

He, on the other hand, enjoyed most sitting there and judging those bad ideas.

To each his own.

Finn, who had drawn the short straw and had been brooding about it all night, leaned back in his chair, water in hand. "I'm too sober for this," he said.

"Think of it this way," Liam said, looking completely unrepentant. "You'll be sober enough to make a move on your woman later."

"I have no problem making a move on my woman whatever the state of my inebriation," Finn said, looking angrily down into his glass. "I might at least trade this for a Coke."

"Things are getting wild over here now," Alex said, laughing.

"I'm surprised you weren't busy tonight," Finn said, leveling his gaze at Cain.

"You know," Cain said, "maybe I'll be the designated driver. Why don't you have a drink, Finn?"

"I'm good, actually," his brother responded. "But, I thought you might want to talk about your current situation."

Liam's eyebrows shot up. "You have a situation?"

"None of your business."

"We're supposed to be bonding," Alex said. "It's good for morale. That's something I learned in the military."

"You all sat around talking about girls in the military? That's some official morale-boosting exercise?"

Alex grinned. "No. But it sounded good."

"Fine," Cain said. "I have a situation. Are you happy?"

"Are you?" Finn said, arching a brow.

"I'm having sex, how could I not be?"

"How the hell," Liam said, rocking back in his chair, "are you having better luck with women than I am?"

"I don't know what to tell you," Cain responded. "Except maybe that women just like me better than they like you."

"Very much not likely," Liam said.

"Except, it seems like maybe they do."

Finn and Alex smirked at each other.

"Stop enjoying this," Liam said.

"I can't help it," Alex said. "It's just so great. Because you essentially admitted that you haven't had any play since you've been here."

"I didn't say that. I just said Cain seems to be having better luck than me."

Cain took a long sip of his beer. "Women like older men, Liam. They like men who know what they're doing."

"It's that redhead, right?" Alex asked. "Alison. Violet's boss."

Cain frowned. "Not your business."

He looked over at Finn who wasn't saying anything at all, but he had a feeling that his brother knew already, seeing as Lane almost certainly did.

"Definitely then," Alex said. "I saw her when she came by the house last night. She was looking for you. And she had some choice names for you too. Which means she's spent more than a little time in your presence. Because let me tell you, they were descriptive names, and they were accurate."

"Did any of them contain the words *big* or *thick*?" He couldn't help it. Something about being in the presence of his brothers regressed him all the way back to adolescence.

"Yes," Alex said, his tone serious. "And *dick*. And also *head*."

Liam snorted. "That does sound about right."

"I think it's great," Finn said. "It's good to find somebody you want to be with."

"It's not like you and Lane. You can stop looking at me like that."

"Hey," Finn said. "Whatever makes you happy."

"You seem so much less concerned with my well-being," Liam said.

"Because you're a jackass," Finn said.

Liam shrugged, then took a drink. "Fair enough."

"Where were you all day?" Cain asked Alex, happy to take the focus off himself.

"I told you, I have some business to take care of. Property that I've inherited."

"You know," Finn said. "Most men don't inherit one giant parcel of land. You happen to get two? How did that happen?"

"Everybody that I've ever loved has died? Oh, and they handily owned large parcels of land. So I guess it's not all bad?"

"Shit, man," Liam said. "I'm sorry."

"Don't be sorry," Alex said, lifting his beer to his lips. "Everybody that enlists understands there's a risk. It could have just as easily been me instead of Jason. It sucks, but there it is."

"Why did he leave everything to you?"

Alex hesitated. "It's complicated. His sister... He wanted to make sure his sister was taken care of. She pretty much would have been better off being left to the care of...anyone else."

"How old is his sister?" Liam asked, an expression of horror on his face. "Did he leave you a kid?"

Alex snorted out a laugh. "Worse. He left me a young twentysomething who's going to be awfully pissed he did. I'm going to have to figure out how to deal with that."

"All right, I officially feel more sorry for you than I do for Cain," Finn said. "Because now Cain is getting laid, and he doesn't have to deal with that mess."

"Wow," Cain said. "It feels good to move up in the world."

"You see why I don't feel sorry for you not being able

to drink," Alex said, directing the question at Finn. "Because I need to drink."

"Have you seen the sister yet?"

"I've met Clara before," Alex said. "But no. I haven't seen her since Jason's funeral." He shook his head. "Yeah, I don't think she's going to take to me owning everything very well. But, oh well. I'm here to make her happy. I'm going to keep her safe."

There was something haunted in Alex's eyes when he said that. And Cain could only figure that Alex must've felt that he failed in that objective where Jason was concerned.

"That sounds so fun," Finn said. "Women love being kept safe against their will."

Alex nearly growled. "I'm honoring the last wishes of my friend. And I'm going to do it no matter how mad it makes his sister." He took another sip of beer. "I just might avoid her for a little while longer first."

Cain laughed, because he couldn't help it. Because it was so rare that someone else's life seemed like a bigger mess than his. But, at the moment, Alex's certainly fit the bill.

Liam looked to the side, his gaze sharpening as his eyes connected with the back of a curvy blonde. She shook her head, leaning against the bar, her rear accentuated by the pose. A few weeks ago, Cain might have been affected by that, in the way that a man was affected by a beautiful woman. Not now though. Now, the only ass that appealed to him was Alison's—not a terribly romantic sentiment, maybe. But then, he supposed that his and Alison's relationship wasn't really about romance. So that was fair enough.

"Excuse me," Liam said, getting up from the table and walking over to the bar.

Finn, Alex and Cain exchanged glances, then they all watched their brother as he approached the woman.

"Bet you ten bucks he strikes out," Alex said.

"You're on," Finn said.

They watched as Liam sidled up to the woman, planting his hands firmly on the bar and turning to face her. Then, she turned to him, and Liam's face changed noticeably. Then went flat. But it was the woman who took three steps back, then abandoned the bar like she wasn't waiting for a drink. Walked straight out the door like she hadn't been there at all.

"Well, damn," Finn said.

Liam turned, rubbing his hand over his face, then looking toward the door. He hung out by the bar, rather than turning to the table right away.

"What the hell was that about?" Alex asked.

"I don't know what it was about," Finn said. "But I do know that was Sabrina Leighton. And I also know that the last time she saw Liam in here she ran out just as quickly."

Cain knew that Liam had spent his teenage years raising a lot of hell, so it stood to reason that there were some casualties that he'd left behind here in Copper Ridge. He had to wonder if Sabrina Leighton was one of them.

"Don't ask," Liam said, as he sat back down at the table.

For once, Cain could tell that his brother wasn't joking. Usually, Liam seemed to take everything pretty lightly, but clearly Sabrina Leighton wasn't one of those things.

It was easy for him to look at his brothers, so long estranged from him, as one-dimensional irritations. Well, that was his least kind way of looking at them. The best he'd seen them as was supportive while he'd worked to rebuild his life, worked to build something new.

He couldn't work the ranch without them. He needed them. But it was still easy to see them as something other than what they were. Which was most definitely men with their own issues, their own wounds.

Alex liked to pretend his didn't exist. Finn had hashed most of his out with the help of Lane when Cain and the rest of the guys had come into town after their grandfather had died. And Liam… Well, Liam was the hardest to get a read on.

And Cain had been so caught up in his own stuff that he hadn't really tried. But then, that was the story of his life, wasn't it?

He didn't ask other people what was happening. Because then they would ask him. He didn't know how to get close. Or maybe he didn't want to.

But this was his family. This was his chance. He couldn't run the ranch without them, and he was starting to think that he couldn't have made it through the past month without them either. Alex and Liam, for all that they were pains in the ass, had come right into that barn with him to get Violet, guns blazing.

"You know her," Cain said, not respecting his brother's boundary. Which was possibly the first time he had ever done that. Not because he was such a nice guy, but because of all that resisting of intimacy he'd spent his entire life doing.

"Obviously," Liam said.

"Old girlfriend?"

Liam treated him to a murderous glare. "Ancient history. Anyway, she was a kid last time I saw her."

"I bet you were a kid too."

He shrugged. "It doesn't matter. But, it does remind me why I've spent so long avoiding living in such damn small towns."

"Something about her still bothers you," Cain said.

"No. I bother her. And here I am, in Copper Ridge, so now she's tripping over me. I'm a jackass, Cain. But I'm not that bad. Just because I couldn't give someone something they wanted doesn't mean I want to be in their face hurting them later."

He took another drink, then glared at the bottle of beer. "I need something way harder than this."

Then he excused himself and went back to the bar again.

"Hey," Alex said. "You almost got Liam to share."

Cain laughed. "I suppose that's about as strange as getting me to share."

"Almost," Finn agreed.

"It didn't kill me," Cain continued. "So maybe it will be a new theme."

"I'm good," Alex said. "I don't need to have sharing hour. Not really."

"You're the one that was asking for details earlier."

"Right. But when I was asking it was because I wanted to hear dirty stuff."

Cain snorted. "Get your own sex life."

"I have two ranches instead. Hoo-fuckin-ray."

"You're the only guy I've ever met who's been pissed off about something like that," Finn said.

"I was in the military for more than a decade. I traveled light. This… Connections… Not really my thing."

"And family is kind of a new thing for all of us," Finn conceded.

Family wasn't really a new thing for Cain. Violet had made him and Kathleen a family sixteen years ago. And since then, things had broken apart, and been shoved back together in strange, mismatched ways. He had lost the wife, gained three brothers he had never really known before. Moved across the country. Met Alison. And something about Alison was changing him.

Yeah, things looked different now. But he wasn't sure that was a bad thing. For the first time, it all actually felt like it might be pretty damn good.

"To family," he said, raising his beer bottle.

Alex followed suit, clinking the bottles together. Finn just sat there and scowled. "I'm drinking water," he said. "I'm not toasting to anything."

CHAPTER EIGHTEEN

"I want to take you out."

Alison blinked rapidly as Cain leaned over the bakery counter, his hands clasped together, his green eyes intent on hers. It had been two days since she had seen him. They had missed each other yesterday, and with some extra work that had come up on the ranch, plus Violet being around, they hadn't managed to connect. But today, he had shown up at the bakery around closing time without texting or calling.

"Is that like... A threat? Are you admitting that you're an assassin? Because that actually connects some dots that weren't quite lining up before."

He laughed. "No. I mean I want to take you to dinner tonight. Unless you have plans. In which case, I suppose I could plan ahead, and stop trying to do the spontaneity thing. But in the past I have been accused of being not spontaneous. I'm trying to change some things."

She frowned. "Are you asking me on a date?" Frankly, the idea that he might be an assassin was less scary.

"Yeah."

"Cain... We talked about what this was." What world was this? Where she was the one having to tell this gorgeous man that it wasn't going to be anything but physical? Why would he want anything more with her? It didn't make any sense.

"I'm not changing the rules. I'm just adding something. You work hard, so do I. Don't we deserve the chance to go out? Plus, you told me yourself you're trying to rewrite your story. You want to change the way people around here see you. Let them see you with a man who wants to do nice things for you. Let them see you being treated the way I think you deserve to be treated."

She tucked her hair behind her ear, taking a step back, trying to ignore the ache in her feet that was centered squarely on her arches, from standing all day on the hard floors. "Are you going to tell Violet?"

He shook his head. "There's really nothing to tell her. Since we both know what this is." He didn't look away from her when he said that, and it made something uncomfortable twist in her stomach. "But if it gets back to her it's not the worst thing in the world. I would have to talk to her about something kind of uncomfortable... But somebody told me just a couple of days ago that I was going to have to be a little more honest with the people in my life. So."

"Really? Somebody told you that?" she asked, fully aware that he was referencing her own advice. "I don't think she's somebody you should listen to. I think she sounds crazy."

"Well, she might be. But she's my kind of crazy."

Would it be so bad to take this? To take this little bit of extra? Part of her thought that it might be. Part of her thought that it was probably a very bad idea to let herself crave anything beyond the physical satisfaction she had found with Cain. But he was so handsome, so tall, broad and gorgeous, and there was a part of her—a petty, small part of her—that was drawn to the idea of everybody in town seeing her wandering around with this sexy man.

Rewriting her story indeed.

"Sure," she said, starting to untie her apron. "Why not?"

"Not the most enthusiastic acceptance I've had to a date, but since it's been about sixteen years since I've been out on an actual date, I'll take it."

That actually helped her feel a little better about everything. Cain was trying to get back into dating, probably. He would want to date other women after her. So this was practice for him. She ignored the hard bite of jealousy that thought brought on.

Of course there would be other women after her. Because they weren't going to be together forever, and Cain was hardly going back to being celibate. Really, it was a waste of sexual prowess for the man not to have sex. His body was a public service. Or it could be if he used it accordingly.

And she had no right to feel possessive or angry about that.

There was nobody in the shop, so she turned the lights off and flipped the sign to Closed. She would take care of any details that needed finishing when she came back home. One of the perks to living right above the bakery.

"If you have anything you want to take care of I can help you with it," he said.

He really was a nice guy. A nice guy who was capable of being a bad boy when the situation called for it. The kind of man that it would be very easy for a woman to start having feelings for.

She swallowed hard. "No. I've got it. I am hungry though."

"Do you have a food preference?"

"I haven't been to Ace's new brewery yet."

"Well, that sounds like a pretty decent plan, then."

He held the door open for her, an act that made her stomach turn over again. The streets were mostly clear as they started down the sidewalk, the little shops on Main all closing early on Sunday.

The sky was a pretty peach color, low-hanging clouds starting to roll in over the sea, rimmed in gold, fading to a dusky color at the center. Part of her wanted to reach out and take hold of Cain's hand, because it seemed like a romantic thing to do. But she wasn't supposed to be having romance with him. She was supposed to be having orgasms.

What are you doing, then?

A very good question.

But she seemed to be intent on doing it, whether or not it was something she should be doing. She drifted slightly to the left, her fingers brushing Cain's, a thrill of excitement rushing through her. Just from the touch of his fingertips against hers. The way that she had reacted, you would've thought that he'd touched her somewhere intimate.

You would have thought there was something much deeper happening than a simple touch on a public street. But of course there wasn't.

And she didn't want him to hold her hand. She ignored the yawning chasm that seemed to open up inside of her that called her a liar. Yeah, she ignored it all the way down the street to Ace's Brewery.

They both paused in front of the door, and Cain reached out and opened it for her. Another innocuous gesture that she felt all the way down to her toes.

She was pathetic, really. That such simple gestures made her all fuzzy inside. It was a testament to how ridiculous her past life had been, and just how much she needed to be on guard now.

She couldn't get lost in the moment. His steady, solid presence beside her. Anticipating sex later. Feeling not quite so…alone. It would be far too easy. And she knew better than that.

The brewery was already crowded, the tables inside full, the tall chairs at the bar occupied. But she didn't mind, because even though it was windy she was happy to take a seat out on the deck that overlooked the harbor.

Except the view blurred when she looked across the rough-hewn table at the man sitting opposite her. But he… Well, he was in distressingly sharp focus.

His dark brown hair ruffled in the wind, the lines around his mouth looking especially deep at the moment as he looked past her and out at the water. There was something sexy about those lines on his face. Lines he had earned, she knew.

There were smile lines around his eyes, grooves between his brows that showed he had spent a good deal of time frowning too. He had probably smiled on his wedding day. And then again when Violet was born. Had probably frowned a lot after his wife had left, and then over the past few years doing his best to raise a daughter on his own.

Absently, she reached up and brushed her fingertips

from the corner of her eye down to the edge of her lips. Trying to see, she supposed, if the events of her life—good, painful and egregious—were written as clearly on her face as they were on his.

And if they were, would he look? Would he wonder? He had asked about her marriage. And she had told him. Had told him more than she had ever told anyone else.

Their waiter appeared suddenly with two menus in hand and the sort of demeanor that told her—before a single word was spoken—that if she dared ask about any of the craft beers on the menu she would be treated to a treatise on the subject. His hair—pulled back into a small bun—only confirmed this suspicion.

He was handsome, in that skinny jeans and band T-shirt kind of way. But Alison had discovered that she was more a Wranglers and cowboy hat kind of girl.

She laughed when Cain made the grave error of inquiring about one of the beers on tap. Which earned him a long-winded explanation that included the words *hoppy* and *notes of pine*.

Cain selected one that Alison noted had not been compared to a tree, and when their waiter was out of earshot he pulled a face. "You know, half the point of drinking beer is because you don't have to get into all that crap involved in wine drinking. Why is a good and simple thing being ruined?"

"Many people would argue that it's being refined," she said.

"I prefer my beer to be sold by a frog or Clydesdale. That's as fancy as I need it to be."

"All the beer is local, or mostly. And a lot of it is made by our very own Ace Thompson. He owns the bar too."

"I didn't figure there was more than one guy named Ace in town."

She smiled. "What are you going to eat?"

"I was hoping you would recommend something, since you're a local."

She laughed. "Are you expecting there to be some kind of local delicacy?"

"Sure. Why not? In Texas we have barbecue. You have…?"

She wrinkled her nose. "Kale? Quinoa?"

"I'm sorry, are you listing foods or are you sneezing?"

She laughed, a strange giddy feeling racing through her. "You would consider these adjacent to a sneeze, I'm pretty sure. But, since we're coastal, I can confidently recommend anything that comes from the sea. Or any burger on the menu made with Garrett beef or steak from the Dodge Ranch."

"What they need on this menu is cheese from the Laughing Irish." He frowned. "And pie from you."

"That would be cool," she said. "But I'm only human. I can only bake so many pies."

"I guess it would require a little bit of expansion on your part."

"Someday," she said. "Someday that might be nice. For now, working with Grassroots on special events is going well."

"Violet really enjoyed helping you with the wedding. At least, I think that's what her grunted responses to my questions meant."

"I'm glad you were asking questions."

Their waiter returned with drinks and took their dinner orders. She got salmon, and unsurprisingly Cain opted for steak and potatoes. She chose to take that as a sign that keeping things casual was good. Because Cain would probably always want steak and potatoes. He seemed like that kind of guy. Sometimes Alison wanted a salmon. And she didn't need a man in her life to tell her she couldn't have salmon.

Not that anything more serious was on the table, and this was just a dinner date. Really, the only thing that was on the table was the salmon and steak the waiter placed before them.

"Good?" he asked as she took her first bite.

"Yes," she responded.

He was looking at her while she took a bite of her vegetables. Just looking. She took another bite, then set her fork down. "Is there something interesting about the way that I chew?"

He picked up his own fork and took his first bite of dinner. "I like looking at you."

As compliments went, it wasn't particularly florid, but she liked it all the better for that. "Thank you. Though it makes me wish that I'd brushed up on my table manners a little more."

"I like your table manners too."

She smiled, her fork poised in midair. "This has taken an odd turn."

"I like you. That's what I'm saying. Is that weird?"

"I don't know." She supposed it wouldn't have been if they were teenagers. Instead of a couple of damaged adults playing at having moments of happiness.

"I'm not good at conversation," he said, finally. "At least, not when I care about how the conversation goes. It's fine when I don't care. When I don't worry about whether or not I'm saying the wrong thing or being offensive, or whatever."

"I take it with your brothers you don't care," she said.

"No. Maybe I should care more. It's not like we have a relationship built on being raised together. It's all blood. Which is kind of a strange thing when you think about it. It takes a lot more than that to make a family. Blood doesn't cover everything. Hell, being with someone for years and years doesn't cover everything. I'm kind of an expert on that. Still, my brothers seem to put up with me."

She was tempted then to ask him for more information. More information about how they had grown up. How he had grown up. What it had been like to know he had brothers out there, but not to be with them. She was an only child, so she didn't really understand the sibling connection.

It was clear to her, though, that the Donnelly brothers had a connection, even if it hadn't been forged by a life spent together. Blood mattered. But she could also attest to the fact that blood wasn't enough. Wasn't the be-all and end-all. Family, love, was more complicated than all of those things.

Blood wasn't sufficient enough to make her parents love her, not really. Raising her wasn't enough to make her parents love her. Marriage vows hadn't been enough to make her husband love, honor and cherish her.

Blood wasn't enough to make things easy between Violet and Cain.

"Nothing just happens," she said absently.

"What does that mean?"

"I mean, love, family... You can't just live in the same house, share the same DNA and expect for those things to create bonds. There's a lot more doing involved than you might think."

"Sure as hell," he said. "My father donated sperm to my conception and then went... God knows where. I saw him a handful of times when I was growing up. Mostly my connection to the Donnelly name comes down to it being written on my birth certificate, and to the fact that my grandfather wanted to know his grandchildren, even if his son didn't want to know his boys. As for my mother..." He shook his head.

She waited for him to finish, but he didn't.

"I was never enough," she said, wrapping her hand around her water cup and turning it absently, watching as droplets of condensation traced lines through the mist that had formed on the glass. "Just never good enough. Not even close. And like I already told you, I rebelled against that idea pretty hard. My house was so quiet, and everybody was so repressed. I remember looking at my father once, with that kind of brutal posture that he had and thinking that if I hugged him hard he might crack into pieces. I didn't think about that much though. Since, you know, the appeal of hugging somebody who clearly doesn't want you to hug them is pretty limited."

She swallowed hard. "Even when my mother was sick...it didn't soften either of them. She died just short of my nineteenth birthday and I kept thinking...if I stayed and took care of her she'd realize that I mattered. That my dad would realize it. It didn't happen. He didn't even hug me at her funeral."

He shifted in his seat, and she sensed a strange recognition growing in the space between them. An intense kind of longing that seemed to rise and swell along with the waves out across the water.

"That's the problem with reaching out to people, isn't it?" he asked, his gaze intense, the muscles in his hands, his neck, his jaw drawing tight. "They might pull away."

She sighed. "I guess I never really asked. I did the caregiving thing just after high school, but I couldn't bring myself to tell my mother I wanted…that I wanted her to love me. Not even when she was dying. When I was younger, I threw myself headfirst into all the messy, intense, dramatic stuff I could find as a teenager. A group of friends who got drunk and stupid in the woods at every opportunity. Who laughed and shouted and hooked up with each other and kind of reveled in the fallout of those things. Because it felt real, and bright, and after spending so long feeling like I had to be quiet, like I had to be a little more dull, a little less loud in order to be acceptable, I just… I liked it. But then it backfired on me. And I found out that aiming straight for the opposite of what I had been raised with wasn't necessarily the best choice."

He said nothing, he just placed his hands on the table, rubbed them together as he looked out at the ocean. Finally, he took another sip of his beer, and then he looked at her. The intensity in his gaze just about knocked her back. Hit something deep at the center of her heart that radiated downward, all the way to her fingertips. She didn't know what it was. She just knew that she felt connected to him in a way that she had never felt connected to anyone before.

"I tried," he said, his voice rough. He lifted his hand, scrubbing his palm over his face. "My mother drank. Well, she still does. She drinks, she gambles, she does whatever she can to waste a few hours of her life, to make it all go as fast as possible. In my opinion, she's waiting around for death to show up."

"That's...grim." Not unlike a point in her own life though. Where she had spent a good amount of time being comforted by the fact that her misery wouldn't last forever, since she wouldn't live forever.

Things were different now, thank God.

"Yeah," he agreed. "Pretty damn grim. I asked her why once. I was a kid, I don't know how old. But I came out of my room and she was getting drunk so she could go out. She did that. Went out after I went to bed every night. Nothing ever happened to me. She didn't bring men back to the house, and I suppose that was her version of keeping me safe." He shook his head, taking another sip of beer, interrupting his own story with a long pause. "Anyway. I asked her why she didn't smile. I asked her why she was always so sad." He looked down into his glass, the corner of his mouth twitching slightly. "She said it was because of me. Because she never wanted a kid, and because having one made everything so much harder. So much more expensive." He lifted his glass, taking another drink. Then he set it back down with a click. "I don't ask anymore. I just don't. I never did, not after that. When something is wrong I never ask, because inevitably I feel like the answer is going to be me. Which is some narcissistic fuckery, I'm not going to lie. But you don't forget your mother saying something like that to you."

Her heart felt like it was unraveling, right at the center where she had felt that sharp stab of pain for him. Now it felt like so much more than just pain. It felt like everything was falling apart, like she was falling apart.

She didn't want it. Didn't want to feel that, didn't

want to be disconnected. To be this bound to a man she couldn't keep, didn't want to keep, had no room for. It was different when she helped women at the bakery, when she heard their stories. When she heard about the men in their lives that had let them down, about the pain and abuse that they had endured. It hurt, but it didn't destroy all the defenses that she had built inside of her. It didn't reach her down in her most vulnerable places, places she had learned to protect out of necessity.

She had walled off things inside of her long ago, things that she knew she had to protect from Jared, from her parents before him. And now she just felt… Open and bleeding, naked in a way, completely unable to blunt the impact of what he had just said to her.

He had heard his mother say the things she had always feared might fall from her own parents' lips. He had asked, and on the other side of that question had not been reassurance, but that dreaded confirmation that seemed to await a special few children who just weren't loved by the people who had created them.

She knew it. Because it was her. She felt it because it was him.

"She feels the same way, doesn't she?" he asked, his voice rough. "Violet. I make her feel that way. Like I might be miserable because of her."

"No," she said, reaching across that space and putting her hand over top of his, the response coming easily, viscerally. "She doesn't. Or maybe she does sometimes, I don't know. Because being sixteen is hard, and it hurts. And you spend a lot of time dealing with worst-case scenarios and trying to hurt your own feelings before anyone else can. But that doesn't mean she thinks that, not really."

"That's the problem. That's the damned problem. I never asked Kathleen what was wrong, I never tried to get to know her, because I was always afraid of what the answers would be. I've done the same with Violet. I did it because I never wanted… But that's the thing. You protect yourself and you end up separating yourself. Separating yourself from the people who need you close."

She closed her eyes, trying to cut through the tangled-up thoughts that were slithering through her mind like eels. "No," she said again, opening her eyes and meeting his gaze. "Because if she asked, you wouldn't say what your mother said. I know you, Cain Donnelly. And Violet isn't the reason that you're miserable. She's the reason you do everything. She's the reason you breathe. If she asked you, that's what you would tell her, and it would be the truth." She meant that more than just about anything she had ever said before. And she was certain of it. Certain down to her bones.

Down to that ratty, unraveling heart of hers that she hated to give any credit. That she really didn't want to trust.

"But she shouldn't have to ask," Cain said. "I need to tell her."

As quickly as the unraveling occurred, it stopped. A band wrapping up tight around all her insides now, as if her body was attempting a hasty repair. But it seemed to wrap around her throat too, almost strangling her.

He was a good guy. A good father. He was just good. She had seen so many people who weren't, they both had. She was…happy for Violet that she had him.

She didn't know happiness could hurt so much. Could make it hard to breathe. Could make it feel like something was stabbing through the base of her throat.

"You should," she said. "Tell her." She swallowed hard, trying to break through that restricted feeling, but only succeeding in spreading it downward toward her chest.

"I will," he said nodding. Then his gaze lingered on her for a little bit longer than she could handle. She looked down at her salmon, which seemed somehow less essential than it had earlier. Less symbolic and more like just a piece of fish.

Cain, on the other hand, seemed a lot more important.

They attempted lighter conversation through the rest of the meal, though Alison still felt like there might be a weight sitting on top of her shoulders. He paid the check, which made her heart do fluttery things and irritated her.

Her heart should be too shredded to flutter. And yet, there it went.

She wondered if that ridiculous organ would ever learn.

"I would like nothing more than to go home with you," he said, when they arrived at the front of the bakery. "But I think I need to go talk to my daughter."

She nodded, feeling annoyed because part of her wished that he would come upstairs with her, even though she wanted him to go talk to Violet now. Annoyed about basically everything, because they were supposed to have a dinner date, and it was supposed to be fun. Fun like the sex they were having. Light and freeing, and not something that took possession of her.

She ignored the voice inside of her that whispered that the sex had never been any of those things either. That it was far too big to be light. And far too life-altering to be fun.

No. She wasn't having that. Wasn't listening.

"You do," she said, taking a step away from him.

"You're not getting off that easy."

He moved in close to her, wrapping his arm around her waist and drawing her up against him. He took hold of her chin, tilting her face up, the motion much more gentle than anything she had come to associate with Cain. He dipped his head, pressing his lips gently to hers. Featherlight. Maddening. She wanted the hard press of his mouth, the hard press of his whole body. Wanted to be consumed by him, possessed by him. Because this, this little tease just left her mouth feeling tingly and swollen and utterly unsatisfied.

Well, not just her mouth.

And frankly, if it was limited to her body, that might have been okay. But it was her heart again. And that just wasn't.

"Good night," he said, his breath hot against her cheek.

"Good night."

Then he turned around and left, and she stood there like an idiot, watching him walk down the street, just barely illuminated by the streetlamps, until she couldn't see him anymore. Then she stood there for a couple more minutes, just for good measure, her fingertips pressed to her lips like a teenage girl who had just gotten her first kiss. Definitely not like a woman in her thirties who had been married, deeply disillusioned, abused and divorced. A woman who should know better.

A woman who was still standing there like an idiot, watching the blank space where the man who unraveled her heart had just stood.

CHAPTER NINETEEN

"HEY, BO."

Cain knocked on the open doorway to Violet's room. It was late, and she had flung herself sideways across the bed, her feet hanging over the edge, one leg tipped up, kicking absently. It took him a second to realize she had headphones in her ears.

He walked forward, gripping the cord that was attached to the left earbud and pulling it out of her ear. "Bo, I want to talk to you."

Violet startled, then rolled over onto her back. "You want to talk to me?"

He did. He really did. There was a mountain of regret between them, and all of it was his. He was the parent, he was the one who had to make things right. Yes, she was being difficult. Yeah, she had disrespected his rules, and him, and in general had been a pain in the ass. But he was the parent.

That meant when there was fixing to be done, at this point, he had to do it. Hell, he was thirty-eight years old and he had just now realized why he did the things he did. He could hardly expect his sixteen-year-old to have greater insight into her behavior than he had into his own.

"I need to talk to you," he amended, sitting on the

edge of her bed. "How has everything been for the past…little bit?"

"Good. I've just been…at home. You have actually talked to me recently."

"I know. But Alison brought it to my attention that I don't do it enough. I've been talking with her. A lot." He didn't know why he was bringing Alison into the conversation. Didn't know why he would even allude to that to his teenage daughter, since what was happening between him and Alison was supposed to just be sex.

Except it's not, and it hasn't been for a while. You just sat across from the woman and spilled your guts to her.

Yeah, that was the truth.

"I like Alison," Violet said.

He wondered if there was a hidden meaning to that, if she was alluding to the fact that she knew something about his relationship with Alison. He was going to choose to think that maybe she did, but he also wasn't going to give any details.

"Me too. But that isn't really what I want to talk to you about. I know that your mom leaving has been hard on you. And I hate that your childhood is screwing you up, Bo, I really do. That was never the intent. I married your mom so that you would have both parents. So that you wouldn't end up with my life. With one parent just off somewhere doing their own thing, rather than raising you like they were supposed to do. I was so focused on not being my father. On being around. On supporting you. So focused on that it meant there were other things I missed. Other things I've forgotten to do. The main one being to make sure that you know you aren't the cause of my stress. You aren't the cause of my hardships."

He reached out and put his hand on his daughter's

shoulder. "You're the reason I breathe. When everything is bad, and hard, you're the reason I get up in the morning. The reason I put one foot in front of the other. I didn't have a father, Violet. Not really. I never saw an example of how to be a dad. But the minute the doctor put you in my arms, I knew that I was going to move heaven and earth to be one to you. To figure it out. It... it kills me that I've done such a bad job sometimes. It kills me that I haven't said these things before. They need to be said. You need to know."

She was just looking at him, her expression blank, her cheeks pale. He couldn't read what in hell she was thinking. He was almost afraid to. Dammit. He was scared of his own daughter. As scared as he had once been to face down his mother and ask why she was sad. As scared as he had been to find out that he was the reason Kathleen hated her life.

He was afraid it was true for Violet too. That no matter how much he might love her, he was more of a burden than anything else. That he would only ever be the cause of people's pain, and never the solution to it.

He was afraid. He was a damned coward. But he couldn't be a coward anymore. Because that cowardice had built walls between himself and the people he was supposed to be closest to. Because that division had caused the kind of pain he had never wanted to inflict on anyone, much less people he loved.

Because it would keep him separate from his brothers. From Violet.

From Alison.

Alison, who had bewitched him from the beginning. Who hadn't been afraid to beat him over the head with his stupidity. To tell him just where he was failing. To force him to share, and to make him want to pry her open in return and learn all of her secrets.

Alison, who was teaching him this new beautiful, painful art of honesty.

"I know that to you it's always looked like I walked away when things got tough. Like I went out and worked the ranch instead of staying where you needed me most. Then I threw myself into working on this house for us on the property. But I never felt like… I never felt like I had much to offer you. Because when the doctor handed you to me in that hospital, not only did I feel the biggest surge of love I've ever felt… I felt afraid. Scared shitless. I've never known how to talk to people, or how to say the right things. I know how to build things. I know how to pound nails. And I know how to work. So I did that for you, as best I could. And it's taken me all this time to realize that it didn't look like love to you. And no matter how I meant it, if it didn't look like love, it wasn't worth much."

Violet pushed herself up into a sitting position, a tear overflowing from her green eye and dripping down her cheek. "No," she said, her lips quivering slightly. "Dad, that's not true. It's not nothing. I knew it wasn't. I did. I get… I get scared. So scared. That you're going to leave me too. And I've been awful. I don't know why. Maybe to try and make you hurry up and leave? So you'll just do it now if you're going to."

He closed the distance between them then, wrapping his arms around her and pulling her against him, cupping the back of her head like he'd done when she was a baby and holding her against him, letting her cry.

"Maybe I don't think that," she said, her voice muffled. "A lot of the time I don't know what I'm thinking at all. It just hurts. And I'm scared too. I'm going to be eighteen, and then I'm going to have to leave, and I don't think I can stand leaving you because you're all I have."

That admission shocked him. He had been pretty sure she'd been counting down the days until she could leave. All of the bitter grumbling and long silences certainly hadn't made him imagine she was afraid to leave home.

"I'm not going to kick you out when you turn eighteen, Violet. As long as you want to stay with me you can. Whatever you need. I'm your dad, not just until you turn eighteen. I'm your dad forever."

She pulled away from him, wiping her eyes, wiping her nose with her shirtsleeve. "Well. It's just hard to... to trust anything."

"I know," he said, his heart squeezing tight. "She hurt us both pretty bad. I think it's made us both wary. But you're right. We have each other. We have each other and even though I've felt that this whole time, I've done a bad job of making sure you knew. And you know... I did move us here for me as much as you. I know I said it was for you, but it was definitely for me too. Because I couldn't stay there anymore. Because I couldn't wait for her to walk back through the door."

Surprise flashed over Violet's face. "Are you... Did you love her that much?"

Ouch. It hurt him that she had seen just how not in love with her mother he had been at the end. "No," he admitted, his voice rough. "Which is a whole other problem. A whole other thing likely related to why she didn't want to be married to me anymore. Her leaving didn't hurt me because I loved her so much. It's because I love you so much. It's because of how badly it hurt you. How wrong and awful it is that she left you. I deserved to be left, Violet. I can't deny that. You don't. You deserve better. Better than her. Better than me."

"Don't say that," she said, tucking her knees up against her chest, her expression miserable.

"It was supposed to make you feel good," he said.

"All I hear is that you don't think you should be with me. I don't want that. You're my dad. That's what I want. I want you to be my dad. And if you think you can do a better job, then do a better job, but don't say I deserve something different. I'm not saying you could do a better job. I mean, I could probably do a better job being a daughter."

"That's the thing. Being a daughter isn't really a job. You're supposed to mess up. You're still figuring things out." He laughed, and shook his head. "I'm going to let you in on a secret though. I'm still figuring things out too. I don't know what I'm doing. I haven't, not from day one. In fact all this time I've only known one thing. I love you. So, since I love you I'm going to do whatever I need to to be a good dad to you. Sometimes that's going to mean bursting into a barn full of drunken hooligans and humiliating you and carrying you back out. So we're clear, I'm not apologizing for that."

A slight scowl appeared on her face. "Okay."

"But for not making sure you knew how much I love you, for not making you feel more secure in the fact that I'm not going to leave… For that I am apologizing. And there I'm promising to do better. If you need to talk, you can talk to me. I want more of what we've been doing. More honesty. Even if it's messy. Even if it does make me mad, and I make you mad. And everybody's mad. We'll both be mad. But, we'll both know neither of us are going anywhere. How about that?"

"Sounds good." She flung herself back at him, wrapping her arms around his neck. "I love you."

He closed his eyes and hugged her back. "I love you too, Bo. I love you too."

CAIN STOOD OUTSIDE on the street feeling like he probably should have texted Alison first. There was a light on in her apartment window above the bakery. Every other window on Main Street was dark, but not this one. It seemed like a sign.

Though at this point he would probably take something as innocuous as a car turning left onto the street as a sign that he needed to be at Alison's tonight.

He shoved his hands into his pockets and let out a long, slow breath, watching as it tangled with the night air, the cool temperature making it look like he was blowing smoke. Or maybe he was, because his blood was running so hot.

But this was more than just arousal. It was more than just sex. Something was changing inside of him, and he blamed Alison. Or maybe he gave her credit, since he really wasn't all that sad about the changes happening inside him.

She had made him want more. Because something about being near her, something about knowing her, had made him acutely aware of how distant he was, not just from her, but from everyone. She had a warmth that he wanted to touch, that he wanted to absorb into himself, and if he was going to do that he had to figure out how to change himself. How to get close to people. How to let them in.

And it was working. With his brothers, with his daughter.

Funny how Alison was the last person he was actually going to make the move with. But, at the end of the day, he felt like this was the relationship that had the most uncertainty. Alison was... Well, she was skittish as a colt.

She had come at him guns blazing when it had come to Violet, and what she felt Violet had deserved. But as soon as she felt like things were changing between them, she retreated. And he understood that, he did. He hadn't entered into this wanting more, wanting a relationship.

But now... Now he didn't want to imagine what his life might be like if he didn't have her in it. She was changing him. Knowing her, being with her, had changed him. But he needed more. More of what she had given to him. This couldn't just end.

Much like that compulsion to get to know her, he couldn't remember ever feeling like this before either. A desperation to hold on to what he had.

He wasn't sure he had ever valued a life, his relationships, the way that he did right in this moment.

He wanted to hold on to this town, his ranch, his brothers, his daughter and Alison with all he had, 'til his hands were bloody. This life, these people, he would fight for. He would lay down a lifetime's worth of baggage for them.

He pulled his phone out of his pocket and started a new message to Alison, mostly because he wasn't exactly sure if she would be able to hear him if he knocked on the door.

Standing outside. Don't have a boom box. Not going full Cusack.

The curtains twitched and he saw Alison's silhouette in the window. Then he saw her lift her phone. He looked down at his screen and saw the dots indicating that she was writing a response.

I've never seen that movie. You're old.

He smiled. You know it's a movie though. So the reference is good enough.

Come back when you have a boom box.

I did bring something else that rocks hard.

What?

He hesitated for a moment. My dick.

In that case come on up.

That worked?

In the absence of romance I will take sex.

He intended to give her both, but he wasn't going to say that. Mostly because he had a feeling that would send her running off into the mountains. He was going to have to seduce her first. But he was up to the task.

Before he went to knock on the door he dialed his brother's house. Finn picked up. "I'll be home late tonight," he said. "If I'm home at all."

"Okay," his brother said slowly.

"Just letting you know. If I'm out all night, I'll probably be late tomorrow morning too."

"Good," Finn said. "Glad to hear it."

"Yeah well. Don't let everything burn to the ground while I'm gone."

"Don't you burn anything down either."

"Not planning on it," he said. "Planning on building something."

Cain hung up, feeling resolute. Then he went to the door, which jerked open before he was able to knock. "It's taking you long enough," Alison said, leaning against the doorframe, crossing her arms and cocking her hip to the side.

He liked that. That fake little bit of confidence she was projecting, while it was clear to him that she was frazzled and trembling a little bit.

"I thought I would stand out here and let the anticipation build."

She rolled her eyes and stepped out of the doorway. "Come on up. My anticipation is built."

He walked over the threshold, then shut the door behind them, immediately backing her up against the wall, pressing his palms against the drywall on either side of her face. "I meant me," he said. "I'm enjoying this. Wanting you. Making myself wait for you."

"Oh," she said, looking down.

"What? You don't like that."

She looked back up at him. "I didn't say that. It's just weird, I guess. To have this. I'm not used to it."

"You're not used to a man telling you that you keep him up at night? That you're all he thinks about. That you make his body burn?"

"No. But you're welcome to keep talking."

"Alison," he said, his voice low, rough even to his own ears. "No matter how much I have of you, I seem to want more." It wasn't just her body, it was everything. And it was beyond words. Something he could only feel. Something he didn't know how to say, because it was just a feeling at the center of his chest. One that felt too big for him to hold.

So he had to try to get it out somehow. And maybe, just maybe, that would be the key. The one that would unlock the door he needed opened. That would give him what he craved with her. Because there was more. Something deeper, something intangible and desperate that flared up when he looked at her.

"I didn't think you were going to come back tonight," she said, clearly uncomfortable with the declaration. Clearly wanting to sidestep it.

Physically, she did exactly what he knew she was hoping to do emotionally, and ducked underneath his arms, moving toward the staircase that he assumed led to her apartment.

"Up this way," she said, tilting her head to the side.

He had half a mind not to let her get away with this. To grab hold of her and take her right here in the doorway so that she couldn't get the distance she was clearly trying to achieve. Instead, he shoved his hands into his pockets and followed her up the narrow staircase.

"Did your conversation with Violet go well?"

He felt impatient, he didn't want to talk about that. Emotionally, he was moving forward, moving down a list of things that he wanted to deal with. He had moved on to Alison, now, and he didn't want to take any of the focus off her.

But he also knew that this—conversation—was part of it.

"It did," he responded. "Better than expected, actually."

"Good," she said. "I mean, I'm glad to know that the two of you are going to be okay. I really like her, and, you know, it's just reassuring to know that when I'm not facilitating communication between the two of you, when I'm not around, everything will be fine."

She took a step backward when she said that, her manner getting a little more agitated.

"When you're not around?"

"Right," she said, lifting a shoulder. "Because she isn't going to work at Pie in the Sky forever. And you and I aren't going to... Well, you know." She turned away from him, heading toward the kitchen that was across the open floor plan living area. "Wine?"

"No," he said, taking three decisive strides across the space toward her. "Bed."

They were going to have to talk. But first... First there would be this. Because it was how they had connected initially. Because still, that raging feeling inside of him existed just outside the bonds of language for him, and he had no words to give to the clawing, tearing sensation that was racking him.

She blinked rapidly, her eyes going wide. "Bed?"

He bent down, scooping her up into his arms, holding her tightly against his chest. "Which way?"

She flailed her arm slightly to the left, and he assumed that was indicating the correct direction. He went that way, not really pausing to take in the details of the house. Later he would. Because he was in Alison's space, and that did fascinate him. He wanted to excavate her. To find out all of the clues he could about her, so that he could continue creating the best, most detailed picture of her that he could.

He was desperate for it. Starving. For every bit of Alison that he could possibly have. Wanted her, needed her. In his life, in his bed, in his soul.

Her bedroom door was already open, and he walked inside, depositing her on the bed, joining her immediately and claiming her mouth with a hard, deep kiss.

If she had any reservations, they seemed to vanish the moment his mouth touched hers. Because she returned it, deep, long, unending. She wrapped her arms around his neck, letting her legs fall apart so that he could settle between them.

There had always been an edge to his physical attraction to Alison, to this heat between them. It had always cut, sharp and deep, straight down beneath his skin, hitting him in a place where no woman ever had before. This was different. It was deeper, sharper, about a thousand times more devastating.

Because the beast inside of him was completely made of hunger now, of want that went so far past the physical it was white-hot and painful to the touch. To her touch. Delicate fingertips skimming over his body, divesting him of his shirt, moving down to work the closure on his jeans, all while her hips rocked against him, mimicking the rhythm that he would establish when he was buried deep inside of her.

Every brush of her hands over his skin was a brand that he knew would mark him forever. In the past, that would have scared him. Would have made him want to run. But here, now, with her, he just wanted to lean into it. Wanted to surrender to it. And he wanted to drag her down with him. He grabbed hold of her hips, holding them tight, imagining that his fingers on her were leaving their own mark, hoping that if he visualized it clearly enough it would be true.

That she would be as ruined as he was, as rebuilt as he was.

They didn't talk, they didn't stop.

Soon, she was naked beneath him, arching upward, rubbing her breasts against his chest, her tightened nipples, the yes on her lips spurring him on, ratcheting up his own arousal to impossible heights.

He skimmed his hands down over her curves, reveling in the feel of her soft skin beneath his touch. Then he pressed his hand between her thighs, growling when he felt how wet she was, how ready she was for him.

He quickly grabbed hold of a condom, protecting them both before sliding into her welcoming heat. And he waited. Waited for the rush of relief to wash over him. For a sense of satisfaction to pervade him, to sink its way down to his bones. Like it had every other time he had been inside of her. Except this time it didn't. This time, being inside of her wasn't enough. He needed more. Wanted more.

They were as close as two people could be. Skin to skin. Joined in the most elemental way. But there was a piece missing. Something vital. And he couldn't for the life of him figure out what it was.

He flexed his hips forward and she gasped, arching up against him, wrapping her legs around his waist, allowing him to sink even deeper inside. And still, it wasn't enough.

He lowered his head, pressing his lips to her neck before scraping the sensitive skin with his teeth. Soothing away the sting he knew he had left behind with his tongue.

She was all around him, her scent filling his lungs, her flavor on his tongue. It wasn't enough.

He moved inside of her then, no rhythm to be found, nothing more than desperation pounding through his veins as he pounded into her. As he chased after the indefinable thing that he knew he would die without.

Except he didn't know what it was. He didn't know at all. He only knew that it was going to be found with her. In her. This was beyond the need for release, beyond the need for satisfaction. Beyond pleasure, beyond pain.

It was something he had never had before, something he had never felt before. Something he had needed, from the day he was born maybe, but that he hadn't truly become aware of until her.

Her fingernails scraped over his back, her breath hot against his neck, the sweet sounds of her pleasure pushing him closer and closer to the edge. The edge of release, but not the edge of satisfaction.

He needed something. Needed it more than air. Something.

He closed his eyes, gritted his teeth, thrusting into her until he found a certain measure of oblivion in the pleasure that took hold of his body. And for a moment at least, as she wrapped her legs more tightly around him, as her internal muscles pulsed around him, as she found her own release and dragged him right down with her, pleasure consuming him like a blaze, the beast inside of him was quieted.

But when the pleasure began to fade, when he became aware of the details in the room… Of her breathing, of her hands resting on his shoulders, of her chest rising and falling beneath his... Of his own heart pounding out a heavy rhythm... That need came back too.

Yet there was something about this moment, like it was the eye of the storm, a storm he could see raging all around him, inside of him, even as he sat here in the calm clarity. There was something about that which allowed him to see.

Which made him understand.

Suddenly all of the pieces clicked into place. The ferocity of the need inside of him, in his heart, and his body, and his soul. And what it meant when it came to this woman lying in his arms.

He loved her.

He wanted her to love him back.

He lifted his hand, tracing a line of concern that marred her forehead. Her eyes fluttered closed, the corners of her mouth turned down slightly.

He wouldn't say anything. Not now. Not because he was afraid, but because it wasn't the time. He brushed a kiss across all that worry written on her face and she sighed, not opening her eyes.

He couldn't dump all of that on her now. Small steps. He would take small steps. He would start by sleeping with her all night. In a bed.

He laughed.

Alison opened one eye. "What?"

"This is the first time we've made it to a bed."

And he wasn't planning on letting her out of it. Not anytime soon.

She closed her eyes again, only this time, a smile curved her lips. "I suppose it is."

She relaxed against him then, and he wrapped his arms around her, holding her against him. And he felt...

satisfied. For the moment. Love. That was the need. That was the ache.

It still ached. Still hurt. But he understood it now.

Love. It was why he wanted to know her. Why he needed to know her. Why he could never get enough of her.

He should have known. Because he'd been discovering that love was the reason for everything. That love always seemed to be the answer to the questions in his life.

Whether it was not showing enough of it, being afraid to talk about it, or needing it, it always seemed to be the answer.

He had a feeling that in this case it might also be the sledgehammer. But he wasn't going to let that hold him back. That was the lesson. He had a damned hard head, but even he learned eventually.

But for now, for tonight, he just wanted to sleep with this woman. This woman he was in love with.

He drew in a deep breath and shifted their positions so that her rear was nestled into the curve of his body, so that his forehead was pressed against her shoulder blades. He felt her stiffen for a moment, and he wondered if she was going to protest his staying the night. Then she relaxed against him.

His last thought before he drifted off to sleep was that it was sure as hell nice to not be alone.

CHAPTER TWENTY

WHEN ALISON WOKE UP her heart slammed against her breastbone, panic firing through her veins. There was a heavy, masculine arm thrown over her body, and the presence of another person in her apartment was just so…so very apparent from the moment she had started coming out of deep sleep, that it was an adrenaline surge that ultimately pushed her into wakefulness.

She wiggled, trying to struggle away from the person in her bed, but she stopped when a pair of warm lips pressed against the center of her back.

"It's just me." The voice was thick with sleep, rusty from disuse overnight. But she knew it was Cain. Immediately. Everything came back then, and the panic abated. A little bit.

"What time is it?" She noticed light filtering in through the curtains, then cursed. She sat up, looking over Cain so that she could see her bedside clock. "Shit!"

She hadn't just slept through the night, she had gone and slept through opening the bakery. She got out of bed, not caring that she was naked, and opened the curtains just a little bit so that she could see down to the street below. She saw Lucinda's car parked against the curb, and breathed a sigh of relief. At least it was open.

She looked at her nightstand, where she usually set her phone before she went to bed, and saw that it wasn't there. Of course it wasn't, because she had been in her kitchen texting Cain, and then he had burst in, and one thing had led to another, and they had gone into her bedroom.

And they had forgotten about all the legitimately important things like her phone, and setting her alarm.

"I didn't mean to sleep all night," she said.

She looked at him, expecting him to say the same thing, because surely he hadn't meant to spend the entire night holding her in his arms. He had cows to feed and whatever else he did back at the ranch, plus a much bigger bed—she assumed—than her own.

"Why not?" he asked, rather than confirming what she assumed. "You were tired."

"Didn't you, like, miss prime milking hour, or whatever?"

"I called Finn last night and told him I might not be home." He sat up, the blankets riding perilously low on his hips. She was helpless to do anything but stand there and appreciate the play of muscles in his back, in his stomach, his arms. Those hands. All of him, basically.

Even in this moment of strange panic, she recognized that he was hot.

"You did?"

He nodded slowly. "Yeah. I came over to spend the night."

She blinked rapidly. "You could have asked."

"Pretty sure I stated my intent."

"For sex. Not for…intimate sleeping arrangements." She was being ridiculous. She heard the ridiculousness coming out of her mouth, and she couldn't really do anything about it. Couldn't feel any differently than she did. Couldn't stop it all from flooding forth like torrents of hysteria.

"Some people assume that intimate sleeping arrangements come with the sex."

"As you pointed out last night, we've never even made it to a bed. So… This seems like a step. And I didn't think we were taking…steps."

"Yeah," he said, making a very male, morning-type noise and slinging his legs over the side of the bed. The covers fell away completely, exposing his body. His aroused body. And heaven help her if she didn't feel a little bit weak, and warm. Very, very warm. "About that."

Right in that moment she felt the floor fall away. She felt like she was falling. Like there was nothing holding her up at all. He was going to do it. He was going to end it. And this. And whatever the hell he had been thinking spending the night in her bed, it was only a tease.

It shocked her, stunned her how much it hurt. To realize she was poised on the brink of the end of this. The end of them.

She opened her mouth to stop them from talking, to say something, but her throat was too tight, and she couldn't think of any words anyway. So she just stood there, staring dumbly at his naked body, his beautiful, glorious naked body that he was about to take away from her forever. It was better than looking at his face. That face that had become so familiar, but was no less handsome for it. And those eyes. Those green eyes that seemed to see all the way through her.

Yeah, she wasn't going to look at those either. As affecting as his muscles were, they had nothing on his eyes.

"The thing is, Alison," he said, and she focused on

his left pectoral muscle, because she couldn't really look away from him, but she needed to not see what his face might look like when he broke up with her, "I love you."

If the floor had been gone before, now the walls were gone too. The street. Maybe the whole damn world.

"What?"

"I love you," he reiterated. "You… You've changed me. In ways that I can't really articulate, because I'm not good at talking, though I'm working on it. You're like…an angel to me. A really dirty, beautiful angel, but an angel nonetheless. Everything in my life had gone to hell, and you helped me figure out how to fix it."

"That doesn't mean you love me," she said, barely aware that she had spoken the words, because somewhere during all of this her face had gone numb, and she couldn't really feel her mouth. "That means you're grateful. It's not the same thing."

"I know the difference between gratitude and love, Alison. I know the difference between love and being in love. Mostly because I've never been in love before." He took a sharp breath, that left pec pitching upward, the motion forcing her to meet his gaze. He was… He was so sincere, so intense it took her breath away. "I cared for Kathleen, and I even loved her. But I didn't crave her. Not the way I crave you. You made me want to know you. Really know you, and to do that, I knew I had to let you know me. I had to let you in to everything, and you know how much I hate that. Because I told you. Because we actually talked about things. Alison, I've never had a relationship like this with anybody before. I've never wanted one. If you'd asked me a few months ago what my worst nightmare was, it probably would have been this. But now... I can't imagine things without you. I don't want to."

It was the longing that scared her the most. Coupled with that breathless moment from about a minute ago when she had thought he was going to end it, with the intense, crushing impact of that pain, it was all a little unbearable.

And here in this space, this sanctuary she had created herself, that she had never shared with another human being like this... It was crushing. Invasive.

This was her life. This place that she had built for herself, this reclamation of herself. And he was here, he was messing with it. He was changing things. They had rules, and he wasn't following them. She didn't want this. She didn't.

Liar.

Yes, she did want this. And that was the real problem.

That she couldn't actually be with this man, sleep with this man without wanting more. But she wasn't actually strong enough to stand on her own like she had allowed herself to believe that she was. She wasn't supposed to need this. She wasn't supposed to need somebody. Not again.

This place, this life, this woman, were supposed to be stronger than that.

But she wasn't.

She was ready to throw herself down onto her knees and beg him to stay with her forever. Beg for it to be true. She had spent so much of her life wanting somebody to love her. The first person who had said it to her she had bound herself to for life. Had bound herself to hideous, awful abuses just for those words.

Cain just said them. Like it was that real and that

easy. He didn't even make her earn them. And that was the headiest, most tempting part. The part that made it seem new and different and safe.

Right now, she realized that if she wasn't careful she would do it all over again.

No, Cain would never hurt her. It wasn't about him. It was about her. About the concessions she would make, the ways in which she would contort herself, the ways she would shrink herself in order to be the kind of woman she thought might be able to keep him. The kind of woman she thought might be able to earn his love.

She would become that thing again. That creature. Colorless. Sapped of life.

No. That was love. She knew it. She couldn't take a chance on it again.

"We talked about this," she said, feeling disembodied from the words that were coming out of her mouth. "That it was going to just be sex."

"I know," he said, his tone maddeningly calm. How could he be calm? Not content to unravel her heart, he was now working on the rest of her. She was falling apart right where she stood.

"Then what are you doing?"

"I'm not doing anything. I didn't plan for this. Trust me, I didn't want it either. But it happened. I fell in love with you, Alison."

She shook her head. "No. You can't have fallen in love with me. You can't." Her parents had spent their entire life staunchly not loving her, and Jared certainly hadn't fallen in love with her, his wife that he had spoken vows to. It was inconceivable that a man could fall in love with her accidentally after so many years of people who should have loved her never quite forming that attachment. It didn't make sense.

"I did," he continued.

"No. I *helped* you. That's what I do, Cain. I help people. It's the way that I've figured I can redeem that tiny existence that I had for so many years, for all that time that I needed help from people, all those times when I needed them to hold me up because I was too weak. I've become that for other people, and I understand how maybe your emotions can get…tangled up in that. But that doesn't mean you're in love with me."

Then he looked angry. A sudden shadow passed over his face and he launched himself from the bed, and she found six-plus feet of angry man walking toward her, totally naked. "Is that how you're going to play it? That we just had therapeutic sex? You offered up your body to me out of pity? Is that just what you do?"

"That's not what I meant. I met with Violet. I talked to you about her, and tried to figure out ways you could get along better. The sex is different. It's separate."

"No. That's where we were stupid. The sex isn't separate. It never is. It never was. It's part of you, it's part of me and it's part of us. There was never a line. It was never me coming to you for advice, and a different me giving you orgasms. It was all just me. And it was all just you. We lied to ourselves, because we were afraid. Because from the minute I laid eyes on you the connection that I felt with you was stronger than anything I've ever experienced in my life. And I needed to have it. I needed to have it, but I sure as hell wasn't going to let myself have it if I acknowledge that." He reached out, his fingertips brushing her chin. "We've both been hurt—"

"No," she said, shaking her head. "Your ex-wife hurt

your feelings. My ex-husband bruised my body. He made me bleed. He broke me, Cain. Not just my body, but my soul. We haven't both been hurt. Don't act like we've been through the same things. Like you can take your limp dishrag of a marriage and compare it to the hell that I lived through."

His head jerked back as though she had hit him, but then he straightened, leveling that green gaze at her. "You're right. I'm sorry. I know what you went through was hell. I do. And I didn't go through hell. But whatever I have to do to convince you that it won't be like that with me, I'll do it."

She shook her head. "I think you misunderstand. I don't think you're going to hurt me. I'm not afraid of you, Cain. I never have been. That isn't the problem. The problem is that I don't want to share my life. Everything I have here? I built it. It's mine. A new life, a new woman. I don't have any room in my life for a man, not in a permanent sense. I like Violet, but I'm not looking for a child either. I'm not looking for ties, I'm not looking for anyone or anything to be beholden to."

Her own words cut her deep, wounded her. She hated herself for saying them. For bringing Violet into it. It wasn't fair, but she also knew it was the one thing that would drive him off. She could probably tell him she didn't want him until she couldn't breathe, until her voice was raw with it, and he would still be there, staring at her, refusing to move. But if she said she didn't want Violet…

He would never fight against that.

"You're lying," he said, his voice rough.

She was. She was. And her heart was twisted up, wrung out, threatening to burst from the strain that was being put on it right now. She hurt everywhere. Pressure building behind her eyes, tears threatening to overflow. But she had to do this now. Or she would never be able to do it. No matter what being with him did to her, no matter how profoundly she lost herself, she would get sucked back into that pattern.

Love wasn't like that for everyone, and she knew it. But she had a feeling that some people just weren't meant to have it. And she was one of them.

So she had to end it now. Had to end it now before it ended later, badly. Before she was left a broken shell again, working to pick up the pieces of her life. She didn't know that woman. She wasn't her. And she would never become her again. Even if it hurt now, she would do what she had to do to keep herself from being decimated later.

"I'm not," she said. "I know it doesn't make sense to you and, in a way, I'm kind of glad," she said, trying to speak around the lump that was forming in her throat. "Kathleen hurt you. But she didn't break that part of you that…can have love. That can have a relationship. Good. Go have one. Go have one with somebody that actually wants to have one with you, Cain. Stop putting yourself in impossible situations and wanting women who are never going to give you what you give them."

"Don't you dare lecture me, Alison. Don't you dare stand there and act like I should love somebody else. I know my heart. I know my mind. I love you. It's not an accident, and it's not because I'm a fool. It's not because there are things in this world I haven't seen. Not because there's pain I haven't felt. You think you're going to wound me? My own mother didn't want me. My wife walked out. On me. On my child. I'm still standing here taking the chance. Because love is worth that. More than that, you're worth it."

She shook her head. "No. No." *I'm not. I'm not.* The echo of those denials rang inside of her, but she didn't speak them out loud. Didn't even stop to analyze them. Couldn't. Didn't want to.

"Dammit, Alison," he said, reaching out, grabbing hold of her arms and pulling her close to him. He didn't hurt her, but all the intensity, all of the pain that he was feeling came through in that hold. "You know what this costs me. I'm doing it anyway. Talk to me. Work with me. Give me a chance."

"No!" She broke his hold on her, turning in the opposite direction and walking away from him. "No," she repeated again, this time the word was steady, as she took a deep breath, found that calm, dead place inside her that she had retreated to for years anytime something hurt too much. Anytime something was too hard. In that moment, that action, this moment of necessity made her feel justified. Made her feel like she really didn't have another option.

Because he had forced her here. He had forced her into this. To that dead, emotionless place that had been her touchstone when the world had been too hard, when her husband had been too cruel. She had to do it now to escape this pain and that she could still access that dead piece of herself was a reminder of how close her trauma was. Of the fact that it was just on the other side of the wall.

It was why she had built the wall in the first place. And Cain Donnelly could not be allowed to destroy it.

"I don't want to," she said. "Can't you understand that?" She whirled around to face him. "You said you haven't been in love before, but I have, Cain. I loved a man with everything that I had, I gave him my trust, and he broke it. He broke me. Don't make the mistake of thinking that I need to be healed, that I'm waiting around for you to show me that I can have what I want. I don't want it. I want my life as I have built it for myself. I want to be free. I don't want to be weighed down by you and all of your bullshit. You have too much baggage. I have enough of my own. And actually, I've figured out how to lay a bunch of it down. Don't make the mistake of thinking that I can't, and that I need you to rescue me. I don't want that. And I don't want you."

The words were sharp and they left an ache in her throat as though they had cut her on the way out.

"Alison..."

"No," she said again. "It has to be this way." She swallowed hard, hating herself for what she was about to say. For what had to be said. "Otherwise...you're just going to end up being the reason I'm unhappy, Cain." She forced herself to meet his eyes. Looking at him felt like dying, but she had to. "We both know that you don't want that."

He didn't react to that. His expression solidified. His mouth firmed into a thin line. Those green eyes that had looked at her with warmth, with passion, with anger, went cold. Like she was looking at dead pieces of jade, so hard and sharp they would cut her if she got too close.

"You're right," he said, his voice tight. "I don't want that."

"I have to go to work."

"So do I."

"Good. Just... Good." She started hunting around for her clothes, panic building in her chest. He needed to go. He needed to get dressed and leave, and if he didn't, then she was going to leave first, because she couldn't be this close to him. She couldn't be. All of her resolve would weaken, and she would collapse. And she just couldn't risk that. She couldn't let this break her like it was threatening to. This was a test, and she was damn certain she was going to pass it.

"Violet is supposed to work later today," he said, his tone hard.

"Yeah," she returned. "I know. This doesn't affect Violet's job, so you know."

"Why would it? Apparently, it doesn't affect you at all."

He collected his clothes then, dressing silently, the anger pouring off him palpable. But he didn't direct any of it at her. And part of her wished to God that he would.

Instead, he just walked out of the room when he was finished. She pulled her shirt over her head, and followed him out into the living area, but by the time she made it there, he was walking out the front door. He closed it behind him with a finality that echoed inside of her.

She should be relieved. It was over. It was done. Everything could go back to the way that it had been before. To the way that she needed it to be.

She wasn't relieved. She wasn't relieved at all.

With shaking legs, she sat down on her couch, her hand pressed firmly to her chest as her threadbare heart beat against her breastbone.

She had told him that he didn't understand the kind of pain she had been through. He didn't, she knew. Not specifically. But in that moment she understood that while Jared had broken her in a lot of horrible ways before, she had never been broken quite like this.

Because no one had ever broken her heart before. And now, she had gone and broken her own.

But it was the only way she could keep the rest of herself whole.

CHAPTER TWENTY-ONE

CAIN WAS NUMB and exhausted by the time he walked into the house an hour after Alison had told him to leave. He was kind of grateful for the numbness, because he had a feeling once it receded, this was going to suck big-time.

He paused in the doorway, shaking his head. Then he pushed his hair back off his forehead, taking a deep breath. She had rejected him. He had told her that he loved her, he had put himself out there, and she had rejected him.

It flew in the face of everything she had taught him over the past couple of weeks like a suicidal bird aiming for a jet. Counterintuitive, feathers and carnage everywhere.

Communication was supposed to work. It was supposed to be the key. His magic key that he had discovered made everything easier. Except today, when it had shattered everything inside of him.

There was probably a lesson in this too. About persisting even though this was terrible. About continuing on in the lessons he had learned regardless of the way that Alison had responded to his declarations. But he didn't really care what the lesson was right now. He was pissed he was being forced to learn it. He didn't want to learn anything. He wanted Alison.

"Dad?" He looked up and saw Violet standing at the bottom of the stairs. "Are you just getting home?"

He wasn't exactly sure why she assumed that, since he could have just as easily been coming in from working outside, but he wasn't in the mood to lie. Wasn't in the mood to sidestep or be defensive.

"Yeah," he said, rubbing the back of neck.

"I noticed that you went out last night," she said, crossing her arms. "Were you going to tell me where you were going?"

He laughed incredulously. "I don't have to tell you where I'm going."

Violet lifted her hands. "I'm just saying, am I going to end up having to drag you out of some barn party late at night while you're three sheets to the wind?"

"Maybe," he said.

"In all seriousness," she said, wrinkling her nose. "Do you want to…talk about it?"

"Are you going to lecture me about safe sex?" The expression on her face actually made him smile, and in his current condition that was pretty difficult.

"Good God. Do I have to?"

He shrugged. "Maybe. I'm kind of curious to hear what that would entail."

"Me locking myself in the bathroom and screaming into the void?"

"That sounds about right." He sighed heavily. "I might go back to bed for a while."

"Are you… Are you okay?"

Violet looked about as shocked to say the words as he was to hear them. "I will be," he said. "There's not much other choice, is there?"

"What happened?"

"Got rejected." He pressed his hand to his chest. "It hurts too. Dammit, I figured I would be done with this stuff a long time ago."

"It's not exactly comforting to watch from this end of the spectrum," she said. "I figured someone your age should be done with that too."

"Thanks."

"Was it… Is there… Is it Alison?" Violet looked genuinely concerned about that.

"Yes," he said, because they were talking now, so he might as well keep going with the honesty. "I didn't tell you because she's your boss and I figured that would be weird for you. It was also just supposed to be… Okay, I'm not going to tell you what it was supposed to be. But, suffice it to say it wasn't supposed to be something you needed to hear about. Stuff changed. At least, for me it did."

Violet bit her lower lip. "Are you in love with her?"

Cain took a deep breath, then let it out slowly. "Yes. But she isn't in love with me."

"That's really stupid," Violet said, her tone earnest. "She should be."

"Thanks. I think so too."

"I can quit. I can quit working at the bakery. If you want me to."

He shook his head. "I don't want you to. I want you to have your job. Because you like it. And I want you to keep your relationship with Alison, because you like her."

Violet scowled. "I'm not sure I like her anymore."

"Things like this happen. That's relationships. One person wants something, the other person isn't ready.

Or maybe it's me. Maybe she is ready, but she needs the right guy. I don't know. Either way… Life goes on."

"But it's stupid." Violet reiterated her earlier stance.

"Good people are stupid sometimes. Just because she doesn't want to be with me doesn't mean she's a lost cause." Privately, he wondered if he was the one that was the lost cause. It was difficult not to. Considering the fact nobody seemed to want to stay with him much.

But no, this was about Alison. He would love to be angry at her—part of him was. But it was hard to condemn a woman who had gone through what she'd gone through. Hard to say what she should do. He knew what it was like to have a marriage go to hell, but he didn't know what it was like to be subjected to the kinds of things she'd been subjected to.

He knew what it was like to have trust broken. To have someone do something that seemed beyond understanding. He would never understand how Kathleen had managed to break ties the way that she had. How she'd walked away from Violet without a backward glance.

"Why are you being so reasonable? You're never reasonable. You're definitely not reasonable with me."

"Good question," he said. "I'm thinking that the unreasonable part comes later." Right now he just felt… Well, still numb. Although, it was starting to fade a little bit at the edges, leaving behind a strange ache that wasn't really preferable.

"If you need me to quit my job, I will. When the unreasonable hits."

"I'm not giving you permission to quit your job, Violet. Nice try though."

"How am I supposed to go into work now? Now it's weird."

"Another unintentional side effect of getting older. Things get weird sometimes. And you have to deal with it."

"Then I guess I have to…go to work and…deal with it."

"Sorry," he said. There was just so much apologizing to do. "This was a good talk, but I'm going to go upstairs and…deal with it."

Cain walked past Violet, heading up the stairs, down the hall toward his room. He stripped off his clothes as he walked through to the bathroom, turning the shower on and stepping beneath the spray before it had fully warmed up.

He wasn't sure what he hoped to accomplish by taking a shower. Maybe he was just hoping to wash the feelings away. To go back to a place in his life where he had been ineffective, but hadn't cared quite so much either.

For the past sixteen years the only person he had really loved was Violet. Now there were more people. His brothers, Alison. And when you had that much, there was a lot more to lose.

Well, he had lost Alison.

That realization sent a sharp stab of pain straight through his chest and down through the rest of his body. Yeah, he wasn't numb anymore. It hurt. Hurt like a son of a bitch.

He braced his hand against the tile wall, steeling himself against the onslaught of pain that rained down on him harder than the water.

He wanted to get right back out of the shower, go back to Pie in the Sky, drag her over the counter and into his arms, kiss her, claim her in front of the entire town. He wanted to fight for her. Wanted to tell her that it wasn't the end, that it couldn't be the end. Because he had finally figured out how to love someone. Really love them. And it didn't seem fair that he had learned it on a woman who wouldn't love him back.

But because it was Alison, because of everything she had been through, he couldn't.

If he was ever going to win her, if he ever had a hope… He had to be the man her ex-husband never was. He had to love her in the way that was hardest.

The way that meant he wanted what was best for her, not what might make him happiest. And not even what he thought might be best for her. But what she felt was best for her. What she chose.

All he could do was what he had done. Tell her.

And wait for her to come to him.

And pray to God she would.

"HI," VIOLET SAID when she walked into the bakery. It was clear to Alison, upon arrival, that Violet was mad at her. And there really was only one reason that could be.

The same reason she was mad at herself. The same reason she wanted to curl up and hide under the counter and cry into a bowl of buttercream frosting. Then cry into a bowl of cookie dough. Then maybe into a bowl of cake batter. Because she had a lot of feelings, and she needed a lot of butter to deal with them.

That made her think of conversations with Cain. And it made her want to cry all the more.

But she was at work, and she was looking at the man's daughter, so maybe she needed to keep it together.

"Good morning," Alison said, trying to sound perkier than she felt.

Honestly, though, a roadkill raccoon was perkier than she felt.

"How are you?" Violet asked, which was something the teenager never asked, because she was a teenager. And the fact that she was asking indicated she knew that Alison might not be doing so hot. Great. Just great.

"Fantastic," Alison returned, putting her focus on the tray of turnovers that she was placing into the display case. "Just wonderful."

"Good," Violet said, her expression slightly stony as she made her way behind the counter and grabbed her apron. "That's good to hear."

"Right," Alison prevaricated, not entirely sure if she should speak the words that were hovering on the edge of her lips. But in the end, she didn't have the self-control not to. "How is your dad?"

Violet's expression went flat. "He's awesome. I've never seen him happier. He brought home a brunette. And a blonde. Pretty sure they're having sex."

Alison knew that Violet was messing with her. It was, in fact, so transparent she didn't even think Violet was trying to make it seem realistic. Even so, the image of Cain wandering in with two different women on his arm right after she had thrown him out of her apartment made her want to take the tray of turnovers and smash it on the ground, kicking pies everywhere.

Which made absolutely no sense. Because she didn't want Cain. At least, not in the capacity that he wanted her to. Well, that wasn't entirely true. She kind of did want that. It was just that she shouldn't. She couldn't. The fact that she wanted it was actually a bad thing. She needed to not want it.

The only real solution to that, the only possible way to deal with it, had been to get rid of him.

He could sleep his way through L'Oréal's entire hair color rainbow for all she cared.

"Good for him," Alison said, knowing that her words sounded as brittle to Violet as they did to herself.

"So I guess… I suppose you don't want to talk to me anymore."

The words shocked Alison. "Why would you say that?"

"Because. You were only talking to me because you wanted to get into my dad's pants, apparently. He asked you to figure out what was wrong with me and you did, because you wanted to sleep with him. But now you're done sleeping with him, so you don't need me."

Alison's heart crumpled up tightly inside of her chest, which a moment ago she would have said was impossible since the organ was already frazzled and reduced. She hadn't thought it was possible to sustain any more damage. And lo, it had been.

"No," she said to Violet. "No. That isn't why I was talking to you. I like you. I care about you. I enjoy your company. I want you to have the best life you can possibly have, and your dad has nothing to do with that."

"I don't believe you. I know how this works. I mean, my own mother didn't stick around when she was done with my dad. Why would you?"

"Because of you. Because of who you are as a person. Because you're bright, and you're talented, and you're really funny. And I wish that you were more confident in the fact that you have value apart from what's happening with your dad."

"I don't…" She blinked, and was clearly doing her best to hold back angry tears.

"Come here," Alison said. "Let's go in the back for a minute."

She led Violet out from behind the counter to the door that went up to her apartment. She opened it, and then stepped in the entryway with her, closing the door to give them privacy.

"Okay. You can yell at me now. Or whatever you need to do," Alison said.

Actually, she would kind of enjoy being yelled at. Cain had not been as angry at her as she needed him to be. Somebody should yell at her.

"I don't want to yell at you," Violet said. "I just don't understand. If you like me, and you like him…"

Alison took a breath, trying to fortify herself. But she had a feeling there was no real fortification to be had at this point. "Remember I told you I was in a bad relationship? My ex-husband was abusive, Violet. And I fought very long and hard to have the independence that I have. It isn't about Cain. Your dad. It's about me. And it certainly isn't about you. I just have baggage, and I need to not be in a relationship."

"Okay. But I'm supposed to let go of everything that happened to me and move on, while you're allowed to be all emotionally scarred?"

Annoyance shot through Alison. "No. This is different. It's relationship specific. Romantic relationship specific. And getting involved…it conflicts with my goals."

"Your goals to be alone? Your goals to not accept the love of a man who loves you? Because let me tell you, I saw my dad when my mom left. He was mad. He's been mad about it for years. But he never looked like he does now. This is different. You're different. He loves you, and being with you… He's different. I like who he is when he's with you. I didn't know that was why, but now I do. And I don't want… I don't want things to go back to the way they were."

Alison gritted her teeth, pain flooding her. She wanted to pull Violet close and give her a hug. Wanted to tell her that everything would be okay. But she couldn't, because she didn't know if it would be okay. The very real possibility that she might have broken this already fragile family wounded her to her core.

"You and your dad know how to talk to each other now. That's a start," she said cautiously. "He loves you, Violet. More than anything. Nothing will ever change that. He's not a man given to flowery speeches, but the closest he gets…he's always talking about you. You don't ever have to worry about losing him. No matter what."

"So that's it?"

Alison's throat constricted. "It has to be. But it's not it for you and me. Understand that. Please."

Violet nodded and turned toward the door that led out to the main dining area. Then she paused. "It just seems to me, though, that if you're still doing things because of what your husband did to you… He's kind of still controlling you. I mean, if you really want to be alone then fine. Be alone, I guess. But if it all just has to do with him… Well, he's still choosing what you do."

Then Violet opened the door and walked back out to the dining room, leaving Alison standing there alone. Shattered. Feeling like she had been punched in the chest.

The words hurt. And they hit way too close to home.

But at the end of the day, Violet was sixteen, and she didn't understand what Alison was dealing with. She didn't.

Somehow, Alison made it gritty-eyed through the rest of the day, all the way until closing time. And that was when she realized that it was girls' night. They had bumped up their time because Lane's brother, Mark, was coming into town for a visit during the usual week.

She made a series of grousing noises while she Saran-wrapped a tray full of leftover pies and angrily stomped to The Grind, where they were theoretically meeting. She did her best to school her face into something more relaxed and a little less feral before she went inside.

She must not have done a very good job, though, because when she walked in they all looked at her as though she had grown fangs.

"Hello to you too," she said, setting the tray of pies down on the counter. "I am late. I forgot."

"You look…" Lane started.

"Like you're ready to eviscerate somebody with your teeth," Rebecca finished.

"Well, I spent the entire day on my feet. It is basically prime evisceration time."

Cassie took a step back. "I think I'll just stay out of harm's way."

"Here. Eviscerate this," Lane said, pushing a tightly wrapped bundle toward her.

"What the hell is this?" Alison asked, poking at the package.

"I don't know. Some fancy-ass brick of a fruitcake that a company in South America sent me as a bonus product with my order today. I am skeptical."

"You offering me a sketchy cake full of raisins is not going to make me less murderous."

"Right. I forgot you had raisin baggage. And apparently some other baggage. At least, I'm assuming by the general state that you're in."

"I'm not in a state," she said, sitting down at one of the tables in the dining room. "I'm just tired."

"Everything going okay with your man?" This question came from Cassie.

"He was never my man," she said, the words coming out more tart than she'd intended.

"What happened?" Rebecca asked.

"Why do you think something happened?"

"Because," Lane said, her tone maddeningly rational, "if nothing happened, you would just say nothing happened. But you're not saying that. You're being cagey. And you're snarling around like a hedgehog."

"Do hedgehogs snarl?"

"If they did it would be like this," Lane said confidently. "What happened?"

"Nothing. I mean, nothing of note. I have ended my physical-only engagement with Cain."

She didn't know what sort of reaction she had been expecting. A round of disappointed noises, perhaps? Something a little more like a movie than she was currently experiencing. She didn't get that. Instead, she was treated to a round of blank expressions.

"And it's fine," she continued, her tone deadpan.

"Right," Rebecca said, clearly disbelieving.

"Of course I'm disappointed. Because he was good in bed. Who wants to lose that? But he and I agreed that it was going to be temporary." For some reason, tears started to form in her eyes, that thick ache spreading through her throat again. "It was only supposed to be physical. And he was supposed to be just as averse to relationships as I was. He changed things, not me, and I had no choice but to end it."

Everyone was still just staring at her. Those same blank expressions on all of their faces. It was judgment, she realized. They were judging her.

"I can't have a relationship. Not like that. I'm not going to…commit myself to some man, let him make all of the decisions about my life. You know what? It's not even that. It's not that he would be controlling, it's that I just… That person that I used to be. She contorted herself into these ridiculous shapes to try and fix a marriage that was so…flawed. I can't go back there. I can't."

"Why do you think you would? Why do you think that being with somebody would turn you back into that other person?" Lane asked.

Alison laughed, a kind of humorless, hysterical sound. "Because I have no evidence to the contrary."

It was Rebecca who spoke next, slowly, her dark eyes serious. "What I'm really wondering is why you think you're two different people."

The words settled between them, layered on top of the uneasy silence. She was… She wasn't used to this. She wasn't used to people challenging her. Normally, her past was a convenient shield that she could use. Nobody questioned it because they hadn't experienced what she had. Because they didn't know what it was like, and they were well aware of that.

Sometimes she had been a little bit resentful of the distance it put between her and other people. But, she had also wielded it conveniently, she couldn't deny that.

But between Cain, and Violet earlier today, and now

her friends, she had been pinned down and examined more times than she was comfortable with. On top of already feeling raw and wounded, she was being subjected to this. It didn't feel very much like support.

She needed support. She was indignant.

"It's easier that way," she said, her tone hard. "I don't like thinking of that person as me. Would you? Honestly, Rebecca, why would I want to think of that horrible, weak woman as myself?" She took a deep, unsteady breath. "She stayed. She stayed for eight years."

"She left too," Rebecca said. "Don't forget that. You were never all weak, Alison, no matter how you felt. No matter how grim your situation was. It was never hopeless, because you were never broken. Not completely. I think you do yourself a disservice by remembering yourself as somebody different."

"Well, if the strength was always in me, then the weakness is still in me now, and I rest my case." Her voice was trembling with emotion, and she felt a tear slide down her cheek. She was resolute. She knew she had made the right decision, so she had no idea why it was so hard for her to deal with the consequences now. Why she was filled with so much regret, when she should be standing firm.

"If you don't love him," Cassie said, "then it doesn't matter. And there's no point beating yourself up over the fact that you're not in a place to be with him or give him what he wants. But if you do love him… If you want to be with him, then I think we're going to have to sit here and figure this out, Alison. This is part of having friends. We don't let you stay in places that aren't good for you. We won't let you settle for less when you could have everything."

Another tear slid down her cheek, and she gave up even trying to control it then. She was miserable. And she had a feeling she knew why. But she didn't know what she was supposed to do about it. She didn't know how to be all of these things her friends claimed that she was. She didn't know how to need somebody without falling apart. Didn't know how to be vulnerable when she needed to be strong.

"I have this whole life," she said, the words coming out broken, which made sense since everything inside of her felt shattered. "The bakery. And this mission to help women who have come out of situations like mine, who have been left feeling like less than they should because they let the idea of love overshadow real love. As they've stopped loving themselves, and they let somebody else have years of their lives. That's important. I don't need more than that. That's more than most people will ever have."

"That's a great mission," Lane said. "And it's important. But at the end of the day that's still just you working for other people. Giving up things that make you happy so you can devote more time to them, because you're comfortable with that. But what do you want, Alison? What do you want for your life, for yourself?"

"What does it matter?" she asked, feeling a little bit desperate now. A little bit afraid. "I'm not…allowed to have…love and happiness. I don't use them right. I don't know what to do with them."

"Maybe nineteen-year-old Alison who got married when her terrible mom died because she was desperately seeking comfort didn't know who she was, maybe she didn't know how to have those things," Lane said, her voice vibrating with intensity. "But don't you think thirty-two-year-old Alison who has walked through the damn fire, who has made new friends, good friends, who has helped so many people find their purpose in life, don't you think she knows how to have that? Don't you think she can?"

For a moment, everything seemed wide-open in front of her, and it was terrifying. There was a certain amount of security in narrowing your focus. In narrowing your life. In cutting yourself off from something entirely. It didn't require a lot of self-control, not in the end. Because it was out of sight, out of mind. And it didn't require any trust.

Opening herself up to those possibilities... It made her feel exposed. Made her feel like she was standing out in the open in the wilderness, soft and ready for any predator who might happen along wanting to tear out her throat.

It made her long for her protection. For her cave.

"No," she said. "No. What if... What if it goes wrong? What if I..."

"What if you get hurt again?" Lane asked, her tone gentle.

"I should be cured of this. I shouldn't want to be in love. I shouldn't want to get married again. I know how it goes. I know how it ends for me."

"No," Cassie said, her tone firm. "You know how it was with him. I know my first husband didn't hurt me. I mean, he didn't abuse me. But if I had decided that all marriages were like what I had with him, then I wouldn't be with Jake now. I wouldn't have my kids. I wouldn't have these beautiful people in my life that I love more than anything."

"That's fine for you," Alison said. "And I'm so glad

you're happy. I am. But I don't…" She stopped talking, not quite sure what she had been about to say.

Until Rebecca looked at her, her expression questioning. "You don't deserve it?"

Yes. Her soul breathed that answer. Before her mind had a chance to think it. It was the truth that lived inside of her, deeper than words, deeper than thought.

"Why would he love me?" she asked, the words miserable, and so self-pitying she wanted to punch her own face. "It doesn't make any sense. He's so gorgeous, and he's a fantastic dad. He's strong, and he's… He's everything. My own parents could hardly bring themselves to pay any attention to me. They disapproved of everything I did. They acted like affection was gold and giving any out would bankrupt them. And then my husband… My husband promising to love me turned into this warped, grotesque thing. Why would Cain love me? Nobody ever has."

"I do," Lane said.

Rebecca nodded silently, and Cassie stood up, walking toward her and putting a hand over top of hers. "Me too."

Now Alison was just a soggy mess, tears flowing freely, sobs shaking her fragile frame.

"You were never a different person," Cassie said, curling her fingers around Alison's and squeezing. "You were always you. You always deserved somebody to love you more than they did. You're strong though. And even in just the years I've known you you've changed. You smile more. You warm up to people faster. You don't look scared. I totally understand why you want to protect that. But…if you stop now… If you stop changing and growing now…"

"I'm still living for him," she said, her tone soft. "And for my parents. I'm still letting other people control my life." It was funny that a sixteen-year-old's words, the words that had been echoing inside of her for the past few hours, were the ones that rang true now.

"And if you don't love him, don't let him push you into anything either," Cassie said. "But I think you do. You don't have to be perfect. You don't have to be perfectly soft, or perfectly strong. You just have to be you. Tell him what you want, tell him how you feel. A relationship doesn't have to stay one way. If at any point it starts to feel oppressive, tell him. But I think… I think you're going to find that when somebody loves you, when they really love you in that way that they should, you'll feel the most free that you ever have." Cassie removed her hand. "That's real love, Alison. It makes you feel stronger. It makes you feel more alive. It breaks down all that fear inside of you. It doesn't ask you to be perfect."

She thought of Cain, the way he had looked at her this morning. The way it had made her feel in those first moments when he had told her that he loved her. He did that. He did all of those things. But she was holding on to fear, and as long as fear was the biggest thing inside of her she was never going to be able to accept that love.

"What if I don't know how to…to take it?" She took a deep breath. "I mean, I'm really scared. It would be so much easier if it was because I didn't trust Cain not to hurt me. But I do trust him. He's a good man. And I… I love him. I really do. I want to be with him. But I'm afraid that I can't be a strong enough woman for him. Or a strong enough woman for myself. I can't just drop my fear and grab onto him, even though I want to."

"My advice would be that you tell him that. You just said that you trust him. You have to trust him with this too."

Alison took a deep breath and closed her eyes. She pictured everything that she had. The bakery, her little apartment, her newfound position in this town as a businesswoman, and not as an abuse victim. Not a victim. She wasn't a victim. So she wasn't going to live like a victim either.

Wasn't going to use her past, her shop, her relationship with the women who worked for her, as excuses for why she couldn't also be with Cain. All of those things, those very good things, had become blockades. Initially, she had needed them, to give herself purpose, to keep herself safe.

Yes, she had needed that cave, the one that created walls and necessary limits, and a sense of security. But it was time to walk out of it. It was time to stand in the sun.

She looked at her friends, her very strong friends, all of whom had banished demons from their past in order to find love. They were flawed. Because everybody was. But that didn't make them undeserving. She could see that easily. It was just so difficult for her to see when it came to herself.

But suddenly, she saw with clarity that, much like when she had left Jared, this wasn't about feeling ready. It was just about moving forward. Because it was the right thing. Because it was the only thing.

Because it was what she deserved.

To be happy. To be loved.

To be with Cain.

Maybe she didn't have to wait until she didn't feel afraid. Maybe she just had to take that step.

"I need to go," she said, standing up, her limbs shaking. "I have to go talk to him."

That earned her the round of unified noises she had hoped for earlier. Only instead of shocked gasps, there were cheers. "Go!" Lane said.

"Yes," Rebecca said. "Go. We'll eat all the pie."

"We'll save you some fruitcake," Cassie added, nodding seriously.

"Keep your fruitcake," Alison said. "Keep it all. I'm going to go tell a man that I love him."

FOR ONCE, POUNDING nails into wood wasn't doing anything to alleviate his tension. Or maybe it never had. Maybe he had just been existing in a stage of deep denial. Keeping all of his emotions in the deep freeze so that he didn't have to deal. And now that he had let them rise to the surface they were causing him a metric fuck-ton of pain.

There was no denying this. No denying that losing Alison hurt with every breath he took. That each gulp of air was a stab of burning agony that didn't seem to end.

Really, no wonder he had avoided this for all of his life. No wonder he had done so much to keep his feelings under wraps.

Theoretically, this letting his feelings out thing might be healthier, but it was like kale. Bitter, available in abundance and tougher with age.

That was the thing. He'd been married before. He had a child who was nearly grown. Everything felt like it was ending. And then this. There wouldn't be another woman after Alison. It was her. Only her. Which meant this was going to hurt forever. Great.

The sun went down behind the mountains and it got

dark inside the barn he was nearly done renovating. He turned on a shop light, flooding the area with light, which also flooded it with heat. He took his shirt off, sweat rolling down his back as he continued to work.

He was so busy, and doing nothing to dampen the noise he was making—it was therapeutic—that he didn't hear anyone come in. Didn't notice anything at all until he heard her voice.

"I thought maybe we could talk."

He whirled around, then dropped the hammer he'd been holding. "What are you doing here?"

"I hope these floors still aren't…"

"I don't give a damn about the floors."

She took a deep breath. "I came to talk to you."

His heart squeezed tight, his fingertips itching to touch her. To make contact with the smooth, perfect skin, to tuck her hair—gleaming like copper in the light—behind her ear before sifting his fingers through it.

Who was he kidding? He didn't want to stop there. He wanted to strip her naked. Wanted to bury himself inside of her so that she would remember. So that she would know what it was like. So that she would ache the way he did. So that she would be full of the same regret that he seemed to be made of.

"I'm not in the mood to talk," he said. "Talking is stupid. I experimented with talking, I didn't like the results."

"Cain…"

It hit him then that he'd never asked Kathleen to stay. Had never gone after her. They'd never once fought all through their marriage, and in the end, he hadn't fought for her.

But Alison mattered too much.

Fuck being a good guy. Fuck her space.

He walked toward her, and this time when he did it she didn't take a step back. Instead, she stood there resolutely, her eyes never leaving his. He wrapped his arms around her, pulled her up against his chest—damp with sweat from the exertion—which was fine with him, she deserved to feel that. She was the reason he was out here.

"Why are you here?" he asked, his tone ferocious. "Did you come to kick me again? Did you come to tell me again that you don't love me?"

She shook her head, and then she reached up, dragging her fingertips across his cheekbone. "No."

The simple touch, so gentle, so small, carrying the impact of a steel beam swung to the gut, stole all of his rage. Stole all of his words.

"I came because… Because I'm scared."

He frowned. "You mean you were scared?"

"No. I am scared. I sort of thought that if I were ever supposed to do something like this, if I were ever supposed to take this kind of step it would feel…easy. And I would feel ready. But I'm not sure why I thought that, Cain. Because there has never been a big change I've made in my entire life—for better or worse, really—that didn't feel hard. That I felt ready for." She took a deep breath. "So I'm scared. But I'm here."

He tightened his hold on her, afraid to let her go. Afraid that if he did she might walk right back out. Of course, he was also afraid that if he held on any tighter she would vaporize completely, prove to be a figment of his overactive imagination.

"Yes," he said, his voice rough, almost a stranger's. "You are."

"I've been thinking. And talking. Talking to my friends. And to your daughter, actually."

"My daughter?"

Alison nodded. "Yes. She was not very happy with me."

"No," he said, not seeing any point in denying that. The fact that Violet had been on his side was one of those victories he was going to take.

"I've spent the past twelve hours trying to untangle everything. And I've come to some conclusions. But mostly? It was all a big ball of fear."

He raised his hands, cupped her face, slid his thumb along the edge of her lips. "You don't have to be afraid of me, Alison."

Her eyes glistened, her mouth pulling tight. She nodded. "I know. It wasn't you. It wasn't that simple. I'm afraid of myself. I'm afraid of what I might find out about my own value if I try again. I'm afraid you'll figure out I'm not worth anything."

Cain shook his head slowly. "Alison, you aren't worth just anything. You're worth absolutely everything."

A tear rolled down her cheek, her lower lip trembling. He wanted to kiss it. But he didn't want to stop her from saying what she was going to say next. "I've been holding on to this idea that he stole who I was. Because it was easy. Easy to think that I was one thing when I went into that marriage, and that he transformed me into something else. But I don't think I ever knew who I was. Everything I've ever done was a reaction. To my parents, to his anger. To my own anger. My own fear. To what I wanted the town to see. But now I want to choose. I don't want to prove anything. I don't want to show the town anything. I don't want to be safe. I just want to be happy. I just want to love you."

A shudder ran down Cain's spine, and he crushed her up against his chest, holding her tight, cupping the back of her head. "Then love me, Alison. Please love me."

"I do," she said, her voice muffled. "I really do love you."

He pulled her back away from him, tilting her face up, watching as tears slid down her cheeks. Tears for him. For them.

"And a very good friend of mine said that I needed to talk to you," she said, a smile touching the corners of her mouth. "Which is funny, because I think we've kind of come full circle now. Since you were the one who did the talking first. And I was a little slow to learn. I'm scared, but I want this. And I'm not going to wait until I feel ready. Because I might never feel ready. Change is hard. And I've made a lot of changes in the past few years. But I sort of bought into this idea that I was done changing. Because change is hard," she said, laughing a little bit. "And I didn't want to have to do it anymore. I wanted to believe that everything was fixed, that I was fixed. But I wasn't. I'm not. I've been married before, Cain. But I don't know how to have a marriage, I don't know how to be in love. I'm not really sure I even know how to accept love. Even though it's something that I want. But I do know that I love you. And that I want to be with you."

"There's nothing to know," he said. "At least I hope not. Because I don't know what I'm doing either. I just know what I feel. And I know it's something I've never felt before. I don't have a map for this. Maybe I'll suck at it. But if I do, I want you to tell me. And we can work on this together. We can make this work together."

"I want to," she said, the words coming out a whisper.

"Then we will," he said. "And if something is wrong with you, I'm going to ask you what it is. And I need you to tell me. Because we're not going to let things get bad. We're not going to let fear get in the way. We're not going to let other people who didn't love us anyway decide what we do with the rest of our lives."

"I told you I never asked my parents for what I wanted. For what I needed. I just rebelled, and acted out, I did things just to make them upset. And when that didn't work, I tried proving myself by changing my plans and giving them everything when times were hard. But that won't be us, Cain. I'm going to try. Because while that scares me, while it terrifies me to cut myself open and bleed all over the place in here, to tell you that I love you, to tell you that I want to be with you, to take the risk that I might get hurt, it scares me even more to think that I might not have you at all. One is a risk I can take. The other one? Not so much."

"The problem with reaching out to people," he said, echoing words from an earlier conversation they'd had, "is that they might pull away."

"And then I did. I'm sorry."

He shook his head. "Don't be sorry. Because I would do it again. And you know what? I think I would have tried. Again and again. I probably would have gotten a boom box."

"Oh, God forbid. Not a boom box."

"Desperate times. And life without you was pretty desperate, Alison." He shook his head. "The first time I got married, commitment chose me. I wasn't looking for it, but Kathleen got pregnant, and it was the right thing to do. This isn't about doing the right thing. This is about going after something that I want desperately, something I wasn't looking for this time either, but something I can't imagine living without."

"Kiss me," she said.

He was more than happy to oblige. He dipped his head, claiming her, long and deep, and pouring all of the love he had inside of him into that kiss. When they parted, her lips curved upward.

Warmth flooded him, love filled him, and he dipped his head and kissed her again. "I love you," he said, his lips still pressed against hers. "And I always will. Always."

"I like the sound of always. I like it a lot."

"Good. Also, I hope you're not averse to living in a barn. Or with a teenager."

"As long as you're there, I think I can handle it. Plus, Violet and I do pretty well. We even bake together, and I am very particular about who I bake with."

He smiled and tightened his hold on her. He'd moved all the way to Copper Ridge from Texas to try to build something new for himself and Violet. For just the two of them. Instead, he'd built something better. A family. A relationship with his brothers.

Cain Donnelly had been alone for four long years. Four years of trying to battle through being a single parent. Four years of going to bed alone. A lifetime of not understanding just how much he could love a woman. But he did now.

He'd wondered—more than once—how his life had ended up at that point. Hadn't been able to connect the dots and make sense of it. But he could see them all now, bright and brilliant.

They had all led up to this. To Alison. To forever.

He understood now. It took more than good intentions and a desire for stability to make a family. Took more than hard work and working the land and pounding nails.

It took love.

"Which one of us gets to tell Violet?" he asked.

"You're her dad," Alison said. "That's all you."

"Should I offer her a chance to be the flower girl?"

Her eyes widened. "Are you proposing to me?"

"Yeah," he said. "I am."

"Isn't that a little bit fast?"

"As my daughter keeps reminding me, Alison, I'm not getting any younger. I need to move fast."

Color flooded Alison's face, along with the kind of happiness he'd only ever dreamed someone might look at him with.

"Ask me why I'm smiling, Cain," she said, a dreamy expression on her face.

And all he could think of was that moment, that one that he had only told one living soul about—her—that moment when he had asked his mother why she didn't smile. And she'd answered it was because of him.

"Why are you smiling, Alison?"

She put her hands on his face, those delicate fingers tracing the lines on either side of his mouth. "Because of you."

EPILOGUE

Violet Donnelly didn't consider herself sentimental. Not really. She was almost seventeen, after all. But still, when she watched her dad exchange vows with Alison at Grassroots Winery, she cried.

It was impossible not to.

Her dad was in a suit, which was something she never thought she'd see, and ultimately was about the biggest testament to how he felt about his new wife. And Alison…well, she was perfect in her simple white gown with its fluttering, sheer cap sleeves and deep V in the back. As far away from an evil stepmother as it was possible to be. The simple, short bridesmaid's dress she'd chosen for Violet to wear was even pretty. Flowing and the same deep green as the trees.

Alison wasn't exactly a stepmother. But a friend. A confidante. The peacemaker when things got turbulent.

And she would stay. That was the most important thing. The thing that Violet never doubted. Not even once.

Sure, stuff had been hard with her dad about a year ago, and things weren't always easy now, but he'd changed. Alison had changed him.

Alison had changed Violet too. She couldn't deny

that. Had stitched together some of the holes that had been torn inside of her when her mother had left.

She watched as the two of them walked hand in hand toward the tasting room, where the cake and food were set out, ready for their guests. And Violet smiled because tonight, Alison wouldn't be serving the guests.

The sunlight filtered through the trees and washed her dad and Alison in a golden glow. Alison's red hair looked like it had a halo around it, her dress fluttering in the breeze. She looked like an angel. Just the one her dad had needed.

Just the one she'd needed.

Right then, Violet felt pretty sentimental, after all.

This was a different side of life than she'd seen before. A different side of love. She'd asked Alison almost a year ago if you had to choose: cake or men.

Commitment or independence. Love or pleasing yourself.

She'd told her then that you didn't have to choose, but over the past year, that had been demonstrated to Violet in a thousand different ways.

She tightened her hold on her bouquet of red and yellow sunflowers and took three long strides to catch up with the happy couple. Alison let go of her dad's hand and wrapped her arm around Violet's waist, bringing her in between them. Violet's dad slung his arm over her shoulders.

They walked into the tasting room to cheers from all of the guests—her uncles cheering the loudest—and Violet felt a surge of the kind of happiness she couldn't remember feeling since she was a kid.

For so much of her life, love had felt heavy. Like a punishment.

But now it felt...well it felt a lot like peace. Like home. Copper Ridge suddenly felt a lot like home too.

She was here with her family. How could it be anything else?

* * * * *

*The Donnelly brothers might be
putting down roots in Copper Ridge,
but the road to happy ever after
is hardly a smooth one.
Look for Finn and Lane's story,
SLOW BURN COWBOY,
available now.
And read on for a sneak peek
of soldier-turned-cowboy Alex Donnelly's story,
WILD RIDE COWBOY...*

VERY FEW PEOPLE would call Alex Donnelly a coward. He had dodged gunfire, survived a rain of mortar shells—more than once—and worn full tactical gear in arid heat that could practically bake a loaf of bread. And a man's brains for that matter.

But he had been a little bit of a coward when he had allowed Clara Campbell to put off their conversation about her deceased brother's will.

The fact of the matter was, he had been a coward for the past couple of months that he'd been back in Copper Ridge and had avoided having the conversation with her at all. He'd had his excuses, that was for sure.

Though some of them were valid. Like the time he'd put into investigating the legality of what her brother has asked him to do. And then the time spent going over the letter Jason had left. The one that clarified just why he wanted things this way, and made it impossible to deny him.

Still, Alex had waited to talk to Clara, even after that.

At first, it had been out of deference to her grief. And after that because he was trying to get his feet underneath him at the Laughing Irish Ranch, which he worked at with his brothers.

Frankly, after losing his best friend and his grandfather, he'd had enough grief to deal with without adding

Clara's. But it couldn't be avoided anymore. And when he had discovered that her cell phone had been disconnected he felt guilty for avoiding it as long as he had.

Clara must be hurting for money. Enough that she had taken a job at Grassroots Winery, and was letting bills go unpaid.

He'd expected her to call if things were that bad. Hell, he'd expected her to call, period. But the way she'd acted at the coffee shop, it didn't seem like she'd spoken to anyone about the circumstances surrounding Jason's will.

Now that he thought about it, if she had, she probably would have come at him hissing and spitting.

She might still. But she was late.

Alex pushed his cowboy hat back on his head and looked at the scenery around him. The Campbell ranch was small, and so was the ranch house. Rustic. From his position on the front porch—which was squeaking beneath his cowboy boots—he couldn't see the highway.

Couldn't see anything but the pine trees that grew thick and strong around the property, standing tall like sentries there to protect the ranch and all who lived there.

"Well, you're doing a pretty piss-poor job," he told them.

Because damned if the Campbells hadn't been through enough. But he was here to make things easier. He knew—was 100 percent certain—that Clara wouldn't see it that way initially. But this was what Jason had wanted, and he knew that Jason had had nothing but his sister's best interests in mind when he had made out his will.

Alex owed it to his friend to see his last wishes carried out. No question about it.

He took a deep breath, putting his hands on his narrow hips as he turned a half circle to take in more of the property. The driveway needed to be graveled. It was slick and muddy right now, even though it had been a few days since it had rained.

There was a truck and a tractor that Alex would lay odds didn't run parked off in the weeds, looking like metal corpses that had been left to rust back into the earth.

The place needed a lot of work. It was too much for him to do by himself, let alone one woman. One grieving woman who had to work part-time on top of doing the general ranch work.

He figured at this point the place wasn't really functional. But he was forming some ideas on how to get it working again. On how to make sure Clara hadn't just been saddled with a millstone.

Or, more accurately, that he hadn't been.

The center of the sky was dimming to a purplish blue, the edges around the trees a kind of dusty pink by the time Clara's truck pulled up the long driveway to the house. She stopped, turning off the engine, staying in the vehicle. She was looking at him like she was shocked to see him, even though he had told her he would be there.

He shoved his hands into his pockets, leaning against the support for the porch, not moving until Clara got out of the truck.

She was such a petite little thing. And she had definitely lost weight since he'd seen her last. He couldn't imagine her taking on a place like this, and suddenly he felt like the biggest ass on the planet. An ass who had stayed away because she was going to be angry when she had clearly been here working her knuckles to the bone.

Jason had been clear on what he wanted. The fact that Alex had screwed it up so far was just about right as far as things went.

"Big wine-tasting day?" he asked.

Clara frowned. "No. Why?"

"You're home late."

She raised a brow, then walked around to the back of the truck and pulled out a bag of groceries. "I had to stop and get stuff for dinner."

"Oh, good, you do eat."

She frowned. "What does that mean?"

"You're too skinny." He felt like a dick for saying it, but it was true. She was on the sadness diet, something he was a little too familiar with. But he'd learned not to give in to that in the military. Learned to eat even when his ears were ringing from an explosion, or the heat was so intense the idea of eating something hot was next to torture. Or when you'd just seen a body, bent and twisted under rubble.

Because food wasn't about enjoyment. It was about survival.

A lot like life in general.

Clara Campbell needed help surviving. That was clear to him.

Clara scowled even deeper as she walked toward him. "Thanks, Alex. Just what every woman wants to hear."

"Actually, in my experience a lot of women would like to hear that." He snagged the paper grocery bag out of her arms as she tried to walk past him. "SpaghettiOs? What the hell is this?"

"Dinner, jackass."

"For a four-year-old."

"I'm sorry they don't live up to your five-star military rations. But I like them."

She reached out and grabbed hold of the bag, trying to take it out of his arms.

"Stop it," he said. "You've been working all day. I'm going to carry your groceries."

She bristled. "You're insulting my groceries. I feel like you don't deserve to carry them."

He snorted, then turned away from her, jerking the bag easily from her hold. "Open the door for me."

"I thought military men were good at taking orders," she said. "All you seem to do is give them."

"Yeah, well, I'm not in the army now, baby." He smiled, knowing it would infuriate her. "Open the damn door."

Her face turned a very becoming shade of scarlet but she did comply, pulling out her keys and undoing the lock, then pushing the door open. He walked over the threshold, and a board squeaked beneath his feet. He made a mental note to fix that.

"There. The dining room is just through there, set the bag on the table." She walked in behind him. "See? I can give orders too."

"While eating SpaghettiOs." But he followed her instructions, then took a look around the room. It was sparse, the floor, walls and ceiling all made with rustic wood paneling. There was a red rug on the floor with the geometric design that provided about the only bit of color to the room.

Other than a big, cheery yellow cabinet that was shoved in the back of the kitchen, packed full to the brim with white plates. It seemed a little incongruous with the rest of the place. And at odds with the rickety dining table and its mismatched chairs.

Alex had never been to Jason's house before. They had met when they were in high school, and consequently, had spent their time hanging out away from the watchful eye of parents and guardians. After that, they had wound up serving together in the military.

The place was... Well, *cozy* was a nice word for it. *Eclectic badger den* possibly less nice but a little more accurate.

"I'm hungry," Clara said, fishing one of the cans out of the bag. "Don't taint my SpaghettiOs with your judgment."

"Wouldn't dream of it."

He watched as she moved around the efficient little kitchen, making small economical movements, getting out a blue-and-white speckled tin bowl and a little pan, then opening up the SpaghettiOs and dumping them in it. She put it on the front burner, turning it to high, then whirled around to face him.

"Okay. What are we talking about?"

"Do you want to wait until you're eating your dinner?"

"No." She turned and opened the fridge, then pulled out a can of Coke, popping it open and taking a long drink. She did not offer him one, he noticed.

"I was contacted by your family lawyer shortly after I found out Jason had died."

Clara turned back to him and crossed her arms, her lips going tight. "Okay, why did he call you?"

"Maybe the question is, why didn't he call you, Clara? I expected you would have talked to him."

She bit her lip. "Well. He did. But we didn't talk." Alex stared her down and her cheeks turned increasingly red as she shifted her weight from foot to foot. "I've been busy," she said defensively.

"Well, if you hadn't been too busy for the lawyer he might have talked to you about the fact that I'm the beneficiary of your brother's will."

"Excuse me?" This was the part that he had been avoiding. The thing he had not been looking forward to. Because his friend had left him with his property, had left him with his earthly possessions, and a letter explaining his feelings that were only that: the feelings of a dead man. Alex had to try to fill in blanks he wasn't sure were entirely possible to fill in. Had tried to reason it all out to decide if he could excuse just defying Jason's wishes.

He hadn't been able to. So here he was.

"All of it," he continued, the words falling heavily from his mouth. "The ranch, everything on it, everything in it, the house. Jason left everything to me." She didn't move; the only indication that she was reacting to what he was saying at all was that her face had gone completely waxen. "Do you understand what I'm saying, Clara? I'm saying that this is my house now, my property. You and the ranch are now my responsibility."

Turn the page for a special preview of
LONE STAR BABY SCANDAL
by Lauren Canan,
a TEXAS CATTLEMAN'S CLUB: BLACKMAIL
novel
available July 2017
from Harlequin Desire.

Resisting her billionaire boss finally becomes futile…
but there will be consequences!

When Clay Everett approached, extending his arm in a silent invitation to dance, Sophie Prescott immediately shook her head in embarrassed refusal. Clay was her boss. Her employer. It was a job she valued highly. There should be no mixing business with pleasure even if Clay was the best-looking man at the charity ball.

His deep emerald eyes gleamed, framed by dark lashes that matched his ebony hair. His five-o'clock shadow and the scar on one side of his face gave him an almost menacing air. Since the accident, he'd presented an entirely different persona: a man who was hard and unforgiving and ate any competition for lunch.

Actually, he had a beautiful smile and perfect white teeth, but people rarely saw them. His demeanor was serious and intimidating. In his five-thousand-dollar hand-tailored suits and white silk shirts, he gave the impression of the consummate businessman. A man of great wealth who was used to the world of glamour in which he lived.

Then there was the Clay of glove-soft, faded jeans, scuffed boots and a thin T-shirt, highlighting his six-pack abs and the muscles in his shoulders and arms, who was disarming in a different way. That was the Clay she knew. He'd come into their office a couple of times in his Western getup and it was a look she much preferred. Like the raging stallions he trained, like the wild bulls he'd ridden to superstardom in his youth, he was a man unlike anyone else.

Refusing to take no for an answer, he grasped her hand, pulled her up from her seat and led her toward the center of the grand ballroom of the new Bellamy Hotel. Her heart rate tripled. Content to watch the antics of the idle rich from the back of the ballroom, Sophie had never expected her boss to find her and propel her right into their midst on the dance floor. She was a secretary, for crying out loud, a woman who had grown up on a farm in the Rust Belt of America. She had no business being here, rubbing elbows with the elite of Royal, Texas.

"Breathe," Clay said in his deep, rich voice, a glint of amusement sparkling in his eyes. "You look as though you're about to pass out. I thought I remembered hearing you say you love to dance."

"I do. Just not here." *And not with you, the president and founder of a billion-dollar corporation and Royal's most eligible bachelor.* His presence alone was enough to make everyone sit up and take notice, but those broad shoulders and incredible good looks caused the crowd to part and make way for him. A few smiled at her sincerely, while others smirked in that condescending manner that only someone in her position could recognize and understand. *Isn't Clay being kind to his poor little secretary? How thoughtful of him.* Sophie could read their minds without much effort at all.

"And what's wrong with here?"

"If you don't know, I won't waste my breath trying to explain it to you."

He chuckled, a sexy sound that drew more looks from

all the women within hearing distance. Instead of allowing them to negatively affect her mood, she closed her eyes and let herself be swept into the music. The ballad was one of her favorites. With Clay's arms around her, they danced to the slow rhythm. He smelled so good. His silken tux jacket felt smooth against her cheek. At some point the song ended and Sophie made a move to return to the small table in the back of the great hall.

"No," he said, his warm breath on her ear. And before she could argue, another song started. He dropped her hand and held her with both arms around her waist, pulled her closer until she could feel every movement, every pulse inside a hard body laden with muscles. More muscles than she'd ever felt on a guy. She didn't know what he did in his spare time, or if such a thing existed for him, but she would bet it wasn't sitting around knitting sweaters.

One thing was clear: he was aroused, a fact that became more obvious by the minute. With every slow step, side to side, he brushed up against her, driving her crazy. A fog of heat enveloped her as she fought to dispel her own body's reaction to his. She was on fire. Her hands clutched his broad shoulders and she drifted back into a dreamworld of his making, letting the mute chemistry between them intensify.

Clay was a cowboy through and through. It was in his stride, his way of talking. It was in those emerald eyes, so piercing they could cut her up into tiny little pieces. And in those full lips just waiting to gobble up and savor each one. The years away from the rodeo arena couldn't take away the cowboy. Even the night the two-ton bull had turned an evening at the rodeo into a nightmare from hell, almost ending his life, couldn't take that away from him.

The doctors had said he would never walk again, but they didn't know Clay. He had surprised everyone. Everyone except Sophie, who knew he was a man who just didn't quit. Ever. After the injuries he'd sustained and the months of grueling physical therapy, it was a pure miracle he was here at all. And he'd astounded everyone tonight when he'd put aside his cane and taken to the dance floor, ignoring the limp and the pain that accompanied it.

His life had previously played out on the rodeo circuit, his talent propelling him to celebrity. Luckily for him—and those around him who jumped on board a good thing—Clay's talent didn't end when his rodeo career did. Today he was a successful entrepreneur, changing his star status from millionaire to billionaire in only five short years. That was just the kind of man he was. If he could imagine it, he could make it materialize. If he wanted it, he got it. And apparently, right now, tonight, he wanted her.

Slowly his hands slid down her back, coming to rest above the surge of her hips, pulling her even closer to him. The feel of his arousal propelled her body to an immediate and impulsive response. She heard his low groan, his breath warm against her ear.

"Let's get out of here," he said in a voice that sounded more like a growl as the third song ended. Without waiting for a reply, he took her hand and led her through the dancing couples toward the exit. When he summoned the elevator, the doors opened almost immediately with a muffled ding. After stepping inside, Clay pushed a button that sent the elevator skyrocketing to the penthouse suite, which he'd rented for tonight, just before he gathered her in his muscled arms.

Sophie had been kissed before but never like this. It was raw, passionate, hungry. His tongue traced the line of her lips, moistening them for penetration. He filled her then, his hand clenching her hair in the back, holding her head exactly where he needed her to be. He was so male. The scars that remained from the near-death accident only served to increase his air of desirability. Even in broad daylight they seemed to highlight a dangerous edge.

He had spent his life dueling with the devil and in spite of impossible odds, he had come out on top. Every time except the last. Even then, Clay had pulled his raw courage from some place deep inside and survived when any other man would have rolled over and admitted defeat. It was part of that rock-hard determination that she felt now, in his arms, his emerald eyes giving off signals as to just what he intended to do to her when they reached his bedroom.

At some point the doors opened with an almost silent swish and they stepped out of the elevator into a vestibule with marble floors and occasional tables laden with huge bouquets of freshly cut flowers. Beyond a black door, highlighted with gold paint, was the penthouse. He guided her through the door with a single-minded purpose. And a few steps beyond that door was the master suite. It was in his face, in his eyes—he was going to make love to her.

And she was going to let him.

This is wrong, said the small voice in her head. So very wrong. He was her boss. Their relationship should be kept strictly platonic. But as she followed him toward the bedroom, the word *no* disappeared from her vocabulary.

"Would you care for something to drink?"

She shook her head. If she was really going to do this, she wanted nothing to mar the memory of this night in his arms. It was a once-in-a-lifetime moment that could never be discussed or thought of again except in her dreams.

He turned a switch and the lights dimmed. He pressed her backward against a wall and his hungry lips again found hers. His shirt and jacket hit the floor before he turned all his attention to her. Leaning over, he kissed her ear, alternately nipping and kissing down her throat until he returned to her mouth, his tongue filling the deep recesses until she couldn't suppress the moan that emerged from deep in her throat. She knew a moment of freedom from the constraints of her strapless gown as it slid down her body to the floor—

"Sophie?" Clay's deep voice brought her out of the daydream. "Sophie! Hello? Are you okay?"

A heated blush ran up her neck and over her face as reality came slamming back. She was seated at her desk, staring blindly at her monitor while the phones rang and Clay called her name. She had to get a grip on this. She kept reliving their one night of passion, first in her dreams, then during the day while she was at work. It had to stop. They were attracted to each other but that night had been over two months ago and it would not be repeated. They never discussed it—as far as Clay was concerned, it was as though it had never happened. It was past time to let it go and move on.

"Yes. Ah…yes. Yep. I'm fine."

"I've been calling your name for five minutes. Are you sure you feel up to working today?"

"Yes. Really, I'm good." She struggled for composure and cleared her throat. If he had any idea of her wayward thoughts, he would never let her live it down. "I just have a slight headache. I'll be fine," she lied and reached for the phone.

Clay laid a file folder on her desk with a sticky note attached bearing instructions. Then pursing his lips as though hiding a smile, he walked out the door.

Sophie hadn't realized she'd been holding her breath and released it now in a sigh. It was almost as if he knew what she'd been thinking. Impossible. He couldn't read minds. Could he?

Clay Everett stood in the massive glass-walled lobby of the main barn at the Flying E Ranch. Around him were countless pictures and awards. There were oversize belt buckles with gold and silver inlays displayed in black velvet-lined shadow boxes. Trophies and large silver cups were arranged on the mantel of the enormous natural-stone fireplace. Still more lined the bookcases around the large room. The walls held dozens of pictures showing action shots of various bulls and horses as they tried with all their might to tear their equally determined rider off their back. If you looked at some closely enough, you could hear the angry cries of the animal, see the fury in its eyes. But the grit and determination in the rider's eyes were fiercer. For the bull, it was eight seconds to kill. For the cowboy, it was eight seconds to walk away a champion.

In the corners of the glass foyer there were silver-embedded saddles on their holding racks with matching bridles hanging over the horn. Amid the trophies were older pictures of a young boy: riding his first bull, roping his first calf, his legs barely reaching the shortened stirrups of the saddle. The largest picture in the room was of a man holding up a two-by-six-foot check, made payable to Clayton Everett in the sum of one million dollars and proclaiming him American Rodeo Champion. Standing next to him were his barn manager, George Cullen, and Sophie Prescott, his secretary and maybe his best friend in the world.

It had been Sophie's idea to move his office to the ranch. At least temporarily. But temporary had turned into permanent after almost two years. Sophie had overseen the move and, as usual, he couldn't help but be impressed. He'd slid into the burgundy leather chair behind the massive mahogany desk like it was still at the highrise in Dallas. Everything, from files to computers to office equipment to Sophie's office, had been set up almost exactly the way it had been at the other location. He could find his way around the new office blindfolded.

Sophie had done it all while he was still in the hospital, his gut torn open by an angry bull named Iron Heart, his left leg shattered by pounding hooves as, in the blink of an eye, he was thrown from the animal and gorged before landing squarely on his head, the compression causing him to break his neck, barely missing his spinal cord. It had taken less than six seconds, from the moment the chute door opened to the crack he heard from within and sweet oblivion, which brought his days as a superstar in the Professional Bull Riding League to an end. It was a bull he'd known would someday come his way. It was inevitable. Nothing went on forever.

He wandered out of the foyer area, down the main

hall to the east wing. After climbing a few steps of the bleachers that overlooked one of the outside arenas and the sloping fertile pastureland beyond, he sat down, marveling at the view all around him. He would never tire of it. Rolling hills, the few that existed in this area, and white pipe fencing as far as the eye could see. In the distance a herd of longhorns grazed on the irrigated spring grasses. In the first part of October, hundreds of breeders of Texas longhorn cattle would gather at the Lazy E Arena in Guthrie, Oklahoma, to find out who owned bragging rights to the bull with the longest horns in the world. Word had reached him that his ten-year-old bull Crackers had horns three-tenths of an inch longer than his chief competitor. That should have made Clay happy. But there was more to life than watching horns grow on a damn cow. No one knew it better that he did.

Clay had to accept that his rodeo days were over and his life was going to change. Hell, it already had. Once he'd been released to come home, it had taken a month of prodding by the stubborn, unshakable, relentless Ms. Sophie to get up off his ass—or words to that effect—and do something. Clay had started tinkering around with some ideas, found one he liked and thrown himself into building a new business—a cloud computing company he named Everest that took off like a rocket, making him a multimillionaire almost overnight with no indication it was anywhere near slowing down. He did it partly to keep his mind off the injuries that were still healing and partly because that was the way he was: a self-made man and risk-taker by nature. And Sophie never let him forget it for a second. He loved nothing more than a challenge, regardless of whether it was a two-thousand-pound Brahma bull or a billion-dollar company. A challenge was still a challenge.

His latest challenge: Sophie Prescott.

As if on cue, she popped her head around the corner. "I thought I would find you here. What do you want for lunch?"

When he merely shook his head, she said, "Then I'll have Rose grill a steak and throw some sides together. It should be ready in about thirty minutes."

"I'm not hungry."

"That's too bad. You've got to eat. Nothing good is going to come out of you sitting around with your head in the clouds."

"I was thinking, not daydreaming."

"Thinking, huh? I'll bet. More than likely thinking about that old bull and how you would do it better if you had a second chance."

He glared. "I'll be in for lunch in a few."

She tapped her watch as a silent way of saying she would expect him sooner than later.

Damn, she was beautiful. For reasons he couldn't understand, she chose to tone down her natural beauty, pulling the amber hair into a ponytail and using very little, if any, makeup. Not that she needed any. Her sky blue eyes couldn't hide behind the glasses always perched on her nose. And those full, slightly pink lips… A man could lose himself in them.

And he had done exactly that almost two months ago, the night of the Texas Cattleman's Club masked ball held at the Bellamy Hotel.

Sophie had always been there for him as a loyal employee and true friend. When his accident brought out the true colors of his money-grubbing fiancée, who promptly dumped him, rage had often filled him. But even when he lashed out, Sophie never batted an eye. He owed her his life. That was a fact no one could dispute. And that made her even more tempting than she'd ever been before.

The problem? She was more off-limits than ever, too.

But even as they do their best to forget it, that one night Clay and Sophie shared will have repercussions to last a lifetime…leading to a scandal that will rock Royal, Texas.

Don't miss LONE STAR BABY SCANDAL
by Lauren Canan,
a TEXAS CATTLEMAN'S CLUB: BLACKMAIL
novel
available July 2017
from Harlequin Desire.